SASHA AND THE STALKER

STEPHANIE KAZOWZ

KAZOWZ PUBLISHING

To my partner Jordan—I love writing the smut and seeing how you react. <3

Playlist
Just Like Heaven - The Cure
Breaking the Law - Judas Priest
Burning Down the House - Talking Heads
Between The Cheats - Amy Winehouse
Just a Friend - Biz Markie
Love in this Club - Usher, feat. Young Jeezy
Never There - Cake
Video Phone - Beyoncé
Truth and Honesty - Aretha Franklin
Somebody That I Used To Know - Gotye, Kimbra
When a Man Loves a Woman - Percy Sledge
One Sweet Day - Mariah Carey, Boyz II Men
You Know How I Do - Taking Back Sunday
Thank You - Led Zeppelin
Good as Hell - Lizzo
I Want You to Want Me - Cheap Trick
Stuck In The Middle With You - Stealers Wheel
White Wedding - Billy Idol

Content Warning
This book includes:
Coarse language
Alcohol use
Drug use
On page panic attack
Fatphobia from a parent
Slut shaming
Biphobia
Side character pregnancy with a precautionary off-page trip to the hospital- everything is fine
Explicit sex
Graphic violence
Blood/Gore
Graphic deaths/murder

ONE

"Fucking talk radio," I grumbled, a white puff of air leaving my mouth. There'd been no time to warm up the car because Luca decided to start the day the right way, and who was I to argue? I sacrificed warmth on the drive to work for hard and fast over the bathroom sink.

I made the right choice.

Forty was surprisingly empty as I cruised into the office. I took the exit ramp, singing along to the hits station blasting over the speakers. "I would—Son of a bitch!"

The brake pedal sunk to the floor. "No. No. No." My little car slowed because I was going uphill, but there was no way it was stopping. With my heart racing, I reached for the emergency brake, knocking my hot coffee all over the passenger seat, and yanked that motherfucker up with all my might. The smell of burning rubber filled the car as I slid to a stop, smashing into the back of a black sports car.

Everything went still. Adrenaline pumped through me, and my hands trembled as I turned on my flashers. Flashbacks of the night I killed Dante Sr. and Luca had Pete cover it up by driving us into oncoming traffic slammed into me, threatening to send me into a full tailspin. Blinking back tears, I cringed as a middle-aged man wearing an expensive suit got out of his car and started yelling. On shaky legs, I stepped into the frosty January morning.

"What the fuck?" His red face contorted into a scowl as he inspected the damage.

"My brakes went out." I gestured toward my destroyed compact.

"Fucking perfect." He shook his head and lifted his phone to his ear. "Yeah, I'd like to report an accident."

Going to the curb, I sighed—what a beautiful way to start a Friday.

Fucking Scott.

I glanced through the glass walls of the conference room to the lobby and then at the clock on my laptop. "Where is he?"

"He hasn't answered my email, text, or phone call." Miranda's long red nails tapped away, organizing the notes she took during our afternoon meeting with people from The Oxford Hotel.

"Well, I have somewhere to be at 7:30, and I can't be late. He's got twenty minutes before I'm out of here."

"You and Luca finally having a date night?" Ashley twisted her braids into a bun at the nape of her neck, somehow still looking fresh after the twelve-hour day we'd endured.

"Yeah. We both got home after eleven last night, and he decided enough was enough. No matter how exhausted I am, we're doing the whole date thing."

"It's been a rough few weeks," Axel mumbled as he sketched in a notebook.

Ashley and I shared a smile.

"Oh yeah? Lots of late nights?" Ashley bit her lip.

Axel looked up. "What?"

"Nothing." She shook her head and pretended to get back to work. "Must be tough staying up past ten."

Miranda snickered, covering her mouth with her hand. Despite being promoted, she still held back when we gave each other shit.

"I regret ever letting you spend the night." Axel's attention fell back to his drawing. "This is why I don't have friends."

"Come on." I leaned back in my chair, folding my hands on my stomach. "You have to admit, we make your life more exciting."

"Sure. Instead of having my nights to myself, I get to work late. Instead of weekends camping and enjoying the great outdoors, I get to work. Exciting." His dark brown eyes held no humor. He was truly sick of us.

Ashley spun her chair toward him. "You knew what you were signing up for. And it's not like you're the only one."

"Great. We can all be miserable together." Axel closed his notebook and rested his hands on top of his head. "Since Scott's an hour late, can we call it a day?"

As the words left Axel's mouth, Scott walked through the front door and past reception. He looked like the morning after— rumpled blond curls, his shirttails hanging out, and his slacks creased as if they'd been carelessly tossed.

I frowned at Ashley, and she pursed her lips, shaking her head. He passed the conference room, his face buried in his phone, not noticing the meeting he was delaying. I grabbed my nearly empty water bottle and tossed it at the glass. The soft thud startled Scott, and in a spectacular feat of uncoordinated flailing, the phone bounced from hand to hand until it hit the glass and then the polished concrete floor.

The four of us burst into laughter as he checked the screen. "Get in here, asshole," Axel yelled.

Scott slid the glass door open, already apologizing, "I'm sorry! I know I'm late. I got caught up."

"Where were you?" I asked with a lifted brow.

"A meeting." He grabbed a bottle of water from the mini-fridge and joined us at the handmade conference table—a perk of working with a master artisan.

Miranda rolled her eyes, tossing her glossy black hair behind her. "The appointment on his calendar's private." She clicked and typed a bit. "The address is a hotel downtown."

"How'd you get my password?" Scott looked at her with wide eyes, his mouth hanging open.

Miranda smiled sweetly and said, "Your mom's name plus her birthday. You had me buy her gift and send it this year."

Ashley sucked her teeth. "You didn't buy your mom's birthday present?"

"Mama Adams is a saint, and you couldn't even buy her a gift?" Axel added, his eyes narrowed at Scott.

"Can we talk about how shitty of a son I am later? How'd the meeting go?"

"You'd know if you were here." I sniped.

"Fine. Let's do this." He straightened his spine, clearing his throat as if preparing for a firing squad. "I was at a late lunch with Nicki, and things got . . . interesting. I'm sorry I'm late, but I'm here now." Scott shifted in his seat as he looked from person to person.

"You can't be serious. Nicki?" I twirled my pen, praying he hadn't just signed his death certificate.

"What? It's not like we're having an affair. It was a one-time thing." He shrugged, chugging half the bottle of water. His pale face flushed with embarrassment, or maybe from thinking about his afternoon of fun.

"Let it go, Sash. It's done." Ashley checked her phone and sighed. "You need to get going. I'll catch Scott up."

I stacked my folders and shoved them in my bag. "Scott, stay away from Nicki. I promise you don't want to be on her fiancé's radar."

Scott laughed. "You mean the accountant?"

"You've never seen Aldo, have you?"

"No. Why?"

"No reason." Giving Scott my back, I turned to Axel. "Can you make sure I have those pictures Monday morning?"

"Yep." He jotted down a note, stood, and left the room without a word.

"Have a good weekend," Ashley shouted, getting only a grunt in return. "Go. Go. I'll send you the Stay Magazine info once we get it from Margot."

"Wait! Stay Magazine?" Scott sat up in his seat, grinning.

"They want a full spread of the new Oxford Hotel Chicago as soon as the renovations are complete. See what you miss when you choose to bang the antichrist?" I joked as I walked to the door.

"She's not so bad," Scott mumbled.

"Uh-huh. Make sure you don't let it happen again. I'm serious." I checked my phone and groaned. Breaking into a power walk that would make my mall-walking grandma proud, I met the car service as it pulled up to the curb.

Somehow, I got myself date ready in under an hour and was only fifteen minutes late getting to Moretti's. As I said goodbye to the driver, I felt eyes on me. One thing I'd learned is there was always someone watching. If you're lucky, it's one of your guys.

Shaking off the nerves, I rushed down the sidewalk, sidestepping patches of melted snow. To my surprise, the awning was dark, and the restaurant was empty. I locked the door behind me, grinning as I slipped out of my coat. Sure enough, only one table was set with rose petals scattered around it—just like our first date.

"Hello?"

"Back here." Grinning, I pushed through the kitchen door. Luca looked up from the stove, his crooked smile crinkling the skin around his eyes, and like always, my heart beat a little faster. "Hey there."

"Hey." I gave him a peck over the counter and settled on a

stool. "I didn't realize I was getting Chef Luca tonight. What's the occasion?"

He frowned as he stirred. "I have to have a reason to cook for you?"

"No, but it's been a while since you busted out the full kitchen press." There were dishes in the oven and pots on almost every burner. "It looks like there are courses to this date night."

"There are. Tonight's menu is inspired by the dishes you've loved the most since we've been together."

"You're making cannoli?"

"Maybe," he sang, turning his back to fuss with a plate.

"You really are the perfect man."

His broad shoulders tensed, but not for long. "How are you feeling after this morning? Any aches or pains?"

"No, at least not yet. I was lucky the emergency brake slowed the car down enough to keep the airbags from deploying. Have you heard from the mechanic?"

Luca shook his head and glanced over his shoulder. "Not yet. Chase assured me he'd be in touch this weekend." He checked his watch. "Why don't you head out to the table and pour yourself a glass of wine?"

"Sounds good." I sashayed away, loving that I didn't need to look to know Luca was staring.

Popping open the expensive wine—wine which I still hadn't gotten a taste for but now understood a little better—I poured us both a glass. I smoothed my hand over the thick tablecloth and smiled at the short flower arrangement in the middle of the table. Every detail had the Luca Moretti touch and was utter perfection.

The kitchen door opened, and bright light poured into the candlelit dining room, creating a halo around Luca's imposing frame. "We're starting with Gnocco Fritto, followed by egg raviolo, then a steak for you and fish for me, and we'll finish with three different kinds of cannoli."

I wiped away an imaginary tear and pursed my lips. "You

know just what to say to a girl to make her feel all warm and fuzzy inside."

He set our plates down and took a seat. Tilting his glass, he swirled and sniffed before finally taking a sip with a quiet hum. The man loved a good wine.

"So, how did the Oxford meeting go?" He set his glass down and cut into the delicate pastry.

I hummed, chewing the buttery, salty perfection. "Great. They loved our ideas, and we got some direction, so we should be all set to finalize the proposal next week."

"That's fantastic."

"Mm-hmm." I stabbed at my appetizer.

"What's wrong?"

Letting out a bone-deep, tired sigh, I set my knife and fork down. "Just Scott acting like a fucking kid."

"What'd he do now?"

I took a sip of wine, knowing Luca wouldn't be happy. "He and Nicki, ya know." I tilted the glass back and forth. "Which is none of my business, but he makes it my business when his fucking around makes him late for our meeting, so then I'm late for dinner with you."

Luca dabbed the corner of his mouth and set the napkin next to his plate. "Nicki cheated on Aldo?" He lifted an eyebrow. I regretted bringing it up, but we'd promised no secrets. His legal counsel cheating on a capo who also handled financials for the legitimate business seemed like something Luca might need to know.

"One time." He grimaced, and I groaned. "And now I'm a snitch."

"Don't worry. I won't say anything. Now that I know, I can keep an eye on the situation." He shook his head. "I'm not so much worried for Nicki, but I hope Scott was being honest when he said it only happened once. Aldo . . . well, Aldo's old school."

The unspoken threat was enough to send a shiver down my

spine. I rarely caught a glimpse of Moretti Luca or the world that went along with it.

"Let's not ruin our dinner worrying about Scott. How's the acquisition going?"

He shrugged. "It would be going a lot better if our appraisals matched. They're asking for a lot more than the casino's worth, and it's getting to the point where we may have to walk away, which would mean a lot of wasted time. I never thought buying a casino would be such a headache."

"I hope it all works out. I'd love to get my hands on the renovations. That place could really shine with the right changes."

"And that's exactly why we need to get it for a reasonable price. It's wildly outdated. Hell, on top of the horrendous décor, the security system needs a complete overhaul. I'm sure we'll come to some kind of agreement. I just need to give them the right incentive."

He finished his plate, collected mine, and carried them back to the kitchen. This casino would be one of the rare crossovers between the two sides of the Moretti fortune. Luca hated the idea, but Marco was pushing hard for it. It was clear he was ready to get out of the restaurant business.

"And here's your egg raviolo."

I cut in, and the yolk oozed out. There were very few things more beautiful than a perfect egg raviolo.

"You have a gift, Luca."

He dipped his chin in thanks and tucked into his plate. His expression was thoughtful, and then he smiled. "I think this might be the best egg raviolo I've ever made."

I didn't answer. Instead, I let my gusto do the talking. When I finished, Luca was still eating, so I caught him up on everything else going on. "I'll be home late the next few Wednesdays because we're running rehearsals for Naughty Gras."

He tilted his head as he chewed.

"It's at the end of February. I perform once with the girls, and then I'm doing a solo show the next night."

"So, it's a whole weekend thing?"

"Mm-hmm."

He nodded and took the last bite of his raviolo. "I'll make sure I'm free."

"You sure?"

I used the freshly baked bread to wipe my plate clean. There was no way I was leaving even a speck of the fantastic cheese combo behind.

"Of course. I love watching you perform." He wiggled his eyebrows and nudged my knee under the table.

"Well, all right. Maybe we can buy some art for the guest room." The idea of guests sleeping under a phallic or yonic painting delighted me.

Juvenile? Absolutely.

Would that stop me? No.

"Whatever you want." Luca's phone buzzed on a nearby table, and he frowned as he stood. "Let me go get our entrées." He smoothly scooped it up on the way to the kitchen.

Frowning at his back, I fished my phone out of my purse and checked my emails. Axel had already sent me the pics I needed to finish all our specs for Monday. I'd have to figure out a way to sneak in some work over the weekend without pissing off Luca.

"Phones away, Ms. Mitchell. Mealtime is quality time." A Luca proverb.

I batted my eyelashes at him as I put it back in my bag. "I'm sorry, Mr. Moretti."

"You're forgiven, but don't let it happen again," he said in a stern voice. Setting my plate down, he switched out my flatware. "Now, let me know what you think of the butter on the steak."

"You got it." My knife glided through the meat, and the first bite made me moan like I was enjoying one of Luca's other god-like talents.

"It's good?" When I nodded, he smiled and finally took a bite of his entrée.

After taking a sip of the white wine he'd poured to go with his fish, Luca cleared his throat. "I want us to go on a trip soon."

Chewing, I mentally went through all of our upcoming deadlines and events. It'd be tight, but I could afford to take a little time off since staffing up at SA Designs.

"I was thinking Paris?"

I swallowed and smiled. "What's the occasion?"

"I promised to show you the world, and I plan on keeping that promise."

"Okay, but I get to plan the next trip. You won't know where we're going until we get to the airport."

"Deal."

We ate in comfortable silence, occasionally gazing at one another, just enjoying each other's presence.

Luca's leg started bouncing when we were nearly done with our main courses. Reaching under the table, I placed a hand on his knee. "You okay?"

He wiped his mouth, leaving half of his meal untouched on the plate—a very odd occurrence for Luca. "Mm-hmm. Just excited to see what you think of dessert."

Frowning, I pulled my hand back and finished my entrée. Just because he was being a weirdo didn't mean I wasn't going to eat. He watched me with the kind of adoration I didn't know I could inspire, especially while gobbling down premium meat.

As I put the last forkful in my mouth, Luca got up and asked, "Done?" Not giving me a chance to answer, he took my plate and headed toward the kitchen.

"What's his deal?" There was no good reason for him to be acting so jumpy. Was it the phone call? Lately, he was getting more and more phone calls that left him on edge, but this was different.

Is he excited?

Before I could dive deeper into possible motives, Luca strolled in, carrying a beautiful plate of cannoli. "Now, these have a special filling." He put the plate in the middle of the table, then grabbed a fresh carafe of coffee—the good shit. Moretti's bought local and bought fresh. God bless them.

I waited for him to sit before grabbing a cannoli and taking a big bite. Covering my mouth, I squealed through a full mouth of pastry and cream. "Tiramisu!"

Luca chuckled. "I'm glad you can taste it. It's always nerve-racking to flavor the cream."

Instead of responding and further stroking his ego, I shoved the rest in my mouth like the classy broad I was. His eyes widened, and he jumped out of his seat, reaching for my mouth just as I bit into something hard, nearly cracking a tooth.

I tongued the thing out of my mouth, losing a dollop of cream on the table. Sparkling up at me was a huge fucking diamond on an antique band.

Blinking rapidly, I waited for it to disappear or turn into something that made more sense.

It was the ring from the closet, the one I'd found a few months ago and promptly shoved into the back of my mind because I wasn't in a rush to get married and was happy with how our relationship was. But holding it in my hand, I knew I was meant to wear the ring.

"Is this?" It took immense effort, but I pulled my eyes from the glittering cream-covered diamond. Luca shot me one of his toothy smiles.

"Sasha," he said as he stood and walked around the table, "I love you so fucking much. Losing you for a year nearly killed me." He cleared his throat. "I know you're my perfect match, and I don't want to wait another second without promising you forever." He knelt beside me. "Will you marry me?"

My eyes burned with tears as I nodded, giving him the ring and holding my hand out for him to put it on my finger. He took it from me, popped it in his mouth, and sucked off the cream before sliding the still-sticky metal on my finger.

Seeing it on my hand broke something inside me, and tears rushed down my cheeks. Luca's big hand rubbed circles on my back as he nuzzled my hair. Gulping down breaths, I calmed down enough to stop the waterworks and finally speak. "I love you, Luca." I looked into his shining brown eyes. "You are everything I didn't know I wanted in a partner. I hate we lost a year together, but I know you're it for me. No matter what, it's you and me."

Luca bit the inside of his cheek and shook his head. "I don't know what I did to deserve you."

Turning in my seat, I threw my arms around his neck and crushed my lips into his. The taste of coffee and cream dominated, but the hint of what could only be described as Luca lingered on my tongue. With a little shove, Luca landed on his ass, and I climbed onto his lap.

I was going to fuck him right there on the floor of Moretti's—the same floor I nearly lost him on. The errant thought added fuel to the fire burning inside me to claim every inch of him.

Twisting my fingers in his lush black hair, I yanked his head to the side and trailed my lips across his cheek and down his neck, leaving a red trail.

So much for smudge-proof.

I pushed the collar of his white button-down to the side and sunk my teeth into the corded muscle there. Sweat from being in the hot kitchen made him salty—his skin the perfect pairing with the sweet confection he'd made for me.

Luca groaned, and I kissed the spot, pulling back to admire the neat crescent teeth marks indented in his skin. Excitement thrummed through me as his dark brown eyes, so open and vulnerable, locked on mine. I knew anything I wanted to do to him, he'd not only allow but enjoy.

Releasing his shoulders, I unbuttoned his shirt, tugging the tails from his pants. Tracing the tattoo over his heart with the tip of my nail, I couldn't help but smile.

Sasha.

Even when we were sure we couldn't be together, he'd been mine. He'd always be mine.

His hands skated under my hiked-up skirt, pulling the fabric until my ass was hanging out. Digging his fingertips into my ample flesh, he spread me. Lace wedged between my folds as I rocked my hips into him.

I closed my eyes to collect myself as Luca toyed with the edge of my panties, dragging them through my wetness. Unbuckling his belt, I rushed to unbutton his pants, tearing the zipper down. He lifted his hips, and I tugged at his pants until he was free.

Gripping the base of his cock tightly, I smiled as Luca's head lolled back and his chest rumbled. His fingers let go of my panties, and they snapped against me, sending a pinch of pain to my clit. I yelped, and his gaze found mine. Gone was sentimental Luca, and in his place was the man that could fuck me to death and have me begging for round two.

He fisted one side of my panties, at first pulling it from my hip, then with a flick of the wrist, they tore from my body, the elastic snapping against me. "Get on my cock, Sasha."

I swallowed, going up on my knees over him. My hands trembled with excitement as I rested them on his shoulders. He grabbed his shaft, rubbing the head from clit to ass, gathering my arousal. "You're so fucking wet. You ready for me?" His voice vibrated through me, creating an ache only he could ease.

"Yes," I moaned, moving my hips, trying to slide him inside. Luca grabbed my ass, keeping me in place as he circled my clit with his wet tip. My head fell back, and I let out a frustrated groan. Now wasn't the time for one of his little power trips. Arching into him, I stopped fighting his hold, and when I did, he thrust up into me, each time getting a little deeper until I sat completely down on him.

"Fuck." I dropped my chin and caught his lips in a messy kiss. My tongue thrust into his mouth, claiming every inch.

Luca's hand wrapped around my throat, the pressure light but present. He guided me back so he could look me in the eye. "I love the way you feel around my cock. You going to ride me?"

As I opened my mouth to speak, he swiveled his hips, grinding into my clit. "Yes," I breathed out.

He put both hands on my hips with a vicious squeeze, lifting me and slamming me back down. It only took him doing it a few times before I gripped his shoulders and started to move on my own. Sliding to the tip and coming back down hard, making him hit so deep it was a little painful.

But fuck, did it hurt so good.

As I moved on top of him, Luca squeezed my ass, moving up my body until one of his giant hands cupped my breast while the other plucked at my tight nipple. He let out a frustrated breath and pulled the neckline of my dress, along with the cups of my lacy bra, down. With my nipples exposed, Luca took one in his mouth, his teeth nipping and tugging, making me lose my rhythm for a moment because I was arching into him.

He slapped my ass, the sting jarring me from the trance his mouth put me in. "Focus." He moved to the other nipple, sucking until I squirmed, trying to ruin his composure. Rolling my hips with every downward movement, he gripped me like a vise, his hands tightening to the point of bruising.

His fingers trailed down the crack of my ass, reaching where we were joined. Wetting them, he slid them back up and circled my asshole. I tensed around him, holding my breath in anticipation. He chuckled against my chest, and with one more brush of his thumb, he brought his fingers to my clit and rubbed back and forth.

Luca's mouth worked in tandem with his hand to make me dizzy. My rise and fall became erratic as I chased my orgasm. As if sensing I needed a little push, Luca tugged my nipple and slapped my ass as I took all of him inside. His dark eyes gazed into mine, maintaining a connection I never thought I would feel—a connection I thought I'd lost.

Love poured between us. Every part of me linked to him. A small pinch of my clit and my whole body convulsed, my pussy clamping down until I was afraid Luca would be stuck inside me forever.

He pumped into me from below with shallow movements as my orgasm subsided, and I collapsed onto his shoulder, panting and sweaty, my thighs burning.

When he slipped out of me, cum ran down my thigh, but I couldn't be bothered with it. Not when I could barely move my limbs.

Luca rested his head against the table leg behind him with a satisfied sigh. "Well, that went better than expected." His eyes shut, and his lips parted as he caught his breath.

Resting my cheek on his chest, I circled his nipple with my nail. Tiny shivers ran through him until he placed a hand over mine.

"You can't tell me you thought we'd get engaged and not fuck." I kissed his collarbone, basking in his scent.

A laugh rumbled through him. "I knew we would, but I thought we'd make it home first."

"When you treat a lady like this—" I picked up a few rose petals and blew them in his face. "You can expect a little action." Without looking, I reached up to the table and felt around until my hand landed on a cannoli. Smiling, I held it up for Luca to take a bite.

"For me?"

I lifted a brow. "Better take a bite now before I eat the rest."

He bit half, and I popped the rest in my mouth.

We sat together on the floor and finished the rest of the cannoli. Once they were all gone and my belly was uncomfortably full, Luca sighed. "I guess we need to get up."

I rubbed my leg. "Probably, although my foot's already asleep, so standing up will be a real bitch."

Shifting me to the side, Luca tucked himself back into his pants and helped me up. Pinprick-like pain traveled up my leg as I shook it, watching him straighten his clothes and tidy up the table. His bare forearms flexed as he lifted the heavy ceramic plate, carrying it to the kitchen. How he made cleaning sexy was beyond me, but he did.

While Luca wrapped the leftovers, I loaded the dishwasher. When the kitchen was tidy and the car loaded with enough food to last the entire weekend, we headed home.

As we turned onto our street, I saw a car parked in front of our house and another in the driveway. "Who's that?"

Luca shook his head and checked his phone. "It's going to be a long night." He offered me an apologetic smile. "And not in the way I was hoping."

TWO

"Boys." I waved at the four hulking men on our porch and headed inside. I wasn't interested in whatever late-night bullshit was interrupting my fiancé and me from enjoying our night.

Luca caught my hand inside the doorway and leaned in. "I'll be right up."

"Mm-hmm." I broke free and headed straight to our room. It wasn't the first time business made its way to our doorstep late at night, and it wouldn't be the last. The first time we lived together, he kept all parts of his mafia business away from me. It was better that he wasn't hiding his other life, but I hated seeing Marco's face when all I wanted to do was ride Luca's.

Sighing, I stripped, adding my dress to the clothes strewn across the floor earlier. *Let his majesty pick them up once he's done with his cloak and dagger shit.*

As I walked to the shower, my thighs rubbed the evidence from our floor escapades together. A perfectly filthy souvenir that, unfortunately, needed to be rinsed away. With enough pressure to turn my skin a wonderful shade of pink, I let the four shower-heads work their magic. The glittering rock on my finger caught my eye, and I stopped washing to just stare at it in amazement. I looked through the foggy glass at the door, and my happiness soured when Luca didn't come walking in, naked and ready for action.

Lotioning every inch of my body, I tried to chip away at my annoyance, reminding myself I'd signed up for whatever it took to be with Luca.

By the time I was cozy between the sheets, I was less angry and more resigned. The faint murmur of agitated voices made it up to our bedroom from his first-floor office. It was clear Luca wasn't coming to bed anytime soon. Since Zoe Chronis went missing, there'd been a massive uptick in violence between the families. Or maybe I just never knew any better, and shit had always been that bad.

Probably something to look into.

I lay wide awake, listening for footsteps that never came. Huffing in frustration, I rolled to the side and then rolled to the other side until my face was buried in Luca's pillow. I breathed in his minty shampoo, like a fucking creep, trying to soothe myself with that tiny piece of him. Disgusted by my pathetic behavior, I screamed, the sound muffled but apparently loud enough for Luca to hear. A stampede of footsteps thundered down the hallway, and the door flew open, slamming against the wall.

"Sasha!"

I squeezed my eyes shut, willing the men I knew were standing at the ready behind Luca to disappear. Of course, it didn't work. I slowly turned my head and gave the group a tentative smile. "Hey, guys. What's up?"

They lowered their guns, Mickey smiling while Marco and Luca frowned.

"What's up?" Luca cocked an eyebrow.

I flopped back on my pillow and stared at the ceiling. "Sorry I scared you. I didn't expect to have company tonight." Lifting my hand in the air, I flashed the ring. "Ya know."

"Congrats, by the way." I could hear the smirk in Mickey's voice, but I refused to look at him.

"Thanks."

"You guys can go back to the office. I'll be right there."

I took a deep breath and slowly released it. What a fucking night.

The door clicked shut, and the bed dipped on Luca's side. "Baby?"

"What?" I kept my eyes firmly on the light fixture overhead.

"Can you look at me?"

I glared at him, and he laughed, scratching his chin. "I'm sorry they popped up."

"Okay."

"Okay?"

"Yeah. Okay. What the hell am I supposed to say?" We stared at each other. Luca studied me, and I could hear the cogs turning, trying to figure out the right thing to say. Rolling my eyes, I shoved his shoulder. "Get back down there so you can finish whatever it is they need and come to bed."

"I love you." He kissed the tip of my nose and rolled away.

Falling asleep without Luca wasn't easy, but I was getting better at managing it.

"Oh my God!" Ashley gripped my hand so tightly that my fingers turned purple. Her eyes were wide as she tilted it back and forth, catching the light. She grinned at Adriana, Sarah, and Jazz. "Sasha is officially locked down."

They raised their glasses, cheering, their voices carrying over the Black Sabbath blasting through the bar. The tables next to us noticed their little celebration, so Ashley showed off my hand like a prized kill.

"Let's actually get to the wedding, and then we can do all this." I snatched my hand away and shook it out.

"Okay, Sash." Jazz rolled her eyes and clinked glasses with my cousin Sarah.

"I mean it! Look at all the shit we've been through. I'm not about to jinx us by celebrating too early."

"Why don't we save your pessimism for another day? Today is for happy, good times." Sarah smiled at me, her face flushed from one too many bottomless mimosas.

"Fine," I relented, knowing they would have their way no matter what I said.

"Great. Now, tell us how he did it." She rested her chin on her knuckles, fluttering her eyelashes.

"It was adorable." I took a sip of my loaded Bloody Mary. "I thought we were catching a late dinner at Moretti's, but he'd recreated our first date."

Ashley let out a dreamy sigh, her smile stretching until her adorable dimples popped. She was too romantic for her own good.

"The entire place was empty, and he'd scattered rose petals around one of the tables."

"Cheesy," Jazz said with no snark in her voice and a big smile. She was like me, a realist, but unlike me, when she found love, she grabbed it with both hands. She and Imani met less than a year ago and already lived together. Jazz even had an appointment with a ring maker to create Imani's dream wedding set.

"The cheesiest."

"I'm surprised you made it this morning." Adriana let out a yawn before taking a sip of coffee.

"Unfortunately, Luca got a call about some overseas issue and spent a good chunk of the night in his office while I was sleeping like a baby." Kind of the truth, but enough of a lie to keep Jazz and Sarah out of the loop. Adriana didn't react. I'd bet good money Marco left her bed to come to our house.

Ashley's eyes narrowed, but true to her southern raising, her bright smile never faltered. "That sucks. Should've put his phone on silent." She pushed the plate of poutine my way. "Any idea on a date?"

I grabbed a loaded fry and shoved it into my mouth. A date?

I'd been engaged less than twenty-four hours, and she wanted a date? "Um. We didn't talk about that. I figure within the year?"

The girls looked at each other, their expressions serious.

"This year? You think you can throw together a wedding to a Moretti in a year?" Ashley squinted her brown eyes and pursed her lips.

"Why not?" I focused on the gravy-covered fries and left them to squabble.

"Dante and I got engaged and married within a year. You'd be surprised what the Moretti name and bank account can get you." Adriana rolled her shoulders back as she eyed the drink menu.

"The real issue is what are we doing for the bachelorette party?" Jazz wiped her hands on a napkin as her dark eyes pierced me, her bright pink lips kicked up in a small smile.

"Yes!" Sarah cheered, holding her hand up for a high five that Jazz begrudgingly gave.

Ashley flipped her braids and side-eyed Jazz. "As maid of honor—" she shifted her gaze to me, and I nodded, "I can assure you the bachelorette will be amazing."

Jazz held up her hands and shook her head, her riot of black curls brushing her bare shoulders. "No disrespect intended."

"I need another drink," I mumbled into my straw as I scanned the small room for our waiter. When I caught his eye, I lifted my glass. "I love this place."

"The food is good, but I vote next time we go somewhere a little less aggressive for brunch. Metal's really not my thing," Jazz said as she eyed the room.

Ashley nodded. "Yeah. I'm sorry to say it, but you Mitchell girls are officially outnumbered. It's time to branch out from Metal Brunch. At this point, I'd take unironic yacht rock brunch."

As much as I loved the place, I knew it wasn't their scene. "Fine. But they better have a spread like this. Otherwise, it won't matter what music is playing. Heads will roll!"

"Thank you, your highness," Jazz said dryly.

A tall man toward the back of the bar caught my attention. I lifted my chin in his direction, not taking my eyes off him. "That guy looks familiar. Where do I know him from?"

Ashley covertly looked over her shoulder and huffed out a laugh. "He looks like he could be one of Luca's cousins or something." Her back straightened, and she turned to me wide-eyed. "Mexico," she hissed.

"What?" I frowned, trying to remember the infamous trip where my blood was about fifty percent tequila the whole time.

She huffed out a laugh. "You really don't remember that first night? Your whole getting over Luca by getting under well . . ." She gestured to the back of the bar, where the man was no longer standing.

"He's gone." Adriana pouted. "Did he really look like Luca?"

"Oh yeah. I thought Luca had followed us to the resort," Sarah chimed in, stealing a bite from my plate.

"Now I regret not staying out with you guys."

I stared at the Judas Priest poster on the wall and wished I could have a do-over of that trip. Nothing says rock bottom quite like sleeping with your ex's doppelgänger and calling out his name during sex. The guy probably caught sight of me and booked it out of the bar, not wanting to run into the one-night stand from hell.

Sarah rested a hand on my arm. "What did Aunt Maggie say?"

"I haven't told her yet. We're having dinner with them tonight, so I figured we'd do it in person. I imagine she'll spontaneously explode from joy, which will be unfortunate because she'll miss out on all those grandbabies she's been demanding."

Everyone froze, and their heads jerked in my direction. The cacophony of "You're pregnant?" "Wait!" and "What?" drew the attention of the surrounding tables yet again.

"I'm not pregnant." I picked up my fresh Bloody Mary and gestured toward my friends and the onlookers, repeating, "I'm not pregnant." As proof, I took a big sip, the pickle and bacon garnish sliding into my nose. "See?"

The whole table relaxed and took a drink of their own.

"I was about to say—" Ashley put her hand over her heart. "That would really mess up the bachelorette weekend."

"I'm glad to see you have your priorities straight."

"I know you well enough to know that if it were up to you, there would be no wedding, just an elopement and a party after. The bachelorette is one of the selling points."

"Guilty."

"But you're excited. You want to do this. Right?"

I gazed down at the ring. "I do." Lifting my eyes, I smiled. "He's it."

"Then it sounds like we have a wedding to plan." Ashley lifted her glass to the middle of the table. "To Sasha and Luca!"

"To Sasha and Luca!"

———

"Stop checking your phone."

I raised an eyebrow and glanced at Luca's phone in his hand. "I'm sorry. What did you say, Mr. Pot? I don't think I heard you right."

He slid his phone into his pocket, giving me a pointed look. Sighing, I tossed mine in my purse and leaned back into my parents' sofa.

For the first time in my mom's life, dinner was late.

Gasp. Shock. Horror.

"It'll be just a few more minutes."

A loud crash came from the kitchen, and Luca frowned. "You sure you don't want a hand, Maggie?"

"No. No. You two relax. Greg?" Mom shouted.

"What?" Dad yelled from the basement.

"Stop messing around down there and get cleaned up. Dinner's in five."

Dad didn't respond. There was just a lot of grumbling and things banging around. Luca and I shared a smile, both fighting back a laugh. They still didn't know about the engagement because when we got to the house, Mom whisked us into the den, and I was wearing gloves.

"She's going to flip when she finally sees this thing." I lifted my hand and tilted it back and forth.

Luca grabbed it out of the air, dropping a kiss right above the ring. "I love seeing you wear my ring." He dropped my hand on the cushion between us, his thumb tapping my knuckles as his gaze burned into me.

When he licked his bottom lip, I leaned in and whispered, "I've got some pretty cool posters in my bedroom. Want to check them out?"

He chuckled and shook his head. "Dinner will be ready in five minutes." Bumping my nose with his, he gripped my chin. "Behave."

Rolling my eyes, I flopped back to my spot. "Almost done?" I yelled toward the kitchen.

"Yep. You two head to the dining room. Greg! Now, damn it!"

"Coming!"

We'd just sat at the table when Dad popped around the corner. "Hey, kids." Luca and I stood and exchanged hugs. "Maggie, you need a hand?" Dad asked, even as he sat.

"Nope, here I am." Mom floated into the room with a platter of pork chops. After a few more trips back and forth, she'd filled the table with baked mac and cheese, green beans, and mashed potatoes. For a woman who dreaded being fat, she sure as hell threw down.

"This looks amazing, Mom."

"Thank you, honey. I hope everyone's hungry."

"Starving." Dad started loading up his plate. "After four days at the firehouse, I'm about to eat my weight in pork chops. Pass those potatoes, Sasha."

Passing the dish, I said, "As long as I get to take home a little leftover mac and cheese, we're good."

"We'll see."

Mom was flushed and preoccupied as she ate. Looking at dad, I noticed his cheeks were almost as red as his hair. "What were you up to before we got here?"

"I was moving some boxes in the basement for your mom." Dad lifted his eyes from his plate. "She's setting up a crafting corner." The corners of his mouth lifted, and he winked at Mom, making her whole face beet red.

Biting my lip, I tried to catch Luca's eye, but he was too busy eating. The sound of cutlery on Mom's fine china, random yummy noises from Dad, and the hum of the washing machine in the mudroom were odd. There'd never been a silent meal at their table. Apparently, Mom and Dad getting freaky and causing dinner to be late was the only thing that could shut Mom up.

Wild.

I twisted around in my chair, trying to strike up conversation. Unfortunately, everyone else was focused on their plate. Fork and knife in hand, I dramatically flourished my utensils and scraped the plate in a move sure to draw my mom from her unnatural silence.

"Sasha Marie! Pick up your knife. Don't scrape my good pla —What's on your hand?" She shrieked the last part, jumping out of her seat and rounding the table. Her hazel eyes were wide with excitement as she snatched my hand, making me drop the fork on the floor, but she didn't care. "You're engaged?" Her head whipped to Luca, and she yelled, "You proposed?"

"Maggie." Dad wiped his mouth with his napkin and settled back in his chair. "There's no need to shout."

She jerked my hand toward Dad, pulling my tits into the mashed potatoes. "This rock is something to shout about, Greg."

"Damn it." Yanking my hand out of her hold, I brushed off the potatoes. Luca's shoulders shook in silent laughter as I glared at him. I lifted my chin at Dad. "You don't seem surprised."

"I'm not." He and Luca shared a meaningful look.

Ah. I narrowed my eyes at Luca. "You didn't."

"I did." He straightened his posture, his jaw tight.

"We'll talk about this later."

He cracked a smile. "Can't wait."

"Great. You know Sasha's engaged. Sasha knows Luca asked for her hand. And I know I'm hungry as hell. Can we eat?"

Mom returned to her seat, leaning over to slap the back of Dad's head. "That's for keeping secrets."

"Yeah. Yeah. Eat your dinner."

Reluctantly, Mom cut off a piece of pork chop and popped it into her mouth. Dad nodded and took a bite.

We ate in silence until Dad reached for seconds. Mom sighed and said, "I'll need to call Rosa tomorrow so we can get the engagement party planned."

"What party?" I asked with a mouthful of mac and cheese.

Luca cleared his throat, balling his napkin in his fist. "My mom said she'd be happy to host at the house."

"Hello? Didn't you hear me? Am I invisible?" Dad made eye contact with me, discreetly shaking his head. The man never willingly got in the middle of any conversation.

"Oh! That's wonderful. I love your mom. This is going to be fun!" Mom bounced in her seat, pushing her plate away and jumping up from the table. "I'm going to go grab a notepad and pen."

"Mom, that's not—"

"I want to make sure we have an idea of what you guys want so that we can make this perfect," she said over her shoulder as she disappeared into the den.

I was invisible. Luca put a diamond on my finger, and I'd become invisible.

Mom sat back down and quickly jotted some notes. "Okay. What are we thinking for colors?" Her gaze finally fell on me.

Wide-eyed, I shook my head, and she pressed her lips into a thin line. Tapping her pen on the paper, she swung her focus to Luca. "What about you? Any ideas?"

Luca's expression went blank. "I figured Sasha would have some ideas. I'm a pretty basic guy."

"Understated elegance." Mom wrote something down. "I like that."

"Green." I blurted out.

"I'm sorry?"

"Green. I like the color green." For someone who made their living creating unique and personalized aesthetics, my mind blanked when it came to imagining my own wedding and the apparent prerequisite engagement party.

"We can do green." Mom grinned.

"Can we finish dinner before you grill the kids about this party?" Dad leaned over the old oak table and snagged another pork chop.

She set the pad of paper next to her and pulled her plate back. "Fine. We have all night."

"All night?"

Luca pulled away from my parents' house well after midnight. "Okay. Let me have it."

"Hm." I crossed my arms and looked out the window. Too tired to lay into him—my silent disappointment would have to do.

"I asked your dad for your hand."

"Mm-hmm."

"I knew you'd be pissed."

"Mm-hmm."

"But I also know you love your dad, and this is the kind of shit he cares about."

I glared at him. "That's a low blow."

He shrugged and merged onto the highway. My parents lived in the county, a solid thirty minutes from our house in the city. "Maybe, but it's true. And I swear to God—he got teary-eyed."

"Yeah?"

"Yeah. He also told me he felt bad for the ass whooping I was going to get for asking him." Luca chuckled. He and my dad were buddies. They'd gone hunting with each other and everything.

"You don't sound nearly as scared as you should be."

"I'm hoping you'll have mercy."

"Mercy?"

"Yep."

I stared at the side of his head, waiting for him to say more. He didn't. Instead, he turned up the radio and hummed along. His calmness only riled me more. I'd usually take any opportunity to fall asleep on the way home, but I picked at my annoyance until I was too agitated to sleep.

When we pulled up to the house, I grabbed my stuff and left Luca to get the leftovers. He was in for a rude awakening if he thought he was getting any engagement bliss sex.

I made my way upstairs, grumbling about men and how embarrassing it was to be in love with one, until I stopped outside our bedroom. "What's this?" I yelled down the stairs.

"What's it look like?" Luca's voice was getting closer.

"Like you begging for mercy."

Luca slid his hands around me until he cupped my soft stomach. His hold on me pushed away all the angst I'd felt in the car. All I felt was him—his heat, his breath on my exposed neck, his cock pressed against my ass.

Biting my lip, I turned in his hold. "You think some candles and rose petals make up for you being an asshole?"

"Maybe?" The corner of his lips tilted up.

"Look, I'm exhausted and don't want to fight—again—on what's supposed to be our engagement celebration weekend. But I need to make one thing clear." I choked up his shirt in my hand. "I am not a piece of property."

"I know that. I—"

"Let me finish. I know you fulfilled this asinine tradition for my dad, and the little girl in me loves you for it, but grown woman Sasha?" I shook my head. "Let that be the last time I'm discussed in terms of a man needing permission from another man to do any fucking thing with me. Got it?"

Luca pursed his lips. "In this house, you will never be treated like property." I nodded and turned, but he caught my hand and pulled me back to his chest. "But I have to be honest with you. You're joining a world where women are not equals. I don't agree with it, but it's our reality. You'll be my wife, untouchable." He paused, his hand cupping my face. "You've seen how my mom's treated."

My jaw tensed. He wasn't saying anything I didn't know, but it didn't make it suck any less.

Stroking my cheek with the rough pad of his thumb, he tilted my face up. His eyes burned into me, searching mine for understanding. "There will be times when I have to step in front of you and handle things. I need to know you'll be okay with that."

"As long as it's only when it comes to Moretti business, I'm fine. You can play Mr. Bossman all you want with them. But here," I gestured between us, "we're equals."

"Of course."

I blew out a breath. "Okay. In that case, let's go have a roll in the petals, and we can both do a little begging."

"Why don't you head to the bathroom? I have one more surprise."

Shooting him a playful glare, I kicked my heels off toward the closet and crossed the room. Luca followed, picking up my shoes and putting them in their correct space. I opened the bathroom door and was hit with warm, humid air. "What did you do?" Surrounded by candles, a steaming bubble bath complete with flower petals waited for me. Gentle music played on a wireless speaker, and my favorite silk pajamas sat folded on the counter.

"This was how I wanted our engagement night to end." Luca's deep timber sent chills through me. His fingers ghosted the back of my neck as he lifted the zipper of my dress and pulled it down. He peppered kisses on the newly exposed skin, making my toes curl against the tile and my eyes shut. "We should've been able to take our time celebrating." The pads of his thumbs spread the back completely open, skimming to my shoulders. "You deserved more than you got, and I plan on giving it to you now."

Never lifting his hands from me, he pushed my dress down my arms, his fingers threading with mine as the soft fabric fell to my waist. Wrapping our arms around me, he held me to his chest. "I love you, Sasha. I'm sorry I made you unhappy, but I'm more than willing to make it up to you for the rest of the night."

My breath stuttered as I tried to rein in my excitement. "Deal."

Cupping my breast with our hands, the tips of his fingers teased my nipples through the lace. "Your body is amazing. Sexiest I've ever seen. Ever touched." I trembled against him. That was Luca's superpower—bringing a bitch like me to her knees.

I arched my back and detangled our hands so I could unlatch my bra. The cups fell away, the cool air from the bedroom pebbling my nipples, and I let out a whimper. I needed him to touch me, to soothe the ache in my body.

Luca shuffled us forward, kicking the door closed and trapping us in the warm bathroom. His large hand spanned my breasts, his fingers toying with my nipples. A shuddering breath left my lips as he nipped my neck. With my arms pinned between our bodies, my torso was exposed for his pleasure.

"You going to let me get naked?" I tilted my face up to kiss the bottom of his jaw.

Luca rested his chin on my shoulder, curling his body around mine. "I guess." He brushed down my stomach, reverently cupping my belly before his hands disappeared under my dress. "You wet for me?" His long fingers slipped into my panties, parting my lips until my clit pulsed under his touch. Using his other hand, he gripped the inside of my thigh, pushing it to widen my stance. "Spread your legs."

Before I could move, he tapped my clit, sending a jolt through my body. He kicked my foot out, the smooth leather of his shoe grazing my barefoot. The brush of his suit on my naked back added to the sensation.

Luca slid two fingers through my folds, framing my clit between his knuckles. He pressed with just enough pressure to make me squirm. "You going to let me take care of you, Sasha?"

"Yes." No hesitation. There was never any hesitation with Luca.

"Beautiful." He pulled his fingers from me, pressing my clit as they passed. His wet digits skimmed up my body to my mouth, the smell of my arousal filling my nose. "Open."

Not being able to see his face added an element of excitement that only spun my excitement higher. I licked my bottom lip, my tongue grazing the tip of his finger. The tang of my arousal exploded on my taste buds, and I eagerly leaned forward, taking his two fingers deep into my mouth, sucking them clean. Luca groaned in my ear and wedged his cock between my ass cheeks.

When he rocked his hips, I pushed back, wanting him to slide into me. I may have gotten carried away because, without too much thought, I bit down.

Luca sucked in a breath but didn't remove his fingers. No. He shoved them deeper into my mouth until I gagged. Grunting, he yanked them free, rubbing the spit on my lips. "No more of that," he murmured against my shoulder blade, giving me a sharp bite.

I groaned, pressing my ass into him.

Luca roughly removed my dress and panties in one pull, leaving me naked in the middle of our bathroom with my back to him. He hadn't told me to stay in place, but it felt right.

"Grab the edge of the tub," Luca rasped. I fought the urge to look over my shoulder to see his expression.

A tremor went through my hands as I wrapped my fingers over the edge. I waited patiently, my eyes following bubbles as they floated atop the warm water. The steam curled my baby hairs, probably melting my makeup.

I nearly jumped out of my skin when a hand ghosted the curve of my ass. A sharp smack kept me in place. This wasn't a new game for us. He knew exactly how to keep me in line. His stubble against my skin nearly sent me face-first into the lovely bath. He kissed the globes of my ass thoroughly, licking, nipping, and full-on biting until every inch had been loved.

A finger slid down my crack, making my knees nearly give out. Luca gripped my ass cheeks, digging into my flesh as he spread me wide. His tongue followed the same path as his finger, only this time he swirled my asshole. I pressed against his hold, offering myself up like a fucking buffet, but he continued down.

I slid my knees out, and his fingers bit into my skin as they kept me spread. Humming, Luca teased me until my pussy fluttered, and I ached for more. His teeth nipped, gently pulling, making me sigh in frustration.

He was playing with me. "Luca," I warned. There was no way to misinterpret my tone.

Immediately, his hand came down with a loud crack on my ass, then returned to its punishing grip. Before I'd recovered, he speared me with his thick tongue as he buried his face in my pussy. I moaned, my hips bucking against his face, trying to ride it despite the hold he had me in. My grip slipped on the edge of the tub, and my hands splashed into the hot water. At the last second, I caught myself by the elbows, saving me from going face-first in the bubbles. "Luca!"

The fucker chuckled, and his mouth moved back to my asshole as he slid two fingers into my cunt, slowly pumping like he was happy to do it forever. Familiar pressure built in my belly, but Luca's languid movements kept me from reaching a climax.

I was a moaning, begging, thigh-shaking mess when Luca pulled away and stood behind me. "Look at me, Sasha."

Bracing myself on the tub, I slid to my ass, my back resting against the cool porcelain. I looked up at him, and my breath hitched.

Still fully clothed with his hair a mess and face shining with my arousal, he looked like a fucking god.

I wanted to suck his cock. I wanted him to tell me to suck his cock. I wanted to gag on him. Choke. But the look on his face let me know he had other things in mind.

There was always time for that later.

"Can you get in, or do you need my help?"

I pushed up and was able to get my feet under me to take two graceful steps into our obscenely large tub. I sunk into the water, groaning as the water enveloped me. "This is amazing." I shut my eyes and leaned back onto the little water pillow he'd affixed to the edge. When he didn't respond, I rolled my head to the side and caught the tail end of my favorite strip show, only this time, he didn't carefully place his clothes in their correct baskets.

No.

His hungry eyes never strayed from me.

"You're getting in?"

He nodded.

"Even though baths are just sitting in your own filth?"

His boxers hit the ground, and he stalked over to the tub. "I will happily sit in your filth."

A chill ran down my spine—he was about to fuck me up.

The water sloshed around as he joined me. Once he was in, he got on his hands and knees, crawling over me until I was pressed against the tub. "Hold on to the sides," was the only warning I got before his head disappeared below the bubbles and his mouth attached to my clit, his fingers sliding into me, moving furiously. First two, then three, all while his mouth worked my clit until I shook. His hand gripped my ass, pushing my pussy more into his face, and then moved behind me. A finger massaged my ass, and I jerked in his hold. Pressing back, it slipped in, adding just the right amount of pressure to shatter me completely.

I reached blindly under the water and grabbed a handful of Luca's hair, pulling him out. He gasped, bubbles clinging to his hair and chin, but he didn't seem worse for the wear.

"What the fuck was that?" I panted.

"Just trying something." He smiled down at me, brushing the hair from my cheek.

"My turn." I pushed him back, climbing on his legs, ready to test my own lung capacity.

I bet I can beat his time.

THREE

It only took my mom and Rosa three weeks to plan the engagement party. I was impressed and horrified when, the day after our family dinner, they sent me a mockup invitation to a close, intimate gathering of one hundred people the weekend before Valentine's Day. They'd created multiple binders of wedding ideas and assured me I wouldn't have to lift a finger.

I'd hope fucking not, considering I didn't want any of the things they deemed "necessary."

"Can you zip me up?"

Luca came out of the bathroom in just a pair of black boxer briefs, drying his hair with a towel—le sigh. The majesty of the wash and go. Of course, I'd spent a few hours primping and preening to make sure I was ready for the grotesque display of pomp and circumstance our moms had put together. But it is what it is.

Tossing the towel in the laundry basket, he joined me at the mirror. He ran a knuckle up my spine to the base of my neck, where he placed a kiss. His lips brushed the shell of my ear as he murmured, "You look beautiful."

"Thank you." I smiled at him in the mirror. "Have you heard

from your guy Chase about my car? I'm getting a little tired of being carted around by Pete."

Luca dragged the zipper up, his body crowding me. "He called this morning while you were out. It looks like your little electric car is totaled."

"Great. Did he say what happened?"

Luca's jaw tensed, but then his face relaxed into a pleasant smile. "Your car was old, and your brakes were worn. You're lucky it didn't happen on the highway."

"Small blessings," I muttered as I fussed with the top of my dress.

Luca's eyes followed the path of my fingers as I moved the clasp of my necklace. "You ready for tonight?"

I sighed. "No. I know it's going to be over the top. Your mom sent over the menu, and my mom sent over the flower arrangements. Spoilers, it's a mini wedding."

"Maybe we can just get married tonight." Luca squeezed my hips before he went into the closet, leaving me to fret alone.

"Could we?"

Poking his head out, he smiled. "Of course not. At least with everything going on with the Chronis family, the engagement party will be small." I rolled my eyes, and he laughed, popping back into the closet. "You're marrying into a family with a lot of traditions. What would it look like if Luca Moretti eloped?" He walked out, unzipping the garment bag that held his suit. "Unfortunately, this wedding isn't really about us."

"Romantic." I sunk into the chair at my vanity.

Luca looked up from where he smoothed his jacket on the bed. "I know." Rounding the post, he knelt before me, taking my hands in his. "I promise you that the honeymoon will be all about us."

While I'd never been too keen to get married, now that I'd met Luca and decided to take the leap, it was disappointing that the entire wedding would be some dog and pony show to install me as the new Mrs. of the boss. I gave him a peck on the lips. "It better be." With a heavy sigh, I shook our arms out and let go of his hands to turn and do one last check of my makeup. A small smudge of my lipstick caught my eye as I asked, "When do you want to get married? We haven't decided, and the dynamic duo is foaming at the mouth."

"I was thinking June?" He slipped on his dress shirt, and I couldn't keep my eyes off him as he made fast work of buttoning it. The fluid motion of his fingers down his body was like a reverse striptease, and I couldn't look away.

"Classic." I licked my lips as he bent over and pulled up his pants. His thick muscular thighs and ass tensed, looking good enough to bite. "So, June next year? Or were you thinking of a longer engagement since we've only been back together a few months?"

It couldn't be normal to get this turned on watching someone get dressed.

He took his time buttoning his pants and sliding his belt through the loops. His eyebrows drew together, and his lips pursed as he buckled it. "I want to get married this June." I choked on air, my ogling interrupted by him being out of his fucking mind. "I've wanted to marry you for a long time." He lifted his eyes and put his hands on his hips. "Maybe since we stood across from each other at Michael and Sarah's wedding."

My lips flapped like a dying fish. It was ridiculous he still left me speechless after all this time.

"You were just talking about eloping."

I nodded.

"But you're scared of a June wedding?" Luca looked confused.

Right there with ya, buddy.

"Four months. We'd only have four months to plan some mafia extravaganza."

He rolled his eyes like he did every time I used the "m" word. "You know my mom has it covered."

I shot up, tossing my lipstick on the table. "It's our wedding.

We should probably be the ones handling the planning. Don't you think?"

"Do you want to plan a wedding for five hundred?" He lifted a brow, knowing damn well I had no interest in that shit.

I threw my arms out wide. "So, we leave it to our mothers and hope they can work a miracle in four months?"

"You'd be surprised what unlimited funds can get done."

My head spun.

Rich people shit.

Luca walked over to the full-length mirror and looped his tie. My gaze was stuck on the way his hands moved the silk into an expert knot, only to untie it and do it again.

"Are you okay?" His eyebrows pulled together as he watched me in the mirror.

Shaking my head, I sat on the edge of the bed with my hands folded on my lap.

"You look shell-shocked." He sighed and came to stand in front of me. "Look, I know this is a lot. And I know it's not romantic, but it's what has to be done. This wedding will solidify my reign and let everyone know the new generation is here. It's not only about us but about Marco and the rest of my inner circle." He tilted my chin up with his finger, ghosting his thumb across my bottom lip so as not to smudge my lipstick. "I hate we have to use our wedding to do it, but that doesn't mean we can't enjoy the day."

The icky feeling in my stomach didn't subside. Luca couldn't sweet talk my worries away. Confusion swept over me because I'd never cared about weddings, but I couldn't ignore the fact that I was disappointed. I wasn't going to have the wedding I wanted. It was a wedding I'd never imagined as a little girl but was becoming clearer in my mind.

I wrapped my arms around Luca's neck, keeping my chin up and away from his clothes. No need to get my pasty ass makeup on his shirt. "Okay."

He leaned back, his hands on my waist. "We can talk more about this after the party. Okay?"

"Sounds good." I managed to smile and finished gathering my things in a clutch that matched my cocktail dress. Rosa and Mom made one concession—the engagement party was black tie optional. I knew the wedding would be non-negotiable, so I got my way this one time.

And damn, was I glad when Luca slid on his jacket. He was in head-to-toe black, with the lines of his suit cut close to his figure. Beautiful Italian leather shoes covered his long feet, matching the belt around his narrow waist. The stubble on his jaw and his tousled damp hair made him look every inch the made man he was.

"You look amazing."

He brushed a flat hand down the front of his jacket and smirked. "You think so?"

I bit the inside of my cheek and gave him a head-to-toe look. Smiling, I sauntered toward him, only to veer off at the last second toward the door.

"Hey!"

"We need to go if we don't want to be late." As I walked down the stairs, I heard mumbled cursing and his steps rushing to catch up.

"What are you doing with the laundry?"

"I'm throwing it in the wash." He frowned at me. "You didn't expect me to leave a damp towel in the basket overnight? Did you?"

A dusting of snow covered the Moretti mansion, and lights sat at the base of the columns, making the already massive home look obscene. The long drive and the street outside the gate were lined with expensive vehicles in an impressive show of wealth and status. Luca passed the valet his keys and joined me on the pathway. "You ready?"

My fingers traced the gems on my neck—the heirloom had become a source of strength for me. The necklace had belonged to Rosa's mom, the underboss's wife who raised five daughters, married them all off to capos or better, outlived her husband, and ensured the family's security. In her way, in her day, she was a bad bitch.

"As ready as I'll ever be." I smiled at him. "How about you? You ready for the Morettis to meet the Mitchells?"

Luca looked up at the house and shook his head with a grin. "I think everyone will get along just fine." He brushed a lock of hair from my eyes. "I'm more concerned about what Axel will show up wearing. I don't know if they make flannel nice enough to keep our moms from shoving him into one of my dad's suits." He pressed his hand to the small of my back, pushing me into motion.

"I'd love to see that. The fabric would be *struggling*."

We entered the foyer laughing, handed our coats to a guy at the door, and set off to find our parents. When we walked into the parlor, the group of people all turned and cheered. Dante was the first person to reach us. He threw his whole body at me, latching onto my waist. The kid was growing like a weed. He'd just turned nine, and I could tell he'd be as tall as Luca.

"Congratulations!"

"Thanks, Bud."

"So, this means you'll be my aunt for real?"

"Yup."

"Awesome! Am I going to get cousins now?"

I barked out a laugh, and my eyes landed on Adriana and Marco heading our way. "We'll see."

Dante frowned, looking back at his mom. "She says I'm not getting siblings anytime soon, so it's up to you."

Adriana blushed. "I didn't—"

"Yes, you did. You said it's Sasha's turn."

Luca wrapped an arm around my waist. "Let us get married, and then we'll talk, okay?"

"Whenever adults say we'll talk about something, they mean no." Dante huffed and sped off toward the kitchen.

"You using me for surrogate siblings?" I smirked at Adriana.

"I mean . . ."

Marco patted Luca's arm and gave him a cute little handshake hug thing. "Congrats." He turned to me with a smile full of genuine joy. Holding his arms out, he fanned his hands, ushering me into a hug. "Congrats, Red. Welcome to the family."

"Thank you." I stepped back and brushed off some powder that had settled on his shoulder. "Sorry about that. The dangers of hugging the pale."

"No worries. Let me grab you guys a drink. A scotch and a . . ."

"Gin and tonic."

"Got it."

Marco left Adriana to offer her congratulations and hugs.

"I'm so happy you guys found your way back together." She whispered in my ear. When she leaned back, her eyes shined with emotion.

"You've always been our number one supporter," I said with a smirk.

Adriana threw her head back with a laugh. It amazed me how far we'd all come with one another.

"What did I miss?" Marco passed us our drinks and stood behind Adriana's petite body.

"Just talking about how Adriana fell in love with me the first time she met me."

"Sounds about right." Marco smiled down at her. What a change from the man I met in the art gallery.

"Luca! Sasha!" Rosa floated into the room, my mom hot on her heels. She gave us each a kiss on the cheek and then took my hands and held them out to the side. "You look lovely."

"Thank you." I blushed as I caught my mom's eye over Rosa's

shoulder. I smiled, but she was too busy inspecting my outfit to notice, her gaze spending a lot of time on my cleavage. "Mom?"

Rosa stepped out of the way, letting my mom take her place. "This color is nice on you." Mom kissed my cheek, gave me one more lingering look, and moved on to Luca. "And look at you. So handsome."

"Thank you, Maggie."

"You two mingle, eat some of these canapés, and we'll round up everyone for speeches." Mom bounced away, talking Rosa's ear off."

"Speeches?" I frowned at their retreating backs.

"Just some short toasts. Aunt Rosa, your dad, Ashley, and me." Marco shrugged.

"Wonderful."

Add speeches about me and my relationship to the shit Sasha hates list.

I spotted Ashley, Malcolm, Jazz, and Imani huddled in a corner, laughing. "Be right back." I patted Luca's arm, then made my way across the room.

"There you are!" Ashley passed her drink to Malcolm and threw her body at me, her face landing in my cleavage. "You look fantastic!"

"Look at you!" I pulled back to admire how the deep purple dress complimented her brown skin. "Had to show me up, huh?"

She put her hand under her chin and batted her eyelashes. "Always."

Everyone laughed as they filed in for hugs and congratulations.

"You guys been here long?"

"We got here about ten minutes before you. Your mom brought us in here and ordered us to get drinks and food." Jazz laughed, waving at my mom, who was cozied up next to my dad in the hallway. "She's an interesting lady."

"Don't I know it."

"Be nice." Imani chastised Jazz, then smiled at me. "Congratulations!"

"Thank you." I nodded and turned toward the rest of the room, smiling even though the sight of so many Morettis staring at me made me uncomfortable. "This is a lot, huh?"

"I can only imagine what the wedding will be like," Imani said in a breathy voice, the idea of weddings and marriage doing something to her. Jazz was waiting for the ring to come in, and then they'd have their own high society parties to contend with.

"A fucking nightmare, I imagine," I grumbled. Ashley dug her sharp little elbow into my ribs, and I swatted her arm. Rubbing my side, I glared at her. "If you don't watch it, I'll step on your little ass."

"Don't threaten me with a good time." She blew a raspberry and took her drink from Malcolm. He towered over her in all his handsome, tailored glory, her fluffy, curly mane just brushing the knot in his tie. Pure admiration passed between them as he dropped a sweet kiss on her hair.

Imani giggled into Jazz's side as she adjusted the top of her black figure-hugging cocktail dress. Her generous pear shape on display, matched with a delicious pair of blood-red heels, made the ensemble the most daring I'd ever seen her wear. "I had no idea Sasha doled out punishments."

"Only to the very lucky." Jazz stage whispered into her ear, wrapping her thin, bare arm around Imani's exposed shoulder, her tall, lean body bending around Imani's short, thick frame. "You ready for all this?" She jutted her chin toward the rest of the room.

"Eh. It's looking like I don't have a choice. Our moms are already in planning mode, and apparently, we're getting married in June."

Ashley nodded, her eyebrows drawn together. "A little over a year. That's not so bad."

"Of this year."

All four sets of eyes fell on me. "Um. That's a quick turn-around." Ashley placed a hand on my arm.

"Yeah."

All five of us took a drink, looking like we were at a wake, not a celebration.

Frowning at my empty glass, I asked, "Where are Scott and Axel?"

Ashley cleared her throat, her hand smoothing down my arm. "Axel was in the bathroom adjusting the jacket Mrs. Moretti forced him into, and Scott is . . . right there."

I looked over my shoulder as Scott walked into the room, wiping the corner of his mouth. Nicki was five steps behind him, looking perfect, except her bombshell waves were more tousled than styled.

"That motherfucker," I muttered, and Ashley sighed.

"Don't."

I glared at her. "Don't? You see the mountain of a man standing by the window?"

Ashley's eyes darted Aldo's way and widened. "Oh."

"Yeah. Oh. That's Nicki's fiancé and the dude that will fucking end Scott if he even *thinks* Nicki's been getting her jollies somewhere else."

Ashley swallowed as Scott approached. He leaned in, wrapping his wiry arms around me, and I caught a whiff of expensive perfume. The kind of perfume uptight, hot-as-hell women wore. "Congrats, Red."

"Nice perfume."

He let me go, subtly sniffing his shoulder. "Jealous?"

"Nope. Concerned. Have you met Aldo yet?"

Scott shrugged and looked around the room. When his eyes fell on Nicki, he tensed. "That's the accountant?"

"Yup."

"Fuck."

"Mm-hmm."

He huffed out a humorless laugh. "I'm dead." His hand

gripped the back of his neck as he turned to me. "Any chance Luca can keep him from killing me?"

I smiled, trying to keep my expression lighthearted. Scott had no idea how much danger he was in and that Luca was, in fact, the only person who could keep him from catching the beating of his life. Fuck, he'd be the only person who could save him from losing his life if Aldo found out he was fucking his fiancée. "No promises."

He ran a hand through his messy blond locks, his cheeks pink as he snuck one last look at Nicki. "Yeah. I'm fucked." The look on his face worried me. It wasn't the look of a man who was appropriately scared.

Tapping on a glass drew my attention away from my self-destructive friend.

"Can I have everyone's attention?" Rosa stood in the door-way, flanked by my parents and Marco. "It's time to make some speeches and toasts, so please freshen up your drinks and meet by the stairs."

The crowd shifted around, and we all congregated in the large entryway where everyone could fit. Rosa ushered Luca and me up the stairs, and we stood a story above everyone. It was all very *Evita*.

"Thank you all for joining us to celebrate Luca and Sasha's engagement. I can't tell you how special it is to welcome another daughter into the family." Rosa smiled down at Adriana, then focused back on us. "Sasha is an extraordinary woman. From the moment I met her, I knew Luca had found his other half. There's nothing like meeting your soulmate." Rosa wiped her eye and cleared her throat. My chest tightened at the way she looked at Luca. I hadn't had a moment of ease around Rosa since I'd killed her husband.

Of course I hadn't.

"Normally, Dante would handle any toasts or speeches, so I'll keep this brief. Please raise your glass and welcome the newest member of the Moretti family."

Champagne flutes raised, and a murmur of congratulations filled the room.

Dad joined us at the railing, practically vibrating with joy. "For those of you who don't know, I'm Sasha's dad, Greg Mitchell. First, I want to thank Rosa for hosting this whole shindig." Rosa smiled and clinked glasses with my mom. The two were thick as thieves after a few weeks of wedding planning. "I don't think we'd all be nearly as comfortable in my den." A smattering of laughter from our family and a few polite chuckles from the Moretti's echoed up to us.

"From the minute Sasha was born, I knew she'd be a hell-raiser." A shocked laugh burst from my mouth. Not sure why I was surprised, but I thought the swanky surroundings would temper my dad.

Not so much.

"As she grew up, she found ways to get in trouble that I could've never imagined. Like in fourth grade when she set up an underground candy bar store in her desk. We only caught on because she tried to take care of the bill at dinner. We found nearly one hundred dollars in a shoebox under her bed."

Dante's mouth hung open as he looked up at me with more reverence than I'd ever received.

"In high school, she told us she was a designated driver when she was actually running a paid service to help kids sneak back into their houses. While I admired her entrepreneurial spirit, we had to put an end to it after a line of parents ended up on our front porch complaining about the money and the fact their kids had been getting away with God knows what."

I laughed, remembering how awkward the "punishment" conversation had been. Dad couldn't bring himself to ground me, so he made me promise to stop and give back the money.

I never gave back the money.

"Luca, you've chosen one hell of a challenge for a wife. You'd do well to remember she's an excellent shot with a mind that can solve any problem." Dad leveled Luca with a stare that was full of amusement and warning. After a beat, he raised his champagne flute in the air, the glass comically small in his worn hand. "To Luca and Sasha. Good luck to him and every happiness to her." He chuckled, his cheeks red and his smile wide as he took a sip. Cringing, he wrapped his arm around me and whispered in my ear. "I love you, kid."

"I love you, Dad."

Marco took a step, raising himself above the crowd. "I guess I'm next." He winked up at me. "Luca—"

A series of buzzing and chimes stopped him from talking, and almost all the men drew their phones, including my dad, uncles, and his friends from the firehouse. Luca frowned at his screen, and then his eyes flashed to Adriana and me.

"There's a fire." Dad looked at me apologetically before visually rounding up his fellow county firefighters. Half the guests moved toward the door, organizing rides. Wives kissed husbands and clumped together, trying to decide whether to stay or go. If they were calling in everyone, it must be a serious emergency. Dad hugged me, then went to my mom and whispered in her ear. Her face grim, she nodded and kissed him goodbye.

Confused, I turned to Luca for answers, but he was already locked in a quiet conversation with Marco. Morettis scattered out the front door and through the house.

"What's going on?" I asked, but Luca and Marco either didn't hear me or ignored my question.

"An entire city block is up in flames. The city's reached out to the county for assistance." My mom's voice startled me.

With my eyes locked on Luca, I asked, "Where?"

"Your dad didn't say."

Finally, Luca turned me and jerked his chin toward the hallway. Dread spread through me as I joined him in front of his old bedroom. "What is it?"

"Someone started a fire in Adriana's home, and it's spread to the entire block." My stomach dropped. "I need to go talk to my mom, and you guys need to wind the party down. Get the caterers and all non-Moretti's out of the house."

I nodded and turned to go to Rosa, but Luca caught my hand and pulled me to him. His lips were on mine before I could ask what he was doing. The kiss was hard, claiming—a testament to being alive. I wound my arms around his neck, pressing myself to him.

He leaned back, our noses brushing against each other. "I love you."

"I love you, too."

Hand in hand, we went to find Rosa, all thoughts about engagements and weddings gone.

FOUR

It took thirty minutes to clear the house of party guests and caterers. Rosa called to push back the cleaning crew, so Adriana, Luca, and I sat in the kitchen surrounded by party mess.

"So, it's all gone?" Adriana twisted a napkin in her hand, her knee bouncing.

"It's not looking good."

Adriana's focus stayed on the white linen sliding between her fingers. Luca and I shared a look, neither knowing what to do or what to say. Tossing the napkin down, she pushed her chair back and abruptly stood. "I should go check on Dante."

Rosa passed Adriana on her way out of the kitchen, the two women sharing tired, tight smiles.

"Marco's waiting for you in your father's study."

Luca sighed and leaned into me, whispering, "Are you tired?"

I shook my head. How could I sleep when someone burned down our family's homes?

"Then, can you keep my mom and Adriana company? Marco and I need time to get some answers."

"Okay, I can do that."

"I know you can." He wrapped an arm around me, and my body relaxed for the first time since Marco's speech was interrupted. I slid my hands around his waist, pressing my chest into his side.

Luca kissed the top of my head and left for the study.

Without Luca's presence, I swore I could feel the ghost of Dante Moretti Sr. watching me interlope in his familial home and business. A shiver went down my spine, and I rushed to the counter to grab another dumpling. Washing down the savory bite with the last of the champagne in my glass, I took a deep breath.

"Tea?" Rosa stood by the stove, holding her red tea kettle. A plate of cookies sat next to her on the counter.

"Yes, please." I took a seat at the breakfast table, clearing a spot for Rosa. "I'm sorry we're keeping you up."

She waved me off and carried the tray holding our tea and cookies over. "It's not the first time family business has kept me up all night, and I'm sure it won't be the last." She handed me a cup and saucer. "Or yours, if we're being honest."

"I suppose not," I mumbled, blowing on my tea, knowing full well I would burn my mouth no matter what I did. Patience had never been my virtue.

"Hm." She took a sip and then went to stand. "I should take the boys some coffee."

I noticed a second tray on the counter and jumped up. "Let me. You've already done enough."

"All right." She gave me a soft smile, but her warm brown eyes bore into me. Since Dante's death, I'd caught her staring at me a lot. The irrational fear she'd figured out what happened to her husband made me jittery. I balanced the tray the best I could and headed toward the study. Raised voices slowed my steps until I stood frozen in the middle of the hallway.

"I want them alive." Luca's voice was cold, harsh. "I don't give a fuck. Make it happen. You have until sunrise."

Footsteps sounded toward the door and then away. "I can't believe Chronis had the fucking balls to do this. All for a daughter he was ready to marry off to the enemy." Marco's voice dripped with disgust.

"You know they don't give a fuck about Zoe. They're just using her as an excuse for all this bullshit. At this point, I wish I would've killed her."

"And you really don't know where she is or what happened to her?"

There was a heavy silence. I moved next to the door, dangerously close to being in the line of sight.

"No. Why would I?"

"You were fucking her."

The accusation hit me right in the chest, and I swallowed thickly, biting the inside of my cheek. I had no reason to feel a way —we'd been broken up for over a year—but shit, if that wasn't a kick in the ass.

"Well, I don't know where she is. I'd put a bullet in her head myself if I did." Luca's tone left little doubt of his words.

There was a beat of silence and a sigh. "I can't believe they burned down Adriana's house. And, fuck, mine! What would've happened if she had been there? Or Dante?" Marco sounded more flustered than I'd ever heard him.

The tray shook in my hands as I let his words settle in. *We could've lost Dante.*

"I know," Luca mumbled something unintelligible and cleared his throat. "They'll pay for it. We just need to buy some time so we can put them down for good."

"I'm glad you didn't marry the bitch. Nothing, not even peace, is worth being tied to that family. I hope you see that now."

"This is the last time we're talking about this. I did what I thought was best while my father was spiraling. We were on the edge of either Chronis wiping us out or the feds bringing us down. The only reason I'm explaining myself to you is that you're more like a brother than Dante ever was. But make no mistake, I *am* the boss. You're my right hand, and I trust you with my life, but I won't have you second-guessing me. Got it?" Luca didn't yell. He didn't need to. The frost in his voice sent a shiver through my body. Luca would never hurt me, but I couldn't say the same for Marco. The threat sounded real as hell.

"Got it. Do you need me here, or do you want me out with Tootsie?"

"Tootsie's tied up right now. Take Aldo and Mickey, but keep them on a leash. I want the fuckers scared and roughed up, not dead."

There was the sound of chairs moving, and Marco let out a humorless laugh. "And to think you wanted to run Moretti's. You're a butcher of a different kind now."

"I was a chef, not a butcher. Get the fuck out of here."

Expensive shoes squeaked on the hardwood, and I sprang into action, reaching the door as it swung all the way open. Marco stopped in the doorway, a frown on his face.

"Rosa thought you guys might need some coffee. You're leaving already?" I asked, keeping my face neutral.

Marco eyed me. Ever since he escorted me out of the hotel room covered in his uncle's blood, he'd paid closer attention to me, which was fair considering . . . "Yeah, but Luca will need that. It's going to be a long night." He patted my shoulder as he passed, and I inched into the study.

"Knock. Knock."

Luca looked up from his phone, and for a split second, I saw the fierce mob boss that forced a man like Marco to yield. With a blink, Luca's face softened, but the heat in his eyes stayed. "Coffee? Perfection."

I placed the tray on the desk and poured him a cup. "Do you need anything else?"

"No. The coffee will do." He took a sip, sucking in a breath when it scalded his mouth. Setting the cup down, he rounded the desk, catching me in a hug. "You should probably go settle in for the night. There's no point in both of us being exhausted tomorrow."

"Wake me up if you need me, okay?"

"You got it." He leaned down, his lips ghosting over mine

before pulling back. "This is not the way I wanted to spend the night of our engagement party." He looked around the richly decorated room. "In my parents' house, up all night overseeing a fucking manhunt."

I caressed his face, my thumb running over a small scar on his cheek. "I understand. Just make sure you take care of yourself. I need you healthy and safe."

"Always." His phone rang, and he pecked my lips before returning to the desk. "Luca," he answered, dismissing me with a tight-lipped smile.

On the way back to the kitchen, I twisted my hands. I needed a moment alone to digest everything I'd heard.

"There you are. I heard the front door close. Are the boys gone?" Rosa nibbled a cookie.

"Just Marco. Luca is still taking calls. He told me I could head to bed, but I don't think I can sleep after all this."

"Understandable. I could never sleep when Dante was handling business." Sipping her tea, she kept her eyes on me as I sat. The family had a habit of watching me like a hawk.

"How did you do it?" I didn't have the right to ask Rosa for guidance, but I had no one else unless I wanted to watch movies and tv shows, and we all know those are full of shit.

"What's that, honey?"

"This. Being the wife of a Moretti. The Moretti."

"Ah. I was born and bred to be the wife of a made man."

I set my teacup down in shock. "Like an arranged marriage."

She nodded with a serene smile. "Yes. It's how it was done, at least in my family and Dante's." She shrugged. "I never knew another life. My momma and papa were an arranged marriage, my sisters were all married off to made men, and I got Dante." She chuckled and broke off a piece of cookie, popping it into her mouth.

"Wow."

"Don't look at me like that. You saw Dante. I was happy as any twenty-one-year-old could be." She sighed dreamily. Her eyes were unfocused as if she were reliving a memory. "All my sisters worried about me marrying the heir to a family, especially the Morettis."

"What do you mean?"

Her smile dimmed, and she took a sip of tea as she collected her thoughts. "Dante was the boss's eldest son, but that didn't mean he was just handed the head of the family. He had to earn it, and we fought tooth and nail to secure our place."

"Oh."

"You shouldn't have any problems. Luca's left no question as to who's in charge. But that doesn't mean there won't be challenges for you."

Suddenly, I was back in that hotel room with Dante's hands wrapped around my throat, fighting for my life.

"Now that you're engaged, you'll be on the radar of every family in the country. I know my son will protect you with his life, but you need to be able to take care of yourself." She shoved the plate of cookies toward me. "Take a bite. You look pale."

Of course I looked pale. Rosa was putting words to all my fears, but her no-nonsense tone snapped me from spiraling. "Thanks."

"I'm not trying to scare you, just trying to make sure you're going in, eyes wide open."

"I appreciate that. It's . . . a lot."

"And it doesn't let up. Someone will always be gunning for Luca and, by extension, you. You don't have the benefit of being raised in the life, so your learning curve is huge, but I'm here to help you." She leaned over the table and placed her hand over mine, the warmth of her soft palm soothing away some of my nerves. "I offer you the same thing I offered Adriana when she joined the family. I'm here to help you grow into your role in any way I can. You're family now, and we take care of family." She squeezed my hand, let it go, and picked up her teacup.

"Were Adrianna and Dante?"

"Arranged?" She bobbled her head back and forth. "Yes and no."

I lifted an eyebrow and waited to see if she would spill.

"You'll have to ask her. Her father arranged for her to marry into the family, but Dante saw her, and the rest was history."

As much as I wanted to know more, I had enough on my plate without adding past dramas. Yawning, I covered my mouth, trying to stifle the sound.

"You should probably head on up to bed. You're dead on your feet."

I nodded, knowing she was right but hating that I was fading. "What about you?" I asked as I stood, stretching my arms out.

"I think I'll stay up a little bit longer. Make sure Luca doesn't need anything else."

"I should probably—"

"Nope. Off to bed with you. You've had a big night, and you're not a wife yet."

I frowned, but she just laughed.

"Don't worry. You'll have decades to stay up all night with Luca. Let me do it this one last time." She rounded the table and gave me another hug. I held her to me, trying to impart a silent apology and give her thanks for taking me under her wing. Without her and Adriana's knowledge and experience, I wouldn't last long in this life. "Good night. We'll catch up in the morning."

"Thank you."

I left her alone, shuffling around the kitchen. Was that what a typical night looked like for her? Ever-present guilt stabbed at my already raw feelings. I had to find some way to ease my conscience. There was no way I'd be able to live with the constant spiraling.

Luca's old bedroom was the same as it was the day of the funeral. My chest ached for all the loss she'd experienced. Rosa had never changed the boys' rooms and was only now considering changes to her own after Dante's death.

Two sets of pajamas, towels, and a small toiletries bag sat on the end of the bed. I was able to remove my makeup and get in bed in no time.

Laying in the dark bedroom, I couldn't turn my brain off even though my body was thoroughly exhausted. More than anything, I wished I was in my own bed, being held by Luca. That's what normal couples do after getting engaged—not have homes burned down and overhear death threats on missing women.

If Luca did have something to do with Zoe Chronis going missing, wouldn't he have told Marco? Of course he would. He trusted Marco enough to cover up my murder of Dante Sr. You don't yank a stiletto from an eye socket, help arrange a dead body in a car crash for someone, just to fuck them over later. Luca had to trust Marco.

But talking to Rosa made me doubt some of what I'd taken for granted when it came to Luca and his family. My understanding of a crime family was obviously airbrushed by pop culture and had little to do with the real ins and outs of the life.

I tried to wait up for Luca, but at some point, I fell asleep, and when I woke up, it was clear Luca had never come to bed. I went downstairs, and Rosa was in the kitchen in a cute, casual outfit, ready for the day.

"Good morning. Want some coffee?"

I nodded and plopped down in a chair. Morning and I didn't get along, and after the night we'd had, I was exhausted despite getting the recommended eight hours. "Is Luca in the study?"

She shook her head, poured me a cup of coffee, and put a piece of coffee cake on a small plate. "Marco came back around five, and the two left. He told me to let you sleep and tell you to stay here until he comes and picks you up."

Taking a bite of the cinnamon piece of heaven, I nodded.

"I thought this would be harder."

"You give me coffee and cake, and I'm good."

"If only everyone were that easy." Rosa laughed, turning her back to me to tackle the dishes.

For a minute, I allowed myself to get lost in the domestic bliss because it wouldn't last. Tomorrow, I'd have to go to work, probably with a bodyguard, and pretend there wasn't an entire group of people who would love to see me dead.

The doorbell sounded through the house, and I put down the last bite of coffee cake and followed Rosa to the door. Adriana was already there, stuck in a standoff with a pissed-off Nicki.

"I told you. I need to get something from the office."

"And I told you, Luca isn't here, and neither is Aldo. Come back when they are."

Adriana started to close the door, but Nicki stopped it with her hand. "Can you drop the scorned woman act for one fucking minute and—"

"Nicki?" Rosa's firm voice carried through the foyer, and Nicki's tan face blanched. I bit back a laugh at the epic turnaround.

"Rosa. I—uh. Luca asked me to grab a folder for him." Nicki's eyes darted behind Rosa, landing on me, and her lips pressed together. The flicker of worry in her eyes and her timid words made me uneasy.

She was lying.

"You know I don't let anyone in the study when Luca isn't here."

"But—"

"No, dear. Have Luca text you when he's back, and you can come by, maybe even have dinner with us." Her voice was soft, but her tone was bitter.

Nicki's eyes widened as she nodded, pulling her hand from the edge of the door. Adriana shut it right in her face and then swung around to us. "The nerve of that bitch to come in here like she has every right."

"She's always been an entitled princess. You can thank Gabe and Dante for that." Rosa turned to the kitchen, leaving us to follow if we wanted to hear what she was saying. "And I doubt she came here for a folder." Rosa tilted her head with a smirk. "I found one of her little lacy pieces in a guest room this morning.

I'm guessing she didn't want us to know she snuck away with that blond boy."

My eyes went straight to the cupboard that held the trash can. "Oh. That's—"

Rosa laughed as she sat back down, picking up her mug. "Don't worry. I won't say anything. Although, you better warn that boy. Nicki's always been one to dabble where she shouldn't." She lifted an eyebrow at me. "But she's never been involved with anyone while she did it. I don't think Aldo would appreciate his fiancée . . ." she waved her hand.

"Right." I sunk into my chair and sighed. "He's been warned." Picking at the tiny bit of coffee cake left on my plate, I struggled to find the words. "So, Nicki has a history of screwing around with taken men?"

Adriana snorted as she poured a cup of coffee. "It's kind of her M.O." The two women shared a heavy look.

"We don't have to talk about this," I said, despite itching to know more. I had my suspicions, but I wanted confirmation.

Rosa shifted in her seat and cleared her throat. "No. Now might be the best time to have this conversation." She pursed her lips, her red-manicured nails tapping the side of her coffee mug. "Marrying into the Moretti family is wonderful, but there are a few unfortunate realities."

"One of them being the Nickis of the world trying to fuck their way into the top spot," Adriana said as she sat down.

"Adriana." Rosa admonished but still slid her a piece of coffee cake.

"What? Do you think she slept with Dante because she loved him?"

"They did date in college."

"I'm not talking about my Dante." Adriana bit back, and Rosa's cheeks flamed. Immediately, Adriana softened. "Sorry," she reached across the table and squeezed Rosa's arm, "but if we're having this conversation, we need to be honest."

Rosa patted the top of Adriana's hand and gave me a gentle

smile. "As much as I want to believe Luca isn't like his father or brother, I think it's best for us to be brutally honest. Being the head of the Moretti family will make him the mark for many ambitious women, and at a certain point, the temptation may become too much for him to ignore."

Nausea twisted my gut. "I see." I didn't, really. I couldn't see Luca *ever* cheating on me. Call it naivety, but he was as obsessed with me as I was with him. He took care of a dead body for me—his father's dead body.

Come on.

"Like Mom said, Luca doesn't seem to be anything like Dante, but it's best to be prepared for the possibility. I wasn't, and it blindsided me the first time I caught him with her." She took a sip of her coffee. "When I met Dante, I was actually dating Marco." She flashed me a smirk. "I'd talked my father into allowing me to pick who I'd marry as long as it was a Moretti, and Marco was the one who caught my eye. That is until I met Dante."

"He was very taken with Adriana." Rosa smiled at her daughter-in-law.

"I knew better than to get involved with him, but he was just so overwhelming. Nicki was on the periphery, but he assured me they were over. As time went by, I realized that was a lie, but by then, I was in love and blind to what a prick he could be." She glanced at Rosa, and Rosa shook her head, understanding in her eyes. "By the time I was pregnant with Dante, it was like he knew I was stuck, and he got sloppy."

"What happened?" I whispered, unsure whether I wanted to hear the gory details.

"It was all pretty cliché. He was working late, and I took him his dinner. He had her bent over the desk. Imagine it! Eight months pregnant and catching your husband banging his ex."

"Jesus Christ."

"Yeah. He assured me he wasn't leaving me, and I needed to think about the baby. No apologies. No excuses."

"How long had they been . . ." The tears welling in her eyes kept me from finishing my question.

"Who knows? I didn't ask. It was clear it would keep happening, and I didn't have a say in it. To think I trusted them working together because how could someone who loved me as much as he did do that? I was so naive." Adriana picked at her coffee cake, focusing on the mess her fingers were making.

I looked at Rosa, hoping for some kind of explanation or reassurance, but was only met with a grim smile.

"After Luca broke up with her in high school, and then Dante in college, she knew she'd never be a wife, but there's a power in being the mistress to the boss." Rosa's voice was rough, but her eyes were clear of tears. "Once Dante Jr. was gone, she became my Dante's lap dog. At first, I didn't think anything of it. She'd been like family."

Adriana frowned at her coffee.

"I know that hurt you, and I'm so sorry." Rosa's voice caught. This was clearly the first time they'd addressed the Nicki situation.

One jerk of her head and Adriana's hair fell around her face.

"At first, I didn't know about my son's affair, but then he was gone, and it was too late to do anything about it. When I brought it up to Dante, he wouldn't allow me to cut Nicki out of our gatherings even though it visibly upset you." She let out a humorless laugh. "That should have been a red flag, but nothing had changed between us. He'd even taken me to Italy for our anniversary. It wasn't until I started finding little trinkets and things around the house, and she started spending more time in the study that I woke up to the truth." Clearing her throat, Rosa ran her hand over her hair. "It doesn't take a rocket scientist to figure out what they were doing."

"That's awful," I said, skeeved out by the whole situation.

"And disgusting," Adriana added, her eyes still on her drink.

Rosa nodded. "A few months before he died, I worked up the nerve to confront him. I had it all planned. I'd even packed a bag if he didn't promise to end things." Her cheeks reddened, and she looked down at her drink. "Unfortunately, it was the same night Luca was shot, and I never confronted him. Instead, it was like almost losing his son snapped him back in shape. Nicki was gone, and we were back in our honeymoon phase. I'm ashamed to say I let myself turn a blind eye to what I knew."

"Was it the first time?" I asked without thinking.

"No." Rosa looked me in the eye. "Nicki wasn't Dante's first affair. But it was the one that made my skin crawl the most. He was her godfather."

The three of us sat in silence for a minute, each sipping our coffee.

"So, she got the complete set?" I murmured.

Adriana's face finally lifted, her eyes blinking rapidly. "What?"

"Nothing."

Rosa bit her bottom lip, a smile playing on her lips. She tapped her nails on her mug as she hit me with a playful glare. "Only you would make that joke."

"I mean . . ."

Adriana finally smiled. "I don't think you have anything to worry about, especially from Nicki. He's not a cheater. He has never been a cheater. Based on how Dante and I started, I should've known better, but Luca? He's rock solid. When he found out Nicki cheated on him, he broke things off. After that, it was a series of serious girlfriends until he seemingly gave up."

I perked up. We'd never really done an in-depth "exes talk," and I was curious. "Gave up?"

"The last was Fern. He met her while he was in undergrad before he went to culinary school. They dated for what?" Adriana glanced at Rosa.

"Five years."

I swallowed. *Five years.* "What happened?"

"When she graduated from law school, the family wanted her on retainer as a defense attorney, and she declined," Rosa said plainly.

"So, they broke up? That seems a bit drastic."

Rosa smiled. "Fern wanted to be a public defender, which is a noble career choice, and we admired her for it, but when she wanted Luca to distance himself from the family, we had a problem."

"Oh."

"Luca planned to work at the restaurant and didn't see any reason to remove himself further from the family, but Fern didn't agree with his choice to stay tied to—" Rosa squinted her eyes, "I think she called us thugs." She laughed and shook her head. "I guess she wasn't wrong, but a man like Luca will always choose family."

Except when it came to me. Warmth spread through me, easing some of the worries the conversation had caused.

Adriana leaned back in her seat, more comfortable now that we weren't discussing her marriage. "He tried working at another restaurant to make her happy, but it wasn't long until he was looking to take over the Moretti kitchen. Needless to say, she wasn't pleased."

"It all came to nothing anyway. Dante died before he could take over, and Luca had to step up."

"She left him?"

Both women nodded.

"Poor Luca." My chest ached for him. The reluctant king lost his partner for the love of his family.

"She wasn't his one. You are." Rosa confidently said, standing and collecting my mug. "More coffee?"

"Yes, please." She went to the counter, and I turned to Adriana. "So, he hasn't dated since?"

"Besides Zoe? Nope."

Zoe. The missing woman my fiancé had fucked while we were separated. A woman who was causing problems between Marco and Luca.

"And that whole Zoe thing was ridiculous. Power posturing with his father," Rosa said, the disdain clear in her voice.

"It looked pretty real to me," I mumbled, believing and not believing my words.

"You need to work on that," Rosa said, setting down my fresh cup of coffee.

"What?"

"Your confidence in you and Luca. You've got the ring, you've got the man. No one can take that from you."

"You're right." She was, but hell if I could make myself believe it.

"Enough man talk. I want to hear what you have planned for my bedroom." Rosa grinned, and the three of us moved on to the renovation I'd taken on as a personal project—a way to make amends without her ever knowing.

"I'll get my tablet and be right back."

I hustled to Luca's room and back, passing the locked, silent study.

"I can't believe you thought that." Adriana laughed.

Chairs scooted across the floor. "What was I supposed to think when my husband left with another woman? As much as I adore Sasha, I did have a moment of doubt and wondered if she tried to get back at Luca through Dante."

Both women laughed, and Adriana said, "I think they were more likely to kill each other than anything else." I stopped in the hallway, leaning one hand against the wall to absorb the blow. There was no way they knew how close they were to the truth.

"You're right." Rosa sighed. "I think he was trying to fix things and undo Luca's agreement with Zoe. If anyone could've broken them up, it was Sasha. Case and point—the ring on her finger."

The shiny rock sparkled at me as my hand slid down the tasteful wallpaper until my shoulder held me up. My chest tightened, and I took slow, deliberate breaths. The edges of my vision became blurry, and I fought the blackness threatening to take me under.

I sat on the floor and kept breathing with my eyes squeezed shut.

You're having a panic attack. It will pass. You're not dying, even if it feels that way.

I rolled my shoulders and pictured my home with Luca, specifically the kitchen. I envisioned him chopping garlic, laughing, and smiling. My heartbeat slowed a touch. I focused on the way Luca's brown eyes glowed in the sunlight. How the skin around his eyes crinkled when he smiled at me. The scene was so real, so vivid, my shoulders loosened. I imagined kissing the scar above his eye, the smell of his minty shampoo filling my nose.

With one last deep inhale and exhale, I opened my eyes. Adriana and Rosa softly spoke just through the doorway but were unaware of my episode on the other side of the wall. I had no idea how long I'd been sitting there, but both my feet were asleep.

Pins and needles traveled up my legs as I stood. I shook my feet as I blotted sweat from my forehead with the sleeve of my shirt, then ran my clammy palms down my thighs. The hallway had a mirror, so I double-checked that I didn't look too rough before joining them back at the breakfast table.

"You okay?" Rosa frowned.

"Yep. I just had to make a quick call." Flipping open the tablet cover, I smiled. "Let me show you what I was thinking for the color scheme."

FIVE

Bodyguards aren't nearly as interesting as books and movies lead you to believe. My protection was none other than Frankie Gambini, Luca's cousin on his mother's side, who was tatted to the extreme and dull as dirt.

That's not fair. I didn't actually know if he was dull because he never spoke. Anything I said received one-word answers and no eye contact.

He was a blast.

"Look. I know you're supposed to be my shadow, but can you wait out here while I duck in for my coffee?"

"No." He held open the door and patiently waited for me to go inside.

"Fine. But know I'm not getting you that latte I know you love."

He grunted. We both knew I was lying.

Frankie posted up at a corner table where he could keep an eye on the whole building while I slid up to the counter and ordered my mocha coffee monstrosity and his classic latte, taking special care to request one of Meghan's latte art pieces.

Standing at the end of the counter, waiting for my order, I

fussed with the sugar packets and cup sleeves, trying my best not to look at Frankie. It's hard not to look at someone that is always watching you. While eye contact may not be his forte, I was always in his line of sight, so I always felt eyes on me. It reminded me of the time Luca and I spent apart.

"New side gig?"

My shoulders stiffened, and I finished straightening the last of the seasonal gift cards. "In this economy, it doesn't hurt to hustle."

Dimitri chuckled, leaning his hip against the counter next to me. "I see congratulations are in order."

"Why don't you sound happy for me?"

"Are you actually asking that?"

Narrowing my eyes, I said, "No. But you could at least pretend."

Shaking his head, he locked eyes with something over my shoulder. "I see he's got one of his goons following you."

"There's been some trouble. But I'm sure you're well aware."

Lowering his gaze from Frankie, he glared at me. "Oh, there's been trouble, all right. One of my warehouses burned to the ground, and I lost a year's worth of earnings. Not to mention priceless art that is forever gone from this world."

"What?" I reached out and placed a hand on his arm. He tensed but didn't move out of reach.

"Someone burned my warehouse to the ground a week after Adriana Moretti's home went up in flames. Coincidence?"

"You think I know who did it?" I pulled my hand away, no longer wanting that tether to him or his accusations.

His face softened, and he stepped closer, trying to close the distance between us. I stepped back without even thinking. His jaw tensed, and he scoffed. "You're scared of me now?"

"No. I just think we should keep our distance."

"Right." He thumbed his nose, glancing over at Frankie and then back at me. "I'm the threat."

"I didn't say that."

"No, but you're looking at me like I'm the enemy."

"Sasha?" The barista slid a carrier with two coffees over and smiled before returning to the register.

"I should go."

"Sasha, wait." Dimitri caught my elbow, his fingers barely touching me. "Call me if you need anything. If you need an out."

Taking a deep breath, I shook my head, looking him dead in the eye to make sure there was no confusion. "I don't need an out. I'm where I want to be."

Undeterred, he stepped closer, his coat grazing my side. "I don't want you to get hurt."

"Luca would never let that happen."

"He's not God, Sasha." Dimitri leaned down so he could whisper, "My family isn't the only threat."

I turned my head so my mouth was buried behind my hair. "What do you mean?"

"We need to get out of here, Sasha. Get you away from Moretti, and then get us both out of the country."

Frowning, I peeked up at him, our noses brushing. "What about Daphne?"

"Fuck Daphne."

"This looks cozy." Frankie's bored voice startled me, and I jumped back into him, the coffees flying into Dimitri's chest.

"Fuck!" He wiped down his coat with a leather-gloved hand, glaring at Frankie.

"Whoops." Frankie turned me toward him. "We should probably get to the office." He didn't waste a second considering Dimitri as he ushered me to the door.

"Remember what I said, Sasha!" Dimitri yelled, but I kept walking.

Frankie held open the passenger door, then went around the hood and got in the driver's side. The entire time, Dimitri watched us through the huge windows of the coffee shop, and I tried to work out what the hell had just happened.

"A piece of advice?" Frankie said, his tone dry.

"Why not?"

"Cut whatever you have with Chronis off. Now."

He didn't wait for me to respond before he turned on the radio and pulled away from the curb. The ride to the office was a blur of nerves, knowing I'd have to talk to Luca about Dimitri and what he said.

Frankie led me through reception, where Miranda sat chatting with Scott's assistant, Brian.

Even though we'd been in the new office and warehouse space for a few months, a thrill worked its way through my body every time I walked into my office, which overlooked the floor where Scott and Axel worked.

"You going back downstairs, or?" I let the question hang as I tossed my coat on the rack and got situated at my desk.

"I think I'll hang out in here. I don't need that girl talking to me."

"You don't like Miranda?"

Frankie looked up from his phone and dead-eyed me. Laughing, I left him on the couch to go find Ashley.

I found her on the floor of her office, surrounded by binders and notepads. "Is all this for the next Moretti property?"

"The Casino."

"Wait, we got the casino?" I patted my pockets, blowing out a breath. "I'll be right back." I walked back to my desk as fast as my stilettos would allow and snatched my phone. I had four voicemails from Luca and a text telling me to call him back. Tapping my foot, much to Frankie's annoyance, I waited for Luca to answer.

"Luca."

"We got it?" I damn near shouted.

"Well, good morning to you too."

"Shut it. We got the casino?"

"Yeah, baby. We got it."

"Yes!" I yelled, and Ashley ran into the room.

"Did you need anything else?"

My brain was already making plans for the card floor and the bars. "Uh. No. See you tonight?"

He chuckled. "I'm making dinner. Love you."

"Love you too."

I set my phone down and stared at Ashley. A huge smile spread across her face. The casino was a whole new level for our company. "You ready for this?"

"You saw the binders. I've never been more ready."

"Let's get started."

The day flew by in a flurry of excitement and planning. Axel and Scott were tied up on the floor, but random outbursts could be heard up in our offices. We had a celebratory lunch and then had to work on other deadlines. By the time I made it home, it was late, and dinner sat on the table.

"Luca?" I hung up my coat and slipped off my shoes.

"Coming."

He joined me in the kitchen as I set my purse on the island. The sleeves of his white dress shirt were rolled up, showing off his muscular forearms, and the top two buttons were undone, exposing a sliver of tan skin and a hint of black chest hair. My fingers itched to undo the rest.

Biting my lip, I sauntered up to him, my hands landing on his chest. "Hey, baby."

Luca smiled down at me, his arms circling my waist and pulling me in. "Hey." He placed a sweet kiss on my lips. "How was your day?"

"Pretty amazing. I can't believe I missed your call about the casino."

Luca's chest shook against me as he palmed my ass. "The one day you aren't taking my calls." I laughed, but Luca continued, "I think you've learned your lesson."

"And what lesson is that?"

He brushed a piece of hair off my cheek and cupped the back of my neck. "Don't let Dimitri Chronis distract you."

I went still, all humor draining from my body. Of course he knew. "Frankie."

"Yeah. Frankie. You know, the guy in charge of keeping you alive."

"It was nothing." I pulled out of his hold and walked over to the island, where there was an open bottle of red and two empty glasses. The excitement of the day had effectively pushed Dimitri and his warnings to the back of my mind.

"You sure?"

I filled the glass to the brim and took a sip. "No." Honesty. We'd promised honesty. "Dimitri told me his warehouse got torched. All that priceless art. Gone." I straightened my spine and looked at Luca. "Did you do it?"

His jaw ticked. "You know he's a black-market art dealer, right?"

"Yes." One of the many discoveries made over the last year.

"So, all that priceless art that was destroyed, he stole."

"Are you really trying to ethics your way out of being the bad guy?"

He scratched the stubble on his jaw, a smirk creeping onto his face. "Sasha, I know I'm the bad guy, but so is he."

"So, you did set that fire."

"Did he admit to setting fire to Adriana's?"

A question for a question. This was all new territory.

"No."

"Did you ask?"

"No. I thought it was best to keep my distance."

"Good girl."

Anger surged through me. "Fuck you." I stormed out of the kitchen and into the dining room. A charcuterie board sat between our two place settings, as well as a few covered dishes. It smelled delicious, but suddenly I wasn't hungry.

"I didn't mean—"

"I'm not some little girl that needs your protection, Luca. I'm not stupid. I know he's a Chronis. I also know he's my friend and would never hurt me."

Luca's face turned red. "Yeah? Even with a brother like Cy Chronis?"

"Just because he's a part of a criminal family, it doesn't mean he's a killer. He's a bullshit art dealer, not an assassin."

Anger vibrated off Luca. His lips pursed as his eyes scanned me. I didn't know what he was looking for. "He's safe, huh?"

"As safe as anyone else in this world. In fact, he was asking me to run away from the Morettis, Chronis, and whoever else wanted to see us dead. I know, for a fact, he hasn't killed anyone, so yeah, I'd say he's pretty fucking safe." As the words left my mouth, I knew I'd fucked up.

The fire in his eyes was raging, but he held himself back, taking a few steps away from me. "That's how you feel?"

"No," I shouted, frustrated that my words weren't coming out right. "I just mean that as far as a Chronis goes, I'm safe with Dimitri. He'd never hurt me."

"He fucking loves you!" Luca roared.

I scoffed. "He doesn't love—"

"He asked you to run away with him! What about his fiancée?"

That stopped me short. Did Dimitri love me? I twisted my hands together, suddenly seeing the exchange in a whole new light.

I was oblivious.

"What?" Luca propped his hands on his hips, watching me closely.

"That was the weird part." He gestured for me to continue. "He said, 'fuck Daphne.' What do you think that means?"

Luca's frown deepened, and he shook his head before leaving the dining room.

"Luca?" He didn't answer, so I followed the sound of his muttering to his office. "Hello?" He raised a hand but kept typing on his laptop. "We were kind of in the middle of something in there."

"And we can go back to yelling after I—there it is." He looked up at me with a grimace. "Come here."

I walked around the desk, my body tense from Luca's bizarre behavior. When I got close enough, he pulled me to his lap. Resting his chin on my shoulder, he leaned forward to be able to reach the keys around my body. "Look at this."

I didn't know whether it was his warm breath on my neck or the image on the screen, but a shiver ran down my spine.

"She's a cop?"

"FBI."

"Why didn't you tell me?"

"You told me you weren't going to talk to him anymore, so I didn't see the point. I'm trying to keep you as separate from this shit as possible."

I fell back into Luca's chest. "Holy shit."

He wrapped me in a tight hold. "Yeah. He must've found out, so that's probably why it's 'fuck Daphne.' More reason for you to stay away from him. The guy didn't even realize his fiancée was a plant."

"I didn't seek him out."

Luca started to stand, gently placing me on my feet before putting distance between us. "But you didn't cut him off." The screen of his phone lit up, and he frowned. "I don't think you completely grasp the gravity of the situation."

"I'm not stupid, Luca."

"Then stop making stupid decisions."

"Are you serious?"

"Are you?"

"What the fuck was I supposed to do? Throw a coffee in his face and storm out? Let Frankie rough him up?"

"Anything that gets you away from a Chronis, *especially* at a time like this, is a better plan than catching up over lattes."

I pressed my lips together, not wanting to say anything else. The whole conversation pissed me off. The worst part? I knew Luca was right, but it didn't change the fact I was in no more danger today at the coffee shop than I was at the grocery store or wherever else. Was I supposed to stay locked in the house?

"Look—" Luca grabbed his phone, frowning as he sent a message. "I need to go."

"It's Thursday."

"I know."

That's all he said.

That's it.

The fucking bastard.

Instead, he grabbed a few things from his desk and left the room. I stayed frozen in his study, unable to wrap my head around what the fuck just happened.

When I finally made it back to the dining room, I fought back the urge to cry. It was empty like I knew it would be, but I hoped Luca would be sitting at the table, ready to gorge ourselves on whatever magic he'd whipped up.

He'd actually left.

He'd never done that before.

I sat in my usual chair and snagged a piece of cheese. Eating my feelings seemed like the best option when your fiancé walks out on you on Valentine's Day.

I carefully lifted the cover on the platter in front of me and let out a sigh. Beef Wellington.

Son of a bitch.

He'd pulled out the big guns, and it ended in a fight and a perfect meal getting cold. Tears blurred my vision, and I muttered a curse as I rubbed my eyes with the back of my hands.

"I'm eating it." I grabbed one with my hands, not too concerned about decorum or what was normal table behavior, and dropped it on my plate. "I'm not letting him ruin this."

Despite being a little cold, the first bite was a revelation. Bite after bite, I shoveled room-temperature gourmet food down my gullet and guzzled the expensive wine like it came from a box. Tears flowed freely as my stubborn heart kept hoping Luca would walk back through that door and we'd make up like always. That same stubborn streak kept me from calling Luca and telling him to come home. I was scared he couldn't, or worse, wouldn't, and I'd still be alone.

I eyed the cannoli with extreme prejudice before picking one up and crushing it in my fist. Cream and flaky pastry went everywhere. I shook my hand out over the table, and a small laugh bubbled up in my chest.

There I was, engaged, sitting alone on Valentine's Day, my hand covered in cannoli and my eyes red from crying. I wiped my hand off and left the table, food and all, to head up to bed. It was only ten, but I was done with the day.

I stripped out of my clothes. Fresh disappointment washed over me when red lace came into view. I'd bought a new set of lingerie, especially for tonight, and now I was the only one seeing it. Well, damn it. I was going to enjoy it. The wine made me a little unsteady, so I sat at my dressing table to take off my jewelry. The bracelets and watch were easy enough to get off, but I tangled the necklace and dropped an earring. "Of course." Sighing, I dropped to my hands and knees and ran my fingers over the plush rug. Unfortunately, I never snagged the diamond stud.

Tilting my face toward the ceiling, I blew the hair out of my eyes. I sat back on my heels, my palms resting on my knees, completely unmotivated.

"Sasha?"

I perked up. "Luca?" I clumsily rose to my feet.

Heavy footsteps were coming down the hall, and I went to meet him at the door. Only when I got there, it was Frankie, not Luca, staring down at my body.

"Not Luca."

Cocking my hip, I put my hands on my hips. "What are you doing here?"

He shook his head, dragging his eyes up from my cherry-painted toes to my face. The heat of his stare caused my skin to flush, but I didn't move an inch to hide myself. "We've got company. You might want to put something on." He shook his head, taking one more look before giving me his back.

"Who's here?" I grabbed my short silk robe from the closet.

"You decent?"

"Yes."

Frankie turned around and raised an eyebrow. "You call that decent."

"Can you see my tits or ass?"

"No."

"Then I'm fucking decent. Now answer me. Who's here?"

"The cops."

My stomach dropped to my ass. I pushed past Frankie and headed downstairs to where my phone was sitting in my purse. "I need to call Luca."

Frankie trailed behind me at a respectful distance. "Already did. That's why I'm in here and not out in my car."

I froze with my hand in my bag. "You were sitting out in your car this whole time?"

He shrugged and looked over his shoulder toward the front door. "You should've come inside."

"No offense, but I don't think Luca would appreciate me hanging out with you on Valentine's Day while you're in your underwear."

"I wasn't—You know what? It doesn't matter. What am I supposed to do?"

"Nothing. I doubt they'll come to the door."

The doorbell rang through the house, and I gave Frankie an unimpressed look.

"Okay. I guess you're answering the door." He looked down at my body and then shrugged out of his coat. "Put this on."

I rolled my eyes but took it and slid it over my robe. It hung slightly lower than the black silk but did a better job of covering my body. "That good enough, Dad?"

"Go answer the door, Sasha."

The doorbell rang again, getting me moving. I took a deep breath and plastered on a big smile before opening the door.

"Ms. Mitchell?" A tall man with black hair and dark eyes stood in front of me, wearing a plain suit. He had the classic good looks you could find in old movies, but something about him made me uneasy.

"How can I help you, officer?" I kept the door cracked, not allowing him access to our house.

"Detective. Is Mr. Moretti home?"

I panicked. Out of the corner of my eye, I watched Frankie pull a gun from behind his back and shake his head no. "I'm sorry he's not." I was proud of my steady voice.

"Any idea when he'll be in?"

"Not sure."

The detective's eyes took a slow perusal of the very little he could see behind the door before reaching for his pocket. My heart stopped, and I started to shut the door as if that would protect me from possible gunfire.

"Here's my card. I've got some questions regarding the disappearance of Zoe Chronis."

I bit back a whimper of relief and kept my hand steady as I took his business card. "I'll make sure he gets this, Detective—" I glanced at the card and then back at him, "Bennington."

"You do that. Happy Valentine's Day."

"You too." I shut the door immediately, uninterested in watching him stroll back to his unmarked vehicle. The small scrap of paper fell from my fingertips as I slid down to the cold hardwood.

Frankie stayed where he'd been standing, muttering something into his phone, occasionally looking at me with a blank face. Finally, he slipped his phone into his pants and squatted in front of me. "You did great." He scooped up the card, flipping it between his fingers.

"Oh yeah. I'm a regular Carmela."

"What?"

"Don't worry about it. Who were you talking to?"

"Luca."

"Is he coming home?"

"Not yet."

I nodded. I thought I was disappointed before, but this was a whole new level of hurt. "I think I'm going to head up to bed." Grabbing the doorknob, I pulled myself up.

"You need me to get you anything?" Frankie frowned and crossed his arms.

"Nope." I shook off his coat, handing it back to him. His eyes instantly fell to the swell of my breasts. "Thanks for the coat. That cop was kind of a creep."

"They all are."

Without another word, I left Frankie at the front door and headed up to bed—alone. The whole day had been surreal, and I was starting to wonder whether my whole life would be a series of exhausting days that ended in lonely nights.

I went through my night routine with my phone face-up on the counter, praying Luca would call me. He didn't.

The bed was too big, and the sheets were too cold without him—flashbacks to before I knew what Luca was hit me hard. I'd spent a lot of nights alone leading up to our breakup. Nights I worried he was cheating or hurt. But now I knew the truth, and the fear that he could be hurt, maybe even killed, was no longer this intangible idea. It was real. Hell, I'd held him after he was shot.

Worry coiled in my stomach, weighing me down until it became apparent I wasn't going to sleep. How was I supposed to sleep when Luca was out in the world with people who wanted him dead?

Not able to fight it anymore, I texted him.

I love you. Be safe.

Three dots appeared immediately.

I love you. I'll be home soon.

He wasn't, and I eventually fell asleep alone.

SIX

Naughty Gras should be the happiest time of the year. Instead of frolicking through erotic art, trying on handmade corsets, and watching a flogging down in the dungeon, I was pouting at the makeup table backstage.

"I take it you and Luca are still fighting?" Jazz glanced over at me as she waited for her eyelash glue to get tacky.

"Yep." I rearranged my lipsticks, pretending to be busy.

"Must be rough to work together when you're in a fight."

"It's not great, but I wouldn't even call this a fight."

"What is it then?"

"A cold war."

Jazz laughed. "You're so fucking dramatic."

"Maybe."

She turned in her chair and bumped my knee. "You want to tell me why you're fighting?"

I absolutely did but couldn't. There was no way in hell I was endangering one of my best friends. But maybe I could give her the watered-down version. "I ran into Dimitri, and we chatted." Not a complete lie, but not the whole truth either.

"Okay? You're friends. Maybe not as good as before, but still friends."

I bit the inside of my cheek. "Luca doesn't like him. Their families have beef, and it doesn't help Luca thinks Dimitri's in love with me."

"Well, he is."

My jaw dropped. Was everyone right? Had I missed the signs?

Jazz tilted her head. "You're serious. You never realized the Greek playboy was in love with you?"

"No?"

She laughed loudly in my face. "The worst part is you're serious."

"This whole thing makes my head hurt. How did we go from being friends that fucked to him loving me? He's marrying Daphne—" *Who's a cop.* "And has never said a damn word."

"When would he have said something? And why would he? Before and after Luca, you were the queen of fuck girls. And I say that with all due respect, Your Majesty." She bowed her head, and the glitter stuck in her curls sparkled in the flashing light coming through the curtains.

I sucked my teeth. Jazz was right, and I hated that there was yet another weird layer to all the bullshit.

"Was that it?"

No. I also defended Dimitri while inadvertently condemning Luca. "Some other stuff was brought up, and then Luca left and didn't come home until the next morning."

She pursed her lips, her brow furrowing. "That's weird."

"Yeah. And since then, we've been avoiding each other."

"Five minutes!" Evie whisper yelled to the entire group, "Five minutes!"

I stood, my ass numb from sitting on the metal folding chair for nearly an hour. "You ready for this clusterfuck?" Bianca rushed past us, her breakaways completely detached.

"I really thought a month of rehearsals would be enough." Jazz adjusted her skirt against her tight stomach, the pink popping next to her dark brown skin.

"It's always a mess leading up to the show, but somehow, we always pull it off."

"Mm." Jazz looked past me to the green room's door, a smirk lifting her full lips. "You've got company."

Turning, I smiled. "Luca."

He weaved in between the performers, his eyes never leaving mine.

"Someone looks ready to make up," Jazz whispered in my ear before slapping my ass and pushing me forward. I glared at her over my shoulder, and she wiggled her eyebrows. "You've got two minutes."

I stepped around a large papier mâché martini olive, careful not to dent it, and was finally face to face with my handsome, if not exhausted-looking, fiancé. He wasted no time pulling me to his chest. "Sasha." His voice vibrated through me.

"You're here," I mumbled into his shoulder, makeup getting all over his jacket.

"Of course I am." His large hand stroked my back as he kissed the top of my hair. "I wouldn't miss it for the world."

I leaned back to see his face. "I wasn't sure."

"We need to talk about the last two weeks. I'm sorry—"

"It's time!" Evie yelled.

Luca exhaled and narrowed his eyes at my pixie friend before looking down at me. His eyes were fierce, and his grip was tight on my waist. "We'll talk when you get off stage." He pecked my lips. "Break a leg."

I nodded, my lips tingling from his light touch and wanting more. Somehow, I made it to the stage.

"You okay?" Chloe whispered in the dark.

"Yep."

The music started, and the lights came up. The shimmy sisters moved in a swirl of colorful sequences and glitter. Bodies of all sizes shuffled and sashayed together, and the audience ate it up. Hoots and hollers carried over the bass, and we somehow pulled together a pretty fantastic routine. When the lights went down, we quickly gathered our stripped clothes and shuffled off stage. Music played through the sound system as we laughed and slipped into our street clothes.

"You about to disappear?" Jazz smirked as she looked at her phone.

"I have no idea."

"Well, Imani and I are going to peruse the art, and I'm going to try and convince her to check out downstairs."

"Imani in the dungeon? Shit. I might have to stick around for that."

"You'd be surprised just how brave my little dumpling can be." Jazz chuckled and picked up her bag. "I'm going to run this out to the car."

The green room had cleared out since we were the last show of the night, and I took my time packing my stuff. Luca had shown up, but that didn't undo all the damage. I hated this part of relationships—the vulnerability, the sharing, the fixing.

"You need a hand?"

I grinned down at my brushes. "Always."

Luca laughed, and the door clicked shut. "I wanted to see what was taking you so long."

"Just finishing up."

He walked up behind me and ghosted his hands down my arms as he pressed his hips into me. "You looked incredible on stage."

A shiver went down my spine. The tiny hairs on the back of my neck stood straight up as his warm breath fanned across my skin. The heat from his body soaked into me, and I leaned back into him. "I know."

"Every time I watch you perform, it feels like the first time."

I smiled, thinking back. "You're not supposed to be back here."

Luca pushed my hands to the edge of the table, caging me in with his hard body. "I know the guy who owns this place." I let out a shuddered breath, heat pooling in my belly as his cock hardened against my ass. He thrust, leaving little question of where his head was at. "I think now's the part where I admit you make me crazy."

"Uh-huh."

"But you already know you make me crazy." His fingers left mine and squeezed my hips. "I'd do anything for you." He moved a hand to the small of my back and pressed down, bending me over the folding table. My tits spilled out of my corset.

"Luca." I pleaded, not sure what I was begging for, but luckily for me, Luca did.

"I know, baby." He smoothed up my skirt, and the room's cool air hit my bare pussy. "Damn it, Sasha." His voice was as rough as his pants rubbing against my sensitive skin.

"Please."

Luca groaned. His fingers dug into my flesh, squeezing my hips before cupping my pussy. I took a step out to make room for him to do whatever he wanted. That was the only way I knew how to be with him—eager.

The heel of his hand rocked into me, and my hips moved against it. Luca wrapped my hair around his fist and pulled me up, his mouth slamming down on mine as his other hand continued its rhythm against me. Two fingers slid between my folds, and I moaned, Luca's mouth swallowing the sound as his tongue moved against mine.

I covered his hand between my legs, urging him to fill me and do anything to relieve the ache, but he didn't. Frustrated, I squeezed my thighs together, trapping his hand.

In an instant, he twisted his hand in my hair and jerked, yanking our mouths apart and turning my limbs to jelly. My scalp burned, but as he nibbled my ear, I couldn't find it in me to care.

"Do you want to come?"

"Yes." You fucker, but I didn't add that part.

"Play with your tits."

I didn't have to be told twice. Heat coursed through my body as Luca's hand moved between my legs. I pressed my ass back into him, his hard cock a welcome pressure as I rolled my nipples and let out a whimper. Luca grunted and finally slid two fingers into me. The fullness was exquisite.

"Yes. Like that." I panted.

"Ride my hand." His voice was quiet, but there was no mistaking the command in his tone. I met each thrust of his fingers as I inched closer and closer to my release. Luca peppered my neck with open-mouth kisses until he reached my shoulder. As his thumb met my clit, he bit down, making my eyes widen, and a strangled cry left my mouth.

"Come for me." He murmured, his tongue grazing the shell of my ear as he spoke.

Like an obedient bitch, my pussy clamped down on his fingers. My hips moved to prolong the fireworks as his thumb lazily circled my clit.

Luca's breathing was heavy against my neck, his hips instinctively moving against my ass. I tried to turn, but he kept his hand tightly wound in my hair and his fingers in my pussy.

"Give me a second."

I tried to nod but couldn't move my head. "Okay."

A knock on the door startled me, but Luca calmly called, "Be right out."

"Okay!" Jazz's sing-song voice made me laugh.

"Déjà vu."

"Yeah." Luca pulled his fingers from my body and took a step back.

I turned around and finally looked at him. His half-lidded stare shone with lust, letting me know we weren't done. Not by a long shot. Falling to my knees, I grabbed his belt buckle and pulled him to me.

He batted my hands away. "Not now." He stood over me, his eyes telling a very different story than his mouth. "God, you're so fucking beautiful." He traced my bottom lip with his thumb, and I flicked my tongue against the tip, tasting myself on his skin, making me hungry for a taste of him.

Luca's fingers curled under my chin, his hold tight as he tilted my face up. "Let's get out of here." He let go, moving away to give me space to straighten my clothes.

"It's early, and I haven't gotten to check everything out yet." I tugged my skirt down unnecessarily hard.

"Then let's walk around."

"Yeah?"

He held out his hand for my bag. "Let's do it."

Outside the green room door, Luca handed off my bag and makeup case to Frankie. "Put this in the car, and then you can take off."

"Got it." Frankie didn't spare me a look as he walked away.

"Bye!" I shouted. Frankie lifted his hand but kept right on toward the door. "I think he's warming up to me."

"I can see that." Luca eyed my bodyguard with interest. "How's that working out?"

"What? Frankie?" He nodded, and I grabbed his hand, pulling him toward the room with all the art. "He's fine. A little weird, but fine."

Luca laced our fingers together and brought my hand to his lips. "I'm sorry." He placed a sweet kiss on my knuckles, his eyes shutting reverently.

Stopping in the middle of the gallery, I grabbed his tie and looped it around my hand like a leash. "Stop it." His lips parted, but I cut him off. "If you're saying sorry, it better be for Valentine's Day, not because you have someone watching over me to keep me safe."

"Okay." Luca was still frowning.

"Let's go look at some erotic art and see if there are any new sex toys to add to my collection. Maybe something for you." I yanked his tie, leading him toward the dealer's stalls. Larger-than-life labia in vivid pinks and purple adorned canvases taller than Luca and ceramic busts sat on the table beside them.

"That's a lot," Luca murmured in my ear, his arms wrapping around my stomach.

"Wonder if your mom would be interested in a more risqué design for the front hall."

Luca's chest shook with quiet laughter, his face buried in my stiff hair.

"Picture it. We take the portraits of Nonna and Nonno down and replace them with a vulva and penis."

Luca lifted his chin at a particularly busty pair of busts. "Replace the vases in the sitting room with those?"

The artist looked our way, and I smiled, holding back my laughter. "I can see it."

We weaved through the booths, eventually picking a few pieces for my office and a gold bust for our living room. Luca's phone stayed in his pocket, and his full attention was on me. It had been a while since we'd had a night out. We usually spent our alone time in the comfort of our home, in comfy clothes or nothing at all. It was nice to show Luca off and spend time with him and my friends.

"You brave enough to go downstairs?" I bumped Luca's arm, lifting my chin toward the line to the dungeon.

He laughed, shaking his head. "I'll let you know if it's too much."

Downstairs was a very different vibe than upstairs. The lights were dim, except where they shone down on the scenes set up around the large basement. The smell of leather and burning wax filled the air, and music played, muffling out the hushed conversations of the spectators.

People stood clustered together watching the show, the newbies with wide eyes and mouths parted in disbelief, while the experienced watched with curiosity and knowing smiles. In the center, a woman was tied up and suspended from the ceiling. Off to the side, a large woman in a leather catsuit flogged a man tied to a St. Andrew's cross. Small stations with candles, cupping, and electric shock wands were along the walls.

Soft moans and grunts kept my attention on the participants.

Not completely sated by our green room romp, the scenes heightened my existing excitement.

"We should get one of those," Luca muttered to himself as the woman brought down a riding crop.

"Yes, please." I cuddled into his side.

He wrapped an arm around me and smiled. "You want to get out of here?"

"Yep. I'm ready."

We made our way to the car waiting outside. "Pete."

He dipped his head. "Ms. Sasha. Having a good night?" He grinned at me as he opened the door.

"We sure are."

We slid into the sedan, my ass thankful for the heated seats.

"Home?" Pete asked as he smoothly pulled away from the curb.

"Actually, take us to The Libertine." Luca gazed at me with a smile that flipped my insides. "It's been too long since we've made a whole night of it."

"You sure? I'm okay, just heading home." The idea of dancing and drinks with Luca was delicious, but going home had certain perks. Like finally getting his cock inside me.

He placed his hand on my thigh, his fingers inching closer and closer to my pussy. "I'm sure." Nuzzling into my neck, he nipped my earlobe, and I swallowed back a moan. Pete didn't deserve to have to put up with our shenanigans.

The Libertine was only a few blocks from the venue, so we got there before Luca had a chance to do more than paw at me. Pete opened my door, his gaze politely diverted, but I didn't miss the smirk on his face—the poor man.

"Let's go through the back." Luca led me past the line wrapped around the block to a metal door. It swung open, and Tommy, one of the young guys I'd seen around, ushered us inside.

The bass traveled through the soles of my feet, my hips swaying to the beat. Heat radiated off the dancing bodies, creating a haze through the flashing lights. Sweat beaded between my breasts, my winter coat far too heavy for the club.

"Want to go upstairs?"

I glanced up to the VIP section, and it was just as packed as the main level. "Sure."

We got drinks and a spot where we could look over the dance floor. I downed my drink, set the glass down, and wrapped my arms around Luca's neck. It never failed to blow my mind how handsome he was. "Hey."

He smiled, wrapping his arms around me. "This is nice."

"It is."

We swayed to the upbeat party music, staring into each other's eyes, the rest of the world falling away. Song after song, he held me, his hands staying on my back, never straying to my ass like they usually did. He held me like I was going to disappear.

"You want to go somewhere and talk?" Luca tucked a lock of hair behind my ear. When I nodded, he smiled tiredly.

The crowd parted for Luca as he pulled me through the club. He lifted his chin at a burly, bald man, and we went inside.

"This is one nice office." The room was dimly lit but clean and quiet. They must've soundproofed it because I couldn't hear the music anymore.

"You sound surprised."

"I am. I don't know what I expected, but it wasn't this." Luca leaned against the door, his eyes following me as I wandered around the room. I walked around the desk, my fingers dragging across the polished wood. "Do you spend much time here?"

"Not much. Mickey handles the clubs. I just pop in to make sure everything is running smoothly."

"Huh." I spun the chair around and took a seat. "So."

Luca pushed off the door, taking his time as he made his way to the chair in front of the desk. He gripped the back of it, his fingers digging into the leather. "So."

"I hate talking."

"I know. Let me start." Luca ran a hand down his face and fell into the chair. "I'm sorry for leaving in the middle of our fight."

"Why did you?"

He tilted his head, his lips thinning as he considered me. "I think hearing you talk about Dimitri, and knowing you were right, fucked with my head. I mean, he's a harmless fucker, and I am, well, the fucking Butcher. Of the two of us, I'm clearly the bad guy. Add to that some business I had to handle, and it was better for me to go."

I leaned my forearms on the edge of the desk, the desire to be closer to Luca driving me to go to him, but I knew if we touched, the talking would stop. "You're a good man."

"No, I'm not."

I blew out a breath. "Fine. I should say you're good to me. I know you would never do anything to hurt me."

"But that doesn't mean you won't get hurt. And it doesn't help that Dimitri feels comfortable enough to approach you. He may not be a killer, but his brother is."

"I promise to walk away next time, okay?"

He sighed, his fingers dragging through his hair. "I feel like I'm ruining your life. I don't want to be that guy."

"You're not ruining my life. You make it infinitely better."

"You have an answer for everything, huh?"

"Have you met me?"

He leaned back in his chair, his legs spread. "You'd tell me if you wanted out, right? Because once we're married—"

"I won't—"

"Being a Moretti is dangerous and as far from a normal life as you can get. You wouldn't be the first person to want out." He grimaced. "The last thing I want is for you to feel trapped. I'd do anything for you, even if it meant letting you go."

Rolling my eyes, I stood and went to him. "Stop trying to push me away." I stepped between his legs and ran my fingers through his hair. "I'm here because I want to be."

His eyes shut, and his frown disappeared. "Okay." He took a

deep breath and opened his eyes. "I believe you. I'm sorry I left you to deal with that detective alone. Frankie said you took care of him quickly."

"Yeah, it was no big deal."

"The fact you can say that lets me know—"

I yanked his hair. "Shut up. Just shut the fuck up. No more of this bullshit." I dropped to my knees. "Aren't you tired of having this conversation? I'm the one that came back to you. Stop thinking I have one foot out the door and accept you're stuck with me." Before Luca could stop me, his belt was on the floor, and his hardening cock was in my hand. "Now, if you're done being a martyr, I'd like you to fuck my face." I smiled sweetly. "Please." Without waiting for a response, I put him in my mouth, sucking and licking until he was completely hard.

He tangled his fingers in my hair, his hips surging up. I gagged, but he didn't stop. His thighs flexed under my fingers, and I dug my nails in, giving as good as I got.

Luca was moaning, mumbling something incoherent when the door swung open, smashing into the wall. I fell backward on my ass as Luca sprung up, pulling a gun from thin fucking air and pointing it at the intruder.

Mr. Big and Bald quickly shut the door, locking it before turning to Luca. His eyes widened when he saw Luca in all his gun-toting, erect glory. "Sorry, Boss. There's been an altercation, and we're securing the inside. Should only take a moment."

Luca lowered his gun. "What kind of altercation?"

The bouncer glanced at me, his eyebrow hitching up for a moment. Schooling his features, he looked back at Luca. "Someone took a shot at Aldo. We lost the guy down an alley, and then a car rounded on outside security and squeezed off a few rounds. Angelo caught a bullet in the arm, but other than that, everyone's fine."

Luca's body stayed loose as he set the gun on the desk. "Cops?"

"Outside. I told them I had to check to see if you were here."

"Good. Give us a minute. I'll be right out."

The bouncer left without another word.

Luca turned around, and my breath stuttered. The lighting was dim, creating shadows around his eyes. His sharp jaw was tensed, and his lips pursed. I stared up at him, not sure I recognized this version of my fiancé.

He extended a hand, and I jumped. Not out of fear. Okay, maybe a little, but it was more out of an instinctual understanding that this man was not the careful playmate I'd initially fallen in love with. This was the shadow—the creature who was capable of extreme violence.

I reached out and grabbed his hand. His jaw ticked as he hauled me to my feet. "You scared of me?" His voice was rough, gravelly.

"No."

"You sure?" His hold on my waist tightened.

I stood on my tippy toes and kissed the underside of his jaw. "Yes."

"Good." Luca held me at arm's length. "It's always going to be you above everything else."

"I know."

He smirked at me, letting me go to tuck his dick back in his pants. Picking up the gun, he shook his head. "I have to go talk to the cops and make sure Angelo's okay." He slid the gun under his suit coat and patted his pocket. "You stay here, and I'll send Frankie up to take you home. I won't be long." He stopped at the door when I snorted. "I mean it. I'll be right behind you."

"Okay. I love you. Be safe."

"I love you too." He opened the door but didn't walk through. "Thank you."

"For what?"

He looked over his shoulder with a tender smile and then closed the door behind him. And with that, I was left in a sequined mini dress waiting for my babysitter.

SEVEN

Deep voices yelling downstairs startled me awake. The words were muffled, but it sounded like Luca and Marco. They'd had enough late-night chats escalate into more in our house for me to recognize the timber of Marco's outrage and Luca's annoyance.

The sound of something breaking, then a voice bellowing, "What the fuck?" got me moving. I struggled to untangle the sheet from my feet and dislodge the pillows from around me. My sleep had been restless without Luca. I tried to wait up for him, but by three a.m., I was out like a light.

Our wooden floors were a little noisy, so I kept close to the bed and stayed on the large rug. When I reached the edge, I tiptoed across the old planks to the door. I slowly turned the knob, lifting it slightly to keep the latch from making a noise. With the door cracked, I could just make out what the loud oafs were saying.

"You're paying for that." Luca huffed.

"Fuck you. Why would you think I took out Yanni?"

"Who else has been pushing me to make that move?"

"Everyone! Not to mention, Cy Chronis is gunning for the top spot. Shit, the shorter list would be who wasn't trying to kill Yanni," Marco yelled.

It got quiet, and Luca asked, "I'm going to ask you again—where were you today?"

"Not killing Yanni Chronis."

I held my breath, afraid even an inhale would get me caught.

"Angelo has a hole in his arm, and the cops are setting up shop across from one of our clubs. Bodies are about to pile up. I need to know you had nothing to do with his death."

"How many times do I have to tell you it wasn't fucking me?"

"As many times as it takes for me to believe some other asshole had the fucking audacity to make the kill without getting the go-ahead from me. You're the only other person in this city who can order that kind of hit without being questioned."

"You're paranoid."

"No, I'm realistic. Shit's happening without my okay, and my underboss is nowhere to be found, missing meetings, not taking my calls, and not at the fucking club when he's supposed to be."

"Mickey said—"

"Mickey wasn't fucking there!" Luca's voice boomed through the house, followed by a thud and groan.

"Where's Tootsie?" Marco asked, his voice dripping with accusation. I pressed against the wall as I got as close as possible to the top of the stairs while staying in the shadows.

"He's handling something for me."

"Interesting."

"What?" Luca's voice was steel. I swallowed hard—worried Marco would say the wrong thing.

"It's interesting that I'm laid out on the floor, and he's nowhere to be found. Who's to say he isn't behind Zoe and her dad? He was the one that drove her home that night while I helped you with Sasha."

"It wasn't him."

Marco scoffed, and the sound of rustling made its way up the stairs. "You know what? Fuck you."

There was a crash, and glass shattered. "One more time, and

you'll be the one with a bullet in your head. Blood or not, I'm not putting up with your disrespect."

I wrung my hands, worried we'd be cleaning Marco off our hardwoods if Luca didn't calm down. My heart raced, and I strained to pick up any clues about what was going on.

"Sorry."

The house fell silent. I needed to get back to our room, but I couldn't risk it.

"Fuck!" Luca yelled. Another loud crash accompanied the outburst. I dreaded seeing the damage in the morning. "We need to figure out if we have someone acting rogue or if this is an outside job."

"Agreed." There was some grunting and shuffling. "Sasha's going to kill us." Marco laughed, and something scraped across the floor.

"Probably." Luca sighed. "This would all be easier if you'd just tell me where you were."

"It's not my secret to tell, but you have to know I'd never go behind your back like that. We'll find whoever this is and take care of them together like we always do."

"Head to the office. I'm going to check in on Sasha. I was supposed to be home hours ago."

Marco chuckled. "Good luck with that."

He said more, but I was too busy sneaking into our room, softly closing the door behind me, and diving under the covers. Nerves and the tense, quick moving I'd just done left me struggling to normalize my breathing.

The door opened slowly, and Luca went into the bathroom. I had a few minutes to collect myself before the bed dipped next to me, and Luca brushed the hair from my cheek. "Sasha? Baby?"

I made a big show of peeling my eyes open and blinking slowly. "Luca?"

"Sorry to wake you up, but I wanted to let you know I was home." He cradled my face, his small smile just visible in the moonlight.

"Thank you." I leaned up and pressed my lips to his. Both of us moved together, content with a sweet, brief kiss. I sighed and laid back on the pillows. "Everything okay at the club?"

"As okay as can be expected. Angelo should be released from the hospital tomorrow morning, so that's good."

"Do you know who did it?" I rubbed my eyes sluggishly, really hamming it up.

"Yeah."

"That's good. Do you know why?"

Luca tilted his head as he examined me. "Zoe's dad, Yanni Chronis, was killed this morning walking out of a coffee shop."

"Wha—"

"Marco's downstairs. Why don't you go back to sleep? I'll be back once we've wrapped up."

"Okay. Don't stay up too late."

"I won't." He kissed my forehead and left the room, shutting the door behind him.

Rolling to my back, I stared at the ceiling, my mind racing.

Luca didn't trust Marco, but he was letting him stay close. Was it some "keep your friends close and your enemies closer" Sun-Tzu shit, or did Luca honestly believe his cousin?

After an hour of laying painfully still in bed, Luca came back. He stripped down to his boxers and climbed in behind me, pulling me to his chest.

"I love you." He whispered into my hair as his hand caressed my thigh, slowing to a stop when he started snoring in my ear. His warm body loosened my tight muscles but did nothing to ease my thoughts.

Yet again, it looked like the threat came from inside the family.

―――――――

"This is one way to spend a lunch," I complained to Ashley as we walked into the bakery. Frankie stopped at the door and lit a cigarette.

"Oh, hush. This will be fun."

Rosa and Mom sat with Luca and Marco at a round table, their chairs crammed together.

"Sasha!" Mom waved and gestured at me to hurry.

"Hey, Mom."

Luca stood and greeted me with a kiss. Marco, sporting a fat lip, stood until Ashley and I were seated.

"Are you excited to pick your cake?" Mom was giddy as hell.

"I'm excited to have cake for lunch. So sure, I'm excited."

Before she could launch into one of her many lectures about diet, wedding dresses, and pictures lasting forever, the baker hustled out of the back.

"Right on time!" Paul's southern twang stood out against the midwestern accents around us.

"Look at you!" I held out his arm, inspecting a new tattoo on the inside of his forearm. "Is that Mrs. Claus?"

He chuckled and pulled me up for a hug. "Yup. I thought it was fitting since I look like Santa. Might as well manifest my own pinup Mrs. Claus." True enough, with Paul's bleach-blond hair and beard, he was a dead ringer for a young St. Nick. His sheer size helped in the illusion.

"I'm here for it. But I swear this woman looks familiar."

Paul's cheeks crimsoned, and he looked over at Luca, sticking his hand out. "I'm Paul Townsend."

"Luca Moretti." Luca's eyes focused on Paul's arm, inspecting the tattoo. "You get that at Golden Ink?"

"I did." Paul grinned. "I get all my work done there. Betty's a genius."

Luca nodded, his hand rubbing over his heart where he wore my name. "Gage did mine."

Paul tilted his head. "You got ink?"

"Just the one." Luca smiled down at me.

"I'm sorry, what?" Rosa popped up from her seat, walking around me to get to Luca. She reached up like she was about to check his skin for imperfections.

"Mom. Why don't you sit so we can start the tasting?" Luca caught her hand and escorted her back to her seat.

Paul took the cue and motioned for a young woman to bring over a tray full of tiny plates and tinier bites of cake.

"What we have here are our vanilla and fruity options." He handed out plates as the woman handed out cups of water and refilled Rosa's and Mom's teacups. "On the tray is a card where you can mark your favorites, and we can go from there. Just holler if you need anything."

"Let's start with the vanilla cake with vanilla icing and go from there," my mom said as she set her card next to the tiny plate.

"A vanilla-vanilla cake won't be it," I mumbled around my fork. It had to be the best cake I'd ever tasted.

"That little moan would suggest otherwise." Luca grinned.

"I mean, it's still cake. I'm going to enjoy it."

We made it through our vanilla flight just as Frankie popped into the bakery. "Boss, I need you outside."

Luca and Marco stood and left us without a word.

"I wonder what that could be about." Mom sat wide-eyed as she watched my fiancé leave. "Is everything all right?"

"Probably." I grabbed the last bite on Luca's plate.

A tray of chocolate samples came out, and I was in heaven. Raspberry coulis, strawberries, and a decadent chocolate ganache made deciding on a flavor or two nearly impossible.

"Should we wait for Luca?" My mom glanced at the door.

"Nope. I doubt he's coming back." I smiled at her, and she shook her head. Luca's disappearing act didn't line up with Mom's perfect image of her future son-in-law.

"So, what do we think?" Paul clapped his hands as he sat in Luca's empty chair.

The door chimed, and Frankie rushed inside. "It's time to go."

"I'm sorry. We're almost done." My mom stuttered out.

Rosa collected her things and headed toward the door, where

Marco waited. "Come on, Maggie. We'll reschedule the rest of the visits for another day."

"Do you want me to box up the extras?" Paul asked, his forehead scrunched.

"No, thank you." I put on my coat, breathing a sigh of relief when Ashley did the same. "I'll call you with our final decisions."

"Sounds good."

Frankie ushered Ashley and me into the car and drove off, speeding down the narrow streets.

"What's going on?"

"We're taking precautions," Frankie said while making a sharp left.

"And what the hell does that mean?" I huffed, pulling on my seatbelt to get some breathing room.

Frankie stayed quiet, and I, for the millionth time, understood why Luca put him with me—the guy gave nothing away.

"Are we safe?" Ashley's eyes widened, and her hands twisted together in her lap.

"You're safe," Frankie said, his eyes never leaving the road.

Ashley fell into my side as Frankie took a quick turn. "It feels like we're in a getaway car."

We flew past dumpsters and back doors with no other cars in view. I held onto the door as the vehicle jerked around another corner. Another five minutes of his stunt driving, and there'd be cake-flavored vomit all over his expensive upholstery.

"Here." Frankie parked in the spot closest to the lobby door, and we got out on wobbly legs. A few dark SUVs were parked along the curb—the Moretti line of defense.

I let him lead us into the building, but once Ashley was in her office and I had him in mine with the door closed, I asked, "What the hell was that?"

"A complication." He shrugged and sat on the couch.

When he took his phone out and started tapping away, I picked up a pillow and chucked it at his head. Frankie glared at me and set his phone down on the cushion next to him.

"Tell me what happened."

He propped his ankle on his knee and tapped his fingers on his shin. His jaw moved back and forth before he pegged me with a vacant stare. "We got a tip that some people were on the way to meet us. That's all."

"That's all?"

"Yep. That's all."

We stared at each other. Me with the fire of a thousand suns, hoping to melt Frankie's ice-cold resolve, and Frankie with a blank face that told me I could go fuck myself.

"You suck," I grumbled and went to my desk. I had casino plans to review since demolition would start in April. We had a month to make sure we took out everything we needed and salvaged what we could.

Frankie buried his face in his phone, not replying. It was weird, but his presence had become comforting. Occasionally, he would mutter or get up and take a call outside, but for the most part, he was glued to my side.

A couple of hours later, my stomach growled. While cake for lunch was fun, it didn't keep a grown person full. I needed something savory. "You hungry?"

"I could eat." Frankie shrugged.

"You want your regular from Young's?"

"Yep. Make sure they put in extra sweet and sour sauce?"

"You got it," I ordered, and Frankie went to the break room for plates and utensils. In no time, we were chowing down.

"You're Luca's cousin, right?"

"Yep. On his mom's side."

I tried to visualize the family tree, but honestly? There were way too many relatives. Rosa told me we would review it before the wedding—flashcards might have been mentioned.

"Any siblings?"

"Four sisters."

He took a big bite of Crab Rangoon, his attention on his phone.

"Are you reading something?"

"Yes."

"A book?"

"Yes."

"Title?"

Frankie sighed and flipped his phone over. "Do we have to do this?"

"Yes."

He let out another long-suffering sigh, and I smiled into my carton of rice.

"I'm reading the autobiography of Grace Jones."

"Sorry, what?" I set my rice down and leaned toward Frankie.

He groaned and flopped back in his chair. "This is going to be a whole thing, isn't it?"

"Um, Mr. Brooding just told me he is reading the autobiography of the iconic Grace Jones. So, uh, yeah. This is going to be a whole thing."

"It's not a big deal. My mom and sisters were reading it for their book club, and it sounded interesting."

I blinked rapidly.

"Stop looking at me like that."

"Nope." I sat back in my seat. "I just found out that not only do you know who Grace Jones is, but you are also in a book club with your mom. That's so fucking precious."

"Sure is." He sucked up a noodle.

"Oh no, you don't. You're not going quiet on me now. Tell me more about your family."

He rolled his eyes and took a sip of water. "My dad died last year of lung cancer, my mom's a saint, and my sisters are fucking ridiculous."

"Sorry about your dad."

"Thanks. It was a long time coming. I've been trying to quit, but it's damn near impossible with all this shit going on."

I soaked in the information. Frankie had said more in the last minute than he had the entire time I'd known him.

"Have you tried vaping?"

Frankie scoffed. "Do I look like a pussy?"

I lifted an eyebrow.

"Fuck. Sorry."

I smiled. "Don't worry about it." Deciding to push my luck, I asked, "Girlfriend? Boyfriend?"

His stoic face split into a grin. "Now, why do you want to know that, Mrs. Moretti?"

"I'm a nosy bitch." I laughed, picking my rice back up. "And it would make this whole brooding thing make more sense if you weren't getting laid."

"You think I'm brooding?" His eyebrows rose, and he laughed.

"You're monosyllabic, always frowning, and you lurk. You're a lurker. What would you call it?"

Without missing a beat, he said, "Dignified."

A surprised laugh burst from my mouth. Frankie's eyes crinkled as he grinned over the desk at me. With an air of triumph, he popped the rest of a Crab Rangoon into his mouth.

"You got jokes. Who would've guessed?"

Mouth full of food, he said, "In this line of business, you have to have a good sense of humor, or you'll go crazy." He swallowed, looking more at ease than I'd ever seen him. "I'd like to think I've struck a good work-life balance."

"You're the king of compartmentalizing."

"I mean, you're the boss's wife. It's probably for the best I keep my distance."

"We're not married yet," I said absently. "But yeah, I get it. It's just weird spending all this time together and not knowing anything about you."

"To be fair, all I know about you is that you're the boss's fiancée, own your own business, and look fantastic naked."

"So, you watched the show?"

"I mean, I was there and have eyes. You're a change for the family. That's for sure."

"Don't I know it." I stabbed at my food and let the silence drag me down. "How am I going to do all this?"

"One day at a time. And you've got Aunt Rosa on your side. No one fucks with Aunt Rosa."

The idea of my future lying in her hands was terrifying. What if she found out what I did? Their marriage was a hot fucking mess, but she still loved the bastard. What if she wanted revenge?

"You going to finish that rice?" Frankie was already reaching for the container, and I pushed it toward him. "Thanks."

"Add 'you're a bottomless pit' to the list of Frankie facts."

He gave a tight-lipped smile, digging into my second lunch.

And like that, our heart-to-heart was over.

Around closing time, Frankie got a call and had to step out. I checked my phone and saw I'd missed a call from Luca.

"You rang?" I wedged my phone between my ear and shoulder while packing up my laptop.

"Hey, baby. I'm going to be late getting home tonight. I had to head out of town, but I'm on my way back."

"Okay?"

"We'll talk when I get home."

I sat back down, tossing my keys on the desk.

"Sasha?"

"What?"

"I love you."

I sighed. "I love you too. Be safe."

"Always."

I hung up. After the weird cake tasting, I'd expected to talk to Luca and discuss what happened, but instead, I was about to go home to an empty house—again.

"You ready to go?" Frankie stood in the doorway, his brow furrowed.

"Yeah."

I waved at everyone on the way out, not interested in small talk.

Once I was settled in the car, I asked, "Where's Luca?"

"Driving home. You know that."

"Let me rephrase. Where was Luca today?"

Frankie turned up the radio, not even looking at me.

Light rain hit the window, obscuring the view. My phone vibrated as we drove past Tower Grove Park, and I immediately flipped it over. BETH lit up the screen, and I frowned.

What the hell does she want?

I sent her to voicemail, knowing I'd never check it. I had more important things to worry about than Beth and her weird bouts of nostalgia.

EIGHT

Luca got home well after three a.m. and stayed in his office. He finally joined me in the bedroom when his clock radio alarm went off.

"Sorry. Sorry." He whispered as he rushed through the door to turn off the eighties rock blaring through the speaker.

"I was already up." I set my phone on the side table and scooted up to rest my back on the headboard. "Sit."

"Let me get out of yesterday's clothes."

I nodded, and he went to the bathroom. The shower turned on, and I blew out a sigh. Avoidance ran both ways with us, and I hated that I had to be the bigger person.

"I called Lauren," I yelled toward the bathroom.

The water shut off, and Luca walked out dripping wet, wrapped in a plush towel. Water ran down his tight abs, my eyes following the trail until it reached the top of the towel.

"What did you say?" His dark brows pulled together as he pushed back his wet hair.

"I called Lauren. I told her you were taking the day off."

Luca took his top lip between his teeth and shook his head. Blowing out a breath, he rested his hands on his hips. "And why'd you do that?"

"Are you fucking serious?"

"Yes!" He threw his hands out, his face twisted in a frown.

"We haven't spent a whole day together since we got engaged. Not to mention, we just made up from a fight Saturday, and by Monday, a threat that Frankie wouldn't explain interrupted our cake tasting. Then, I spent the better part of my evening lying to my mom. Luckily, she loves you enough not to connect the dots. After all that, I'd say we absolutely need a day together without outside interruptions and bullshit."

His tight jaw relaxed, and he came around to my side of the bed. "I wish you would've said something."

"When?"

He gave me a resigned nod and turned toward the bathroom, dropping his towel at the door. He used his foot to push it around, sopping up the puddles on the floor. I laughed as he inched across the tile, his ass flexing with each slide of the towel. He peaked his head out of the doorway and smiled. "You didn't think I'd leave the floor all wet?"

"Never."

"Get dressed. If we're taking the day off, we're doing it in style."

"Yes, sir!"

"This is my idea of a day off."

Luca stepped behind me as I stared at the Rothko. "I'm glad you like it. Let's head downstairs."

"Yes, please!"

We paid the attendant and went into the first room of the immersive Van Gogh exhibit. Shades of blue and yellow surrounded us as we walked through Starry Night.

"This is amazing," I murmured.

Luca took my hand and laced our fingers together. "It really is. Thank you for calling off today. I needed this. We needed this."

"My pleasure. Thank you for going along with it."

"Anytime."

We strolled along in comfortable silence. A class of elementary school kids darted around us while their teacher tried to rein them in. It was all very wholesome.

"These kids are lucky." I pointed to a trio of girls side-eyeing us as they whispered and giggled. "We never came to the art museum, but we sure as hell went to The Arch."

"Right? How many times can one kid go up in that shaky elevator?" Luca laughed. "I have a thing about heights but refused to admit it. So, year after year, I tortured myself to prove I wasn't a wuss."

"Couldn't be the kid in tights and afraid of a national monument."

"Ha. Ha. Ha. You're not so fearless yourself, Ms. Mitchell."

"You got nothing."

"Okay, then you can change the air filter next time."

I gasped and slapped his arm. "You wouldn't make me go into that creepy basement."

"You're right. I wouldn't." He wrapped his arm around my waist and pulled me to his side. "You're lucky I love you."

I gazed up at him, his dark brown eyes shadowed by the deep blues lighting the room. His lips spread into a breathtaking smile, and I fought the urge to kiss him. "I am."

"Thank you for letting me love you."

I ghosted my lips over his. "You're welcome."

Luca's laugh let out a warm burst of air against my face. "Keep walking before I scar these kids for life and catch a charge." He discretely patted my ass and moved us forward.

I couldn't help but smile at the two kids in front of us discussing the exhibit.

Will we have artistic kids, or will I have to learn to like sports?

As if his brain was on the same wavelength, Luca said, "If we have kids, I want to do stuff like this with them."

"If?"

His cheeks reddened, and he looked away. "We've never really had that talk, and I don't want to assume."

"You've met my mother."

He laughed, and his hand squeezed mine. "But she's not a reason to have kids. If we have them, I want us both to be one hundred percent sure."

I tugged Luca away from the crowd and made sure I had his full attention. "I'd never thought too much about kids until you. But now? Now, I know I want kids with you. I want the whole family thing. At my last annual visit, I had my IUD removed and am back on the pill. I figured it'd be easier for when we're ready to try."

"Yeah?" Luca grinned, running his hands up my arms.

"Yeah." I bunched the front of his coat in my hands and pulled him down to me, our lips meeting in a mind-numbing kiss. His lips, so full and soft, claimed mine like he was about to knock me up right there in the museum. He tangled his fingers in my hair, tilting my head until my neck hurt, but I didn't care. I'd take a little pain if it meant he kept kissing me like he owned me.

"Ew!" A chorus of little voices brought us back to our senses.

"Probably should cool it before we get arrested," I whispered into Luca's mouth.

"You ready for lunch?"

"I could eat."

I followed Luca out of the exhibit and museum. The early spring air was still cold, but at least the sun was out after morning thunderstorms.

Luca opened my door and helped me get into his low-sitting sports car. We'd taken out one of his favorites for the day, and it was a chore to get my ass in and out of it, especially in the dress and shoes I was wearing.

I checked my phone as Luca walked around to the driver's side, pleased to see no urgent emails or messages. Ashley really was an MVP.

"You ready for a make-up cake tasting?"

"Really?"

"Mm-hmm."

"I trust you have real food coming too?" I side-eyed him as I buckled my seatbelt.

"I know my baby."

The drive to the bakery was quiet until Luca's business phone rang, and he shot me an apologetic smile before answering, "Yeah?"

Someone went on for a minute, but the hourly news update on NPR blocked any possibility of hearing what was going on.

"I can be there after seven."

We got to the bakery, and Luca hung up with a grunt. He tapped his fingers on the steering wheel, his jaw ticking. "I have to go out tonight." He swung his heavy gaze my way. "I know you wanted the whole day, but—"

I put my finger on his lips. "Hush. Don't ruin the next—" I checked the dashboard, "four hours by being all broody." I stuck out my bottom lip.

"Don't try to make me laugh."

"But I like your laugh. It's way better than this pout."

The corners of his mouth twitched, and he dropped his head back on the headrest. "I'd rather spend tonight with you."

"Same, but you're the boss man, and with that comes responsibilities." I grabbed his hand and raised it to my lips. "I get it. We'll be good as long as you're willing to have days like today."

Inside the bakery, Paul had a table set with soup, sandwiches, and cake samples.

"You are a god." I patted Paul on the shoulder as I passed him to the feast he'd prepared for me.

Luca pulled out my chair and sat next to me. His shoulders relaxed as he filled my plate and then his own.

I always came first.

Paul hovered in the background but never approached. Instead, he let Luca lead the tasting. I tried the same cakes as before but noticed an extra as we worked our way through the plates. My lips twitched with a smile. "Is that . . .?" I pointed at it with my fork.

Luca grinned at Paul and then pushed the cake in front of me. "Tiramisu."

"In public?" I playfully gasped, throwing my hand over my heart.

"Just taste it." Luca's gaze burned into me, making me shift in my seat.

My fork glided through the cake, and I made a big show of lifting it to eye level and smelling it. Paul chuckled, but Luca raised an eyebrow, clearly over my antics.

As soon as the airy sponge hit my tongue, my eyes shut. Paul had somehow enhanced all the delicious tiramisu flavor I'd grown accustomed to in my time with Luca.

I chewed slowly, not wanting the delicious cake to ever leave my mouth. When I finally swallowed, I opened my eyes. The look Luca gave me sent my body into a tailspin. He wet his bottom lip and swallowed, his throat bobbing, capturing my attention. Our knees touched as I shifted toward him. Despite the innocent surroundings, the decadent dessert on my tongue and the brutally handsome man in front of me ratcheted up my arousal. It wasn't lost on me that Luca's mouth would be on me if we were home.

"We have a winner?" Paul's voice startled me.

"I believe so," Luca answered for me.

I drank the rest of my water and cleared my throat. "How did you do that?"

Paul laughed and came around the table next to Luca. "I can't take any of the credit." He slapped Luca's back like they were old buddies. "This guy sent me the recipe."

I narrowed my eyes at Luca. "Either my memory is terrible, or that cake is even better than the last time I had it."

"I had a lot of free time last year to perfect it." His gentle tone softened the blow, but not enough to keep my stomach from dropping. "Paul, can you wrap up a couple of pieces for us to take home?"

"You got it, Boss."

When Paul left, I kissed below Luca's ear. "I love you."

"I love you too."

"This cake is the most romantic thing anyone has ever done for me." I leaned back so he could see my face. "I want you to know I missed you every day we were apart."

"We don't have to talk about that."

"Maybe we do."

Luca frowned and adjusted in his seat. "I don't—"

"Here we go." Paul set a to-go bag on the table and rushed off to the kitchen.

Luca blew out a relieved breath. He'd been dodging this conversation since we got back together. "You ready to go?" He was already standing and putting on his coat.

"Sure."

I wanted to reassure him. I wanted to let him know I'd not only broken his heart but my own. But it was clear he didn't want to talk about our breakup.

The levity we'd found at lunch was gone as he drove us home, and I didn't know what to do.

He parked in the driveway and shut off the car but didn't get out. Tapping the steering wheel with his finger, Luca finally said, "The year we were apart was the hardest year of my life. I knew you were it for me, and it killed me to know you were out in the world without me. I spent all my free time cooking, trying to find a new normal. In the end, I cooked my way through our relationship and perfected your favorite dishes."

"I'm sorry." The words felt wrong and awkward, but I needed to say something. I knew I did the right thing when I left him, but the right thing wasn't what I wanted.

Luca finally turned and looked at me. "I'm sorry about yesterday. I knew I needed to make it up to you, so I sent Paul the recipe. I'd never planned for anyone but you to taste that cake, but I thought maybe it was perfect for our wedding."

"I hope you had him sign an NDA." I joked, trying to relieve some of the tension in the car.

Luca chuckled. His hand cupped my cheek, and I leaned into his touch.

"Why don't we make the top tier tiramisu and do the boring flavors for everyone else? That way, it stays a little secret between us."

"I like that." Luca smiled.

"Good." I kissed his palm and trailed a hand down his jacket to his belt buckle. "Now, we should finish what Mr. Clean interrupted the other night."

"Mr. Clean?" He watched my hand loosen his belt and unbutton his pants. As if an afterthought, he said, "You mean Paulie?"

"Sure. How the hell would I know?" When I couldn't maneuver his dick out of his pants, I sucked my teeth. "So much for driveway head." I flopped back in my seat.

Luca's phone buzzed, and he groaned. Picking it up, he frowned. "I promise when we're on our honeymoon, this fucking phone will be on 'do not disturb' because this is ridiculous."

As Luca tapped away, I shivered. The temperature in the car was getting chilly, and if I wasn't going to suck his cock, then there was no reason to freeze my ass off. "I'm going inside."

"I'll be right there."

I grabbed my purse and the cake bag. There was no telling how long Luca would sit in the car, and I didn't want to interrupt him when I started jonesing for another piece.

Ryan met me at the door, meowing up a storm.

"What's up, buddy?" I kicked off my shoes and hung up my coat. Ryan circled my feet, headbutting my shin like I wasn't already looking at his goofy ass. "Let's go check your water bowl."

He followed me to the kitchen, his meows continuing all the way there. Sure enough, he was out of food and water.

Luca snuck up on me as I gave him a small bonus scoop of food. "He's going to get fat."

"And?"

"The vet said he needed to lose a pound."

I rolled my eyes. It was easy for him to keep Ryan on his diet. He wasn't the one the damn cat followed like a shadow until he got what he wanted.

"I need to head out," Luca said to my ass because my face was deep in the pantry.

"All right."

"I'm sorry."

I stood up, shaking my head. "You've got to stop apologizing. It's your job. I understand."

He closed the distance between us in three steps, pinning me against the refrigerator, the cold steel sending a shiver down my spine. "You're amazing."

He fisted my hair as his lips crashed down on mine. Pinned against the fridge, I fought to arch against him. Answering my frustration, he slid his thick thigh between my legs, immobilizing me completely.

My clit throbbed, the pressure of his leg both perfect and not enough. He tugged my hair at the root, making me gasp, and his tongue swiped inside my mouth. The sweet cake and bitter coffee from the bakery added a delicious flavor to our kiss.

He gently wrapped his hand around my throat, his thumb grazing my racing pulse. His lips left mine, and I tried to follow, but his hold stopped me.

"Open your eyes." Luca's rough voice demanded.

I swallowed, my chest rising and falling as I looked up at Luca. The naked hunger in his eyes sent a shot of pure desire through me.

"You want to suck my cock?" He punctuated his words with a circling of his hips, his hard length pressing into my stomach.

I nodded, licking my lips in anticipation.

"Use your words." Luca's hands tightened ever so slightly.

"Yes." My voice was husky, dripping with need.

He stepped back, and I sagged from the lack of support. "On your knees."

I dropped immediately to the cold, hard tile. My hands grabbed the waist of his pants and pulled his hips closer. While he caressed my hair, I traced the outline of his hard cock with the tips of my fingers. I looked through my lashes as I slowly dragged down the zipper. "I want you to come in my mouth."

He flexed his fingers in my hair as I nuzzled his bulge.

Never breaking eye contact, I pushed down his boxers and kissed the tip. My lips slowly spread as I slid the head between them. Luca groaned, his head tipping back, only to snap back, his gaze locking on me.

I took him as far back as I could, my cheeks hollowing as I sucked him in. I did it again, this time taking a little more. Pulling back until just the head was in my mouth, I circled it with my tongue as my hand moved up and down his shaft.

Luca's fingers tightened in my hair, the jolt of pain making me moan around his cock. "Touch yourself." Luca's deep voice sent heat through my body.

I squeezed his balls before raking my nails down his thigh, and a tremor went through his body. Spreading my thighs wide, I raised up on my knees to keep his cock in my mouth. I gasped when my fingers touched my clit. It wouldn't take much for me to come all over my hand.

I popped my lips off his cock, spit stretching from my lips to his tip. "Fuck my face."

Luca didn't have to be told twice. He twisted my hair around his hand, grabbing his cock with the other. My mouth fell open, and he traced my lips with the head. "Fuck yourself with your fingers."

Sliding two fingers into my pussy, I moaned, and Luca thrust into my mouth with a grunt. He paused a moment at the back of my throat, and I adjusted my breathing. Wrapping his other hand in my hair, he pumped into my mouth. I moved my fingers in time with his thrusts, my arousal dripping down my hand.

"Fuck, look at you." He grunted, his abs tensing. "I'm coming." Luca gritted out, moving my head to meet his thrusts. He bottomed out in my throat only a moment later, shooting cum down my throat. I gagged as I swallowed as much as I could.

Luca pulled out, cum dribbling out of the corner of my mouth. His hands fell from my hair, and he used his thumb to wipe it away. "You come, beautiful?"

I shook my head, my fingers slipping from my pussy.

"Let's fix that." He lifted me off the floor and hefted me onto the counter. Picking up my wet hand, he licked my knuckles. His eyes shut like he was tasting the most delicious dish as he sucked each finger clean. He hummed in satisfaction, and the vibrations through my hand made my breath stutter.

Luca put my hands on the counter and placed a hard kiss on my lips before abruptly pulling away. My eyes fluttered open in time to watch him sink to his knees. He roughly shoved my legs apart, his fingers digging into my soft thighs. "So fucking pretty."

"Thank you."

He chuckled as he kissed up the inside of my thigh, his nose nudging the wet satin between my legs. His lips latched around my clit over my panties, and he sucked. Oh lord, did he suck.

My legs turned to jelly, and my head flew back into the cabinet with a thud. I grabbed a handful of his coarse, black locks, trapping him between my thick thighs. Luca turned his head, biting me hard. Moaning, I bucked my hips as he pushed my panties aside and thrust two fingers in easily.

"Fuck!" I grunted, fucking his hand right back.

"Watch yourself ride my hand, baby."

I opened my eyes, and Luca shoved my skirt out of the way. My belly blocked my view, so I leaned forward and gripped the edge of the counter for balance. The sight of his thick fingers disappearing and then gliding back out set me off. I clamped down on his fingers, and he pressed his thumb to my clit, sending a second shock through me. I cried out, falling back against the cabinet.

Luca's fingers continued to work me, helping me ride out my orgasm. When the fluttering stopped, he pulled his fingers from me.

"I fucking love you," I panted out.

Luca gathered me off the counter and into a hug. "I fucking love you too."

We stood in the kitchen holding each other until the doorbell rang. Luca sighed. "That'll be Marco and Frankie."

I buried my face in his chest and mumbled, "Don't go."

He laughed, the sound vibrating through me as he squeezed me tightly. After a few deep breaths, we reluctantly parted, and he helped me get decent before tucking himself into his pants. "I guess I'll go let them in."

I poured myself a glass of water and sat at the kitchen island. The guys all came in a moment later.

"Sorry to interrupt," Marco said.

"No, you're not."

He shrugged and leaned against the counter where Luca had just made me see stars. I smiled into my glass.

Frankie went straight for the fridge, not even a wave in my direction. While he rifled through the drawers, I asked Marco, "So where are you two off to tonight?"

"Nowhere special."

"Awesome."

And that was the last bit of conversation we had until Luca came into the kitchen in a fresh suit.

"Ready to go?" Luca passed an envelope to Frankie while talking to Marco.

"Yeah. See ya, Red."

"Ugh."

Luca came over and gave me a kiss that held remnants of the heat we'd had. His lips tasted like me. I felt a possessive satisfaction that he would be out in the world with me on his tongue.

"Be safe," I mumbled into his lips.

"Always."

It wasn't until Luca was out of view that I turned toward Frankie, who leaned on the island, his face in his phone.

"Frankie."

"Sasha."

"How was your day?"

He glanced up from his phone without lifting his head. "Really?"

"Yes."

"It was fine. I had to take a drive out of town, but other than that, pretty uneventful."

"Where'd you go?" I went to the sink to refill my water.

"Not here."

"Cool. Good story."

"We don't do stories, babe."

"You're a babe guy?"

"If the babe fits."

I scoffed and headed to my bedroom for a pair of fresh panties. Frankie followed me as far as the living room.

"I'll be back down in a bit."

No answer from Frankie, because why would he answer? Better to let me talk to myself like a loser.

Closing the bedroom door behind me, I stripped out of my clothes and quickly cleaned myself up. In no time, I was sitting comfortably in bed.

After a cleansing breath, I pulled out my laptop and opened my email. As much as Luca leaving bummed me out, I had a lot to do, and taking a day off was going to be a bitch to make up.

As I scrolled through requests from clients and vendors, my phone lit up next to me with the name Malcolm.

"Hello?"

"Sasha?"

"Yes."

Never one to doddle, Malcolm got straight to the point. "My brother-in-law has been following you."

NINE

The stars aligned, and Frankie went outside right as Malcolm showed up at the office.

"Talk fast. I don't know how long he'll be gone."

"Someone is paying to have you followed." He handed me a manilla folder. "I'm still digging into who because apparently, Shane took cash and an alias."

I flipped through the pictures and notes, my hands clammy as I lifted a picture of Luca and me at the Art Museum the day before. "Has he handed over any information yet?"

"No. I came across this file on you before he delivered it."

"That's good, right?"

Malcolm pursed his lips. "Not sure. It worries me someone hired a PI so closely related to you. Either they trusted Shane to get the inside scoop without tipping you off, or they wanted you to know they were watching."

"Yeah, that's not good."

"You need to tell Luca."

"I will."

He flattened his palms on my desk, bending his ridiculously tall frame to bring us eye to eye. "I mean it. No rogue shit this time."

"Okay."

Malcolm searched my face for any signs of deceit—which he wouldn't find. I was one hundred percent telling Luca someone was watching me.

Dipping his chin, he tapped the top of my desk. "I guess I'll head out then."

"Not a word to Ash." I rushed out.

He stopped with his hand on the door handle and looked over his shoulder. "Obviously. She's just now getting over the fact you're marrying into the mob. I don't expect she'd appreciate you having a stalker."

"Have I told you how much I love you two together?"

He gave me a blinding smile. "Not today."

I laughed and shook my head. "Get out of here before Frankie or Ashley catches you."

Malcolm slipped out, and I took a steadying breath, shoving the folder into a drawer. I snagged a stack of old notes and fed them into the shredder sheet by sheet. The buzzing soothed me in the way only office machinery could.

"You're shredding without me?" Frankie's voice startled me, and I spun my chair around.

"Sorry, I forgot you're eight."

He covered his heart with his hand, his face blank as ever. "Ouch."

"If it'll make you feel better, you can shred the documents Miranda digitized last week."

Frankie spread out on the couch and tilted his head toward the door. "What'd the giant want?"

"Tips for Ashley's birthday present. He's going all out."

Frankie's eyes narrowed as he studied me. "I have to head out of town for a few days. Pete's picking you up and taking you home, and the Marino twins will be your protection until I get back."

"Two for the price of one?"

"Between the two of them, they should be able to bring you to work and back with no problems."

"If you say so."

He leaned forward, his elbows on his knees. "You planning on causing trouble?"

"Never." I glanced at my phone, seeing a missed call from Luca. "When do you leave?"

"Now. Luca should be here in a few."

"Wow. Personal protection courtesy of the boss? I'm a lucky girl."

"No arguments here."

I answered several emails, hoping to get a little time with Luca before he left. As if my thoughts had conjured him, Luca stood in the doorway in his black tailored suit, looking like a dark angel. "You can go. I've got it from here."

Frankie got up to leave, and I yelled out, "Have a safe trip!"

"Yeah, yeah, yeah," he said as he walked around Luca and out of my office.

"He's just so chatty."

"It's why he's your bodyguard." Luca grinned.

"Is that jealousy?"

"Nothing to be jealous of. Frankie's as loyal as they come and as social as Ryan on his diet."

I got up from my chair and met Luca in the middle of the office. Wrapping my arms around him in a tight hug, I sighed. His hugs were next level. "I bet he gives shitty hugs."

"Let's not find out." Luca's deep voice rumbled through his chest.

I smiled up at him. "He's probably all ass out and has limp-noodle arms."

"Exactly." Luca lightly pressed his lips to mine, clearly in no hurry. "You about done for the day?"

"Just need to finish an email to a client, and we can go, but I need to tell you something."

Luca frowned, shutting the door behind him and leading me

to the couch. "What's going on?" He tucked a lock of hair behind my ear.

"I'm being followed."

His hand dropped, and his stare sharpened. "Come again?"

I stood and went to my desk. "Malcolm came across this file. His brother-in-law is a PI, and apparently, someone paid him to investigate me. To follow me."

Luca took the folder, silently flipping through the pictures until he got to the last one. "I'll handle this."

"Okay?"

Luca set the folder down and pulled me between his legs. "You trust me?"

"Of course."

"Then don't worry about this."

I bit my lip, uneasy by how well he'd taken the information. "I'll try not to."

"Good." He smiled. "You said you had an email to finish, right?" I nodded, and Luca popped my ass, pushing me toward my desk. "Then get to it. I'm hungry."

The change in mood was jarring, but I had to trust that if there were a problem, Luca would handle it, and if he was Mr. Chipper, it must not be a big deal. "Are you cooking tonight, or are we getting takeout?"

"I'm cooking."

"Well, hot damn. Give me five minutes."

Writing an email to a pissy client was very difficult with Luca sprawled out on my tiny office couch. The same couch we'd had a few magical late nights on. But tonight wasn't the night for hanky-panky.

Once I had everything shut down, we made our way out to the waiting town car. Pete jumped out and opened the door. "Ms. Sasha."

"Pete. When are you going to drop the 'miss' business?"

He grinned, the lines on his face deepening. "Never. After the wedding, if you'd like, I can call you Mrs. Moretti."

I shook my head, smiling, and slipped into the car.

"I like the sound of that," Luca murmured in my ear as he squeezed my thigh.

"I hope you like the sound of Mrs. Mitchell-Moretti because all I can promise is a hyphen."

"Baby, I'll take you any way I can get you."

I kissed him, my tongue tracing his lips, parting them. We pushed ourselves closer together, our hands exploring as he wedged his knee between mine.

Pete cleared his throat, and we pulled apart slowly.

"Sorry, Pete." I laughed. It wasn't the first time I'd mauled Luca in front of him, and it wouldn't be the last.

"No problem at all. Would you like me to raise the partition?"

"That won't be necessary. We'll be home soon." Luca adjusted his pants.

"How's Maria?" I asked, trying to take my mind off Luca and what his slacks were hiding.

Pete smiled at me in the rearview mirror. "Great. She's planning a trip for us to Paris for when you two are on your honeymoon."

"That's amazing."

"I'll give you a list of the best places to eat," Luca said, pulling out his phone to make a note.

"Thanks, Boss."

When we pulled up to the house, Luca told Pete to be back at ten.

"How many days will you be in Chicago?"

Luca sighed as he shrugged off his jacket. "Hopefully, just two, but knowing Marco, we'll be there until Sunday."

"I thought you were in charge." I smirked as I shoved my shoes under the coat rack. Luca reached for me, but I took off toward the kitchen. I stopped with the island between us. "What'd I say?" I asked innocently.

He loomed over the counter, his palms flat on the butcher block. "You have five seconds."

"To what?" I pressed myself against the edge, putting myself almost within reach of his ridiculous arm span.

"To get out of my kitchen so I can make dinner."

My shoulders slumped, and I shuffled away. "Okay."

"Quit your pouting."

"I'm not pouting."

"You are, but it's cute. Now go get out of those clothes, and I'll have dinner ready in thirty."

An idea popped into my head as I hurried upstairs.

Purple lingerie.

I got gussied up, choosing my highest fuck me heels, and slid on my short silk robe.

"Luca?"

He wasn't in the dining room or the kitchen.

"Luca?" I found him at his desk, scowling. "You okay?"

"Yeah, but I need to leave immediately." He typed furiously on his laptop.

The front door opened, and Pete rushed in, followed by Frankie. I tightened my robe around me, suddenly regretting my dinner attire.

"Your bag is in the car." When Pete finally looked my way, his eyes widened, and he coughed. With pink cheeks, he dipped his chin and spun around, leaving the way he came.

"You didn't have to get all dressed up for me." Frankie winked at me, not at all phased by my little outfit.

I stuck my tongue out and turned back to Luca, who was finally looking at me—well, glowering at me.

"Frankie, go wait for me in the car."

"You got it."

Luca waited until the front door closed before asking, "What are you wearing?" He stood, laptop bag in hand, and rounded the desk.

"A going-away present, but it looks like there isn't enough time." I opened my robe, letting him get a better look. "Too bad, huh?"

He stalked toward me, his body forcing mine back into the wall. "Yeah, too bad." Trailing a finger down my sternum, he grazed my belly. My breath stuttered, and I gasped as he roughly cupped my pussy. "How am I supposed to leave you here like this?"

I shook my head, my fingers digging into his arms to keep me upright. Luca's lips crashed down on mine, teeth nipping until his tongue thrust into my mouth. All too soon, he stepped away, and I stumbled forward.

"What the fuck?"

"I've got to go." He snarled, his eyes burning into me, setting my body on fire. "I love you." It sounded a lot more like I hate you.

"I love you too. Be safe," I said my voice just above a whisper.

Luca gave me one more hard look and shook his head before walking out of the room. From the hallway, he shouted, "Pictures. I want pictures, maybe a video."

I let out a surprised laugh.

"And I told those Marino fuckers to stay out of the house, so shoot them if they take one step inside." And with the dramatic flair of a man who was used to getting what he wanted, Luca slammed the front door.

"Well then."

"Why don't you two stay in the lobby with Miranda?" I mumbled as I stared at the scantily clad pic I'd sent Luca. The sexting arms race was ramping up to what I hoped would be an explosive finale when he got back.

The Marino twins looked at each other and shrugged. They left my office silently, and I could finally take a full breath. Their presence was the exact opposite of Frankie's. The two behemoths would loom around me, silent like a pair of statues. One would ride in the back of the car while the other rode upfront with

Pete, never saying a fucking word. For two days, I didn't know peace, just quiet. Even at home, I was painfully aware they were sitting right outside because it was the only time I heard their voices.

Ashley's head popped in the doorway, and she visibly relaxed when she saw I was alone. "Thank God. I don't know if I can handle any more of the beefcake twins."

"They're a lot." *Understatement of the year.*

"I never thought I'd say it, but I miss Frankie." Ashley sat and set her laptop on my desk.

"He's not so bad. And after those two, he's looking more and more like Prince Charming. Luckily, they're only temporary."

"Ah, the life of a mob wife."

I bit back a smile. I tried to keep that part of my life away from Ashley, and for the most part, she never spoke about it once Luca and I got back together.

"Not a wife yet."

Ashley frowned. "You having second thoughts?"

"No! I just mean, I haven't gotten married yet."

"Has it been hard? Entering his world?"

I pursed my lips, not sure how much to share. I didn't want Ashley to think I regretted my choice to get back with Luca. "Parts of it. There's a lot more to it than I imagined, and there's a lot less." Her brow furrowed. I was clearly making zero sense. "Nothing has fundamentally changed besides the extra security, but there's an extra mental burden now that I know. Does that make sense?"

"I think so."

"Eventually, people will have expectations for me, and that terrifies me."

"And the only person you have to help you figure it out is Rosa."

This was the closest we'd ever come to talking about that night. Once I was discharged from the hospital, I regretted telling her the truth. Maybe it was the concussion, the pain meds, or my broken heart that made me blurt out everything, but it was a burden she didn't deserve.

"I guess that's my penance."

Ashley looked back at the closed door. "Fuck that. You did what you had to." Her lips thinned until her dimples dipped in her brown cheeks. "Can I be honest?"

"Of course."

"When you went back to him, I was pissed."

"You never said anything." But I knew. Of course I knew. What friend and business partner wouldn't be pissed about being forced into bed with the mob?

"What was I supposed to say?" She shook her head, her eyes on her hands. "I love you, and I want you to be happy." She looked up at me with shiny eyes. "I know Luca makes you happy. But I can't help but be scared for you. For the business."

I reached across and patted the desk until she gave me her hand. "I promise you nothing will happen to me. Or the business."

"You can't promise that, and you know it." She squeezed my fingers, a plea to make the problems go away.

I swallowed, my stomach turning. "What can I do?" An idea that would break my heart but ease her concerns popped into my head. "I could sign over my quarter of the company and become an employee. Then, there are no ties to Moretti Properties beyond vendor contracts. Same as any other business in the area."

"No!" She leaned across the desk and grabbed my shoulders. "No. That's not—"

"Admit it. You'd feel better. Don't make this about our friendship. As a business owner, you can't say this wouldn't make you feel more secure."

She sighed and sat back in her chair, her hands twisting together. "I need to think about it."

"I'd do it. Just say the word."

Ashley blew out a breath. "Let's look over these blueprints."

And like that, we pushed aside the future of our collective

dream and started talking open concept and window options. I needed to protect my friends and the company we'd built, and I'd do whatever it took to do it, even if it meant giving it all up for them.

"Where'd my shadows go?" I asked Miranda when I was leaving the office.

"I don't know. They left without saying anything. Big surprise." She rolled her eyes as she shut down her computer.

"Weird." I eyed Miranda's dress. "You going out with the guy from your business class tonight?"

She gave me a huge smile. "I am." Pulling a mirror from her drawer, she freshened her lipstick. "So far, Oscar's really great. It's early days, but so far, so good."

"Fingers crossed he's not a mouth breather like the guy you brought to New Year's."

She chuckled. "Sasha, I respect your business acumen, but before Luca, you were a hot mess when it came to relationships. So maybe you aren't the best person to be giving relationship advice."

I grinned. "You're not wrong."

"Don't worry. We went hiking last weekend, and he seemed to do all right."

Scrunching my nose, I glanced down at my phone as it lit up. "I don't get how you enjoy doing that. Nature, sweat, and the chilly Midwest spring? No, thank you."

"You've never been. How would you know you hate it?"

We made our way out, waving at Axel as he unloaded wood from his truck. Now that it was March, the sun was setting a little later, so the sky was a riot of color.

"It combines so many of the things I avoid. I'm making an educated guess."

"Well, next time a group of us go, I'm dragging you along."

"I'm too old for new hobbies."

"You're only seven years older than me." She deadpanned.

Pete opened the backdoor for me, patiently waiting.

"And wiser."

Miranda rolled her eyes. "You're ridiculous. See you Monday."

"Drive safe!"

She waved and hurried to her car, tapping away on her phone.

"Pete," I said as I slid into the backseat.

"Ms. Sasha." Once he got in the car, he turned around. "Where are the boys?"

"No idea. I figured you would know?"

He stared at the building like he could summon them with his mind. When his wise guy magic didn't work, he grunted and started the car. "Let's get you home."

At a stoplight, he texted someone. "When was the last time you saw the Marino brothers?"

"Probably a couple of hours ago?"

Pete got quiet, which made me nervous. When we got to the house, he inched up the driveway. Two enormous shadows that I assumed were the Marinos sat on the porch.

Pete backed the car up and parked on the street. "You stay here," he said as he took a gun from the glove box.

"Wait!" I hollered as he got out, but he ignored me. He marched toward the house with his gun pointed, and the Marino twins jumped up. My body tensed, waiting for gunshots.

Pete shouted, and then, to my relief, the twins laughed. Pete came back to the car, his face flushed. "They're here." He huffed as he held the door open for me. "I'm going to walk you in."

Pete escorted me to the front door. The Marino twins stood on either side of us, facing the street—no greeting, no smile, no nothing.

Once inside, Pete closed the door, and his shoulders sagged. "I need to go to the office for a minute." He turned and pointed at the phone in my hand. "Call Luca and let him know. Always check with Luca if someone is coming or going without him telling you."

I hit Luca's contact, and he picked up on the second ring. "Hello?"

"Uh, Pete told me to call and tell you he was in the house and going into the office."

Luca chuckled. "Perfect. Thank you. You doing okay?"

"Yes?" I was beyond overwhelmed.

"Sasha?"

I blinked rapidly, refocusing my vision on Pete's worried face. "Sorry. It's been a weird day."

"You want to talk about it?" A muffled voice on his end said something, and Luca responded, "Give me a minute."

I wanted to tell him I missed and needed him here, but what good would that do? "We can talk later."

"You sure?" More voices started talking on Luca's side.

"Yep. I love you. Be safe."

"Love you too. Talk soon."

I stared at my phone's black screen, wondering when I'd hear back from him.

"Ms. Sasha. Are you okay?"

The stress ball that had been twisting in my gut the minute Luca left tightened. "I'm okay. Luca said it's fine for you to go into the office."

"I'll just be a moment."

"Okay."

I took out one of the meals Luca prepared for me to eat while he was gone. The adrenaline from expecting the worst pumped through my veins. There was no danger, but seeing Pete in all his gun-toting glory had opened the floodgates.

The microwave plate spun, and I could practically hear Luca scolding me for not using the oven to heat up his culinary masterpiece.

"I'm heading out."

I leaned against the counter and gave him a small smile. It was the best I could do. "All right. Be safe."

"Remember, I'm only a phone call away."

"Thank you." And I meant it with every fiber of my being. Since day one, Pete had been a constant, and I didn't doubt his loyalty for a second.

As I sat down to eat, my phone rang. "Of course." Leaning across the island, I grabbed my phone.

"Hello?"

"Sasha, do you have a minute?" Rosa's cheery voice sent a wave of discomfort through me.

"Sure." I stirred the noodles around.

"I need to get out of this house—away from everything—so I thought I'd spend the week at the lake. I know Luca will be gone a few more days, and I wondered if you wanted to head down with me for the weekend."

My appetite vanished, and I pushed the bowl away. "I, uh—"

"We can go over wedding plans, and I can get you better acquainted with the family." I desperately needed to learn about the rest of the Morettis, but I also had no desire to spend alone time with Rosa.

Searching for the words to let her down easily, I paused long enough for her to twist the knife. "Please, Sasha? I'm feeling extra lonely. Monday is Dante's birthday, and I need a distraction."

Internally cursing, I put a smile on my face so my voice would be upbeat. "Of course, Rosa. I'd love to. When were you thinking of heading down?" I looked at the clock, and it was only six-thirty.

"Whenever you can be ready. Sorry for the last-minute plan, but once it was in my head, I thought, 'What the hell, let's do it!'"

"I could have a bag packed in thirty."

"Perfect! Mickey's here and will drive us down. We'll head your way now."

"Actually, I think I'll drive myself. I'm not sure when I'll need to come back, and it'll be easier if I have my car."

There was muffled talking on Rosa's end, like her hand was covering the phone. "Mickey said that sounds fine. Just make sure the Marino boys are tailing you."

"You got it."

"Thank you, Sasha. See you in a few hours."

Try four hours, but I wasn't one to argue with the queen. Who was I to say no if she wanted to take a last-minute trip to the Ozarks on a Friday night?

I called Luca, but he didn't answer. Not uncommon, but annoying. After scarfing down my dinner, I packed a quick weekend bag and left the house. My phone lit up in my hand when Rosa sent me the address and the codes for the door and the alarm system. As the garage door opened, a deep voice startled me, calling out, "Where are you going?" The slightly larger twin emerged from the darkness of the porch, scaring the bejesus out of me.

"The Ozarks with Rosa. You're supposed to follow me."

They both huffed but went to their big-ass SUV parked behind my brand-new eco-friendly compact. I was speeding down Highway forty-four in no time, my eyes constantly drawn to my rearview mirror.

Are the twins the only ones following me?

TEN

It wasn't until I made it to Warrenton that my shoulders loosened up. Not to my usual carefree, loosey-goosey level, but at least I wasn't wearing them as earmuffs anymore.

I turned on the radio and tried to focus on anything but the impulsive drive I was on and who could be following me, but unfortunately, the dark highway offered few distractions.

It was a little after eleven when I pulled off the main drag through the tourist area and started my trek down the winding tree-lined back roads. It took me a minute to realize there were no cars behind me.

Where the fuck were those assholes?

Dread settled in my stomach as I focused on the dark road ahead. I was pissed the trees blocked out the little light the moon provided—even more pissed that I was alone in a place that had probably seen its fair share of unsolved mysteries.

I gripped the steering wheel tightly with one hand as I held my phone in front of my face so I could still kind of keep my eyes on the road.

No messages, no missed calls, no service.

Biting the inside of my cheek, I brought up the directions I'd screenshot in case I lost reception.

At least I prepared for that.

As I came around a narrow curve, the most incredible cabin came into view. At least two stories, all made of glass. Despite it being late, the place was lit, and I could see the entire main floor through the wall of windows. "I swear to God, if those assholes got here first and left me alone in the fucking woods, I will kill them."

I slowed, inching closer, until it was apparent Rosa's SUV was nowhere in sight. In fact, there were no cars visible. A cold sweat broke out across my forehead, and my eyes widened to take in my surroundings better. I held my breath as if I could hear better without my tiny act of taking in the oxygen necessary to live. An enormous figure moved through the main floor to the door, and I swallowed a scream when it stepped outside. Their features were shadowed because of the darkness and the bright house lights behind them, but based on their size, I figured it was a man, and much to my horror, he was holding a gun.

Easing down on the brake, I parked the car and reached over the seat to the glove box, where Luca kept a small handgun. My hand was steady around the handle, but my composure was slipping. White knuckling the steering wheel with one hand, the gun resting on top of it in the other, I started to turn around. The gravel driveway was lined with trees and overgrown bushes, so it would take at least a three-point turn to get the hell out of there. I'd turned halfway around when the tires hit something, and I was stuck.

"Fuck," I muttered, licking my lips as I kept an eye on the house. I put the car in reverse, but whatever I'd driven over kept the wheels from budging. "Worthless, fucking, piece of shit compact—"

The large man got closer, and I ducked down in the seat, pressing the gas pedal to the floor—it was my last chance. With one final surge, the car reared back right into the thick trunk of a tree. The tires continued to spin, but the tree kept it in place.

Over the squealing tires, a deep voice yelled, "Sasha?" He

dipped his head to peer into the car, sticking his gun back in the holster at his side.

"Tootsie?" I screeched. I put the car in park but kept it running. Eyeing him, I rolled the window down a crack. Based on what I'd heard between Luca and Marco, no one was above suspicion. "What are you doing here?"

"I could ask you the same." Tootsie frowned down at me. "Does Luca know you drove out here? Alone?"

"I'm not alone. The Marino twins, Rosa, and Mickey should be here any minute, and I left Luca a message."

His jaw twitched, and he looked over my car into the woods. "Let's go inside." He turned his mammoth body from me and walked ahead, not waiting for me.

"Okay," I mumbled, dropping the gun into my purse. Slowly, I got out of the car and grabbed my overnight bag. "Sorry for crashing your weekend in the woods. Rosa wanted to get away," I said, raising my voice at his back.

He rubbed his shoulder, tilting his head from side to side. "Ah." He stopped me at the front door, his features severe. "Let's get you settled. Then I need to check on my guest."

"A little romantic getaway, huh?" I elbowed his side as I passed. "You don't need to worry about me. Rosa, on the other hand . . ." My laugh petered out as I made it past the front door. "Holy shit." The cabin was an absolute dream. Beautifully stained woods lined every inch of the open-concept main floor. The full kitchen, dining area, and living room were furnished with over-sized furniture in earth tones with white accents. The décor was sophisticated while still mirroring the natural beauty right outside.

"Wait until you see the bedrooms."

I pulled out my phone, and notifications popped up. "Well, it looks like you're safe from Rosa's prying. She said they're staying in St. Louis." Tootsie visibly relaxed. "Apparently, Adriana caught Dante's stomach bug and got sick during dinner. That would've been useful information a couple of hours ago." Deciding to call

Luca once I was heading back to St. Louis, I shoved my phone back in my purse. "But where are the twins? I'm not sure when I lost them."

Tootsie shook his head. "That, I don't know. You want something to drink? I just made fresh coffee." He picked up a full pot from the counter as I sat in an overstuffed chair that faced the whole space.

"Coffee sounds great." I brushed my fingers over the soft throw on the arm of the chair. "I guess I should call—"

"Oh! Someone's here!" an airy voice called out.

Tootsie bolted from behind the kitchen island and up the stairs, but it was too late. Zoe Chronis floated down, stopping abruptly when Tootsie's huge body blocked her path. I blinked as if it would turn Zoe into someone who should be in the Moretti cabin.

Standing in the middle of the staircase, a cocky smile on her face, was the same blond goddess I'd met at Dimitri's engagement party. She was as beautiful as ever, only now she was dressed in an oversized shirt and leggings.

The truth smacked me in the face. Luca was a fucking liar.

"I told you to stay in the room," Tootsie gritted out as he tried to turn her shoulders.

Zoe grabbed onto the railing, her neck twisting to peek over his shoulder at me. "Well, she's seen me now, so let go!" She jerked out of his hold, sliding past him and rushing down the last steps.

Tootsie hung his head, dragging a hand down his face. His broad shoulders dropped as he leaned against the railing. He was pissed off and directed every ounce of anger at the woman making her way to the couch.

I stood with my purse gripped tightly in my hand. "What are you doing here?"

Zoe stopped behind the couch, all her confidence slipping away. Her mouth opened and closed, but she said nothing.

Shooting Tootsie a look, I softened my voice. "What is she doing here?"

"Sasha—"

"No. Both of you sit down and tell me what the fuck is going on." The ticking of a rustic clock on the mantel counted off the seconds while the two silently battled.

Tootsie sighed, stomping down the stairs to our abandoned mugs. "Zoe, sit."

"I'm fine right here," she sassed as she leaned against the wall.

He brought my coffee over, setting it on the table while pinning her with a stern look. "Sit."

Zoe's eyes narrowed, but she gingerly sat her ass on the edge of the cushion. He handed her a mug and went back to pour himself one. Once he was situated next to Zoe and taking up two-thirds of the loveseat, he turned to me and said, "Zoe's alive."

I snorted and eased back into my chair. "Obviously. Now tell me why in the hell she's in my fiancé's cabin."

"Technically, it's the family's cabin," Tootsie muttered. I glared at him, and he held up his empty hand. "Okay, sorry. I brought her here after the engagement party, and we've been here ever since."

"That was months ago."

"Tell me about it." Zoe rolled her eyes and shifted away from Tootsie.

"The news said your apartment was ransacked. Is that why you ran?" Zoe's eyes darted to Tootsie, and her lips thinned. The silent conversation between the two of them lasted longer than my patience. "What? Jesus. I know she's here. Just tell me why!"

"That night, when I went to drop Zoe off, a guy was waiting in her apartment." Tootsie's hand landed on the space between them, inches from Zoe's thigh. Her eyes followed the movement, her own hands unclasping as she smoothed her pants. "Long story short, he was there to kill her, probably to frame Luca or the family and start a real war, and I kept it from happening. She recognized him as an associate of her cousin Cy." A tremor went through Zoe, and Tootsie rested his hand over hers. "I got her out of the city, and Luca agreed it was the best option."

"Who else knows she's here?"

"Her dad and brothers."

I frowned, confused that he was talking about Yanni as if he were still alive. "So, who's starting fires and shooting up clubs?"

"My guess is Cy and his flunkies because Yanni has agreed to a cease-fire with Luca until they kill Cy and we return Zoe."

Again, Tootsie talked about the dead man like he wasn't buried six feet under. "I'm sorry, returned?" I frowned at the Greek Princess. "I thought you were here by choice."

Her cheek twitched, and a flush crept up her neck. "That's how it started." She shot him a glare full of fire as she swatted his hand from her thigh. "But now it seems I'm a bargaining chip."

Tootsie sighed as he reclined further into the couch, his eyes rolling to the ceiling. "You are not a bargaining chip. I'm keeping you safe."

Zoe leaned back, her spine bending to the shape of the arm of the couch. "From whom? My family?"

"Yes!" Tootsie shouted, turning his body and creating a distance between them. "We don't know who is siding with your cousin."

"And what about your family?" Zoe's hand jerked toward Tootsie, then me. "I'm sure the Morettis would be thrilled the boss has his number three holed up in the middle of nowhere protecting a Chronis."

"She's got you there," I murmured, and their heads swung my way. "What? She's right."

"Real helpful, Sasha."

"Never claimed to be helpful." I shrugged, finally taking a sip of the coffee. Grimacing, I put it back down. "That tastes off."

"It's decaf," Tootsie said, his eyes returning to Zoe. "She doesn't drink caffeine."

"Ah. Interesting." Licking my lips, hoping my cherry lip balm would erase the weird flavor, I struggled to find a nice way to address the elephant in the room. "Why?"

"Caffeine can cause insomnia and—"

"No, Zoe. Why is Luca sticking his neck out for you?" Her mouth fell open in shock, so I tacked on, "No offense."

Zoe let out a humorless laugh. "None taken, I guess." She pulled her upper lip between her teeth and slid her legs under her t-shirt as if she'd suddenly caught a draft. Resting her chin on her knees, she huffed. "Luca's nice. He's a nice guy."

"Okay?"

Zoe cringed, her fingers twisting the end of her intricately braided blond hair. "Last summer, we became friends. He needed an in with my family. I needed a future husband who wouldn't kill me in my sleep. It was a win-win." Tootsie stiffened, a frown making his brutish features even more severe. Zoe smirked and added, "It didn't hurt that he's gorgeous."

"He is." I pinned her with a stare, and the smirk fell right off her rosy lips.

"Right. Sorry. Luca showed up a few days later, before his father's funeral, and we hashed things out. I would stay here until my dad and brothers handled Cy, and then things would go as planned, and we would unite the families." Her eyes dropped to my hand. "But things changed. Congratulations, by the way."

"Thanks."

Zoe nodded. "Luca called me and told me he couldn't marry me, but he would keep me safe like he promised. So here I am until the men in charge tell me it's safe to go home." Her expression of utter disdain landed solely on Tootsie.

The two of them simmered with anger toward each other. Tootsie's hands flexed as he stood, picking up our mugs and taking them to the kitchen. Zoe didn't spare him a glance as she quietly sipped her coffee. From the other side of the counter, Tootsie watched Zoe with the kind of intensity that led to either fighting or fucking. I'd put money on the latter.

My feelings were all over the place. I was mad Luca hadn't told me—a tiny and jealous part of me screamed it had to mean something. My more charitable side worried about Zoe's safety, especially if Marco found out where she was. Then, there was the obvious fact that Zoe didn't know her dad was dead. There was no way in hell I'd be the bearer of that bad news.

I was exhausted.

"Are you okay?" Zoe asked, her eyes soft.

"Yeah. I'm fine."

She tilted her head and said, "You're worried about Luca and me?" Before I could answer, she chugged right along. "Because anyone that's seen that tattoo knows Luca is all yours."

I bit the inside of my cheek, fighting the urge to dive into an interrogation where I held a gun to her head as she explained why she saw Luca's bare chest. I settled for a simple, vaguely threatening, "As long as that's clear."

She solemnly nodded. "Crystal."

The tension building between Tootsie and Zoe was thick, and I wanted to get the hell out of there. I slapped my thighs and stood. "Welp. I think I'm going to head out."

Zoe untangled her legs from her shirt and hopped up. "You can't go! It's almost midnight!" She looked at Tootsie. "Tell her she has to stay."

"I don't think anyone tells Sasha what to do," he said with a chuckle but turned his dark stare to me. "But Luca would kill me if I let you leave this late. He's going to have enough dead bodies to contend with once he gets his hands on the Marinos."

They were right, and I hated it. "Okay. Is there a guestroom?"

"Nope," Zoe said, carrying her mug to the sink.

I grabbed the soft throw blanket and sighed. "Couch it is."

Zoe laughed. "Sorry, I meant there are no guestrooms because that's where we're staying, but the main bedroom is free."

I looked between the two of them. "Why aren't you guys staying in the main?"

"We aren't—"

Zoe said at the same time Tootsie said, "That's Luca's room."

I smirked. They were banging or would be soon. Lucky sons of bitches had this whole banging paradise to themselves. "Well, I guess I'm heading to bed."

"Night."

"Night."

I peeked my head in every room until I reached the last door. My interior design heart nearly stopped. The room was the perfect balance of rustic charm and decadent elegance. I wasn't usually a fan of so much wood in a room, but with the lighting and décor, I would've been happy to spend time there, especially if I was trapped with Luca.

The adrenaline I'd ridden throughout the day petered out when I caught sight of the glorious bed. I snapped a quick picture and sent it to Axel—a little treat for him to wake up to.

Calls and texts from Luca continued to roll in, but I had zero interest in talking over the phone. I wanted to tear into his ass face-to-face.

As soon as my head hit the pillow, I fell asleep. Early the next morning, I woke up to my phone vibrating in my hand.

AXEL LAPUSAN

Who made the frame? Where are you?

Get the name of the craftsman.

I'm serious.

I didn't respond. He woke me up so he could wait. Exhausted, I shuffled downstairs. Tootsie stood at the counter, sipping from a mug.

"What's the point of drinking that?" I grumbled. The fact that Zoe didn't drink caffeine was a huge red flag for me. The woman wasn't normal.

"This is the good shit." He jerked his chin toward the coffeepot.

"You're an angel." The early morning light streamed through the windows, creating a warm glow throughout the cabin as we drank our coffee in peace. As I poured a second cup, I glanced at the stairs and asked, "Does Zoe know about her dad?"

Tootsie sighed, sitting on a tall barstool on the other side of the counter. "No."

"Don't you think she should know?" I leaned my hip against the counter, checking the stairs again.

"Yes, but what good would it do right now? It's not like she can just run home. It's not safe for her."

I scoffed. "So, your solution is not to tell her? What happens when she *can* go home?"

"Then I'll tell her."

I shook my head and put my mug down. "She's going to hate you for keeping this from her."

"She'll get over it."

"Jesus. You really believe that?"

"I can help her through it. I just need some time. We need to figure out who in her family wants her dead."

"Not to mention, keep her from the entire Moretti family."

Tootsie grimaced. "At least Luca's on our side."

Our side. They had a side.

I rolled the words around in my head. Tootsie was in deep, and I wasn't sure how this could end well for either of them.

"I wouldn't be so sure. With everything going on, I don't know how long Luca can back Zoe, even if it's on the down-low."

"You heard something?"

"No. I mean, I had no idea Zoe was here, but tensions are high between Luca and Marco, and if Marco found out you were here with her—I don't know if either of you would survive."

"I won't let anything happen to her." He glanced at the stairs and then back at me. "Do you understand what I'm saying?"

It was clear that while he may be a Moretti by blood, his loyalty was to his Greek princess.

"I do."

I set my mug in the sink and rocked on my heels. "I think I'm going to head out. Who knows how long the loser twins will be MIA? It's probably best they don't make their way here and see you two."

"I still can't believe they let you drive all the way here without an escort." He walked with me to the door.

"It's not the first time they've not been where they're supposed to be, so I'm guessing they'll have their asses handed to them."

"If they're lucky." Tootsie's face was relaxed as if he wasn't discussing the potential demise of two men. He picked up my bag and carried it to the car. "You all set?"

"I think so. Thanks for getting my car unstuck. Should've probably gone for the bigger car."

He laughed. "That's probably true." He patted the roof and stepped back with a nod. "Drive safe, and let me know when you get home?"

"You got it."

The drive home gave me time to digest the information Zoe gave me. Cy Chronis and Dante Moretti Sr. should've been pals because their similarities just kept piling up.

Psychos who tried to murder innocent women? Check.

Assholes who ruin family members' lives for power? Check.

Fuckers who needed to be handled so everyone else could go about their business? Check.

With Yanni Chronis dead, Zoe's brother Nikos headed the family with his brother Alex's support—the Chronis equivalent of Luca and Marco. I didn't know how close the brothers were to taking out the asshole ruining their family or if Yanni's death and all the recent kickups would make them focus on payback for the Morettis.

The longer Zoe stayed "missing," the closer the cops came to arresting Luca. We needed their asses home yesterday.

After hours of driving through hilly then flat Missouri, I hit the St. Louis city limit. As I passed the welcome sign, police lights flashed in my rearview mirror, and sirens blared.

Hundreds of miles of speeding, and it was only once I let my foot off the gas that I got clocked. I let out a harsh breath and pulled over, leaving my hands on the steering wheel. The sun was high in the sky, so I had to squint at my side mirror to see the cop in street clothes strolling up to the car.

Tap. Tap. Tap.

The fucker used his nightstick to knock on my window.

Deliberately, I lifted my left hand from the steering wheel and cracked the window.

"Turn off the vehicle."

I turned the keys and looked through the window. Detective Bennington smirked at me in all his douchebag glory. My stomach dropped, and for the first time, I wished the Marino twins were here.

"Ms. Mitchell. Did you get a chance to give Mr. Moretti my card?"

It'd be wise not to poke the bear.

"Sorry, no." I looked past him to the empty city street. "Was there a reason you pulled me over?"

He leaned his forearms against the car, his face leaning in so close I could have caught his nose if I rolled up the window. "I wanted to check in. Make sure you didn't need anything."

"Nope. I'm good."

His smile fell. "I want you to think long and hard about your choices from this point forward."

"Is that a threat?" My voice was far more confident than I felt.

"No. It's a fact. You can either go down with your fiancé or save yourself." He pushed off the car and reached into his pocket. My mind went immediately to the handgun in my bag. I wouldn't have enough time to draw and protect myself if he went for his sidearm.

Detective Bennington took out a business card and passed it through the small crack in the glass as an upscale sedan stopped in front of my parked car. He let out a chuckle and straightened as the Marino twins approached him. "Boys." Bennington dipped his chin and strolled back to his unmarked vehicle.

They waited until he pulled away, then turned to me, the one with a scar through his eyebrow glaring. "What the fuck was that?"

Not what I expected. I thought they'd say something about leaving me alone in the sticks.

"It's the cop that came to the house. Ask Frankie about it." I turned on the car and rolled up the window. The twin with perfect, thick brows frowned and used his arm to move his brother back and out of my way.

As I drove away, Scar-brow pushed his brother, shouting something and gesturing to the back of my car. Externally, I was cool as a cucumber. Internally, I was terrified of the cops, the twins, everything. I blindly reached into my bag, wanting to feel the cool reassurance of Luca's gun, but I came up empty-handed, and my stomach fell to my ass.

Where's the gun?

When I got home, I searched the car but came up empty-handed. In a panic, I dialed Tootsie.

"That was quick."

"Did I leave a gun there?" I whispered, despite being alone in my house.

"Uh. I haven't come across one. Let me check the bedroom."

I paced the kitchen, my eyes darting to the French doors every two seconds.

"Found it in the bedroom. Must've fallen out of your bag."

I let out a huge breath. "Thank God. Uh. Can you put it somewhere safe?"

Tootsie laughed. "Sure. Anything else?"

"Nope. Be Safe."

Tootsie hung up, and I stared at our perfect backyard with my palm resting over my wildly beating heart.

ELEVEN

After a weekend of cleaning up vomit and warming up soup for a sick Dante, Adriana, and eventually Rosa, I was back in my living room waiting for Luca to get home. At eight p.m. on the nose, Luca came through the door.

He hung up his coat with a wry smile and set his bags neatly under the hallway table. "Honey, I'm home."

I stood but made no move to join him at the door. "Explain."

He shook his head, his eyes narrowing at me. "You haven't been answering your phone."

"And you've been a lying bastard. Now that we have that cleared up explain why Tootsie's holding Zoe Chronis hostage at your cabin. What the fuck, Luca?"

"It's business. I told you I would keep you out of Moretti business."

"Then why are you lying to Marco?"

"Because Marco will gut her for all the trouble helping her has caused. He doesn't realize we'd be in this mess whether or not I helped her."

That made sense. Marco saw the world in black and white when it came to the Chronis family. He wouldn't be moved by Zoe's story or recognize they were always going to start a war.

"Then why not tell me?" I asked, hurt evident in my voice.

Luca loosened his tie, yanking it from his neck as he undid the top button of his shirt. "What part of it was business isn't clear."

I rushed around the couch to get in his face. "What part of I'm your fiancée, and she's the bitch you were going to marry, don't you understand?" My chest rapidly rose and fell. As much as I tried to beat back the jealousy and trust in Luca, a part of me demanded Luca be only mine.

"So, we're doing this." He balled up his tie. "I planned to marry Zoe, but I never fucked her." Luca raised his voice, inching close enough that I could feel the anger radiating off him. "I haven't fucked anyone but you since we met!"

Shocked.

I was shocked.

Too bad it wasn't enough to calm the storm already brewing inside me. Jealousy and anger twisted together, making me want to lash out and release the fear and tension weighing on me. "It doesn't change the fact you're risking our future together for another woman. Another woman who told me all about the tattoo on your chest." I was wrong, abso-fucking-lutely bonkers, but the words tumbled from my mouth. "How does a woman you've never fucked see that?"

Luca's chest heaved as his hands fisted in the air inches from my elbows, just short of grabbing me. "You have some fucking nerve." His anger wrapped around me, choking out my will to fight. "I have *never* mentioned the people you fucked while we were apart. I wouldn't do that." His voice was deep and full of menace. "But you—" He chuckled, cupping my cheek, running his thumb over my bottom lip. "You have the audacity to be jealous over—"

"I'm not jealous," I mumbled.

"You're as green as your eyes, and it's bullshit."

"I—"

"I don't need to hear it." He scowled. "I already know."

Guilt left me scrambling for something, but what could I say?

Sorry I fucked around because I was hurt and lonely? Sorry, I'm raking you over the coals about dating someone else while I self-destructed?

Luca's face softened, and he caught one of my hands in his. "I know." He sounded resigned and sympathetic all at the same time.

Feeling absolutely miserable, I poked at the fears that had surfaced as soon as I saw Zoe. "You would've fucked her once you got married."

He shrugged. "Probably." I reared back, my hands landing on his chest to create space that he immediately closed by pulling my hips to him. "It doesn't matter. It never happened and never will."

"But it almost did. You almost married someone else." The tears I'd blinked back rolled down my cheeks, and Luca brushed them away.

"And you almost died."

I sighed and looked up into his beautiful brown eyes. "Are you sure nothing happened?"

He eyed me, his head tilting as if seeing me in a new light. "This is the last time we're discussing my blip of a relationship with Zoe. Nothing ever happened. She got to my place early one night and caught me before I was dressed."

I raised an eyebrow. "So, she saw you in a towel?"

"Sweatpants."

"That might be worse."

He smiled. "Shut up." Pushing my hair back, his smile dimmed. "We were friendly, and when her family tried to kill her, Tootsie took her to the cabin, and I approved it. I didn't think too far past that. With everything going on with my dad's funeral and us, she kind of fell off my radar."

"I'm sorry." I kissed his chin.

"Why?"

"For doubting you."

"I get it. It must've been pretty shocking to see her."

I pushed him down on the couch and climbed on his lap. "It was."

"I'm still trying to strike a balance between what I should and shouldn't tell you." He slid his hands to my ass, smacking both sides hard. "From here on out, you'll know any business that has to do with an ex."

"Good." I ran my fingers through his hair. He shut his eyes and leaned his head back against the couch. "So, what's going to happen to her?"

"I don't know. Right now, she's safe from her family and ours, but I don't know how long that'll last." I tugged on his earlobe, and he gave me a drowsy smile.

"You'll make sure she isn't hurt, right?" I tried to keep my tone light and conversational—like we weren't discussing Zoe's future.

"I'm going to try, but Marco wants her drawn, quartered, and put somewhere as a message not to fuck with us."

"But that would only help them justify an all-out war. Her brothers know she's safe. Isn't it better to keep them happy?"

"I'm not sure if the brothers have everything under control. And it's clear Cy Chronis doesn't give a shit about his cousin. He's been using her disappearance to make unsanctioned moves against us. After the club shooting, we have every reason to seek retribution. Marco would see Zoe as the ultimate fuck you. We might as well do the crime if we're paying for it."

"He'd do that?"

Luca nodded, his expression deadly serious. "We're not good men, Sasha. Marco would do a lot of things for the Moretti name. So yeah, Marco would kill her to send a message. The tension between our families since Dad died isn't sustainable. Eventually, someone is going to go too far."

"Would you let Marco kill Zoe?" The million-dollar question.

Luca looked away from me, but his hands continued to knead my ass. His cock hard beneath me, and I couldn't help but rock on him, ashamed I was getting off at a time like this. "I wouldn't have a choice. So, yes. I'd let him kill Zoe."

My mouth went dry as he moved against me.

"You'll leave this, yeah?" He wrapped his hand around my neck, a gentle pressure to keep my eyes on him—as if I could look away.

"One more thing, and then I'm done." I waited for Luca to nod before I continued. "If you aren't going to protect Zoe, I think Tootsie will."

"Did he say something?"

"Yes."

A thoughtful look passed over his face. "Thank you for telling me. I'll talk to him." Conversation over, Luca stroked my pulse with his thumb while he slid a hand under my shirt. When he cupped my breast and squeezed, I arched into him. He broke our kiss and smiled up at me. "You miss me?"

"What do you think?" I rolled my hips on his lap, my thighs spreading wider so my clit rubbed along the ridge of his hard cock.

"I think not seeing you for days fucking sucks." He pinched my nipple, and I shrieked.

"Do it again."

"What? This?" His fingers pulled a little more this time, and my eyes snapped shut. The sharp, quick pain sent a jolt through my body all the way down to my clit. I worked my hips a little faster, my hands resting on his chest.

"Turn around." Luca's hands gripped my waist and lifted me.

I stood in front of him, and he trailed his fingers down my legs and then back up until he reached my panties. Snapping the band, he looked up at me. "I need these off."

"Say please." I teased, pulling the lace away from my body.

He lifted a brow and settled back on the couch, unbuckling his belt.

I narrowed my eyes at him. Toying with the edge of his old t-shirt I was wearing, I bit my lip. "Where are your manners?"

Luca pulled the belt from his pants and then flicked the button. I licked my lips as he slowly unzipped them. "Take your panties off so you can ride my cock. Please."

"That's more like it." My lips twitched as I inched my shirt up to under my tits. My stomach hung out, the squishy flesh he loved to touch. "And the shirt? What should I do with the shirt?"

He reached into his pants and pulled out his cock. Long and thick, it bobbed at me as if to say, "Hello! I believe I have an appointment with your cunt."

"I'd prefer it off, so I can see your ass."

I yanked it off, my chest bouncing with the movement.

"You are so fucking perfect." With his eyes heavy-lidded and full of hunger, Luca stroked himself.

I kept my eyes on him as I slid my panties down and stepped out. "You want me—" I turned around and glanced over my shoulder. "Like this?"

Luca's eyes dropped to my ass. He bit his lip and reached out, pulling me back to him.

A sharp pain made me jump, but he held me in place. "Did you bite my ass?" I stared at him, open-mouthed, and he grinned.

"Yeah. Touch your toes." He smacked my ass, and I shivered.

I leaned over, my nails grazing my ankles as Luca dug his fingers into my cheeks, spreading them wide. Nothing happened for a moment, and my legs shook in anticipation.

When Luca's warm tongue brushed against my ass, my nails scored my ankles. He hummed against me, and I reached out for the coffee table for support.

"Your toes, Sasha."

I swallowed, took a small step out, and bent my knees, finally reaching my ruby-red toenails.

Completely exposed and vulnerable, I stared at my thighs. Luca didn't make me wait long. His tongue circled my asshole while two of his fingers rubbed my clit.

"Luca!" My tits were in my throat, and I shook, trying to stay bent over.

Luca guided me back to his lap as if he could tell I was about to wipe out. His arm caged me against his chest as he slid a hand between my legs, two fingers circling my clit. "You're so wet," he murmured in my ear as he slipped his fingers inside me.

His cock pressed against my ass as his fingers lazily moved in and out of me. It felt good but wasn't enough. I bucked against his hand, but the angle wasn't right.

Huffing out a breath, I stopped trying as Luca's chest shook against my back. "Are you laughing at me?"

"Yes."

"Fucker." I tried to get out of his lap but only succeeded in standing enough for Luca to spread my thighs and impale me on his cock. We both moaned, his rumbling through me, going straight to my pussy.

His hand came down hard on my thigh, and then he dragged his fingers to my clit and pressed down. "Fuck me, Sasha."

I didn't have to be told twice. Balanced on the balls of my feet, I raised up and came down hard. Luca's fingers rubbed in time with my movements. His arm dropped, and his hand explored my torso. Blunt nails trailed down my stomach, goosebumps following in their wake.

I leaned forward, changing the angle, and grabbed his knees for leverage. He grunted behind me as I rolled on top of him. Our bodies moved against each other, slick with sweat. My calves burned, but I wasn't going to stop.

"I need you to come," Luca gritted out, his hold on me bruising.

"I need—I need—"

As if understanding my incoherent begging, Luca sunk his teeth into my shoulder as he pinched my clit.

"Luca!" Stars flashed behind my eyelids as my body shook.

When the flutters finally stopped, I sagged back into Luca's chest. He kissed my shoulder and murmured, "I love you."

"I love you," I said between panting breaths. My legs throbbed like I had done an intense workout. When I opened my eyes, I caught sight of the cherry on a cigarette through the window. "Is Frankie out there?"

Luca's nose brushed against my shoulder. "Yeah. Why?"

"He just got one hell of a show."

"For all my complaining, I'm really getting used to being chauffeured to meetings. Especially when it's not Frankie." Ashley spread out in the backseat of the town car. "It's good to see you again, Pete."

Pete and Ashley shared a smile. "You too, Ms. Brooks."

I laughed, adjusting the leather carryall bag Luca got me for my birthday. "I'm glad you're finding the perks."

"I'm an optimist." She bit her straw while she grinned.

"You've had too much caffeine today."

Ashley rolled her eyes and took another sip of her iced latte. "Have you seen Beth's latest ad?"

"Yes. So fucking cornball. How many shots at the base of the Arch does one mayoral candidate need?"

"Approximately a billion. It's like she wants everyone to know she grew up in the county."

I laughed and scrolled through some notes I needed to pass on to Michael. One perk of the project was all the construction being in house. Moretti Constructions, a subsidiary of Moretti Properties, would handle the demo and rebuild under the direction of SA Designs. It would be the largest project I'd managed, the largest we'd taken on as a company, and I was both terrified and elated.

I looked up as we drove past the Arch and took the waterfront exit.

"You excited to do the final casino walk-through before demo?" Ashley asked as she repeatedly jerked the straw out of the cup and pushed it back in, squeaking up a storm.

I placed my hand over hers to stop the noise. "I am. It's going to be a lot of work, but it will be beautiful when it's all done."

"I'll be happy to see that damn red and yellow carpet go."

I chuckled, gathering my bag as we pulled up to the main entrance. "Same. But, it's fun to think about how in style it was when they built it."

"True. I hope our plans don't end up on someone's future hate list."

"I don't think we can avoid that."

Luca beat Pete to my door, so he went around to Ashley's. I stepped out, and Luca immediately wrapped his arms around me. "Hey."

I leaned up and gave him a brief kiss. "Hey."

"You ready for this, Boss?"

"I like the sound of that." I swatted his ass and darted around the car, away from my grinning fiancé.

Frankie leaned against the wall of an out-of-order water fountain. As always, his eyes were glued to his phone.

"Frankie!"

His lips twitched at the sound of my voice, and he looked at me through his dark lashes. "Ms. Mitchell."

I groaned, looping my arm through Ashley's. "Not you too."

"It's a show of respect." Frankie shoved off the fountain and joined us at the front door. "Michael's waiting inside." He pulled the tarnished brass handle and gestured for us to go in.

My cousin Sarah's husband, Michael DeLuca, ran the construction branch of the company totally on the up and up.

"Sasha!" The goofball bounded toward me like an overgrown golden retriever puppy, scooping me in a hug once he reached me. "How are you?"

I patted his solid back and laughed. "I'm doing okay. How are you?"

"Excited to start the demo." He put his hands on his narrow hips, surveying the dated but grand lobby. "This is going to be fun." His grin was infectious, and soon even Frankie looked like he might enjoy living.

"Did you have a chance to look over my notes?"

"I did. I think we can swing most of what you want. There are just a few places I need clarification." Michael took out his tablet, and we started the slow walk-through process. The casino had been built and decorated in the eighties with a minor facelift in the early two-thousands, so we kept very little.

After a few hours, we'd covered the entire property and reviewed the building and design plans.

Michael locked up, positively buzzing. "I'm glad we could wrap up our other open projects. I was worried we wouldn't start until this summer."

"Not going to lie. I was kind of hoping we'd start once I was back from my honeymoon, but someone's an overachiever." I playfully nudged Michael.

He got a mischievous glint in his eyes. "Well, I have an incentive to get the bulk of this job done before November."

"She's not!" I covered my mouth with both hands.

Ashley frowned at the two of us. "What are you talking about?"

"Nothing," we said at the same time, not at all playing it cool.

"Secrets, secrets are no fun," Ashley chided.

"Only if you're not in on them." I pushed her toward the car and turned back to Michael. "I assume she's not ready for people to know."

"Not yet. Sarah wants to wait until twelve weeks, but you're family, so I figured . . ." He gave me a sheepish look. "Don't tell her I told you. I don't want to steal her thunder."

"No problem. I'll act completely surprised when she tells me."

He breathed out a sigh of relief. "Thank you. I'm having a hard time not telling everyone."

"No kidding?" I gave him a quick hug. "Well, congrats. I'm thrilled for you guys."

"Thank you." Michael stepped back, and Luca joined us. "I

better go. I need to drop by the office before I head home. Do you need anything else from me?"

"Not that I can think of." Luca wrapped his arms around me from behind. "Will you be able to make the tux fitting?"

"Yep. Looking forward to it." Michael did a little finger gun wave and went to his car.

"I cannot believe he's related to you."

Luca laughed and spun me around. "The Colombo side of the family is a little weird. You want a ride home?"

"Sure. Let me tell Ashley, and we can go."

Luca kissed my forehead and released me.

"Ashley, I think I'm going to head home with Luca. Pete will take you back to the office?" I looked at him, and he nodded.

"Works for me. See you tomorrow!" She jumped in the back-seat, said something to Pete, and they drove away.

I took my time walking over to the car. The shadow of the Arch shaded the parking lot, and a cool breeze came off the river. Within the span of a few years, my career had catapulted to a level I hadn't ever considered. We were rising in prominence not only in St. Louis but in the region. We were getting featured in industry magazines and had companies singing our praises. But nothing would compare to the attention we'd get once the casino opened.

My chest swelled with pride, but fear wormed its way in. Our plans were terrific, but this project was larger than anything we'd ever attempted. Add to that the fear that I wouldn't be where I was without Luca and the opportunities he offered, and my nerves were frayed.

Self-doubt wasn't something I was used to, but the building looming behind me opened up a part of me I thought I'd put to rest.

When I reached Luca, he frowned. "Are you okay?" He brushed a lock of hair from my face.

"Yeah." I tried to smile, but instead, my eyes started to burn. "Just reality setting in."

He dipped his face down so we were at eye level. "It's going to be great. You're going to be great."

I bit my lip and sucked up a sniffle. "You're right. I'm just overwhelmed."

"Why don't you get in the car so we can get home, and you can take a bath while I make us dinner?"

The vise around my heart loosened at his sweetness, but I couldn't fully shake the bad vibes. The opportunities Luca provided me were the source of a lot of my doubts. This was something I needed to work out for myself. I needed to own the fact that, yes, Luca was the reason I got the contracts, but I took them and ran.

Of course, that's easier said than done.

TWELVE

Five huge Italian men and a redhead walked into a tux shop, and it went exactly how you'd imagine.

"Is there anything blacker?" I asked the sales associate.

"I have a few more swatches in the back." The young man rushed to the back room, leaving me with Luca and his groomsmen.

"You know, we could've picked out our tuxes." Marco groused as he flipped through silk ties.

"You could've, but then I wouldn't get to harass you and catch the fashion show."

"Here, I think this might be what you're looking for." The twenty-something waved the scrap of fabric in the air like a prize.

I took it from him, rubbing it between my thumb and fingers. "Yes! Talon, this is it!" Turning to the towering men, I smiled. "Now that we have this, it's time to choose the cut."

Michael stepped out of a dressing room, grinning. "This is almost identical to the one I wore to my wedding. You know, the reason you guys met." He waggled his eyebrows.

Luca looked over at me, the heat in his eyes putting me on edge. That night was intense—the beginning of a life I never knew I wanted. The longer he stared at me, the higher the chance that his closest friends and family were about to get a live sex show.

Digging deep, I found the strength to pull my eyes from Luca. "You do look handsome, but I'd like to see something a little more classic?" Talon grinned, already heading toward a rack of pre-selected options.

"I have just the thing. Very Bond, but like, less violent." Talon's back was to the group of smirking men.

I rolled my eyes while Mickey nudged Aldo—the only Moretti wedding party member not smiling.

Aldo never smiled.

It was one of the things I loved about him. He was engaged to Nicki, and she had to deal with a man who never smiled or laughed.

They were the blandest couple in town. Well, except for the cheating.

"Ma'am?" Talon jarred me out of my less-than-charitable musings by presenting a beautiful tux.

"Perfect." I pointed at Luca, who was still stuck in some salacious memory. "You. Get in that dressing room."

He strolled toward us, his eyes devouring me. "You going to help me try it on?"

My cheeks heated, and my mouth went dry.

Talon cleared his throat, and Luca's gaze shifted to him. "I—uh—I need to help you so we can check the fit. I need to take measurements, too."

Luca didn't respond, but he did walk toward the dressing room, a dazed Talon in his wake.

While the other guys quietly chatted, Marco—who'd been a grump all day—excused himself and stepped outside. I wanted to talk to him and see if there was any way to ease the tension building between him and Luca. Without a plan, I followed Marco out the door.

"Send me the address. Uh-huh. He doesn't need to know. I'll handle it." Marco looked up as I passed him, cocking an eyebrow in question.

Panicked, I held up my keys and jingled them with a smile. He gave me the tightest lip, most stick-up-the-ass smile I'd ever had the displeasure of receiving, and I booked it to my car.

Marco's voice carried to where I sat in the driver's seat, bent over as if searching for something on the passenger's side. "I need you to go with Luca tonight." He pushed, and when he spoke again, it sounded like he had turned away from me. "I'll be back in the morning."

I searched the floorboard for a scrap of anything. "Now, what in the hell can I bring back inside?" My hand ran across a hair tie, and my heartbeat finally slowed.

Sitting up, I adjusted my top and got out of the car. Marco was off the phone, so his sole focus was on me as I locked the car.

"Hair tie." I twirled it between my fingers. "It's hot in there."

He nodded and held the door open for me. Marco was one of the sharpest guys I'd ever met. There was a real chance he didn't believe me, and the thought made me sweat. The room was suddenly unbearably warm. At least that part wasn't a lie anymore.

As I struggled with my curly mane, trying my damnedest for a smooth, high ponytail, Luca walked out looking like a fantasy. "Holy shit," I mumbled, unable to take my eyes off him. My arms ached, and I dropped them from my hair.

"You like it?" he asked, but his face let me know he knew just how good he looked.

I leaned back on a glass display case, feigning nonchalance when my whole body was reacting to the sight of him in a tux. "It's all right."

"I have one other design that could work." Talon rushed in between us, his eyes searching Luca for any imperfections. "But I don't think it'll be better than this."

"I'm just kidding, Talon. It's perfect."

The kid's shoulders relaxed, and he smiled at me. "I'll start taking measurements. We should be able to have these in by your June date."

The owner joined us with a clipboard, and the two went to work measuring all the guys. As I drank champagne and joked around, I kept an eye on Marco. He maintained his distance all day, his phone glued to his hand.

He was so distracted that the owner stuck him with a pin because he was moving. "Son of a bitch."

"I'm sorry, Mr. Moretti," the elderly man said in a thick Italian accent. "But if you'd just stay still, I'll be done in a few minutes," he scolded like Marco was a child.

"Apologies," Marco gritted out, his jaw tensing as he looked at his phone.

In no time, everyone was measured, and our information was in their system. "Thank you for fitting us in under such short notice." Luca shook Mr. Zito's hand.

"My pleasure." Then the two of them had a little conversation in Italian that had everyone else smiling and occasionally chuckling, but I had no fucking idea what they were saying.

Talon shook his head and shrugged. At least I wasn't the only one in the dark.

I really need to get on that Duolingo membership.

"You ready to go?" Luca's question drew my attention from my clueless companion.

"Yes, sir!" I joined him and stuck my hand out toward Mr. Zito. "And thank you for everything. Luca's going to look perfect."

Mr. Zito took my hand and flipped it, placing his thin lips on my knuckles, his eyes sparkling up at me. "The pleasure is all mine, Mrs. Moretti."

Butterflies hacked away at my stomach as if they had tiny glittery machetes.

Mrs. Moretti.

I was in a daze as we said our goodbyes and got in the car.

"You okay?" he asked as he pulled onto the busy city street.

"Yeah, just daydreaming about my dreamy fiancé in his tux." I flashed him a saucy smile.

"Yeah?"

"Yeah. And your four merry men."

Luca laughed loudly and shook his head. When his laughs turned into soft chuckles, I pressed my luck. "Is everything okay with Marco?"

Silence filled the car.

I waited him out.

"He's fine."

I fought back a disappointed sigh. "Good. He just seemed distracted today. Maybe it's something with him and Adriana."

The turn signal clicked loudly before Luca sighed and said, "We haven't been seeing eye to eye lately. It's causing some friction."

"Is it about Zoe?" I kept my eyes on the passing buildings.

"Partially."

"I overheard Marco on the phone. He asked someone to go with you somewhere tonight because he'd be gone until morning. Oh! And that he had an address. You think there's anything to that?"

"What did I—"

"I wasn't snooping." *Liar.* "I was getting an elastic for my hair." I pointed to my messy ponytail.

"The number of times you just so happen to overhear something is troubling."

"Whatever. Should we warn Tootsie?"

Luca side-eyed me. "We?"

I sunk back in my seat. "Right. Business."

Luca nodded and turned on NPR, effectively ending the conversation. He showed no signs of being worried, which made me more anxious.

When we got home, Luca headed to his office, and I rushed to our room. Quietly, I went into the bathroom and shut the door, cringing when the lock clicked. My stomach flipped as I sat on the toilet lid, my cell phone in hand. One call and I would be officially going against Marco and possibly Luca. I glanced at the door, gnawing my bottom lip.

Fuck it.

I tapped the contact and then pressed the phone so hard to my ear that it created a suction. Eyes locked on the door, I turned on the shower and stood at the edge of the glass.

"Yes." Tootsie's deep voice picked up after one ring.

"It's me," I whispered.

"I know."

The steam from the water filled the room, making everything clammy, specifically my face, which was within mist range of the showerhead. "I think Marco knows where she is."

He cursed under his breath. Despite the loud rush of water in my ear, I could hear him moving around and a door closing on his side. "What do you know?"

"Uh." I suddenly felt silly, like I might've blown what I heard out of proportion. "I overheard him ask someone to send him an address, that he'd handle it, and Luca didn't need to know."

"That sounds pretty vague."

"Sorry, I—"

"The fuck? I gotta go." The line dropped.

I pulled the phone from my face and stared at it in disbelief. Blinking away the moisture from my eyes, I let out a little laugh.

"Sasha?"

I jumped, dropped my phone, and watched in horror as it bounced on the tile. "Shit!" I whispered and scrambled to save it from the water.

"Baby? What's happening?" He tried the handle. "Why's the door locked?"

"Uh. I must have hit it on accident. Give me a second." I yanked my shirt over my head and ripped my jeans off, wrapping my phone in my clothes. I shimmied out of my underwear and hopped under the stream of water.

"Sash?"

"Coming!"

I stepped out of the shower carefully, avoiding the bathmat and bypassing my towel. When I swung the door open, a blast of cold air chilled my wet skin. "What's up?"

Luca's eyes trailed down my body, and he licked his lip. "Where's your towel?"

"On the rod?"

He glanced behind me at the trail of water from the shower and my balled-up clothes on the floor. "Let me just—"

"I'll clean it up." My nipples pebbled under the cold air. Goosebumps prickled my skin, and a shiver ran down my spine. "I'd like to get back in the shower, so what's going on?"

"I need to leave a little earlier than I thought. Something came up, and Mickey needs me down at Red. Apparently, Marco isn't picking up." Luca frowned, shaking his head. My heart raced, but I kept my face neutral. "You're on your own for dinner."

I smiled and leaned in to kiss him, keeping my wet body from touching his pristine clothes. "Sushi it is."

"You're a cruel woman. Now finish your shower. I'll call if I'm going to be late."

"Love you. Be safe." I took a step toward the shower, and Luca landed a firm slap on my ass. Scowling, I rubbed the sting away.

"Love you too." He strolled out of the room, all sexy and in charge, while I wilted against the door frame.

I finally relaxed as I took a shower and finished my beauty routine. If something was wrong, I wasn't the person who needed to handle it. It was a reality I needed to come to grips with before I pissed off the wrong guy.

An hour later, I was cuddling with Ryan on the couch, reading a book, when my phone vibrated. Tootsie flashed on the screen, and I shot up, snatching it off the table.

"Hello?"

"Whoa." Tootsie chuckled. "No need to rupture my eardrum."

"Not the time for jokes. What's going on?"

"We had some company and slipped out the back," Zoe mumbled in the background. "Zoe says thank you."

I sagged in relief. "Nothing to be thankful for."

"All the same. Look, I have to go. It's probably best if you don't reach out again. I've got it from here."

"Makes sense. Be safe."

"Will do."

The line went silent.

I looked around the living room, unsure of what to do with myself. Zoe and Tootsie were safe, and now I needed to tell Luca that Zoe was gone. I texted him to call me and waited.

And waited.

And waited.

The news played in the background, but I didn't hear any of it. Dinner was tasteless as I zoned out. My mom texted to confirm the big dress trip, and all I managed was a thumbs-up emoji. All I wanted to do was get this info off my chest and onto Luca's big, capable shoulders.

Sometime after four a.m., Luca and Marco bust through the front door, slamming it behind them.

"I don't know why you're so upset!" Marco yelled.

I peeked over the back of the couch.

"Are you serious? Not only did I just drive for seven hours, but those assholes burned my cabin to the ground, and they found puddles of blood! What happens when they find bodies?"

Confused, I sat up, hoping they would notice me.

They didn't. Instead, they kept bitching back and forth.

"Yeah. The Chronis bitch is out of the way. That's a good thing."

Luca's jaw ticked, and his hands fisted at his sides. "But she died on my property. Why would you tell them to do it there?"

Marco took a step back, his forehead furrowing.

"Are you trying to fuck me over?" Luca took a menacing step toward him.

"No!" Marco raised his hands in defense. "I told them to go get her, but apparently, Tootsie made trouble."

"Yeah, because he had orders to keep her safe until I said otherwise."

"Well, he should've fallen back when Tony told him they were bringing her to me. I was doing you a favor. It's been months, and you weren't handling the bitch."

"You didn't do shit. You sent those pieces of shit to kill an innocent woman. And now Tootsie is dead!"

Marco swallowed but didn't back down this time. "They were supposed to bring her to Jeff City. Things got out of hand."

"Yeah, two soldiers killed a capo—our fucking cousin."

"And I'm sorry about that. But what the fuck was he doing protecting a Chronis to the death?"

The two men silently stared at one another, their chests rising quickly.

"I'm sorry, what?" My brain was in a full tailspin.

They both turned toward me, their hands resting on their holstered guns until they saw it was me.

"Jesus, Sasha. Why didn't you say something sooner?" Luca's hand brushed through his hair.

"Oh, I'm sorry," I said, standing from the couch. "I should've just shouted my way into the convo."

"You shouldn't have heard any of that." Marco frowned, his fingers still hovering over his side piece.

"Lower your hand or lose it." Luca gritted out.

Marco's arm immediately fell, and he took a step toward the door. "It's been a long night, and things are tense. Let me go handle the twins and the cops. You stay here."

"Why should I trust you to handle this? As it is, I may go down for a double homicide."

Marco rubbed his jaw. "I know things look shady, but I would never do that to you." He reached for the doorknob. "Trust me."

Luca glared but let Marco leave without another word.

I rounded the couch and met Luca in the entryway. "What the hell is going on?"

"Everything's going to shit." Luca sighed and pulled me to his chest.

"Is Tootsie really dead?"

"It seems that way. They haven't gone through the ashes yet, but I'm guessing they'll find a couple of bodies. It's how I would've handled it."

I bit my lip, unsure whether or not to believe it. "I talked to Tootsie just a few hours ago. He said they got away."

Luca blinked rapidly. "Why would you be talking to him? Damn it, Sasha!" He let me go and stalked over to the couch.

"I thought he should know what I heard."

"What you heard? It was nothing!"

"It wasn't nothing. I was right!"

"But you didn't know that at the time, and now you're involved. What if Tootsie and Zoe aren't dead, and Marco finds out you spied on him and reported to Tootsie? You have to fucking think, Sasha." He gripped the top of the cushion and dropped his head. "You need to stay out of this." Rolling his shoulders, he lifted his dark eyes to me. "Promise me you're done."

"I promise," I said with no hesitation.

Luca studied me before giving me a slight nod. He pushed off the couch and gathered me in his arms. "What the fuck was Tootsie thinking?"

The words "he loves her" were on the tip of my tongue, but that wouldn't help a goddamn thing. So instead of talking, I burrowed my face into his chest. The smell of smoke, cologne, and perfume weaved into the fabric of his shirt.

"Let me get changed. I smell like a nightclub."

I rested my cheek over his heart and took a deep breath. "I don't mind."

"Yeah, well, I need to wash off the day." He squeezed me tight and then let go. Taking the stairs slowly, he sagged as he went to our room.

"I'll be up in a minute."

I turned off the TV and lights before I went upstairs. Passing the closed bathroom door, I went into the closet. My fingers skimmed the expensive fabric on Luca's side as I thought about Tootsie. We'd already cut him from the wedding party because of his "extended absence." I had no idea how Luca explained away months of him being gone—that wasn't any of my business.

But now people would know.

The family would find out Luca had been hiding Zoe. I gripped the arm of a suit coat as worry filled me. How would this go?

"What are you doing in here?" Luca startled me, and I let out a scream. He dried his hair with a towel, frowning as I stood in the back of the closet, wrinkling one of his fine suits.

"Getting pajamas." I reached into a drawer and took out the first oversized shirt in the pile.

We got dressed, both of us lost in our own worlds.

Moving in sync, we climbed into bed, shutting off the lights and curling into one another.

Luca kissed the top of my head, his damp hair brushing my forehead. "Night, Sasha."

"Night. I love you."

He exhaled, his body completely relaxing under me. "Love you."

Luca fell asleep in a matter of minutes while I was wide awake, worrying. Had Tootsie gotten away? Or had they been caught after he called me?

It took me thirty minutes to work up the nerve to get out of bed. I slowly inched away from Luca until I was free of his hold. I rolled myself off the edge, landing lightly on my feet. Luca moved, and I froze like a statue.

When he let out a loud-ass snore, I shook my head and inched toward the door, stopping every so often to check over my shoulder. Sneaking around my own house felt ridiculous, but I made it to the kitchen with no problem. I kept the lights off and bounced on my feet as I called Tootsie.

He didn't answer.

I sagged against the countertop with the phone clutched between both hands, devastated and unsure of what was to come.

THIRTEEN

"Just try on the princess dress, then your mom will leave you alone," Ashley whispered, our heads pressed together in a rack of gowns.

"Here's the thing. I don't want to."

"I don't think that matters. Your mom is determined to see a princess, so you better give her a princess."

I rolled my eyes, snatched the closest cupcake dress from the rack, and walked it to the consultant, Chloe. "Can we try this or something like this?"

My mom's eyes lit up when she saw all the tulle in my hands. "Oh, Sasha, that's lovely."

"Glad you think so." I followed the chipper dress consultant to the dressing rooms.

After a lot of wiggling, pulling, and adding a panel of fabric to hide my ass, I waddled out to the platform surrounded by mirrors.

I stepped onto the dais and kept my eyes on my ridiculous reflection. I looked like a ginger Cinderella.

"Oh, honey!" My mom gushed, jumping up from her seat, champagne sloshing over the rim of her glass. "You look like a princess!" Her hands fussed with the layers of the skirt as I stood with my jaw on the floor.

SASHA AND THE STALKER

"You like it?"

She looked up at me in the mirror, her hands smoothing the fabric on my waist that bunched because the sample size didn't fit me, but they could order my size. The designer was a rarity that focused on midsize and up, but of course, the store only had the smallest size available to try on.

"Like it? I love it!"

Positive words while trying on clothes were a rarity with my mom, so the urge to agree was strong. I looked back at my reflection, trying my damnedest to like it, but the dress was absolutely horrid. "It's . . . nice," I forced out.

My mom gave me a watery smile, laughing. "You hate it. But thank you for trying." She wiped under her eyes and shooed me back to the dressing room. "Go try on one of those sexy, lacy, silky things you girls picked."

We all laughed as I hustled back into the dressing room. Everyone was having a good time and enjoying each other's company, and I was positively floating by the time we got to the last dress.

As soon as I slid the satin mermaid number over my body, I knew. The dress was made for me—well, once they cut one to my measurements.

Chloe smiled sweetly and held up a tissue box. "Should we go out there and show them how amazing you look?"

I took a tissue and twisted it in my hands. Blinking back tears, I cleared my throat. "Let's do it."

She swung the door open, and I took a step out. All conversation died when they noticed me. I tried to keep my hands from shaking as Chloe helped me onto the platform. My three reflections confirmed I looked terrific.

As the seconds ticked by and no one spoke, my nerves won out, and I looked behind me. "You guys." I choked out a sob.

Adriana, Jazz, Ashley, and Sarah held hands, tears welling in their eyes.

"Oh, Sasha. You're gorgeous." Mom covered her mouth with her hands while tears poured down her cheeks.

Rosa stood, ever the stoic lady, and joined me. "You're a vision." She took my hand and squeezed it. "Chloe, dear, this is the one."

"Absolutely, Mrs. Moretti. I'll be right back."

Adriana brought me a champagne flute and raised her own. "To Sasha's perfect dress!"

"To Sasha's perfect dress!"

Chloe took my measurements, and then we tried on some bridesmaid dresses since we'd found "the one." Trying to find a color that flattered Jazz's dark brown skin, Ashley's medium brown skin, Adriana's natural tan, and Sarah's pale complexion was excruciating.

"I give up." I reclined on the stiff couch.

"How about we let the girls pick their own color and cut, and they can make sure the fabrics match?"

I rolled my head toward Rosa. "You sure, Rosa? Does Sasha and the gemstones fit the theme?"

"It's your wedding, honey." Rosa smiled at Mom. "I think we can make it work. Right, Maggie?"

"I think so." The two women smiled, sharing some telepathic conversation I'd never be privy to.

Jazz flopped next to me and grinned. "So, we get to pick our own dresses?"

"Yes. The pressure to choose is too much for me."

"Great." She cupped her mouth and yelled toward the dressing rooms, "I call gold!"

A chorus of okays came back to us. I smiled and searched my purse for my phone, coming up empty-handed. "Ugh. I'll be right back."

Frankie was nowhere to be found when I stepped out of the boutique. In my experience, just because I couldn't see him didn't mean he wasn't there.

After digging around, I found my phone wedged between the seat and door because things can't ever be easy.

"Need a hand?"

Startled, I jumped, bashing my head on the dashboard. "What the hell is wrong with you?" I stood, rubbing the sore spot and glaring at Detective Bennington.

"Now, now, Ms. Mitchell. That's no way to talk to an officer of the law."

I closed the door and locked it. Taking a step onto the sidewalk, I scanned the street for Frankie. "You're right. What I meant was, what the fuck is wrong with you?"

The sleazy bastard smirked and shoved his hands in his pockets. "I assume you heard about the fire?"

I looked anywhere but at the douche in front of me. My phone lit up. Unfortunately, it wasn't Frankie or Luca but Beth. Again.

"You want to know what I think?"

I gave him a blank stare.

"I think Luca was keeping Zoe Chronis a secret in their little forest love nest. He went down there for a romantic weekend and caught his cousin messing around with her."

Clueless. The dude was clueless.

"In a jealous rage, he kills them and realizes he needs to cover his tracks. Am I close?"

I rolled my eyes and caught sight of Frankie making his way to us. Finally.

Bennington smiled, dipping his chin. "Once we get confirmation on the blood and they finish searching what's left of the cabin, you might need to postpone that big wedding you're planning."

Frankie silently grabbed my elbow and ushered me back to the dress shop.

"Where were you?" I hissed.

He waited until we were across the street from the cop before he said, "Waiting for the douche to make his move."

"Excuse me?"

Frankie brought us to a stop outside the shop. His eyes stayed on Detective Bennington as he asked, "What did he say?"

"Some bullshit about Luca killing Zoe and Tootsie in a fit of jealousy and then torching the cabin to cover his tracks. He said once the blood is IDed, I'll need to postpone the wedding."

Frankie's jaw tensed, and I followed his line of sight. Bennington waved and then sauntered away, completely unbothered. I swear to God—the motherfucker was whistling.

"Is Luca going to be charged with their deaths? What proof could they even have?"

"None. He'd be in custody if they had anything. There's no proof of foul play. Hell, Luca has an alibi for the night of the fire."

"Has the fire department submitted the incident report yet?"

Frankie's body relaxed. "Not yet."

"Well?"

One side of his mouth kicked up, and he gestured toward the door. "Let's just say the incident report will go our way."

"So, I shouldn't worry?"

"Does it matter what I say?"

I rolled my eyes and walked into the boutique because nothing he said would keep me from worrying. Until the authorities found some bodies or Tootsie and Zoe surfaced, I would be a ball of nerves.

"You ready for lunch?" My mom beamed at me from across the room.

"Yep. The Glutton still sound good to everyone?"

A chorus of yeses came from the changing rooms.

Chloe sweetly smiled and joined me at the door. "We'll call you when your dress is in." She leaned in and whispered, "And if you want, we can send you pics of what dresses your bridesmaids choose."

I suppressed a laugh. How many Bridezillas had Chloe dealt with to know she needed to make the offer? "That's okay." I lifted my chin toward Rosa and Mom. "You should probably keep them in the loop, though. It's their circus—I'm just the clown."

She nodded and made her way over to the actual women in charge.

My mind was stuck on what Detective Bennington said about there being no wedding. Would all of this be for naught? Would I lose Luca?

"Let's go! I need a cocktail!" Ashley hollered.

Jazz looped her arm through mine, and we left the shop. "What's going on?"

"Huh?" I looked at my car, expecting the cop to pop out and bother me again.

"You've got this vacant stare thing going on."

I cleared my throat. "I'm just a little overwhelmed. We found a dress at the first place. It feels too easy."

"What did you expect? You booked an appointment at the bougiest bridal boutique in town. If it wasn't here, you'd be walking down the aisle butt-ass naked."

"There's a thought."

"I mean, I think only your family would have a problem with it." She nudged me.

"All the more reason. You riding with me?"

"Sure, even if you do drive a matchbox." She folded her model height into the passenger seat. With a huff, she slid it back as far as it would go, which didn't add much space because I'd had Frankie riding shotgun earlier.

"You guys have got to let up on my car."

"And you should have let that rich hubby upgrade you when the last one was totaled."

"I can buy my own car," I grumbled and waved at Mom and Rosa as they drove by. "My mom is so excited for a girls' day."

I pulled a U-turn and followed them to the restaurant.

"She's cute. She keeps asking me about Imani." Jazz laughed and pulled down the visor. "Was she like that when you were with Beth?"

"Ha! Not even close. I think mom is loosening up now that her queer daughter is on the straight and hetero. Don't even try to explain to her that just because I'm marrying a man doesn't mean I'm straight. The eye glaze is real."

Jazz laughed as she cleaned up her lipstick. "One perk of my parents. They are one hundred percent on board with Imani and me living out our lesbian auntie fantasies. You all have the babies, and we'll spoil them and send them home."

"I can see it now—future baby Sasha coming home with the latest in kiddie fashion and a stack of newly released kids' books."

"So, you are having babies?" She flipped the visor closed and put all her attention back on me.

My cheeks flushed, and I shifted in my seat. "That's the plan."

"Huh."

"What do you mean, 'Huh?'"

Jazz gently laid a hand on my arm. "Not a bad, 'huh.' An 'I'm surprised that I'm not surprised,' huh."

"Uh-huh."

"No, I mean it. You're kind, intelligent, hilarious, and just enough of a weirdo to raise some top-shelf gremlins."

My lips twitched. "Thanks."

She squeezed my forearm, her lips twitching. "You're practically the poster child for reformed fuck girls. Buying homes, getting married, talking about kids. You could become a life coach to the commitment challenged."

"I plan on starting a YouTube channel. Secrets of a former fuck girl."

"I'd watch it."

"You could co-star with me."

"Bitch." Jazz smirked. "Who would've guessed we'd end up here? Marrying two squares."

I nearly choked. There was a real possibility that Jazz and the rest of the world would know the truth about Luca if this fire and everything blew back on him. Life would be easier if he were a square.

"This is totally random, but who is the best criminal defense attorney in St. Louis?" Internally, I kicked myself for being so abrupt, but I trusted Jazz. She was an excellent corporate attorney with connections all over town. On top of that, she was the daughter of a federal judge.

She threw her head back and laughed. "You planning on killing someone?"

"No. Just curious." I kept my eyes on the street, scanning for a parking spot.

"I guess that would be Fern Robison." My mouth went dry, but I stayed quiet. "We went to law school together. A smart girl, but a little over the top on the granola shit, if you know what I mean."

"What?"

"Oh, you know—Birkenstocks, vegan, PETA loving." She paused, and her face scrunched up. "Lots of bandanas."

I shook with laughter. "So, you weren't besties?"

"Nah. That rock deodorant is where I draw the line."

"I'm sorry? Rock deodorant."

"Look it up. It's wild." Jazz fluffed her hair, the curls bouncing around her face.

Parking the car, I watched my mom and Rosa laughing as they walked toward the restaurant. "Get ready to see Maggie Mitchell tipsy. It's truly a gift."

The hostess seated us at the back of the restaurant at a long table under a lit-up "Glutton" sign. Frankie and Pete sat at two top next to us, where they had hushed conversations and kept their phones within reach.

"Are you sure you don't want a drink, honey?" Mom patted Sarah's hand as she took a sip from a fussy vodka number.

"I'm all right." She gently pulled her hand away, resting it on her stomach. If she wasn't careful, everyone would know her good news before she was ready.

"I think we should make a toast." Ashley lifted her martini glass and winked at me. "To my best friend, finding the perfect wedding dress and bringing together the ultimate bridal party for an amazing day. To Sasha!"

"To Sasha!"

Smiling, we clinked glasses, and I took a sip of my pink gin and tonic.

"Sasha?" A voice cracked, drawing the attention of our entire table and the guys.

"Beth?" I set my drink down but made no move to stand. Uncomfortable from her intense stare, my eyes drifted to the people with her. Senator Cooper stood at Beth's elbow with a fake-ass smile stretching her thin lips. A plain woman in a basic suit had her hand on Beth's lower back.

The corners of my mouth twitched, but I fought back the urge to smirk at her.

"You're getting married?" She took a step closer to our table.

"I am." I flashed my ring, and Ashley hid a grin behind her glass.

"To Luca Moretti?" Beth swallowed, her hands twisting in front of her.

"Yep." I took another drink.

"Are you serious?"

I was about to deliver another monosyllabic answer when Mom popped up from her seat. "Oh Beth, so lovely to see you. Congratulations on the election!"

Beth shook her head, clearing her throat as she reached for Mom's hand. "Thank you, Maggie. It was a close one."

"I'd say. Those last-minute campaign contributions must have helped."

"They were a blessing."

Mom nodded and turned to Senator Cooper. To say the two women hated each other was an understatement. "You must be very proud that your daughter is finally following in your footsteps."

The Senator smiled, looking at her daughter with what the untrained eye would see as love and admiration, but anyone schooled in the Coopers knew it was merely mild interest. "I couldn't be prouder. This is just the beginning."

Beth's lips pursed, but she recovered quickly with a practiced smile. "I was just elected mayor. Let's not get ahead of ourselves."

Beth won the election? How'd I miss that?

The engagement.

The fire.

The shooting.

The other fire.

The blood.

Yeah. I'd been busy.

"It's never too early to plan your future, darling." She patted Beth's arm and checked her watch. "We should sit down and order. You have that meeting with the incumbent at three."

Beth bit her lip, indecision in her eyes as she studied me and then the ring shining on my finger. Straightening her back, she took another step away from her mom and the silent woman and said, "We should catch up sometime."

Not in a million fucking years. "Sure. Give me a call." *That I will never answer.*

She frowned like she heard my thoughts, and the three women walked to the front of the restaurant.

"Now, why would you tell her to call you?" my mom scolded as she sat next to Rosa. "You know that girl is obsessed with you." Her eyes darted toward their table.

"I've been dodging her calls for over a year. I can keep on doing it. At least now I know why she kept calling me."

"Who is that?" Rosa peeked around my mom.

"Sasha's ex." Sarah nibbled a piece of bread, eyeing the charcuterie board.

"Oh."

Mom sat up tall like she was preparing to defend me, but Rosa only nodded and took a piece of cheese from the board.

After the Beth run-in, the conversation was more subdued

than before. Even when we got our food, no one was particularly chatty.

"Well, this is just awkward," Adriana mumbled around her straw.

"Huh?" Jazz asked as she licked her fork clean.

"Sasha's ex is just staring at us. I don't know if she's blinked once in the last half hour."

As if on cue, we all turned toward Beth's table.

"Don't everyone look!" Adriana hissed, and we all looked at her. She rolled her eyes and stood. "I have to use the restroom."

"You want dessert?" I asked as the waiter cleared the plates.

"No, thank you. I'm stuffed." She patted her stomach.

"It's creepy that the mayor-elect is just staring at you," Jazz said as she side-eyed Beth.

"Would it be less creepy if she wasn't the next mayor?"

"No. I guess not."

Our desserts came, and we demolished them, but Adriana still hadn't returned from the bathroom.

"I'm going to go check on Adriana." I tossed my napkin on the table and tried to ignore the eyes burning holes in the side of my face.

I knocked softly. "Adriana?"

There was no answer.

"Adriana?" I knocked a little louder.

Still no answer. I tried the handle, but it was locked. "Fuck."

Rushing back to the table, I grabbed a waiter. "Our friend went to the bathroom, and she's not answering. We need a key."

"What?" Alarmed, Rosa got up and followed me.

The waiter ran back to the office, and we met him in the hallway. When the door swung open, Rosa gasped, and I rushed in. "Adriana!"

My hands ghosted over her, afraid to move her. "Call 9-1-1!"

The waiter nodded and rushed past Rosa.

"Her pulse is weak." I blinked back tears as I held my fingers to her neck. It wasn't like I had any medical training, so who knew if I was checking it right, but I had to do something.

Everyone crowded around the door as we waited for the paramedics. Adriana's breathing was shallow, but her chest moved steadily.

"Ma'am, can you give us the room?"

A stocky man helped me up, and I made room for the paramedics. They worked quickly, and within minutes, Adriana was on a stretcher and being wheeled out to an ambulance. The paramedic helped Rosa into the back, and they took off down the street, sirens blaring.

Frankie touched my shoulder, and I jumped. "I'll drive you to the hospital."

I nodded and went over to my mom. "I'm not going to make it to dinner tonight."

"Of course, honey. Please let me know when you hear anything."

"You got it."

I said goodbye to Sarah, Jazz, and Ashley with promises of updates, and then Frankie and I took off for the hospital.

"She's going to be okay," he said, breaking the tense silence.

I wasn't sure if the pit in my stomach was because of Adriana or the mess the rest of my life was becoming.

FOURTEEN

When I got to the hospital, Rosa was pacing and barking out orders in the waiting room. "She's a Moretti. Make it happen."

A nurse scampered away, shooting worried looks over her shoulder.

"Rosa?"

She breathed out my name and wrapped me in a tight hug. "I'm so glad you're here."

"How is she?"

Rosa sighed and walked me over to the polyester chairs. "Awake but confused."

"That's good. Any idea what happened?" I set my purse in the chair beside me, ready for a long wait.

"As of now, just dehydration."

"Hm."

An hour went by with no updates.

"I'm going to get some coffee. You want some?" Rosa smoothed out her shirt and grabbed her wallet.

"Yes. Please."

I checked my phone for the millionth time. Luca hadn't called me back, and Frankie was somewhere in the hospital doing whatever the hell he did when he pulled a disappearing act.

"Family of Adriana Moretti?"

"That's me!" I jumped up to join her.

She eyed my hair and height and asked, "And your relation?"

"She's my sister-in-law."

The doctor looked toward the hallway. "Let's wait for Mrs. Moretti."

I pursed my lips and stared in the direction of the coffee machine. Awkwardly, we stood together, side by side, waiting for Rosa. When she finally rounded the corner with a coffee in each hand, we started walking toward her.

"Mrs. Moretti."

Rosa's face lit up, and she rushed to us. "How is she? Is she okay?"

"Adriana is fine. We gave her fluids and are waiting for a few results, but so far, so good. You can see her now."

I took the coffee, snatched my purse, and followed Rosa's disappearing back.

Adriana gave us an embarrassed smile, and the doctor left us alone in the small fluorescent-lit room.

"Hey, sweetie, how are you?" I rubbed her blanket-covered shin.

"I've been better. I wish I hadn't passed out in a public bathroom." She shivered. "The thought of what I laid in is troubling, but what can you do?"

"The doctor says everything's looking fine." Rosa fussed over Adriana, fluffing her pillow and straightening her blankets.

Adriana looked past her, the peaceful mask falling for a moment, a flash of something in her eyes I couldn't place.

"I just overdid it. Too much champagne, not enough water." Adriana chuckled and made a big show of gulping down water.

Bullshit. She'd nursed the same glass of champagne at the dress shop and only had half a cocktail at the restaurant.

Rosa and Adriana chatted back and forth while I became more and more concerned. When my phone vibrated, I was thankful for a break from Adriana's fake chipper voice and Rosa willfully ignoring it.

"Hello?"

"Is she okay?" Luca rushed out.

"Yes. As far as we know."

He blew out a breath. "Thank God. The last thing we need is a health scare."

"Right."

"Keep me posted and let Adriana know I have Dante, and he's all set up at the house."

"Will do. I love you."

"Love you too."

"Luca?" Adriana yawned as I put my phone down.

"Yep. He wanted you to know we've got Dante for as long as you need."

A tired smile graced her lips. "Thank you. I'm glad he has you guys." Her eyes welled up, and she took a shuddering breath.

I sat in the chair next to the bed and patted her thigh. "Of course he's got us. That's my guy."

"It's looking like I'll at least be here overnight. Rosa, do you think you could go get me some pajamas?"

Rosa's face relaxed now that she had something to do. "Of course! And I'll check in on the boys."

"I'm sure they're fine."

"I know. I know." Rosa waved Adriana off as she gathered her things. "I just want to make sure Dante knows his mama is all right." She did a quick eye sweep of the room, no doubt seeing if she could bring anything else from home. "All right, I'm out of here. I'll be back in a little bit."

We watched her glide out of the room, leaving behind a trace of Chanel. I turned back to Adriana, and her smile melted away.

"So, what's going on?"

She fidgeted with the stiff blanket. "I haven't been taking care of myself like I should." She shut her eyes for a long moment before hitting me with her sad gaze. "Who doesn't realize they're dehydrated? I'm so embarrassed."

I picked her hand up and kissed it. "You've had a lot going on —your house burning down, staying with Rosa, and now you're setting up a new home. That's a lot."

Adriana nodded and blew out a breath.

"Let's get you back to normal, and then we'll sort the rest out."

"Okay." Adriana shifted around in the uncomfortable bed, finally rolling her eyes with a huff. "This bed is the worst. It reminds me of when I had Dante. If he wasn't crying, the lumpy bed kept me from sleeping."

I laughed and hopped up to look in the closet for another pillow. "Do you need anything? More water, TV on, trashy celebrity magazines?"

Even with my back turned, I felt the energy in the room shift.

"Adriana." Marco exhaled, his large frame taking up the doorway.

I looked between the two and bit back a smile. "I'm going to get you a snack." I picked up my purse and went to the door, but Marco didn't move. "Uh, Marco?"

He startled and stared down at me like I appeared out of thin air. "Sasha?" Shaking his head, he stepped into the room, leaving enough space for me to slip by him.

"Are you okay?" Marco's deep voice was rough, and it took everything in me to walk away from the show. Their relationship had been undefined and low-key, but anyone with eyes could see that Marco wanted more.

I found a small room full of vending machines and a television playing in the corner. As I bought a little bit of everything, the five o'clock news started.

"Good evening, St. Louis. Tonight, we have an interview with the mayor-elect about her ideas for revitalizing the city without sacrificing our history."

I rolled my eyes.

Beth.

She'd always talked about wanting to run for office. It was one of the many reasons she disagreed with my dancing and political activities. The weird part was hearing that she'd done it made all those old feelings of inadequacy pop back up. Beth was a few years younger than me but poised and positioned to take office younger than her mom ever did. The reason she hadn't run years before was me, and she never let me forget it.

I grabbed the coke from the bottom of the machine as Beth's voice filled the small space. "Thank you for having me, Mandy." Leaning against the warm plastic, I cracked open the can as my beautiful ex delivered talking point after talking point, zoning out until her words were no more intelligible than the parents in a Peanuts cartoon.

"There have been calls from some of the community to stop the opening of yet another casino on the river. Any comment on the renovation and future reopening of The Palace?"

I shoved off the soda machine, dread souring the sweet drink on my tongue.

Beth smiled brilliantly, the same "gotcha" smile she'd give me when I'd argue myself into a corner. "We're a long way from the doors opening. There's a lot to consider."

My jaw ached from clenching it so tightly. *Like hell they'd stop the doors from opening.*

They went on to discuss St. Louis's annual Fourth of July celebration and the changes coming to this year's festivities, but I checked out. Suddenly, not only was my personal life under attack but so was my professional life.

In a daze, I carried the armful of treats to Adriana.

"Where'd Marco go?" I dropped the bags on the tan mobile table next to her bed.

She sniffled. "He left."

"Why?" I looked around the room, shaking my head in confusion.

"I told him to leave." She swallowed hard, her hands ringing in her lap.

Gently, I sat down and laid a hand over hers. "Why would you do that?"

Adriana's cheek twitched, and her glossy eyes rolled to the ceiling. "It's all too much with him. It always has been."

I stayed silent, allowing her to fill in the gaps.

"He loves me." Her red-rimmed eyes turned to me, the lines on her face deepening. "And I don't know if I can match his feelings. I never could." She shook off my hands and pushed back her hair. "He says he doesn't care and that he'll take me any way he can have me, but that's not fair. That's not what I want for him or me. He deserves to be someone's first choice."

I frowned, grabbing a bag of peanut M&Ms. "And that could never be you?" I fussed with the edges of the pack.

Without a moment of hesitation, she answered, "No."

I pointed the open candy to her, and she shook her head, so I popped two M&Ms in my mouth and leaned back in the chair. My eyes wandered to the muted TV in the corner. Beth wasn't on screen anymore. Instead, there was an info-graph about the city's police budget.

"I wish I could." Adriana's voice came out in a whisper.

"So, what are you going to do?"

She leaned back into the pillows. "What can I do? I told him we're done."

"Think he'll listen?" I threw a few more pieces of candy in my mouth.

A smile tugged at her lips, and she picked up some sour candies. "No. He never has before."

I turned to her and raised an eyebrow.

"Nothing like that." She laughed and chewed thoughtfully. "Marco's too noble to ever do that to a family member or with a married woman, but that didn't stop him from being my shadow for the last ten years."

"He does like to lurk."

"He's the best at it." She gave a pained smile and shook a few candies in her hand. "He told me he'd wait."

"I never pegged him for a romantic."

"Then you don't know him."

"I guess I don't."

The house was dark when I pulled into the garage.

"Luca?" I dropped my purse on the counter. "Dante?"

I slipped out of my heels, my feet throbbing. "Anybody?"

Heading into the living room, I found Luca and Dante passed out on the couch, the TV asking if they were still watching, and an elaborate snack spread on the coffee table.

"Hey, guys?"

Nothing.

A little louder, I said, "Guys?"

Luca's face twitched, but his eyes stayed decidedly closed.

"Guys!" I shouted.

Dante shot up—his curls flattened on one side, impressions from the blanket on his pink cheek. "Aunt Sasha?" He rubbed his eye. "Is Mom here?"

"No, honey. She's staying the night at the hospital for observation, but she'll be home tomorrow."

"Oh, sh—shoot." Luca frowned down at his phone and then up at Dante. "We missed a call from your mom." He handed Dante his phone, and the kid immediately called her back.

Luca joined me behind the couch and kissed me on the forehead. "Everything okay?"

I sighed and leaned into him, watching Dante talk to his mom. "I think so? The doctors sent out for a bunch of tests. By the time I left, Adriana seemed to be doing much better."

"Marco rushed out of here like his ass was on fire."

"Yeah." I flashed him a look. "We'll talk later."

"Mom sounded okay." Dante smiled up at us and handed Luca his phone. "Can you make us dinner?"

Luca chuckled. "Sure. How does pizza sound?"

Dante fell back on the couch and grabbed the remote. "Perfect." He started the next episode of the anime they'd been watching, effectively dismissing us.

We went back to the kitchen, and Luca pulled out the ingredients for the dough, and I hopped on a barstool at the island. "So, Adriana ended things with Marco."

Luca looked up from the yeast he was measuring with a frown. "She didn't."

"Yeah."

"Well, fuck." He poured warm water over the yeast and leaned against the counter as it proofed. "Now's not the time for his head to be a mess."

"Luca." I frowned.

"I know. That's shitty, but I need Marco to be focused, and this will only distract him."

Luca started chopping veggies for the toppings as I grated cheese.

"Maybe they'll work it out."

Luca mixed the dough, his brow furrowed, and his full lips pursed into a thin line. "I doubt it."

"Why?"

"Watch your fingers." He dipped his chin at the sharp grooves of the grater that my fingertips were dangerously close to being scraped against. "They did this before."

"Oh." I corrected my hold.

His forearms flexed as he kneaded the dough. Every fold and flip mesmerized me. There was nothing like Luca in the kitchen to arouse my every attention.

"Sasha?"

I looked up at Luca. "I'm sorry, what?"

He chuckled. "I asked you to grab a jar of pizza sauce from the pantry."

"Got it."

Luca jarred his own sauces in big batches, something I'd never considered until I lived with the ex-chef. Our shelves were lined with every kind of tomato product you could imagine.

"Did you know Beth won the election? I can't believe I forgot to vote. I've never not voted." I set the jar down next to his workspace and sat back on my stool. "She told me the *good news* when I ran into her today."

Luca popped open the jar, dipping a spoon in to take a small taste of the sauce. Nodding, he ladled it on the dough. "We donated to her challenger in the primary. Unfortunately, the Cooper name carries weight in this city."

"Well, she was on the news talking about our casino and rethinking if the city really needs another."

Luca grinned. "I'd like to see her try to stop us."

"So, you're not worried?"

He sprinkled cheese on and started to arrange the toppings. "Not in the least. The casino is a boon for the city. Jobs, tourism, the taxes? She'd be a fool to stand in our way."

I sighed. "That's what I'm worried about. You didn't see how weird she was today. You'd think we broke up yesterday, not years ago."

Luca's black eyebrows pulled together as he focused on me. "She give you trouble?"

Waving him off, I picked up a pepperoni and tossed it at his picture-perfect pizza. "No, nothing like that. I just don't think we should write her off."

"You know her best. I'll take your word for it and keep an eye on her."

"Thank you." I leaned across the countertop, careful not to dip my front in the pizza. "I love you." I pecked his lips and fell back into my seat.

"I'm going to put this in. Why don't you get changed? I'll get Dante in here to help with the salad."

"Sounds good."

As I changed out of my clothes from the day, my phone buzzed and lit up. Peeking at it through the neck of the shirt I was putting on, I saw it was an unsaved number texting me.

+1 (314) 555-1010

Call Me — D

You block a motherfucker, and they just text on a different number.

I quickly blocked the new number Dimitri texted from and went to Beth's contact to double-check that she was also blocked. I was done dealing with people that were against my relationship with Luca. We'd all made our choices, and now we're left to live with them.

FIFTEEN

Ashley, Axel, Scott, Miranda, and I sat around the conference table, eating takeout and wading through the minutiae involved with the final rollouts for The Oxford Hotels in five cities.

"It might be worth sending Miranda to Chicago to oversee the final touches." I stabbed a hunk of General Tso's and pointed it at her. "Can you head up there on Sunday?"

She cringed, setting down her rice. "Is there any way I could oversee Philly?" She dipped her chin. "Oscar wants me to meet his family, so we're supposed to fly out Friday night. I could stay on next week?"

I smiled at her, already nodding. "We can make that work." I looked around the table. "I'll take Chicago then?"

"Thank you," Miranda breathed out, her long black hair doing little to hide her reddening cheeks.

"We're family," Scott said around an egg roll. He chewed quickly and swallowed. "It's what we do. Now the question is, will we be ready for our part of the casino reno by the beginning of September?"

Axel pushed a packet of paper toward Scott, staying silent.

"I guess that's a yes from our carpenter." Scott flipped through the pages. "I've got a good idea of the types of upholstery

I want and some pretty amazing wallpaper. I'll need to review Ashley and Sasha's big-picture plans to make sure it all gels, but that shouldn't be a problem. What are you thinking, Ashley?"

We all turned to her, and she pursed her lips. "Let's get through the next week before we leap into the next project. I don't want to fumble this job because we're facing that behemoth." She cracked a smile and started stacking her binders. "I assume I'll be handling things here and fielding calls?"

"If you don't mind." I tossed a fortune cookie her way.

"Not at all. If there's nothing else, I'm going to head back to my office. I have a few things to wrap up."

"I think that's it. Keep your phones on and be ready to have your entire weekend ruined!" I stood and gathered my trash.

As soon as I got to my office, I called Luca.

"Sasha?"

"Hey, babe. You got a minute?"

"Just."

"Okay. I need to go to Chicago on Sunday for the final rollout of The Oxford. Do you want to come with me or . . .?"

"Uh . . . I can make that work. I'll have Lauren book our travel."

"I can—"

"Nope. It's done. Anything else?"

"I'm not wearing underwear."

"Sasha." His tone told me to stop, but I couldn't.

"Think you can sneak away for a few minutes?"

A door opened on his side, and a few muffled voices filtered through the phone.

"Or I could come to you."

"I wish." Luca mumbled something, then said, "I have to go. I love you."

"Love you too."

Ten minutes after our conversation, Lauren sent over the travel itinerary. The woman was possibly the most impressive executive assistant I'd ever seen.

The week went by in an anxious blur of vendor mess-ups and a Saturday night spent drinking in Scott's workshop while he scrambled to source more hand-painted, white wallpaper. Sunday morning, Luca and I were seated comfortably in first class.

"It's a thirty-minute flight. First class is a bit overkill, don't you think?" I dug through my purse for the five-dollar gum I'd bought at the newsstand by the gate.

"No. Thirty minutes or thirty hours—we're too tall to fly economy." Luca stretched his long legs out to prove his point.

"I guess—Aha! Want a piece of gum?" I waved the package around.

"I'm fine."

"Are you taking any meetings this week?"

He frowned down at his phone. "A few."

"Oh?"

"With everything that's gone down with Tootsie, my Uncle Telly wants to talk about how . . . people are being handled. He never wanted Tootsie to come to St. Louis, so now I have to smooth things over with him and my cousin Taz."

"That makes sense." I paused, visualizing the family tree Rosa had given me. "So that's Telemaco and Tazio, and Tiziana is Taz's twin? The Adamos?"

"Someone's been studying."

"The wedding's coming up, and I want to make sure I at least know your aunts, uncles, and first cousins."

"There's a lot of them, and most are a pain in the ass." He slapped his phone on his lap, throwing his head into the headrest. "But I think you'll like Tizzy. She's the family wild child."

"Can't wait."

Luca picked up my hand, kissed the back of it, and set it on his thigh. "I was trying to keep this week wide open so we could have some fun in between you putting out fires." Rolling his head toward me, he smiled. "You've been my rock for the last few months. I want to be there for you while you're busy being a boss."

"You're too much. I hope I have time for some fun. Everything should go smoothly, but the more we scale up these projects, the more opportunity there is for problems."

"I'm sure you got this."

"From your lips to God's ears."

Monday and Tuesday went off without a hitch, and we were on track to finish two days early.

"I can't believe we're pulling this off," Scott shouted over the noise of his workshop.

"I can. We put in the work, had the plans and the backup plans, and Miranda absolutely crushed Philly." Ashley sneezed for the hundredth time, and Malcolm's deep voice in the background told her to lie down. "I'll lay down when the clock hits five. Leave me alone."

"Be nice." I wedged the phone between my shoulder and ear while I signed for a delivery.

"You try to be nice when you've got some control freak barking orders."

Scott broke into a fit of laughter. Even Axel scoffed.

"Why are you two laughing?" Ashley sniffled.

"Pot meet kettle. That's all I'm saying," Scott rushed out, talking over Ashley's objections. "As much as I love this 'yay us' conference call, I need to get back to work."

"Okay. Check in at the same time tomorrow?"

"Sounds good."

We said our goodbyes and hung up.

"Sasha, there's a delivery on the side entrance." The hotel manager, Margot, grinned at me. She'd been our contact for months, and we'd built a strong connection. She was a hotel professional with thirty years of experience at every level of the industry.

I loved her.

"Perfect. Let me wrap up here, and I'll meet you out there."

She tapped her clipboard on the table and left me alone in the business suite.

Blowing out a breath, I finished signing yet another dozen forms and filing them away for the time being.

The hotel was absolutely gorgeous. The lobby was a combination of navy and forest green with dark woods and gold accents. We'd pulled our inspiration from a fabulous smoking jacket I'd bought Luca—a jacket he said he loved but had never worn. The rooms were individualized by themes while having a cohesive look that kept the renovations from being a total nightmare.

Walking through the small but beautiful event space, I noticed a few missing items that would have to be found.

"Let's see what you got!" I hollered up into the long truck.

Margot's head popped into view. "It's the rugs!"

"Finally!" I pulled myself up into the trailer. "Let's send them in by floor. That okay with you guys?" The delivery guys agreed, and Margot and I matched the rug to the room and sent them on their merry little way for the next hour.

Margot hopped down from the truck with an enthusiasm that I couldn't even begin to match. "Be honest with me."

"About what?" She helped me down.

"Is it cocaine? You snorting nose candy?"

She cackled and shoved me toward the door. "Cocaine? What is it? The eighties?"

"I wouldn't know. I was born in eighty-seven."

Margot's mouth fell open with a choked laugh. "You know what?"

Suddenly, the familiar pops of gunfire echoed down the alley. On instinct, I pushed Margot to the ground behind the truck's massive wheels.

"Are those gunshots?" Margot shrieked under me.

"Yes! Stay down."

She drew her hands over her head, and I tucked my face in her neck. The shots grew closer, and suddenly, more gunfire sounded from in front of the truck. Margot's body shook under me, so I hugged her tighter.

The street went quiet, and the scuffing of shoes running down the alley toward us had me pushing Margot under the truck and crawling on my belly behind her. A set of shiny black shoes stepped right in our eye line. Margot's lips parted, and I clamped my hand over her mouth with a terse head shake.

"Sasha?"

My body sagged in relief. "Frankie?"

His face replaced his shoes. "Oh, thank God. Get out from under there."

I crawled out, but Margot didn't follow. Peering under the tailgate, I felt ill. Margot was curled up in the fetal position, silently shaking.

I cursed under my breath and looked up at Frankie. He shrugged, his eyes darting to the street.

"It's safe to come out." I bit my lip as I heard her scrapping across the asphalt. Standing with my arms wide, I watched as her limbs trembled under her, struggling to get upright. The usually tamed salt and pepper curls were all over her face, but I could still make out the tears running down her cheeks. When she lifted her brown eyes to me, my stomach turned.

"Are you okay?"

My words snapped Margot from her daze, and she threw herself at me, sobbing. I looked over her shoulder at Frankie, but he was on his phone. "It's okay, Margot. It's going to be okay."

"You saved me!" Her fingers dug into my arms. Wild-eyed, she peeked over her shoulder at Frankie, then back at me. "We need to call the police. Is he calling the police?"

As if on cue, red and blue lights sped past us, their sirens drowning out Margot's rambling. "And what—"

"Why don't you head inside? I'm sure the police will be looking for someone to talk to. I'll meet you in there."

Margot's head bobbed, and she wandered inside, tripping on

the threshold. I let out a relieved breath when the door shut. If she was inside, she was safe. I had to believe that.

"It's Luca." Frankie startled me, shoving his phone in my face.

"Luca?" I murmured.

"Sasha. Are you okay?" His voice was low, serious.

Without warning, a sob broke free from my chest, followed by another, until I clutched Frankie's phone like a lifeline and cried nonsense at Luca.

"Baby, give Frankie the phone."

"But, but—"

Frankie shoved off the wall and held out his hand.

I shook my head, giving him my back. "I need you."

"I'll be there soon. I love you. Now give Frankie the phone."

Reluctantly, I passed the phone off.

Frankie watched me carefully while he listened to Luca. "Got it. I'll keep an eye on her." He slipped the phone into his pocket and tilted his head. "You okay?"

I nodded.

Rolling his eyes, he opened his arms and waited.

"I don't need it," I croaked.

He sighed and closed the distance between us, wrapping me in a hug. I tried to pull away, but he tightened his hold until all I could do was give in to the totally unexpected show of affection.

Rocking us side to side, he shushed and murmured kind words while I sniffled against his chest. When the waterworks stopped, he dipped his chin. "Feel better?"

I smiled, wiping under my eyes. "I guess. Where'd you learn to hug like that?"

"Pretty good, huh?"

"One of the best."

"Thank my sisters."

"Of course, the book club sisters."

"They'd appreciate the nickname. Let's head inside. You can harass me some more in there."

"Promise?"

"Until Luca shows up, I'm at your mercy."

I wrapped an arm around his waist and squeezed. "Thank you, Frankie. I mean it."

"Yeah, yeah."

The lobby was a flurry of officers and employees. I cringed at the sound of shoes scuffing the floors. Thank God we hadn't buffed them yet.

"Sasha!" Margot waved at me from reception.

"Does that woman ever relax?" Frankie whispered.

I waved back. "As long as she's not crying, I'm good."

When I reached Margot and the two officers, I was relieved to see she had pulled herself together. Hopefully, she wasn't too scarred from the whole incident.

"Officers, this is Sasha Mitchell. She was with me in the alley when we heard the gunshots. She saved my life." Margot gripped my hand, squeezing so tightly that my fingertips turned red.

"I don't think we were in the line of fire." I patted her hand and gently slid mine away.

"Do you have a minute to give your statement?"

I checked with Frankie, and he dipped his chin. "Sure, but do you mind sitting? I'm still a little shaky, and my shoe choice isn't exactly helping."

"Of course." The officer gestured toward the sitting area. Margot broke off to speak with an employee while Frankie and I sat with the two cops. "Why don't you start from when you heard the first shots?"

I went through the whole incident in excruciating detail, considering I hadn't seen anything, and the shooting was a block away. As we stood to say our goodbyes, trading business cards in case they needed more info, Luca pushed open the door and walked in like he owned the place.

When his eyes met mine, his face softened in relief. "Sasha." His voice boomed through the room, and without missing a beat, I rushed to him, throwing myself into his chest.

"Thank you for coming."

"Always. I will always come for you." He kissed the top of my head and loosened one of his arms. "Officers." He shook their hands and then wrapped me back up. It probably looked ridiculous, but I was beyond caring.

"Mr. Moretti, we were just taking your fiancée's statement, and now we'll be out of your hair."

"Thank you." Luca's deep voice vibrated under my ear as I stayed plastered to him. "If you need anything, call my cousin."

"Of course. I hope the rest of your stay in Chicago is less eventful."

Luca rubbed my back.

"Are they gone?" I spoke into his jacket.

"They are." He lifted my chin and stared into my eyes. "Are you okay?"

"I am now."

He gave me a tight-lipped smile and pecked my lips before turning his attention to Frankie. "You ready to go? We need to head back to Taz's house."

"Car's around back."

"Let's go."

Luca walked us toward the kitchen, but I dug in my heels. "I need to finish up here."

"No. You need to come with me."

"But—" I glanced to where Margot and a good chunk of the staff stood watching us.

Luca bent down and quietly said, "It's safer for you and them if you come with us. I'm not sure what's going on, and I don't want this to blow back on your business."

Too late.

"Well, let me at least let Margot know I'm leaving."

Luca checked at his watch and clicked his tongue. "Make it quick."

"Yes, Mr. Moretti." I rolled my eyes and headed toward the group. "Hey guys, I need to leave early, but I'm just a phone call away." I went around the desk and grabbed my computer bag. "Seriously, if you need anything, just call."

"You got it, Sasha." Margot hugged me tightly. "Thank you for everything."

"Of course." I patted her back and broke away. "I'll see you all first thing in the morning."

"See you then!" She shooed the staff away, dismissing everyone from the lobby.

The three of us walked to the car in silence. Frankie took the driver's seat while Luca and I slid into the back.

A few blocks from the hotel, I asked, "What's going on?"

Luca frowned at his phone. "Someone tried to kill Cy Chronis."

"And you don't know who?"

Luca's jaw ticked, his hand fisting his phone as he looked at me, fire in his eyes. "So far, no. But I have my suspicions."

His phone rang, and he answered it in fast, angry Italian. As much as his stern tone and aggressive body language should scare me, it was unbelievably sexy.

Luca ranted the entire way to his cousin's house. When we got there, the door swung open, and Taz Adamo greeted us with a grim smile. "Come in." He turned and went inside, Frankie following in his wake.

I started toward the study, but Luca gripped my elbow. "Wait. Why don't you head up to our room? I'll be up shortly."

"Oh. Okay."

He kissed my cheek and left me at the foot of the stairs.

"It's for the best," I mumbled to myself as I made my way up the ornate staircase. Our room was at the back of the house with a beautiful view of their garden. I sat at the window and stared at the flowers, clearing my head from the hectic afternoon.

The tranquility was short-lived when Luca stormed into the bedroom, seething and muttering under his breath, pulling me from my daze.

"You okay?" I stood by as he paced the room, yanking his tie off.

"Oh, I'm fine. It's Marco you should be worried about." He tossed his tie on the bed. "The son of a bitch is fucking dead once I get my hands on him."

I jumped up, grabbing his arm to stop his frenzied moves. "Woah. What are you talking about?"

"Marco! I'm talking about how we just got a call from the cops, and several witnesses are describing a man who looks a lot like Marco at the scene of the shooting."

I shook my head, patting his chest to get his attention. "Don't take this wrong way, but what did they tell the cops, tall, dark, and asshole? At a glance, all you guys kind of look alike."

Luca's frown morphed into a blank stare of disbelief. "You think we all look alike?"

"I mean, there certainly is a family resemblance. Freakishly tall, with black hair, and probably wearing a black suit? You're telling me you don't see it?"

His eyes narrowed, but the corner of his lips twitched. "What does Marco say?"

All the calming I'd done was out the window, and Luca jerked away and started roughly unbuttoning his shirt. "That's the kicker. He's not answering his phone, and no one can find him in St. Louis. Where the fuck is he?"

Luca's face was red as his hands flailed. I shoved his shirt down his arms before pulling his undershirt over his head. "Why don't you wait to hear from Marco before signing his death warrant?"

"You could've died." His hands framed my face, the rough pads of his thumbs caressing my cheeks. The intensity in his dark brown eyes made my heart race.

"Those gunshots were nowhere near me. I was fine."

He slid his fingers into my hair, tilting my face up. "Stop trying to make me feel better."

"Stop blowing things out of proportion."

His eyes dipped to my lips, and he shook his head. "You still don't get it." His fingers tightened in my hair, making my scalp tingle. "You are my fucking life." He swallowed and licked his lips. "Anyone who tries to take you from me will fucking die. Family included. You're it, Sasha. You're my everything."

My bottom lip trembled, and I curled my hands around his forearms. "Wow."

Luca snorted. "Wow?"

"Yeah, wow." I leapt at him, my lips crashing into his with no finesse. He groaned into my mouth, one of his hands moving down my back and gripping my ass. I hooked my fingers in the waist of his pants, blindly feeling for the belt buckle.

Luca broke away, his eyes wild as he searched my body. "Where's the fucking zipper?" he asked as his hands ran over my body. I lifted my arm, and he let out a puff of air. His big fingers fumbled with the tiny tab. "Fuck."

"Let me."

The zipper snagged. "Of course," I grumbled. Giving up on the zipper, I grabbed the hem and lifted the skirt. The bodice wouldn't budge over my chest. "Well, this is just ridiculous." I dropped the fabric, and it bunched around my bust. "I've been stuck in clothes before, but this—this is ridiculous."

I jumped when his thumbs brushed where the waist was wedged under my bra. "I can work with this." He kneeled before me, his hands spreading across my soft stomach as he placed a kiss under my belly button. "Sit."

Luca guided my hips back until I was perched on the edge of the mattress. His head disappeared under my cotton skirt as he slid my panties down. I jumped when his lips touched the inside of my thigh. My knees knocked into his ear, and he fell backward on his ass.

"Sorry." I held back a laugh.

Luca leaned back on his hands, assessing me like I was one of his little cooking experiments. Standing, he unbuckled his belt, toeing off his shoes. "All right." He kicked off his pants and tugged his socks off.

The afternoon light streamed through the gauzy curtains, making Luca's skin take on a golden glow. His muscles flexed as my gaze followed the lines of his tall frame, from the dusting of black hair on his chest where "Sasha" was tatted down to where his cock twitched under my attention. Even after all this time, he was the most beautiful creature I'd ever seen. "Come here."

Luca obeyed, closing the distance between us in two steps, his lips slanting over mine as we fell back on the bed. I ran my hands down his back, greedily touching every bit of exposed skin. Grabbing his ass, I pulled him closer, his hard cock rubbing between us. He groaned into my mouth, more of his delicious weight settling on top of me.

"I love you, Sasha." He murmured against my lips.

I opened my eyes, looking right into his warm brown gaze. "I love you."

"I can't lose you."

"You won't." I tilted my hips up. "Now, show me how much you love me."

A hint of a smile played on his lips as he brushed the hair from my face. His hand disappeared under the rumpled cotton between us and dragged the head of his cock down my slit before nudging it in. Slowly, he rocked back and forth until he slid completely inside.

We both groaned, and I arched into him. Nothing ever felt as right as Luca and me together.

Luca set a slow and steady pace, his thumb brushing my clit while he peppered kisses down my neck. He yanked the neck of my dress down, making the straps dig into my shoulder, creating a pinch that curled me toward him. His mouth circled my nipple, his teeth gently tugging while his tongue teased the stiff peak. I fisted the hair at the back of his head, unsure whether I wanted to pull him away or keep him right where he was—teasing the ever-loving hell out of me.

"Luca," I whined, rotating my hips as much as his weight would allow.

He pushed up on his hands, creating space between our bodies, and my skirt fell on my face. Chuckling, he twisted the loose fabric in his hand and pinned it next to my body. With one arm trapped, I used my other hand to drag my nails down his chest and abs until I reached where he moved in and out of me. Luca watched my fingers brush his cock as it disappeared inside me, then circling my clit until my pussy fluttered around him.

His jaw tensed as his gaze moved up my body, his hand following as he palmed my jiggling belly with reverence. A shiver went through my body, goosebumps prickling in his hands' path. Cupping my breast, he roughly squeezed as his thrusts came harder. He raised a knee to the bed, hitting me at a new angle, tearing a scream from me.

I turned my head, trying to cover my mouth.

"Don't," Luca demanded, grabbing my jaw so I had no choice but to look at him. He studied my face, drinking in my response to each snap of his hips. There was no holding back. I moaned and groaned, my eyes watering as he worked my body as only he knew how.

Luca's thumb brushed my bottom lip, and I caught the tip with my teeth, showing no mercy as I bit down. He grunted and started pounding into me. I couldn't catch my breath, and Luca didn't want me to. I dug my nails into his shoulders, holding on for dear life. His eyes bore into me, the love, admiration, and possession in his stare pushing me over the edge. My body shook, and I bowed into him, shouting his name.

Luca planted his hands on either side of my thrashing head, his chin falling to his chest as he fucked me through my release, finally finding his own with a groan. He nuzzled my ear, whispering, "I love you."

There was a knock on the door, and Luca sighed against my neck, making me shiver. "Maybe if we stay quiet, they'll go away."

Frankie's voice boomed through the door, "We found Marco. He's downstairs."

SIXTEEN

I'd never seen Luca dress so quickly. He was out the door before I could slide my panties back on, his voice booming through the house. I smoothed my dress and rushed downstairs.

"What do you mean you can't tell us where you've been?" Luca was nose to nose with Marco, while Frankie and Taz stood nearby, both posed at the ready.

"Exactly what I said. I can't tell you where I was."

"Someone shot at Sasha!" Luca barked at Marco, spit flying as he shoved him into the wall.

Marco frowned, clearly surprised by Luca's words.

"No one shot at me." I cautiously walked toward the standoff. All four men turned toward me, Marco taking a step my way before Luca's arm shot out, holding him back.

"You okay, Red?" Marco looked me head to toe, his posture relaxing once he saw I was whole.

"Just peachy."

"Sasha, go upstairs." Luca's tone left no room for my usual back talk, and Taz was paying close attention to my reaction.

I swallowed my anger at Luca's tone and smiled demurely, turning to ascend the stairs like the perfect Mrs. Moretti. The silence behind me was the only thing making the whole situation less humiliating. Everyone was Luca's bitch.

When I made it to the room, I kept the door cracked.

"You really think I'd hurt Sasha?"

"I don't know anymore. You're making moves behind my back, and now you just so happened to be in Chicago when someone tries to take Cy Chronis out, blocks away from my fiancée?"

"I'm your cousin!"

"And that's the only reason we're having this conversation, instead of me putting a bullet between your fucking eyes. Now, I'm only going to ask you one more time. Why the fuck are you in Chicago?"

I held onto the door frame, my ears straining to hear what Marco said, but he stayed silent. The distinct sound of a gun cocking echoed up the stairwell.

"Luca?" Taz's voice was low and tense.

"What good is family if they stab you in the back?"

"I would never—" The doorbell cut off whatever Marco was about to say.

"Go see who it is," Luca ordered.

A woman's frantic voice filled the downstairs. "Luca! What are you doing?"

"Go upstairs, Adriana."

"I'm not going anywhere until you listen to me. You had a couple of guys snatch Marco off the street! Are you crazy?" Adriana's shrill voice cut through the house.

"Adriana, I'm not going to say it again. Go—"

"He was with me!" She screamed and then, in a more respectful tone, added. "He was with me."

"Doing what?"

"It was a surprise weekend away."

There was a scoff and a loud thud.

"What the fuck, Luca?" Marco's voice was muffled.

I inched down the hallway, leaning against the wall at the top of the stairs, just out of sight.

"I don't know what the fuck's going on, but I don't buy this bullshit about a romantic getaway for one second." Luca's voice dripped with disgust.

"It's true!" Adriana pleaded.

"You willing to put that on your life?"

My mouth went dry. The threat was obvious, and I couldn't believe it was pointed at Adriana. She was like a sister to him, the mother of his nephew, and he was talking to her like she was the enemy.

"Yes. I put that on my life."

I held my breath, my heart thumping violently in my chest. The silence was deafening while I waited to hear Luca's verdict.

"Okay."

"Thank you," Adriana sobbed.

"Don't make me regret this."

"You won't." Marco was brave to speak up.

Footsteps coming up the stairs had me racing back to our room. Panting, I tiptoed to the bathroom and quietly shut the door. I flushed the toilet and turned on the faucet to wash my hands.

"Sasha?"

"Just a minute."

When I opened the door, I found Luca staring out the window. "Luca?"

"I'm really struggling here." His attention stayed on the garden.

I stood in the middle of the room, unsure of what to do.

"Marco is closer to me than any brother, but now I'm not sure if I can trust him. And he's pulled Adriana into whatever he's doing."

"What—"

"Don't. I know you were listening at the top of the stairs."

I narrowed my eyes at him. "How do you know?"

He finally looked my way, the corner of his mouth curving up. "I know you."

"Fine." I rolled my eyes and perched on the edge of the bed. "Did you ever consider maybe he's protecting Adriana?"

Luca rubbed his forehead. "Great. The idea of Adriana having secrets is really helping."

"Luca. You know, whatever she has going on is probably everyday people's shit. Not . . ." I trailed off as I waved my hand around.

Luca shook his head and looked up at the ceiling. "You're ridiculous," he huffed. "Someone's going after Cy, and it's not me." He sighed, walking over to me.

I grabbed his hand and kissed it. "You'll figure it out. You always do."

He hummed, running his thumb over my knuckles. "You'll be done tomorrow, right?"

"Should be. We're running ahead of schedule, and even if we weren't, we have to be done by Friday."

"Reservations?"

"Yep."

He inhaled deeply, his eyes shutting. "Okay. I'll have Lauren move up our return. I don't think an extra couple of days is a good idea under the circumstances."

"Okay."

My phone buzzed across the room, drawing both our attention.

"Get it. I need to go downstairs and sort some things out."

"Okay."

Luca strolled out of the room, his posture tense, but at least he wasn't on a rampage ready to kill someone.

"Hello?"

"Is everything okay?" Ashley rushed out.

I swallowed and slumped into a chair in the corner. "Yes, yes. Everything's all right."

"Margot said two huge men showed up and took you away. I

assume she meant Luca and whatever lackey he had on you today."

I barked out a laugh. "I'm sure Frankie would love to know he's a lackey." She chuckled, and I added, "But yes. They were in the area and scooped me up after the cops got done questioning us."

"Hm."

My eyelid twitched. "What are you thinking, Ashley?"

"Was this about, you know?"

"No!" A lie. I dialed back my intensity. "No. Unrelated as far as I know."

I'm going to hell.

"Okay." Her tone dripped with doubt.

"Look. I've decided—"

"Nope!" she interrupted me. "We aren't talking about that right now. I'm still thinking."

"But you're clearly not okay—"

"Let me decide that."

"Fine, just stop interrupting me."

"Then stop trying to break up with me."

"I'm trying to protect you."

"I know."

I knew what I had to do. As soon as I was back home, I'd have Jazz draw up the necessary papers to give Ashley complete control of my shares. If I were lucky, she'd allow me to stay on as a consultant or employee.

"Well. I should probably call Margot and see if she needs anything. She was pretty shaken up."

"I can't imagine being shot at!" She let out a laugh in disbelief. "I heard you were quite the hero."

"She's exaggerating."

"Psh. But I'll let you go. Malcolm just got here with dinner. Call me if you need anything."

"You got it, Boss."

"Oh! I like that. You should call me boss," she said, away from the phone.

Malcolm's deep voice rumbled through the phone, "We could try that. Or you could—"

"Gotta go!" Ashley squeaked and hung up abruptly.

Smiling, I got out my laptop and got to work.

"I'll pick you up at seven?"

"Yep. Mom said we could stay for dinner if we want."

Luca yawned, shaking his head. "After the week we had and the flight, I'm worn out. Let's pick something up on the way home."

I gasped, a hand covering my chest. "Why are you suggesting we hit a drive-thru, Chef Moretti?"

He let out a tired laugh, his head resting on the seat. "No. I'll call in our order at Blue Waves. Sushi sound good?"

"Sure." Pete pulled up to my parents' house. "You go rest. Ruling the world can wait." I pecked his lips a few times.

"Fine." He yawned again. "Have fun with your dad."

I smiled. "See ya, Pete."

"Miss Sasha."

"Ah! So close." I winked and slid out of the town car.

When I walked into the house, it was quiet. "Dad?"

"In here!"

I followed his voice to the kitchen, where he was eating a sandwich over the sink. "I'm guessing Mom isn't home." I lifted a brow.

He chuckled and shoved the last bite into his mouth.

"You didn't have to rush on my account."

Chewing quickly, he brushed his hands together, then chugged a glass of water. "Our reservation's for four. If we're late, Doug will give the slot away. He's a real prick."

"Ah. Good ole Doug. So, he's still hung up over Mom." I wiggled my eyebrows at him.

Dad scoffed, puffing up. "Who wouldn't be? There's only one Maggie Mitchell." He emphasized Mitchell as if I needed to be reminded she was *his* wife.

"Yeah, yeah, yeah. You love mom. She's the best. I'm going to go clean up a little, and then we can go."

"Make it quick."

"You got it."

I was hanging the guest hand towel back up, smiling because I knew Mom would lose it when she saw it all rumpled, when my phone vibrated with a text.

> +1 (314) 555-1456
>
> Call us. Z&T.

I dropped my phone, and it clambered to the floor. My shaky hands fumbled it, dropping it two more times before I was able to keep hold of it. With my heart racing, I unlocked the screen. Of course, there was no more to the message, but I reread those words like they held a second meaning I could decipher with time.

"Sasha?" Dad knocked on the door, and my phone fell into the wet sink.

"Fuck," I muttered. "Just a minute!" I roughly dried it off on my sleeve.

"We have to go now!"

"Hold your horses!"

Dad grumbled but left me alone.

There was no way I was calling them in my parents' bathroom. I smoothed out my red waves and patted my face. Stress on stress on stress made me an absolute mess. Straightening my back, I left the bathroom and joined Dad by the front door.

"You look like shit, Kiddo."

"Thanks, Dad." I laughed, loosening up my stance.

"I mean, you do." He shrugged. "You feel up to this?"

"Nothing would make me feel better."

"You still got it!" Dad shouted over the loud pops as I hit the outline's head before sending a few to the chest.

"You don't lose what comes naturally."

"One hell of a girl you got there, Greg." Doug, never one to read the room, hovered behind us. "Amazing."

"Don't you have something you could be doing, Doug?" Dad groused.

I laughed and took off my ear protection. "Let's get a drink. I'm thirsty."

"Fine. I trust you'll hold our spot?" Dad towered over Doug, daring him to disagree.

"Of course! We can't have our champion shooter waiting among the riffraff."

Dad grunted but couldn't hide his pleasure at Doug's compliments.

We got a couple of sodas from the vending machine and then stepped out into the warm spring evening. Dad took a deep breath. "Smells like rain."

I took a swing of cola and nodded. "It's that time of year."

"Almost wedding season." His green eyes sparkled as he hid a smile behind his can.

"That it is."

"You ready to be someone's wife?"

I laughed and leaned against the brick building. We stood in silence, listening as the bugs started to hum and buzz.

"How do you balance it?"

"Balance what?" He flicked the tab on his can, looking at the cars passing.

"Being a husband and a firefighter."

"Well, your mom always comes first. No question. The

community is important, but my work would mean nothing if I didn't have your mom to come home to."

I looked down at my hands as I rolled the can between them. "I'm giving my shares of the company to Ashley." I blinked back tears. "She deserves them, and I can't put all we worked for in danger."

"I can't say I'm surprised."

"Dad—"

"I'm not judging, but I've heard some things since you've been with Luca. You're signing up for a hard life." His eyebrows bunched as he took a drink. "You need to be sure it's what you really want. Once you're in, you're in." He turned his serious stare on me.

"He's what I want. The rest, I can handle."

Dad chugged the rest of his soda, crushing the can. "Then we better get back inside and work on your shot."

And just like that, my dad gave his blessing to me becoming the wife of a mafia boss.

"I'm so tired!" I threw myself back into the seat.

"I told you to reschedule."

I shut my eyes. The windshield wipers beat back and forth, lulling me to sleep. "Couldn't. Dad's on for the next few days, and we have so much wedding stuff to do. I don't think Mom would let us run off to the gun range." I struggled to find a comfortable position, giving up when it became evident the tiny car wouldn't accommodate a quick nap. "No, it had to be today, but now I just want to curl up in bed and—"

"What the hell?" Luca mumbled, braking two houses down from ours.

The abrupt stop sent my head into the window. With wide eyes, I looked at Luca and yelled, "Jesus—"

"You stay here. I'll find out what's going on." He kept his eyes on the scene in front of us as he turned the car off.

"Okay?" I rubbed the sore spot on my head.

Luca got out of the car and approached a cop standing on the edge of the tape. It was too dark and the rain too constant to see their faces—the flashing lights were not giving me enough time to catch any expressions. Luca shook his head and moved deeper into the crowd of cops.

Tapping my nails on the dashboard, I leaned forward, hoping to catch a glimpse of him among the uniformed men and women, but I couldn't see a damn thing. There was no use guessing what was going on. Taking my phone out, I tried to distract myself until Luca returned. I absentmindedly scrolled through pictures of my friends out and about.

A loud knock on the glass made me jump, and I whipped my head toward the window, where an asshole cop smirked down at me.

Detective Bennington.

I glared, waiting for him to say something. He made the universal roll your window down gesture, which was a bit dated in this day and age because I hadn't even seen a crank handle in nearly a decade.

I shook my head. "How can I help you?"

He kept winding, so I waved my hands around. "Cars not running."

"Crack the door."

Rolling my eyes, I opened the door a sliver. "Yes?"

"Sasha Mitchell?"

This motherfucker.

I took a calming breath. "Yes?"

"Can you step out of the vehicle?"

"Why?"

"I have a few questions."

"I think I'll wait until my fiancé comes back." A thrill ran through me when Bennington's posture straightened. I closed the door and locked it with a smile.

He shook his head, running a hand through his damp hair. "Fair enough. Let me go get him."

Luca came marching back about five minutes later, the smug cop following in his wake. He stopped at my door and waited with his hand hovering over the handle until he heard the lock click. He crouched down until he was at eye level. "You okay?" he asked, his eyes trailing over me as if something could've happened to me in the car.

"I'm fine. What's going on?"

He looked over his shoulder. "The cops got a call. Apparently, they found a body on our lawn."

"Huh?" I heard his words but couldn't understand them.

His jaw twitched. "There's a dead body in our yard." I could see the barely concealed rage in his eyes.

"Someone we know?" I whispered.

Luca nodded once, his lips thinning until they nearly disappeared.

Glancing behind him at the cop, I grimaced. "So, what's the plan?" I swung my eyes back to Luca.

"We're going to my mom's tonight while they sort this whole thing."

"Can we run in and get an overnight bag?"

"No, but Mom will have what we need. We can come back to the house tomorrow. Just give me a minute."

Luca pecked my forehead, then closed the door. He walked up to Bennington and said something that made the cop's smile fall. Shoulders straight, stride slow, Luca walked to the car. There was no way around it. The man was showing them he was leaving because he wanted to, not because he was being told to.

"What was that all about?" I asked once he was in the driver's seat.

"Just reminding him of a few things." Luca inched past the squad cars and our neighbors, staring at the scene in front of our house. Mouths agape, they huddled together, pointing at our car and shaking their heads. Not one to shy away from scrutiny, I wished our windows weren't tinted. I wanted to give them a little wave, maybe blow them a kiss.

"Assholes," I grumbled, slumping in my seat.

Luca grabbed my hand and pulled it to his thigh. "Rich people, am I right?" He chuckled and kissed the back of my hand.

"You're the one who said we needed to move to this neighborhood. Now, look at us, the hottest and most judged couple on the block."

We drove out of the city toward the land of McMansions and HOA fees. The rain lightened to a drizzle. Before I could work up the nerve to ask who died, Luca turned up a long drive, stopping at the gate to enter the code. Further down a private lane, Luca's parents' house came into view, and Rosa was standing in the doorway.

"I told her to stay in bed," Luca mumbled.

"You know you can't tell that woman what to do."

"A man can dream."

We got out of the car, and Rosa rushed to my side, catching my hands in hers. "Are you okay?"

I squeezed her fingers. "We're fine. What are you doing coming out here in the rain?"

"Don't worry about me. Are you hungry?" Rosa looked around me to where Luca took two big bags of takeout out of the backseat.

"Got it covered." He lifted the bags. "You want some?"

Rosa screwed up her face. "Sushi? No, thank you. I've already eaten. Let's get you inside."

Luca set us up in the kitchen, much to Rosa's disapproval. *Dinner should be eaten at a proper table.*

Once we were alone, I put down my chopsticks and stared at Luca until he noticed. He gave me a sad smile, wiping the corner of his mouth. "Are you not hungry?"

"Who?"

"Sasha, I don't—"

"Tell me."

Luca cleared his throat, tossing his napkin on the table. The sorrow etched on his face turned my stomach. "It was Pete."

I sagged in my chair, the air whooshing out of me. My vision blurred with tears as I tried to make sense of what Luca said. "Pete?" I croaked out.

There was no way Pete was dead.

Luca came around the table, pulling me out of the chair and into his arms. "I know, baby. I'll handle it."

"What about Maria?" I sobbed into Luca's chest.

"Marco's over there right now with Maria. Once you're done eating, I'm going over there."

"I'm done." I leaned back and wiped my eyes. "Let's go."

Luca's eyebrows pulled together as he wiped a stray tear away with his thumb. "You want to go?"

"Of course! Maria will need all the support she can get. If you're going, I'm going."

"Thank you." Luca kissed me softly. "It'll mean a lot for you to be there."

I swallowed, trying to clear the lump in my throat. "Pete's gone."

Luca pulled his top lip between his teeth and nodded.

"Who would do that?" It was a worthless question. Lots of people wanted Pete dead. Lots of people wanted Luca dead. Hell, lots of people wanted me dead.

Fuck 'em.

"Never mind." I cleared my throat and slid out of Luca's hold. "We should box this up for later."

I started moving food back into containers as Luca watched me. "You know I love you, right?"

All I managed was a tight-lipped smile as I scooped up a rainbow roll. My phone buzzed in my purse. "Can you get that?"

Luca dug through the junk in my bag until he found it.

Frowning down at my phone, he muttered, "What the fuck is this?"

I licked eel sauce off my thumb before folding the box closed. "What is it?"

"An unsaved number texting you." He tapped on the screen. "For the second time. Why didn't you mention this?"

"Oh shit! I totally forgot."

"How do you forget this, Sasha?" He waved my phone at me. "Z&T? Have you been in contact with them? Have you known they're alive all along?" Luca's face turned red, his voice getting louder and louder.

"No! I haven't talked to them since the night we thought they were dead. I've been a little distracted today. I meant to tell you earlier."

He ran a hand through his hair, staring at the phone like the texts would disappear. "This is the last fucking thing I need."

"Should we call them?"

Luca shook his head. "There's no we, Sasha. I'll handle it."

I rolled my lips in as I carried our food to the refrigerator. "Tootsie doesn't trust you."

"We're family."

"And both families are trying to kill them."

Deep in thought, Luca wiped the table down as the grandfather clock in the entryway chimed nine times.

"We better get over to the Abates." Placing a kiss on his chin, I hugged him tightly, enjoying the feel of him in my arms. Our breathing synced up, and we rocked back and forth until he took one last deep breath and let me go.

"I love you." He tugged my earlobe, a serious look on his face as he leaned in, softly pressing his lips to mine. "It's you before everything." He whispered against my lips, the gentle brushing sending a delicious tingle down my spine.

"I love you. Now, you better stop being all cute and sweet before your poor mother sees something that will scar her for life."

Luca chuckled and let me go. "You're such a good daughter."

He was quiet as we left the house, not bothering to tell Rosa. It wasn't until we were on the highway that he spoke. "Okay."

"Okay?"

"You can call them, but I'll take over once Tootsie and Zoe understand I had nothing to do with whatever happened at the cabin."

"And you're going to help them, right?"

"Now that I know they're alive, I'll do my best."

I linked our fingers together. "That's all I can ask."

SEVENTEEN

Beautiful white flowers filled the front of the church and covered the closed casket. Due to the violent nature of Pete's death, a traditional open casket was impossible and only added to the anger simmering under Luca's skin. He died checking on an alarm at our house, and on a regular night, I would've been there. Guilt became a constant companion, but I kept it to myself. Everyone had enough to deal with without me adding my bullshit to it.

Getting ready for Pete's funeral was a surreal experience. Rosa prepped me for what was expected, as it would be my first big event as the soon-to-be Mrs. Moretti. She filled me in on family trees and showed me pictures of Pete's mom, Mrs. Abate, so I would recognize her without an introduction. Entering the church, people walked a fine line between gushing over our upcoming wedding and offering condolences to Mrs. Abate and Maria.

A short, round woman, Mrs. Abate had a stiff upper lip and didn't shed a tear during the service. The priest motioned for her to say a few words, but she shut it down with one jerk of her chin, her hand remaining locked in Maria's. In her place, Luca stood. It occurred to me he'd speak, but then again, I had no idea how a boss handled the death of one of his soldiers. Calling Pete that felt wrong, but it's what he was. To survive in this world, you couldn't shy away from the truth.

Dressed in a beautifully tailored black suit, his shoulders broad and his back straight as an arrow, Luca exuded power. His eyes held none of the softness you'd expect at a funeral. No, they were full of quiet anger and the promise of retribution. "Pete is gone too soon. A man with a big heart, he loved his family more than himself. He will not be forgotten, not now," Luca looked at Mrs. Abate and then at Maria. "Not ever." Both women dipped their heads, Maria's eyes full of tears.

With those brief words, he left the pulpit and joined me in the pew. I laced our fingers together, needing a connection to him.

Person after person got up to say their goodbyes. Luca leaned over as the speeches winded down, his lips grazing my ear as he whispered, "You need to get up and say a few words."

Nodding, I stood and smoothed my dress. I'd prepared a little something, just in case.

"For those of you who don't know, I'm Sasha Mitchell. Pete —" Taking a breath, I smiled at Maria. "Pete was one of a kind. He was kind and quiet but had his own unique sense of humor. No matter how much I begged him, he refused to call me Sasha. First, it was Ms. Mitchell, then Ms. Sasha, and every time he said it, there was this little twinkle in his eye because he knew he was driving me crazy." Reserved laughter echoed off the high ceilings of the church.

"Most recently, he took to calling me Mrs. Moretti." I looked at Luca, tears making him a dark blur. My face heated up, and I looked up at the ceiling and swallowed the lump in my throat. Gaining some semblance of control, I cleared my throat and continued. "Pete took me under his wing and showed me the ropes. He treated me like family, and we all know what a privilege that is." I smiled at Luca, but his face stayed a blank mask. "When I met Luca, I didn't know just how big my family would become. Today, we say goodbye to one of our own, but we will never forget the amazing friend, son, and husband Pete was."

I patted the lectern. Instead of returning to my seat, I went to Mrs. Abate. She stood, and before she stopped me, I pulled her into a tight hug. "I'm sorry for your loss. If you need anything, you tell me."

Her stiff hair rubbed against my cheek as she nodded. Holding her shoulders, I looked her in the eye. There were no tears, only all the pain of losing her son. "I mean it. I don't want to hear about you struggling or not taking care of yourself. We got you."

Her eyebrows scrunched together as she took me in. "Okay."

Nodding, I turned to Maria and, for the hundredth time, wrapped her in my arms. "I'm so sorry, Maria. He loved you so much." I swallowed, holding back the emotion, trying to escape. "I'm here for whatever you need." Maria trembled as she let out a shuddering breath into my neck.

We hugged for maybe longer than was appropriate, but the church remained silent as we had our moment. I wouldn't be the one letting go. This was for Maria. The church full of people could wait until this grieving wife was ready to stand on her own.

When Maria's hold loosened, she discreetly wiped her eyes and grabbed Mrs. Abate's hand. The older woman softened as she brought her daughter-in-law to her side. The three of us shared one more sad look, and I returned to my seat. No one moved to give another speech, so the priest dismissed us. Luca raised an eyebrow, and he leaned down and kissed my forehead, murmuring into my skin, "Good job."

Outside the church, Rosa joined us, and we stood behind Mrs. Abate and Maria as people gave her their condolences. Then we followed her out and joined them in the town car behind the hearse. Rosa told me Mrs. Abate was a second cousin of Dante Sr., and her husband had passed. Pete was her only child, so his death left her with only Maria.

"How are you doing, Flo?" Rosa asked, patting her hand.

"I'm ready for today to be over." Her deep, smokey voice surprised me.

"Well, don't worry about the repast. We have it handled."

"Thank you." Her voice didn't waiver for a moment.

We rode in silence until we reached the cemetery. Luca got out first, then helped his mother and Maria, leaving me alone with Flo.

"What you said about my Pete was nice." She patted my knee. "You're a good girl."

It was the first time anyone had ever called me a good girl and meant it in a non-sexual way. Completely gobsmacked, I slid out of the car and held Luca's hand to the gravesite. The first tremors spread through Mrs. Abate's body when the pallbearers pulled the casket from the hearse. Her chin dipped, and a tear rolled down her cheek. Maria quickly curved around her, sharing her strength.

My own eyes burned, and I swallowed hard. I didn't hear anything the priest said because I was so focused on Mrs. Abate. The woman who had been so calm and collected at the church crumbled in Maria's shaking arms. Their sobs and cries became loud enough to drown out the prayers.

Biting my lip, I held back tears. I had no business blubbering, but watching Pete's mother and wife fall apart broke my heart.

The ride to the Abate's house was a blur. Flo and Maria whimpered and wiped at their eyes while Luca sat in stony silence. He escorted us into the generous two-story brick home, then disappeared to God knows where.

"Can I make you a plate?" I asked Flo as I got her set up in the living room in what seemed to be her chair.

"I'm not really hungry."

I persisted. "How about a cup of coffee?"

"That sounds great. Thank you."

"Maria?"

"I'm fine."

I left them to chat, running into at least six people who introduced themselves. I twisted my hands, anxious to get to the refreshments, making my apologies and dodging more people to get Mrs. Abate her coffee.

The whole day crashed in on me as I stood in line, staring into the distance, wondering where Luca went.

"Oh, sorry!" A small body bumped into my legs, and I looked down into warm, brown eyes.

"Dante." He grinned up at me, and I hugged him to my hip. "Where's your mom?"

"Somewhere around here. She told me to come find you."

I scanned the room and found her standing very close to Marco, frowning while he yammered on about something. "You hungry?"

The impatient nine-year-old sighed and rolled his eyes. "Always."

Ruffling his hair, I pointed him toward the buffet. "Go make a plate and find somewhere to sit out of the way. I'll find you in a bit."

"Okay!" And he zipped away, adults dodging him but not saying a damn thing to the Moretti prince.

"Careful!" I whisper-shouted, and he threw a hand up in the air but didn't slow down.

Shaking my head, I made Flo her cup of coffee and took it to her, not interrupting the conversation she was having with a handsome older man. Her cheeks were as red as the tip of her nose, and I smiled as I left the two of them to chat.

I roamed the main floor, politely smiling and accepting congratulations. At the back of the house was a less formal living room, and that's where I found Luca and some of his top guys lounging with cigars and talking.

Luca looked up from the tumbler of amber liquor in his hand and smiled. "There you are."

"Here I am," I said, doing jazz hands.

The men chuckled as Luca captured my wrist, pulling me down to his lap. I settled in against his chest, finally able to relax my shoulders and forget the hundred people milling about the house.

He kissed my cheek and asked, "Did you eat?" His hand slid around to palm my stomach.

"No. I was about to, but I wanted to see if you needed anything."

The corners of his mouth turned up. "I'm okay. I just need you to take care of yourself. In fact—" Luca shuffled me off his lap and onto the empty cushion between him and Marco. He gave Marco a blank look, then smiled down at me. "I'll be right back." He dropped a kiss on top of my head and left me with Marco, Franco, Mickey, and Frankie.

"You did a good job today," Marco said as he swirled his drink. "Very First Lady." He chuckled, but it wasn't mocking, just sad.

"Pete was a good one." I crossed my legs, leaning away from Marco. Luca hadn't told me if he'd settled things with his cousin, so I was unsure how friendly I should be.

"That he was." Mickey raised his glass, and the guys did the same and drank. Marco handed me Luca's glass from the table, and I took a sip. We all sat in silence, Pete's memory hanging over us.

Franco straightened up in his chair as he assessed me. I didn't know much about him other than he was Luca's cousin on his mom's side, one of the few who worked directly for him. Most of his mom's family was in Chicago and New York. "Congrats on the engagement."

I dipped my chin with a measured smile. "Thank you." I felt like Miss America trying to answer in a way that was both respectful to the occasion and appropriately excited to be engaged.

"You ready to join the family?" Franco asked.

"As ready as I'll ever be. Are you all ready for me?"

"Sasha, I don't even think Luca's ready for you, let alone the whole family." Marco was making fun of me, but it was a welcome change from Franco's serious expression.

"You love me, don't lie."

"Yeah. Yeah. You just keep Luca happy, and we'll be good."

"That, I think I can manage."

"I'm sure you can." Mickey laughed as he wiggled his eyebrows. Nudging Franco, he pointed at me with his drink. "You should catch one of her shows."

Marco shook his head at his brother's big mouth, his eyes looking over Mickey's head to the doorway where Luca stood with a plate of food piled high and a smirk on his face.

"Yeah?" Franco asked, his stare contemplative, not the gross leer I was used to with dudes when they talked about my dancing. Not like the looks Mickey gave me.

"Oh yeah. Totally worth twenty bucks."

"Glad you think so," Luca said.

Mickey flinched, his smile turning into a grimace. Slowly turning around, he peeked over the back of his wingback chair. "Hey there. Just talking about how talented your fiancée is. Congratulations again."

Luca didn't say anything—just walked past Mickey and handed me the plate of food. In two quick steps, he was in front of Mickey with his hand raised.

SMACK.

"I think you should find a different way to spend your twenty dollars."

Mickey held his cheek, his jaw working back and forth. "You got it, Boss."

"Why don't you check in with Gio and text us his location?"

"Sure thing." Mickey hopped up, and while he didn't run out of the room, he did move pretty damn fast.

"Anyone else have a compliment for my fiancée?"

I bit back a smile when the guys stayed quiet.

"Good." Luca reclaimed his seat and nudged the plate in my hand. "Eat."

Rolling my eyes, I scooped up some mostaccioli. While I ate, the tension in the room grew. No one spoke, but the looks they gave each other seemed to work just fine. "If you guys need to talk, I can go," I mumbled around the pasta.

"Yes."

"No."

Marco and Luca answered at the same time.

"No," Luca repeated. "What we need to discuss can wait."

So, they continued their bizarre standoff while I filled up on the best Italian buffet I'd ever had. Or maybe it was the fact I hadn't eaten an entire meal in a few days. Funny thing about stress and grief, they can obliterate your appetite.

Setting the plate on the coffee table, I stood up. "I'm going to check on Maria. You guys do whatever you need to." I kissed Luca's cheek and gestured to the still-full plate. "Finish that. You didn't eat breakfast."

The men all stood as I left the room, a move that would take some getting used to.

The walls at the front of the house were lined with photos of Pete, Maria, and his family. One picture, in particular, caught my eye.

"That was our tenth anniversary." Maria's soft voice made me jump, and she placed a hand on my arm. "Sorry, I didn't mean to sneak up on you."

I waved her off. "No, I was spacing out." Turning back to the photos, I pointed at the one I'd been staring at. "Is this London?"

Maria smiled, her puffy eyes squinting. "It is." Her long fingers skimmed the frame. "We went for our tenth wedding anniversary." Her smile grew. "Pete decided it was time to kick start our travel." She grinned and led me down to another picture. "This was just last year when we went to Morocco. I can't explain how beautiful it was. This picture doesn't even do it justice. Next year was supposed to be Japan."

"You both look so happy."

"We were." Maria blew out a breath. "I was actually coming to find you. Can you help me with something upstairs?"

"Of course."

She passed me and started up the stairs. "There's a box of things Pete would want Luca to have. I figured it'd be safe to give it to you."

She led me into a bright, cozy bedroom. While the rest of the house smelled like marina and bread, the bedroom reeked of Pete's cologne as if she'd sprayed it on every surface. Framed prints from around the world hung on the walls, while knick-knacks from their travels were displayed on lovely handmade shelves.

"Let me see." Maria reached under the bed, feeling around until she smiled. "There we are." She pulled out a small white box and stood up. "It's just a few little things, but . . ." She shrugged and handed it over.

"I'm sure Luca will love whatever it is."

Maria nodded and sat down on the edge of her bed. "I don't think I can stay here."

"I'm sorry?" I sat next to her as she glanced around the room.

"Without Pete, I don't know if I can stay in this house. Once I get Ma settled, I'm going to take off for a few months."

I covered her hand with mine, following her eye-line to a picture on the nightstand.

"They say your wedding day is the happiest day of your life, but it was just one of many perfect days with Pete." She chuckled. "You know, on our fourth date, I worked up the courage to tell him I didn't want kids, and if he expected me to, it was best for him to find someone else. I was ready to walk away heartbroken because I was already half in love with him." Maria turned to me, tears welling in her eyes. "Pete just laughed and asked me why I thought he wanted kids. Of course, I didn't have an answer. A month later, he proposed."

What do you say to something like that? Something so heart-breakingly romantic and funny?

Nothing.

"These men—" she said after a beat, gesturing to the door. "Are some of the best men you'll ever meet. They'll love you harder than you can imagine and make all your dreams come true if you let them, but loving them comes at a price."

I tilted my head, letting her know I was listening.

"Pete gave me the world and showed me a good chunk of it, but it came at a cost. He'd be gone for days at a time. His hours were irregular at best, always waiting for a call, and when he was home—" She swallowed, her face solemn. "When he was home, it was my job to share the burden of his soul. Good men like Pete and Luca don't make it through this life unscarred. It falls on us to create the bright side, the part of their life that helps the ugliness fade, at least for a little while."

"Can I ask you something?"

Maria laughed, wiping her eye with a wrinkled handkerchief. "After that lecture? Please."

"How did you keep your own life outside of all this?"

"Ah." She looked around the room before settling on my face. "It was easier for me. I'm a nurse, and Pete," she cleared her throat, "Pete wasn't exactly a boss."

"What about your family and friends?"

"My Mom passed away a few years ago, but she loved Pete. Everyone else either didn't know or made a quick exit out of our lives. The beauty of the Morettis is they become your family and friends." She laid a hand on top of the box. "If you let them."

Maria was so candid that I didn't doubt she believed what she said. The picture she painted was lovely, but I wasn't sure it was real, especially after everything I'd experienced. I wasn't about to shit on her vulnerability, so I smiled and tried to hand her a tissue from the nightstand.

"Oh no, I'm fine." She waved the rumpled, soggy handkerchief. "This was Pete's."

Maria went back to staring at her wall of memories, and I twisted and tore the tissue, ready to stay with her all night if that's what she wanted.

I'm not sure how long we sat, hand in hand, soaking in whatever Pete vibes remained. The dull hum of the crowd downstairs dwindled as the front door opened and shut. By the time the house was quiet, the room was dark, but neither of us switched on a light.

Loud shouting and stampeding heels on the stairs broke through our silent vigil.

"Sasha!" Adriana rushed into the room, panting. "I need you downstairs." Without waiting for a response, she was out the door and thundering down the stairs.

The sound of something heavy crashing to the ground and loud masculine voices got both Maria and me to our feet and down to the living room, where Luca and Marco traded blows like prized boxers. Dante Sr.'s inner circle—Gabe Ricci, Alessandro Russo, Giuseppe Moretti, and Antonio Bruno—stood around the outside of the room, sipping their drinks and occasionally muttering to one another. Luca had slowly retired his father's most trusted associates from decision making, replacing them with his most loyal cousins. It had not been a pleasant transition, and these old bastards did nothing to hide how much they enjoyed the new boss and underboss beating the shit out of one another.

Marco yelled something in Italian and then socked Luca in the stomach. Luca growled and tackled him into the curio cabinet. Tiny spoons and glass flew everywhere. Slivers of wood clung to their black suit coats as they rolled around on the floor.

"Enough!" I shouted, and they went still. "Get off the floor right now," I gritted out. "Look at this place!"

The beige rug under the decimated coffee table had red splotches all over it. Lamps and plastic cups surrounded the side tables and couches that had been shoved feet from their rightful spots.

Maria surveyed the room, a smile playing on her face. "I guess it was time for a new rug." A giggle spilled from her lips, followed by a chuckle, and then Maria devolved into a full belly laugh. She fell onto the couch, holding her stomach while Luca and Marco climbed off the floor, watching her with concern.

"Maria?" Luca approached her, but she held up a hand, hiccupping while telling him she was fine. He looked at Marco, who was equally confused.

"What happened?" Mrs. Abate stood in the doorway, a kitchen towel over her shoulder. Her eyes darted from the two bloody men to the destroyed furniture to her daughter-in-law doubled over. "Oh, Maria." She breezed past me and sat next to Maria, drawing her into a tight embrace. "It's okay."

Maria lifted her head, shoved her dark hair from her face, and showed Flo that she was crying, but it was from laughing so hard. "Pete always threatened to smash my tiny spoons. I guess they did it for him." Another loud burst of laughter followed, and the rest of us awkwardly stood there, waiting for a sign from the great above to tell us what we were supposed to do.

Mrs. Abate apparently had a direct line to the cosmos because she looked at me and jerked her chin toward the kitchen.

"It looks like your drinks could use a little freshening." I eyed the former underboss, waiting for a response. Wisely, he dipped his chin and left the room, the other men following in his wake.

With the tension in the room sky-high, I turned to the couch. "Why don't we clean you guys up?" I motioned Marco and Luca away from Maria, giving Adriana a look. "Come on!" That snapped them out of their daze, and the four of us left the Abate women to laugh or have a breakdown—whatever Maria was doing on that couch.

"Is she going to be okay?" Luca said in my ear as we followed Marco and Adriana down the hall.

"I have no idea. What the fuck is going on between you and Marco?" I rasped.

Luca nudged me along. The kitchen was a mess of half-empty serving trays and bowls. Adriana read off a piece of paper, "Be back in an hour to clean up. Signed, the wives." She rolled her eyes, placing the note back on the counter. "They could've just told us. *The wives*. What's that?"

I scoffed. "Get Rocky and Rocky two some ice. I'll check the

bathroom for a first aid kit." Marco and Adriana were gone when
I got back, and Luca was packing the food away. "You should be
icing your eye. Leave that for now."

"I'm fine." He didn't look up, just kept moving down the
counter.

I set the case down and leaned against the cabinets. "You
going to tell me what that was all about?"

He filled the sink with soapy water, bracing himself against
the edge as he leaned. "We were working out a few issues."

"All over Maria's living room?"

He shoved off, turning toward me. "I'll get her a new rug."

"What about Marco? You going to get him a new nose?"

"Breaks give a face character." He thumbed the tip of his nose.
"Don't worry about Marco."

"Just like that?"

"Just like that. It's amazing how cathartic a few punches can
be." Luca's eyes flared as his jaw tensed.

I opened the first aid box, pulling out a cleansing wipe.
"Come here." Luca shuffled next to me. We both leaned a hip
against the counter as I went to work, wiping away the blood
from his lip and cheek. "You're lucky you're so fucking beautiful.
Not many people can pull off the beaten look."

Luca scoffed, grabbing my hips and bringing me flush with
him. "Who got beat? It was just a little tussle."

Pursing my lips, I rubbed the cut above his eyebrow a little
too aggressively, and he winced. "Sorry. I don't like seeing you
hurt." The scars on his body told the story of a man who'd been
put through enough violence for a few lifetimes.

"I'm okay."

His nonchalance in the face of everything going on broke
something inside me. "And that's the fucked-up part." I tossed the
used wipe on the counter and glared at him. "You shouldn't be
okay with being hurt, Luca. You shouldn't be walking around
with black eyes."

Luca dropped his chin to his chest. "Baby—" He let out a

harsh breath, looking back at me with a pained stare. "That's my life. That's this life."

"Family shouldn't hurt family." I cupped his cheek gently, avoiding the cut.

"No. But Marco and I are like brothers, and that's how we settle shit. It's been that way since we were kids. It's what we were taught."

"Might be time for family therapy."

Luca let out a humorless laugh. "I'll think about it."

"Our kids won't be brought up like this." I pinched his chin. "You hear me?"

He frowned, his fingers digging into my fleshy hips. "Of course. No one will touch a hair on their heads. Our family is untouchable. Precious."

"You're precious too."

He leaned down and kissed me hard, paying no mind to his split lip, turning to press me against the counter. The granite was hard and cold at my back, while Luca was hard and hot, molding me to his body. I twisted my fingers in his hair, craning my neck to meet his lips with fervor, not minding the hint of copper on my tongue.

The day had put so much into perspective. So much about our future was unknown and out of my control, but here in Luca's arms? Things were clear. Maybe it was fucked up, but we existed for one another. Our year apart proved we could survive without each other, but I didn't want that. I wanted this. I wanted to fucking thrive, to live my life to the fullest.

Luca broke our kiss, his eyes shining. "Thank you." He pecked my lips.

"For what?" I kissed the corner of his mouth.

"For loving me like no one else ever has."

I tugged his hair. "How could I not?" I sighed and looked at the sink. "We should finish up here."

Luca kissed me one last heart-stopping time. "Let me. You go check on Maria."

"Okay."

I found Mrs. Abate alone in the living room, making tidy piles of broken furniture and décor. "Oh! Let me help."

She let out a heavy sigh and wiped her hands on her thighs. "Leave it for tomorrow. Maria's gone to bed, and I'm sure she'll want to look through all this." The older woman gave me a sad smile. "You did good today. You'll make a fine Mrs. Moretti." She patted my shoulder as she walked past me to the stairs.

"Thank you," I said to her back, getting no response.

I spotted my purse on the couch and grabbed it before heading back to the kitchen. Checking my phone, I nearly ran to the kitchen. "They texted again!"

Luca put a plate in the dishwasher and wiped his hands on the towel next to the sink. "We need to go." He looked around the kitchen and grimaced. "I guess we'll leave the dishes for *the wives*."

The front door opened, and the middle-aged wife brigade stormed into the kitchen, pushing past me.

"Oh, Luca, honey. What are you doing?"

"You shouldn't be cleaning up."

"Sasha, how could you let him clean up?"

The wives of the Capos sounded off. The old guard hated me and used every opportunity to remind me I didn't belong.

Too fucking bad. Soon, new would completely replace old, and they could retire their old-fashioned bullshit criticism.

"Ladies," Luca hollered over the squabbling, quieting the wives of his father's inner circle. "Sasha and I were just leaving. The mess is all yours." He dropped a kiss on each of their cheeks, took my hand, and pulled me from the house.

Once we were in the car, he called Marco. "I need you at the house in fifteen."

"Got it."

And that was it. The car ride home was quiet, anticipation building. Tootsie hadn't answered any of our calls, and Luca worried the Chronis Family had caught them or whatever traitor was inside the family.

Marco stood on our porch when we got home, and the three of us silently went to Luca's office. I couldn't help but stare at Marco's face, marveling at the destruction Luca's hands delivered. "Are you okay?"

Marco frowned, wincing when the cut on his cheek pulled open. "I'm fine, Red." He turned to Luca. "They called?"

"No, they texted Sasha again. Ready?"

I nodded, and we all hovered over the desk as the phone rang. The line picked up, but no one spoke. Luca lifted his chin at me.

"Uh. Hello?"

"I'm on speaker?" Tootsie's harsh voice came through, and relief flooded my body.

"You are."

"Hello, Luca." Tootsie let out a humorless laugh.

"Tootsie, it's good to hear your voice. I assume Zoe is okay?"

"She's fine, no thanks to you."

"I had nothing to do with it."

"Sure you didn't. I want to speak to Sasha alone."

Luca glared down at the phone. "No. There's no reason for that."

"Are the Marino twins still working for you?"

Luca and Marco shared a look. "It's being handled."

"Like Cy Chronis was handled."

"We didn't have anything to do with that."

"That's not the word on the street. It's being pinned on the Morettis."

"You say Morettis like you aren't one."

"After all this, am I?"

Marco rolled his eyes, but Luca immediately answered. "Yes. I understand you just wanted to protect Zoe."

"You been telling stories, Sasha?" Tootsie's tone was playful, the relief in his voice palpable.

"I told the truth." I looked at Luca, and he nodded. "Luca wants to help you guys. It does no good for you to be out there alone."

A soft feminine voice said something, and Tootsie sighed. "Even if I believe you and the Morettis aren't a threat, Cy still tried to kill his own cousin. Until he's handled, we aren't coming back."

"We can keep you safe." Luca gritted out, glaring at Marco, the tension between the two rising yet again.

"No, you can't."

And the line went dead.

"Fuck!" Luca slammed his hands on the desk. "This is why we don't do secrets."

"I know," Marco said, his voice strong and clear. "At least we have confirmation they're alive. I'll try to get a bead on them. They're going to need money. There's no way Tootsie called just to chat."

"Do that. Besides us and those fucking Marino twins, no one on our side knows they're alive. Keep it that way." Marco nodded and left, taking the remaining tension with him.

"Are they going to be okay?"

Luca sat in his leather chair, looking exhausted. "I don't know. He should've told us where he was. I can't help him if I'm in the dark."

I rounded the desk, perching on the edge of the desk. "He'll come around."

"I don't know. Marco and the twins fucked up big time."

"Why are they still around?"

Luca smirked. "Their time is coming."

I kicked the arm of his chair, pushing it back a little. "So mysterious."

"Nope. Just keeping my promises."

EIGHTEEN

"Can we talk?" Ashley stood in the doorway of my office, not bouncing in like usual, which made me sit up in my chair.

"Sure. Frankie, can we get a minute?"

"You got it. I'll be in the lobby."

Ashley closed the door after him and stood in front of my desk.

"You going to sit?"

Her face twisted with indecision before she finally sat in what was, in my mind, her chair.

"You're freaking me out. What's going on?"

She blew out a breath, her gaze on the candy bowl between us. "We need to talk." That was it. That was all she said.

"Okay?" I shifted in my chair, waiting for the hammer to fall.

"Malcolm's brother-in-law, Shane, is in the hospital. He was jumped."

My stomach turned. "Oh?"

Her eyes narrowed, and she pinned me with a glare. "Yeah, *oh*," she scoffed. "Malcolm's pissed that he got involved—" Her voice lowered, and she said, "With the mob? Did Luca do this?"

"I don't know." Shame prickled through my body. "Someone paid Shane to follow me."

She scoffed. "So, he deserved to get his legs broken?"

"No! When I told Luca, I didn't think—"

"That's the thing, isn't it? You don't think. You've been so wrapped up in your own world for the past six months that I don't even know when you're coming or going. I'm constantly worried about you getting hurt, and now Malcolm's family is in the mix?"

The tears shining in her eyes and her heaving chest made me sick to my stomach. She was upset, and I'd done this to her. Going around the desk, I kneeled in front of her and took her hand in mine. "When Malcolm told me someone paid to have me followed, I had to tell Luca. Ash, I am so sorry. I didn't know it would go that far. I've been a shitty friend, and you don't deserve that."

Ashley nodded, pulling a tissue from the box and dabbing the corner of her eyes. "I just hate this. Everything feels like it's spinning out of control. I don't like fighting with you."

"Me neither. It's unnatural."

"Can you grab dinner tonight?"

"Yes," I answered immediately.

She snorted out a laugh. "Don't you need to check your calendar?"

"Nope. If anything's there, I'll reschedule it." I mentally crossed my fingers that Mom would understand.

"Okay. I've got to get ready for a meeting with the Westons." We both stood and hugged. It had been a long time since I'd gotten an Ashley Brooks hug. "I love you," she said into my chest.

I angled my chin to keep from eating her fluffy hair. "I love you too."

"Okay, I'm off to replace the nineties in yet another office building."

"Godspeed, Ms. Brooks." I saluted her as she left my office.

Frankie wandered back in as I packed up my computer bag. "You have an appointment?"

"This isn't what I do, Sasha." Jazz fell back into her leather office chair, holding my folder in the air. "We've been friends for how long? And you still don't know what I do for a living."

"Okay. The theme of the day is Sasha's an asshole." Jazz laughed as she looked over our original contracts. "I had no idea there were so many facets to corporate law. My only other point of reference is Nicki, and well, I'll admit, I zone out when she talks."

"You really are an asshole," Jazz laughed as she quickly typed on her laptop. "You're in luck. Ka has a free hour."

"Oh, thank God. You think she can have the papers drawn up by tonight?"

"Probably. You sure you want to do this?"

I nodded and looked at the beautiful piece of modern art just over Jazz's shoulder. "I have to."

"Is this about the investigation?"

Startled, I dropped my gaze to her concerned face. "What are you talking about?"

She scoffed, her eyes going to the wall of windows next to her office door. "My dad's a federal judge. I know who the Morettis are."

"You've never said anything."

"*You've* never said anything." She raised an eyebrow in challenge. When I didn't say anything, she asked, "You got a dollar?"

"What?"

Rolling her eyes, she extended her hand, palm up. Baffled, I grabbed my wallet, fished out a dollar, and slapped it in her hand.

"Okay, I'm officially on retainer. Now spill."

"Oh! Like they do it in the movies."

She grinned.

"It's not that I don't trust you, Jazz. I just don't want to pull anyone else into this mess."

"I get that, but I think you need someone on your side.

Someone you can be open with. Now you don't have to worry about confidentiality or me getting into trouble."

I pursed my lips, fiddling with the snap on my wallet.

"Fine. Let's ease into it. Are you sure you want to give up your share of SA Designs?"

"I have to. I told you about the shooting in Chicago, right?" She nodded, and I huffed out a breath. "It wasn't directed at me, but it wasn't random. Then you have Scott fucking Nicki, who's engaged to Aldo. And what happens if they arrest Luca over all this shit? It's not a good look for one of the owners to be married to someone up on murder charges. My personal life is bleeding into my work life, and I don't see it ending well."

"I think you're giving your clients too much credit. There are plenty of people willing to do business with murderers. How else would Moretti Properties be the billion-dollar corporation it is today?" She gave me a gentle smile. "You're too honorable for your own good, Sasha Mitchell."

I snorted. "Yeah, real honorable." I rubbed my forehead. "I didn't know about all of it. You know?" Guilt settled in my stomach, and the dull ache behind my right eye intensified. "When we signed the initial contracts with Moretti Properties, I had no idea. After discovering who Luca really was, he assured me there wouldn't be any problems—that they've never had any issues. But now, with everything else going on, I don't see how SA Designs comes out unscathed."

"I assume Ashley knows?"

"Yeah." I shut my eyes, thinking about the look on her face when she rightfully read my ass for filth that morning.

"Did she ask you to do this?"

"No. It's my idea. She told me no before, but I don't imagine she'll put up too much of a fight after today."

"What happened?" Jazz leaned on her forearms, her perfectly shaped brows pulling together.

"Malcolm's brother-in-law has two broken legs, courtesy of my new family."

"Uh oh."

"Yeah." I wiped my hand on my thigh and dropped my wallet into my purse. "I think I finally understand the realities of being with Luca. One of them being that I'm no longer just Sasha Mitchell. I'm a Moretti."

"Is that what you want?"

Without hesitation, I said, "Yes. There's no one else." Her face softened, and the corner of her lips tilted up. "That being said, becoming a Moretti is my choice. Ashley doesn't deserve to have her dreams suffer for my choice."

"Then let's get you unincorporated." Jazz lifted her chin, and Ka joined us.

"Sasha. Good to see you again." Ka Chan sat in the chair next to me, taking the file from Jazz. "Let's see what we have here." She flipped through the pages, her face neutral, and then she snapped the folder closed. "Seems simple enough. Let me go work up a new contract, and I'll get it over to you by the end of the day?"

"That would be perfect."

Ka nodded, her shiny black bob swinging, and left just as quickly as she came.

"Bye!" I called after her.

"She's one of our most billable attorneys. She's doing you a favor by not chatting. You'll thank her when you get the invoice."

I laughed. "Well, let me drop some more cash on lunch. My treat for bothering you."

"Sorry, can't. I'm having lunch with Imani and her mom, but I'll take a rain check. I feel like I haven't seen you in forever."

"Yeah. It's been brought to my attention that I've been MIA."

"I know you think you have to keep your new life separate from your old, but that's not sustainable. You need to trust us."

"It's not about trust. It's about keeping you all safe."

Jazz dipped her chin. "Sasha. My father is an elected official. He's put away some dangerous people. Being your friend isn't something I'm scared of."

"But Ashley—"

"Is with Malcolm, who does some shady shit, and she knows the truth. You've got to stop this martyr shit and let us decide what's right for us. Ashley had no problem setting a boundary, right?"

"Right." I fidgeted with my skirt.

"So, maybe, just maybe, we know what's best for us." I opened my mouth to speak, and Jazz held up her hand. "And by keeping us in the dark, you might actually put us in more danger. I'll let you know if it gets to be too much and I need to step back. Until then, stop pushing us away."

I bit the inside of my cheek. "I hadn't thought about it like that."

"Of course you hadn't. You were too busy ghosting us. No more. I get you stepping back from the business, but no more keeping stuff from us." She waved the dollar in my face. "I'm your attorney."

Relief washed over me, and I laughed. "Well, let me get out of your way, and thanks for setting me up with Ka."

"Anytime. Tell Luca he could do so much better."

"Yeah, yeah." We hugged and kissed each other on the cheek. "Tell Imani if she wises up that I'm just a phone call away."

Jazz shoved me toward the door, laughing, "Get the hell out of my office."

"Bye!" I sang, wiggling my fingers.

"Oh! Appetizers. I'm getting the queen treatment." Ashley sat in the seat across from me with a big smile. "Sorry, I'm late. Axel needed a hand with a client."

"No problem."

"I swear, I don't know how I found his whole stoic thing attractive. He's annoying."

I laughed. "Maybe we should stock the conference room with booze. We all know he gets loose enough after a drink."

"It's the dancing for me." Ashley chuckled and took a sip of the fruity cocktail I'd ordered for her, doing a little shimmy. "He has no business being that good a dancer."

"A total Dr. Jekyll, Mr. Hyde situation. All quiet and brooding, and then you get a few shots in him and, BOOM, he's the life of the party."

"Mrs. Kline was less than impressed by his lack of conversation. Good thing I hadn't left the office."

"Ashley to the rescue!"

"Always." Ashley grinned and picked up a piece of bruschetta. "I'm guessing you already ordered?"

"I thought we'd do the chef's tasting. Is that okay?"

"Perfection. Now, tell me what's going on with you."

At her words, I immediately took out the papers. "Promise not to get mad."

Ashley exhaled and took a large swig of her drink. "Okay. I'm ready."

I slid the contract over to her. "I'm signing over my part of the company to you."

"No." She pushed the papers back at me. "I told you I didn't want this."

"And I told you it's what's best."

Ashley sucked her teeth, her eyes darting away. "What's best?"

"I will not let my choice to marry Luca ruin everything we've built. I don't want there to be any problems if something happens."

"What kind of something?" Ashley's eyes narrowed.

Jazz's words fresh in my mind, I summoned the courage to be honest. "Luca's under investigation for murder. It might just be a scare tactic, but the police think they've got him."

Ashley's hand covered mine on top of the contract, but she didn't say anything.

"If Luca's charged with murder, I'm standing by his side."

"Of course you are." She frowned, shaking my hand. "And you're worried about us."

"SA Designs is doing well, but we're still new. I don't want anything to taint what success is coming."

Reluctantly, she nodded. "Does this mean you're leaving the company, too?"

"Not if you don't want me to."

Ashley squeezed my hand, then pulled her own back to her lap. My heart sank. I knew she was about to make the right choice, the only choice.

"I don't want you to leave."

Surprised, I let out a harsh breath. "Are you sure?"

"Yes. I can't imagine doing it without you."

"If the worst happens, I'll leave. No fuss, no muss."

She gave me a small smile and picked up another piece of bruschetta. I did the same, and we bumped them together before taking a big bite. "Delicious," she mumbled, covering her mouth.

"I don't know how what is essentially fancy toast is so good."

"Don't let Tim hear you." Ashley stage whispered, much to our waiter's delight. The new chef at Moretti's was a jerk. Luca had been bitching about him for weeks, loathing that Tim would be catering our wedding.

"One perk of marrying Luca is I'm the future Mrs. Moretti, which means Tim can suck it."

Ashley cackled, and we polished off our drinks and crusty bread app. "I need to use the restroom before they bring out the next course." She got up just as the waiter dropped off fresh drinks.

Sipping my gin and tonic, I scrolled through my texts, responding to my mom's guilt trip about canceling our plans.

"Sasha?"

My eyes widened, and I lowered my phone to the table. "What the fuck are you doing here?" I whipped my head toward the bar, where Frankie chatted up the bartender.

Dimitri sat in Ashley's seat, and Daphne took the one beside him. "We needed to talk to you."

"So, you thought you'd come to Moretti's? Do you have a

death wish?" I hissed, leaning over the table to make sure they heard me.

"We'll make it fast," Daphne said, her eyes scanning the room.

I slowly sat back in my chair, giving them the floor.

"I'm an FBI agent," Daphne whispered.

Blinking, I waited for more, but apparently, that was supposed to be shocking. "Oh, I know."

Daphne's tan face became ashen as she looked at Dimitri in panic. Licking her lips, she turned back to me. "How?"

"You really want to talk about that right now?" I peeked at Frankie, and thankfully, he was wrapped up in whatever Warren was saying. "I suggest you get to the point before Frankie notices or Ashley comes back."

Dimitri's lip curled. "You need to get away from these people, Sasha. Luca will be arrested. It's just a matter of time. And with the nature of his relationship with Zoe, there is talk of bringing you in for questioning. They think you're an accomplice." He gazed at me, his usually cold, gray eyes full of concern. Daphne observed him, the corners of her mouth pulling down.

I stayed silent. It was news that I was being investigated as an accomplice, but I already knew the other stuff.

"Are you listening? You're being investigated like a criminal, and they have an eyewitness placing you at the cabin days before the fire." Dimitri was getting more agitated.

Determined to hide how much I was freaking out, I pressed my lips together. Dimitri and I were no longer the kind of friends that confided in one another. He seemed to have missed the memo because he looked at me expectantly, his hand inching toward me.

"Damn it, Sasha!" His voice was strained, the tendons in his neck popping. "I don't want to see you lose your freedom because of *him*. Let me help you." His hand touched my arm, and I shrunk away. Hurt flashed in his eyes as his fingers curled into a fist, landing on the table with a soft thud. "You're really choosing him." He swallowed thickly.

"Dimitri." Daphne's voice made him flinch. When he looked at her, it was like he'd forgotten she was there. She lifted her chin, her shoulders tensing. "We told her. It's up to her how she wants to handle her life."

He glanced at me one more time, studying me like it would be the last time we saw each other, and then he nodded. They both stood, and Daphne walked toward the door while Dimitri stopped and came back to the table, bending to bring us face to face. "If you change your mind, I will always come for you." He cupped my cheek, placing a quick kiss on my lips before rushing out of the restaurant.

I touched my lips, confused by what had just happened.

"Are you okay?" Ashley asked as she sat.

"I think so?"

She glanced at the door. "Who was that?"

I checked the bar, and Frankie was gone. "Um. Dimitri and Daphne."

"Weird."

"Yeah." I paused as Frankie stormed back into Moretti's, glaring at me. "You know what? I'm getting really tired of people fucking with me."

"Okay?" Ashley gently set down her drink. "What do we need to do?"

"There's no we. I need to start pushing back. I can't let these fuckers take everything I want away from me."

NINETEEN

"Luca?" I yelled the minute I walked through the front door, Frankie hot on my heels.

"Why didn't you come and get me?" Frankie shot back.

"Why didn't you notice a Chronis in Moretti's? Luca!"

Frankie scoffed, and Luca came out of the kitchen.

"What's going on?" Luca caught me by the shoulders and looked me head to toe. "Are you hurt?" His eyes hardened as he glared over my head at Frankie. "What the fuck happened?"

"Dimitri Chronis crashed Sasha's dinner with Ashley." Frankie leaned against the wall, an ugly scowl on his face.

"At Moretti's?" Luca's grip on my arms tightened.

"Yeah. And she didn't let me know when they sat down. I caught sight of the asshole as he was leaving. They were gone by the time I got out to the street."

Luca turned his incredulous look my way, his hold getting uncomfortably tight. "What did they want?" I took a step back, and Luca loosened his hold with an apologetic head shake.

Rubbing my arm, I said, "To let me know the cops are close to arresting you and that I'm being investigated as an accomplice. Apparently, there's an eyewitness to my little trip to the Ozarks." I darted past Luca, rushing to our bedroom. "I'll pack our bags while you get the jet. We're going to Vegas. We're getting married now. These fuckers aren't going to keep you from being my husband."

"Fuck." Luca ran a hand over his face, then pried the suitcase handle from my grip. "Baby, we don't have to go to Vegas." He turned toward Frankie, who was leaning in the doorway. "Get Father Anthony on the phone."

Frankie nodded and left us alone.

"Sasha, I'm so sorry."

"It's not—"

"It is." He took my hand and kissed my knuckles. "I'm going to ask you something, and I need you to be honest."

"Okay?"

"Are you sure you still want to marry me?"

"Yes. Hence, the "let's run away to Vegas" frenzy you just witnessed."

He smiled at the lack of hesitation.

"Even if I spend the next two decades in prison?" His warm brown eyes burned into me, searching for any sign of doubt.

"Yes, Luca. Even if you spend the next two decades in prison. Even if I spend the next two decades in prison." My stomach turned at the thought of doing hard time.

"I won't let that happen. They don't have enough on you to put you away. They're trying to scare you."

Frankie came in, his focus on his phone. "Father Anthony will be here in fifteen minutes. Marco's pulling up now."

Luca turned to me with a gentle smile. "I hate to do it this way, but if you want to marry me, we need to do it now. There's no telling when they'll take me in, and I don't want to leave you without my protection if that happens."

My heart thumped against my ribcage, and I was lightheaded. "Protection?"

He cringed. "If we're married, we get certain legal protections, and you'll be untouchable as far as the family goes. I know it sounds archaic, but it's the reality of my world, our world."

Pulling away from Luca, I stiffly walked to the bed and sat. He followed, kneeling between my knees with his hands on my thighs. "Baby, if you want to walk away, now's the time." His lips twisted into a pained smile.

His words were like a slap to the face. "I'm not walking away. It was my idea to elope. I'm just a little shocked because the reality that we're getting married in twenty minutes is setting in."

"I know. I'm sorry it's not going to be the day we've planned." He gave me a sarcastic smile.

Rolling my eyes, I shoved his shoulder. We'd both lamented giving our mothers free rein on the wedding planning. "Move. I'm going to go freshen up."

Luca helped me up, kissing the top of my head. "I love you."

I smiled and pushed him out of the room. With limited time to get ready, I prioritized cleaning up my makeup and touching up my hair. The doorbell rang as I slipped into the sparkling blush gown I'd planned to wear to our rehearsal dinner.

Taking a deep breath, I started to walk down the stairs.

"Thank you for coming, Father Anthony."

"Of course, Luca. Now, where is—" The priest's mouth fell open when he noticed me.

Luca turned, and when our eyes met, a shiver went down my spine. The connection between us was a live wire, and being with him was worth anything the world would throw at us.

"Sasha," Luca said roughly. Meeting me at the bottom of the stairs, he took my hand and pulled me to him. In my ear, he murmured, "You look beautiful."

"Thank you." I fluttered my eyelashes and smoothed the lapels of his suit coat. "Are you ready to make an honest woman out of me?"

"It would be my pleasure."

He presented me to Father Anthony. The middle-aged priest

schooled his expression back to the serene smile I was accustomed to. "It's good to see you again, Sasha."

"You too, Father Anthony. Thank you for coming so late. We really appreciate it."

"Oh, it's no problem. Where do we want to do this?"

Luca and I shared a look and said, "The dining room." Smiling, we lead Father Anthony, Marco, and Frankie through the living room to the formal dining room.

Father Anthony stood in the large archway that led to the kitchen, and we all stood in front of him—Frankie next to me while Marco took his spot next to Luca. "Are we ready?"

"Let's do it," I said, squeezing Luca's hands to expel some nervous energy.

Father Anthony nodded and opened his little book. "Luca and Sasha, have you come here to enter into marriage without coercion, freely and wholeheartedly?"

"I have," we said in unison.

"Are you prepared, as you follow the path of marriage, to love and honor each other for as long as you both shall live?"

Smiling ear to ear, we both said, "I am."

"Are you prepared to accept children lovingly from God and to bring them up according to the law of Christ and his Church?"

"I am." *Or, at the very least, we'll let the grandmothers take them to church.*

Father Anthony then led us in our vows.

Luca's eyes shimmered with tears as he gazed at me, his hands warm and steady as he recited his vows. "I, Luca, take you, Sasha, to be my wife. I promise to be true to you in good times and in bad, in sickness and in health. I will love you and honor you all the days of my life."

Those vows had been said a billion times by a billion other people, but Luca saying them to me cracked my heart wide open. Love flowed through me until I was about to burst. I hiccupped, and Luca cupped my cheeks, his thumbs wiping away the happy tears. Covering his hand with mine, I leaned into his touch.

"I love you," he said, his voice clear and strong. Then he leaned down and pressed a kiss on my lips.

I smiled into the kiss and leaned back. "You better hurry up, Padre."

Luca smiled down at me as we stood chest to chest, and I recited my vows. "I, Sasha, take you, Luca, for my lawful husband, to have and to hold, from this day forward, for better, for worse, for richer, for poorer, in sickness and in health, until death do us part." One of Luca's hands slid down to my neck, his other into my hair.

"I now pronounce you man and wife," Father Anthony added, which was different from what we'd discussed, but without a full mass, there was room for improvisation.

Luca didn't wait to be told. He dipped his head and guided my lips to his. I wrapped my arms around his neck, arching into his body. Our lips met in a fierce kiss as if we had been waiting years instead of minutes. His fingers twisted in my hair, holding me to him. I nipped his bottom lip, and he groaned, giving me the chance to slip my tongue into his mouth.

A throat clearing brought me back to reality, a reality in which I was mauling my fiancé—no, my husband—in front of a priest.

Leaning back, I tried to create space between us, but Luca's hold didn't loosen. I ran my thumb under his mouth to wipe away the lipstick smeared there. His heavy-lidded stare sent a thrill through my body, and I was ready for our guests to get the fuck out.

As much as Luca's tight hold would allow me, I turned my head and smiled at Father Anthony. "Do we need to do anything else?"

"Just sign the certificate." He gestured to the table where they'd all already signed.

"Luca?" His gaze lifted from my lips, and he slowly blinked. "You need to let me go."

The corners of his lips twitched, and he released me. I walked to the table on wobbly legs and scribbled my name. Luca stood dangerously close, waiting to sign. Reaching around me, he pinned me against the beautiful table—an Axel Lapusan original —while he signed his name. His hardening cock pressed against my ass as his arm wrapped around my lower stomach.

Luca shoved the piece of paper down the table. "Get out." He pushed my hair to one side and kissed my neck. The three men must have left, but I had no fucking idea because Luca's hand slid down and cupped me over my dress. "Mrs. Moretti." He groaned in my ear.

"Mrs. Mitchell-Moretti," I panted out, planting my hands on the table to keep myself upright.

He chuckled, taking a step back. "So, you decided to hyphenate." His knuckles ran down my spine, goosebumps following in their wake.

"Yes."

Luca gripped my hips and turned me. "I love it." He crowded me. The edge of the table dug into my ass when he stepped between my legs, a thick thigh pressing against me. "God, look at you. So fucking perfect." His fingers ghosted over my cheek. "I love you, Sasha. I'm going to make you so fucking happy."

I caught his hand and kissed his palm. "You already do." Tugging on his suit coat, I brought him down for a kiss. This was where I belonged—safe in his arms.

He squeezed me from hip to ass, his touch harsh and then gentle as he kneaded, moving my body so I was grinding down on his thigh. I rode his leg, fisting my skirt, tugging it until the soft wool of his pants met wet lace.

Moaning, I broke our kiss and tugged on his tie until he swatted my hands away. "Wait," he grunted, his eyes following the roll of my hips. Shaking his head, he pushed me back. "Follow me."

"Where are you going?" I said to his back.

"Come on!" he shouted from the front door.

Grumbling, I shuffled off the table, righting my skirt. When I got to the entryway, the door was wide open, and Luca smiled at me from the front steps. "What are you doing?"

"We almost forgot an important tradition."

I paused just inside, my hands on my hips. "What? Announcing it to the neighborhood?" Frankie and Marco leaned against their cars, smoking. "And what are you two doing?"

Frankie cackled, stubbing his cigarette. "We were just leaving."

"Sasha, come here." Luca's tone drew my attention. He crooked his finger, the corner of his mouth pulling up.

I rolled my eyes and stomped down the stairs. "What—Luca!" I squealed as he scooped me up into his arms. "Put me down!"

"No," Luca laughed, taking the stairs with steady steps, Marco and Frankie's laughter following us into the house.

Luca kicked the door closed behind him. "There. I carried you over the threshold." He slowly lowered me to the floor, my body sliding down his, the hem of my dress getting stuck on his belt.

"Oh." I smiled at him, cupping his cheeks. "Such a romantic."

His hands skimmed down my back, landing on my ass with a slap. "Always making fun of me."

"You make it easy."

"So many things I could say."

"Shut up!" I swatted his chest and broke away from his grasp, holding my skirt up so he could watch my ass jiggle as I sashayed back to the dining room. Looking over my shoulder, I smiled. "You coming?"

He glanced at the staircase and tilted his head, his forehead scrunching up.

"We covered the cliché tradition. Now let's do one of our own."

Luca was at my back in five steps, guiding me to the table. "It's a hell of a tradition." He smoothly slid the zipper on my side down, his fingers creeping across my ribs, tickling me. "Fuck, you smell amazing." Nuzzling my hair, he inhaled deeply, his chest brushing my shoulder blades.

"Mm-hmm." I shrugged the straps down, the cool air a relief on my heated skin.

"Let me." Luca took over undressing me, skimming his hands down my sides and legs. "Step out." I took an exaggerated step toward the table, turning to face him. His gaze traveled down my body as he hung my dress over the back of the chair.

I cocked my hip, dragging the tips of my fingers from my thigh to my cleavage. Luca's eyes followed the movement as he shrugged off his jacket. "We're married," I muttered in disbelief.

Luca worked his tie loose, pulling the silk from his neck and draping it on the growing pile of clothes on the chair. "We are." Button after button came undone, and tan skin peeked out between the stark white dress shirt. My fingers itched to touch him. "You freaking out?"

"Not even a little bit. How about you?" I closed the distance between us, yanking the tails of his shirt from his pants before hooking my fingers in his belt and tugging him closer.

"I would've married you that first day." Luca's brown eyes were full of honesty, and warmth bloomed in my chest.

He traced the top of my bra, dipping between my breasts. I sucked in a trembling breath and looked up at him through my eyelashes.

"The minute you came down the aisle, I was done. You were the most beautiful woman I'd ever seen." He chuckled, dipping his chin to watch his finger follow the white lines on my stomach. "And when we finally spoke, you knocked me on my ass."

"I was drunk and belligerent."

"And completely charming."

I tossed my head back and laughed.

Luca took the opportunity to unhook my bra and drop it on the floor. He palmed my breast, his thumb grazing my hard nipple. "Fucking perfect."

I licked my lips, giving him a dopey grin. "I love you."

"I love you. Now, ass on the table."

"Yes, sir!"

I tripped backward, distracted by Luca's hands easing my panties down. My ass hit the edge of the table, and I lifted one generous cheek at a time as the lace got caught on my ankle. Luca grunted in frustration until they went flying into the kitchen.

"I like these shoes." He rotated my ankle, the light catching the stones. "Are you wearing them on the day?"

I frowned down at the stunning heels. "I was going to, but now . . ."

"What?" Luca eased the shoes off, carefully setting them aside, and moved between my legs. His hands smoothed up my calf, squeezing away the tightness.

"I mean. Are we still going to have a wedding? We're already married."

Luca kissed the freckle on my knee. "Oh, we're having the big, monstrous wedding our mothers are planning. But I can't lie and say I'm not happy we got to have this for us. I'm embarrassed that it didn't occur to me sooner to elope."

"Who says I would've said yes?" I teased, and Luca slapped the outside of my thigh. The jiggle caught his eye, and he licked his lips.

Placing a kiss where stretch marks lined my soft skin, he hummed. "So fucking pretty." His fingers splayed across my thigh, and he shook it. "Damn." He licked his bottom lip. "You have no fucking idea what you do to me."

I dipped my foot down, dragging my toe over the obscene bulge in his pants. "I think I have an idea."

Luca gripped my knees, forcing my legs wide. I fell back on my hands, heat spreading through me as Luca's eyes devoured me. With just a look, he had me aching.

He massaged up my thighs—his fingertips harsh, then soothing as he went. I gasped as his hands framed my pussy, his thumbs pulling my lips open. "You wet for me, baby?"

The tip of his thumb brushed my clit, and I jerked, letting out a shaky "Yes." Luca's tongue ran up my slit, and I shivered. The light touch made me want to crawl out of my skin, but Luca's heavy hands kept me still.

After a few gentle licks, Luca devoured me. My fingers curled into my palms, the sting barely noticeable when Luca's tongue speared me and his thumb circled my clit. I leaned on one hand, twisting my other in his black waves. "Luca," I moaned, lifting my hips to force his tongue deeper.

Luca ran a hand up over my belly and pushed me back, his hand settling under my belly button. My head fell back into the ornate metal basket in the middle of the table. "Ouch." I shoved the decorative stuff away and flattened my spine against the cold wood.

"You okay?" Luca's breath sent a chill through me. He grabbed one of my ankles and set it on the edge of the table. "Keep that there."

With my thighs spread as far as they would go, Luca kissed, licked, and nipped until I was quivering under him. Only then did he slide a thick finger inside. I groaned, and he added another, pumping and curling them as his hand pressed down on my stomach, creating a delicious pressure. His lips closed around my clit, and he sucked, making my back arch as my body exploded in waves of pleasure. Panting, I struggled to open my eyes.

Luca smiled down at me, his hands moving from my hips to my ribs. His cock nudged my sensitive pussy as he leaned over and kissed me. I parted my lips, letting his tongue slide against mine as he thrust inside me.

We both moaned, our mouths falling apart.

"Fuck, Sasha. I'll never get tired of this." Luca stood up, grabbed my hips, and pounded into me, my back sliding on the smooth tabletop, only to be pulled back to Luca. One of my legs was raised, my ankle resting on his shoulder. The new angle made him hit deeper, curling my toes.

I needed to be closer to him, to touch him, so I struggled to push up, and he dropped my leg so I could sit. Wrapping my arms around his shoulders, I kissed him as he continued to thrust. He reached behind me, roughly grabbing my ass.

I tore my mouth away and panted out, "Sit down."

Luca licked his lips, sliding his hands under me and lifting me before taking one step and sitting, impaling me on his cock.

I screamed out, my fingers gripping his shoulders.

Luca's eyes shut, and his throat bobbed.

I eased up and then sat down hard, jarring him. His hooded eyes were hazy as they opened, and his lips parted. Luca's thumbs caressed the curve of my stomach as I started a slow up and down, my fingernails digging into his shoulders.

Luca traced the lines on my stomach, moving under to my clit. He pressed down with his thumb and flexed his hips up to meet me. I reached behind, gripping the edge of the table, and bounced faster. My calves burned as I moved on the balls of my feet. Inching closer and closer to my climax, I rolled my head back.

Luca's hand came down on my ass hard. "Sasha, eyes open."

I groaned, looking down at him. "You know what my eyes look like."

"But I've never seen my wife come on my cock."

My heart fluttered. There was no mistaking the love in his gaze. After all this time, it was hard to believe that Luca was all mine. I slid my hand from his shoulder, letting it settle over his heart. The ornate black tattoo of my name peeked through my spread fingers.

Luca's hand covered mine, and I stared into his dark eyes. Our bodies slid against one another, our heavy breaths mingling, adding to the heat between us. "I'm yours, Sasha." He squeezed my fingers. "Forever." He thrust up, and my mouth fell open with a moan. My palm slipped from the edge of the table, and he gathered me up in his hold, his hips slamming up into me while I remained pinned to his chest. "And you're mine, Sasha."

Tears blurred my vision as I clung to him. "I'm yours. Forever."

A fire lit in his eyes, and he gripped my hips tighter, his fingertips digging into my thick hips. "Mine." The possessiveness in his voice curled around me, making me shiver. "Your heart," he panted as he impaled me on his cock. "Your mind. Your soul. Mine." He thrust over and over until my orgasm careened through me with a violence I'd never experienced. Every part of my body trembled, leaving me a shaking heap on his lap. I crashed my lips into his, kissing, biting, and licking as Luca chased his own release.

He groaned, breaking away from our kiss. His hand circled my throat, his grip tight enough to hold me in place. "Fucking perfect. You should see yourself." Luca licked his lip. Beads of sweat trailed down his temple as he continued his assault between my legs. His serious gaze never left mine as his features twisted in blissful agony, his movements becoming jerky until he stilled under me.

Sliding his hand up, he brushed his thumb under my eye, wiping away a tear. "You okay?" He placed a sweet kiss on my lips.

I snorted. "My legs are noodles. I'd say I'm more than okay."

He chuckled, shifting in the chair, reminding me he was still deep inside me. We both groaned, and I rested my forehead on his shoulder. "Give me a second."

Falling into a fit of laughter, we hugged each other close, neither of us eager to break away.

From somewhere in the next room, an alarm sounded on my phone. "Ugh. Give me a minute." I awkwardly stood, and Luca slipped from my body.

As I turned, Luca caught my hand. "Don't take it." He eased off the chair, pulling my back to his chest. Resting our joined hands on my stomach, he contentedly sighed against my neck. "I can't wait to see you pregnant with our children."

I bit my lip, knowing he wouldn't like what I was about to say. "I don't think now's the right time."

"Why not?" I frowned over my shoulder, and he shrugged. "I don't see any reason to wait."

Rolling my eyes, I stepped out of his hold and faced him.

"Oh, I don't know. The fact we just eloped because we know the FBI is closing in around us?"

Luca shuffled closer, his hands running up and down my arms. "Around me, and now we're protected if the worst happens."

"Exactly, the worst could still happen."

"I've got you. Everything will be fine." Luca's words did little to calm me. "Just think about it. Okay?" He kissed my forehead.

"I will."

Luca's pants buzzed, and he pulled me into a tight hug. "I'm going to check that, then meet you upstairs?"

I nodded under his chin, the coolness of the room chilling my ass as he let me go. Soon enough, I was alone in the dining room, stark naked and wondering how Luca could be so optimistic.

Sure, his family had probably gone through things like this, but to contemplate bringing a baby into this mess? He had to have lost his mind.

I crossed the cold hardwood to the kitchen tile, my phone still chiming on the counter. Turning it off, I grabbed my birth control pack. One little pill, and I would be free to bang another day without worrying about bringing any kids into this fucked up situation.

Tapping the case on the butcher block, I stared out the window at the backyard.

Would it be so bad?

Yes.

I popped out the pill and dry swallowed. Luca would have to wait until he wasn't being investigated for murder to knock me up. I gathered our clothes and went up to the bedroom, where Luca was already brushing his teeth in the bathroom.

He didn't ask about the pill, and I didn't mention it. We went about our regular bedtime routines and fell into a heap in bed.

Luca wrapped me in his arms, his fingers twisting my engagement ring. "I can't believe we're married. Sucker."

I laughed and slapped his stomach. "If anything, you're the sucker."

"Agree to disagree," Luca mumbled into my hair.

"You really think everything will be okay?"

Luca took a deep breath and traced a hand down until it rested on my ass. "I do."

I nuzzled into his chest—my nose pressed to his skin so I could only smell him and a hint of my perfume. "Okay." My gut told me he was wrong, but for one night, I figured it was okay to believe Luca's pretty words.

TWENTY

"I can't believe we're on a private jet!" Sarah squealed, linking her arm with Imani's as they looked around with wide eyes.

"Luca said he wouldn't have it any other way." Ashley grinned as she reclined in her chair, pointing to the controls as she waved Miranda over.

"The perks of marrying Mr. Moneybags." Jazz laughed as she sorted through the overflowing basket of expensive chocolate, fruit, and other snacks.

"Says the girl that had a debutante ball," Adriana whispered not so quietly to me.

Jazz glared at her, but her lips quickly curled into a smile.

"So, where are we going?" I said as I flopped into a cushioned leather chair.

"Ah. Ah. Ah." Ashley wagged her finger. Somehow, these loudmouths had kept the bachelorette weekend a complete secret. "You'll know when we land."

"This is ridiculous."

"It's fun." Sarah handed me a glass of champagne. "Now finish that before it's time for take-off."

Gio and Tommy, our security detail for the weekend, boarded last and took the seats between us and the cockpit.

A few bottles of champagnes polished off and a luxury gift basket demolished, we landed in Puerto Vallarta, ready to make the most of the next three days.

"We've got the top two floors." Ashley smiled at me as we stared up at the boutique beachfront hotel.

"Let's go!" Sarah pulled her luggage, a white floppy hat bouncing in her face. As the only one of us not able to drink, she was prepared for a weekend of eating, reading, and catching some sun—and, if I knew my cousin at all, making fun of our drunk asses.

The two suites had three bedrooms, a living room, and a full kitchen. They were open air with no walls, so the pool and hot tub sat just past the roof. It was amazing.

"Everyone, get ready. We have dinner reservations in an hour!" Ashley shouted at Tommy, Adriana, Miranda, Jazz, and Imani as they left the elevator. "I can't wait to eat a real meal."

"I told you to eat before the flight." Sarah dug through her purse, eventually finding a single-serving package of almonds. "Here. I keep snacks handy for the all-day sickness."

"Thank you." Ashley hugged them to her chest.

We split off into separate rooms and got ready for our first night in paradise. All glammed up, a car service picked us up and took us just blocks from the hotel. The restaurant was on the ground floor of another hotel, but instead of being seated at one of the opulent tables inside, the hostess walked us out to the beach, where lanterns and ornate flower arrangements created a cozy dining room on the sand. Tommy and Gio sat at a table next to ours. Close enough to be protection and far enough to give a false sense of freedom.

"This is unbelievable." The crashing waves created the perfect white noise to keep conversations private. I took Ashley's hand and squeezed. "Thank you for arranging all this."

She grinned, her dimples popping. "It was nothing."

Once our first round of drinks was delivered, I tapped my knife against the glass. "I'd like to make a little speech." The group playfully groaned. "I just wanted to thank all of you for being here this weekend. Before I met Ashley, I'd never had a best friend. And before all of you, I'd never had a group of close friends. You're the sisters I never wanted—" They laughed, and Jazz threw a tortilla chip at me. "But I clearly needed. You're some of the most amazing people I've ever met, and I am grateful you all keep putting up with my ass." I raised my glass. "Cheers, you're stuck with me."

"Cheers!" We clinked glasses.

Jazz cleared her throat and added, "And to Luca, the one desperate enough to legally bind himself to Sasha."

I laughed and tapped my glass against hers.

Looking around the table, I couldn't believe how lucky I was to have so many people who loved and cared about me. My parents loved me and did their best to accept who I was, but these women embraced me in a way that only your chosen few could.

"You okay?" Ashley pushed a bowl of salsa my way. "You've got a glossy eye thing going on."

"Yeah. Just soaking it all in."

She gave me a soft smile and then turned to the loud debate over the menu and which apps we should get.

"Get all of them." I shrugged. "Why choose?" Tommy's deep laugh caught my attention, and I noticed that the two Moretti soldiers had quite the spread. In a very ladylike move, I leaned over and snagged a taquito. "How do you already have food?"

"We weren't busy being sentimental," Gio said, completely straight-faced.

"You're boring."

"I know." He bared his teeth. I suppose it could've been a smile, but it was more like a predatory warning to move along.

So, I moved along.

After a delicious meal and too many drinks, we headed to a club to dance. Standing in a tight pack, we dissuaded dance partners with wild dance moves and the occasional outburst of hysterical laughter.

"I need to use the bathroom," I shouted in Jazz's ear. She followed me to the small hall at the back of the club. Three women stood outside the women's bathroom.

"Let's just use the men's." Jazz lifted her chin toward the door.

Flashbacks of the last time I'd used the men's room ran like a reel in my mind, and I shook my head wildly. When Jazz frowned, I added, "I'd rather avoid piss on the floor."

The short redhead in front of us spun around with a big, drunk grin. "It's all urinals. I checked."

Jazz laughed, and I blew out a sigh of relief.

A bleary-eyed coed threw her arm around the short woman and lifted her chin at us. "We're just here for moral support, so you're two closer to peeing."

"Good to know."

"You don't have a lighter, do you?" she yelled over the loud music as she patted her pockets.

Jazz and I shared an amused look. "Sorry, no." I reached into my clutch and pulled out a matchbook with the hotel's logo. "But I do have these."

"You're a goddess." The younger woman gushed as she snatched them from my hand. "Tiff and I were going to head out back and—" She made the universal sign for smoking a joint. "Since you provided the fire, it's only right you come with us."

Smoke what I was sure would be skunk weed in the alley with two college kids?

"Sure, why not? I really do need to pee, though."

The DJ dropped a song with thumping bass, and the crowd got extra rowdy, so the four of us awkwardly danced, unable to hear each other over the ruckus. As we entered the bathroom, the two hallway girls and their friend left, repeating their invitation to join them in a bit of puff, puff, pass.

"You're not really going to the alley with those kids, are you?"

Jazz asked as she checked her lipstick. Her dark eyes watched me in the small sink over the mirror. "I'd bet good money they have that weak ass weed they sell on the beach."

I let out a deep sigh. "No, which makes me feel old."

"You're ridiculous."

"I know." I searched my small bag and huffed. "You don't, by chance, have a tampon, do you?"

Jazz dug through her purse. "Last one." The bathroom was not even a four-by-four square, so she easily handed it to me from the sink.

"Thank God. I didn't want to have to fashion a toilet paper pad."

She turned and fluffed her big waves. "Only you would be lucky enough to get a bachelorette weekend period."

"At least I won't have to worry on the wedding day. That'd be a hassle." I washed my hands as Jazz leaned against the door. "I'm glad Luca isn't here to be disappointed."

"Are you already trying for a baby?"

I pulled half a paper towel from the dispenser and dried my hands the best I could. "No. But he doesn't know that." Tossing the useless piece of paper, I wiped my hands down the skirt of my dress. I took a step toward the door, but Jazz didn't move.

"What?"

"He wants to start trying now. I thought we should wait until he's not under investigation for murder."

"Ah." Jazz sagely nodded.

"What?"

"Nothing." I moved to open the door, and Jazz stayed in my way. "Just seems like the kind of thing you should tell your soon-to-be husband."

"Well, I plan to, just after the wedding."

"Good." Jazz stepped away, but instead of leaving the smelly, tiny bathroom, I took her spot.

"When are you planning on proposing?"

Jazz smirked. "After the wedding."

I shook my head and grabbed her hand. "We have so much in common." Jazz laughed, and we joined the gang on the dance floor. I proceeded to get drunk and sweaty with my best friends.

As last calls rang out at the bar, we shuffled out the door.

"Where's the car?" Ashley slurred as she hung on Sarah.

"Tommy's bringing it around."

"I want to walk," I whined, shifting on my heels.

"No," both Sarah and Adriana said. Sober friends are never as flexible as you'd like.

"But it's so nice, and we could walk up the beach."

Imani, drunk as could be, wrapped her arms around Jazz and smiled up at her. "That sounds romantic."

Jazz gazed lovingly down at her, and my chest tightened. Separate bachelor/bachelorette parties were the worst. I missed Luca.

"What my baby wants, my baby gets," Jazz practically cooed as she threaded their fingers together and took off toward the pier at the end of the street.

"We'll give them a minute and follow," Ashley loudly whispered, which caught Gio's disapproving stare. Miranda leaned on his shoulder, her eyes shut.

"You guys can head back to the hotel. We'll be there in a little bit."

Sarah and Adriana looked relieved. Of course, the pregnant lady and the mom would want to be in bed before sunrise. Tommy pulled up in the sprinter, and Gio helped them in, situating Miranda by an open window. He said something to Tommy and then gestured toward the beach.

When Ashley and I made it to the pier, we slipped off our heels. The warm sand between my toes and the sound of the crashing waves grounded my drunk ass.

"This is the best night," Ashley slurred.

"It's up there."

"Pretty soon, we won't be able to just take off to Mexico."

I frowned down at her. "What do you mean?"

"Life." That's all she said, her face solemn.

What started as a sputter turned into a full-on belly laugh.

"What?" Ashley stopped walking, staring at me like I was out of my mind. "Sasha!"

"I'm s-sorry." I wiped under my eyes. "That was just so movie of the month. I'm getting married, not being sealed in a tomb."

"First, it's getting married. Then it's babies." She started down the beach, and I snagged her hand.

"Do you have something to tell me?"

"No. Just pointing out we're growing up."

"We're thirty."

"But we've never acted like it."

I wrapped my arm around Ashley's shoulders and pulled her to my side. "And we won't. We'll be eighty and still raising hell. I foresee being kicked out of several retirement communities. These poor men that have chosen to love us."

"Oh, Sasha, they never had a choice." She peeked up at me with a smirk on her sweet face.

We flirted with the shoreline the rest of the way back, Gio grumbling in the background about his shoes and the water.

Back in our suite, we hugged and went to our rooms while Gio posted up on the fashionable but comfortable coach, ready to protect us should it come to that. I struggled through my night routine before falling into bed. The light from the main living space snuck through the curtains on the floor-to-ceiling windows.

Sometime after dawn, I woke up with a shout. The glass door to my room slid open, and Gio stood with his gun pointed toward the ensuite bathroom. "Sasha?"

Not two seconds later, Ashley ran past him to my side. "Are you okay?"

I fisted my t-shirt and felt the thump-thump of my racing heart. Sweat soaked my collar and dripped down my back. Through ragged breaths, I said, "I'm fine." I wasn't fine. Mentally, I was back in that hotel room, fighting for my life.

"You were screaming." She climbed into bed, hugging me to her chest. "Gio, you can put down the gun." At the mention of his gun, I shivered and tried to shrink in Ashley's arms.

Silently, Gio left the room.

"I-I don't—"

"Shh, honey."

I panted into her soft tank top, the warm scent of her body butter soothing my frayed nerves. The skin-on-skin contact comforted me until I was breathing more easily. Chuckling, I pulled back and patted her thigh. "I needed that."

"Anytime." Ashley's brown skin glowed in the early morning sunlight pouring through the open door, her face shiny with product. She adjusted her bonnet with a cautious smile. "Are we getting up or trying to sleep a little more before the chef gets here?"

I scooted back down the bed, fluffing my pillow. "More sleep."

Ashley nodded and made herself comfortable next to me. Face to face, I couldn't help but smile. "It's been a while."

"Yeah." She tucked her hands under her cheek.

"Thanks for being here."

She rolled her eyes, but a small smile tugged at her lips. "Where else would I be? Now, go back to sleep. Your breath is nasty."

I tucked my lips and fought the laughter bubbling up. She shoved my shoulder and rolled onto her back. It didn't take long for her to fall asleep, but I couldn't shake the feeling of Dante's hands on my throat.

After listening to Ashley's snores, I gave up on getting more sleep and shuffled out to the living room. Gio spoke softly on the phone, the crashing waves making it impossible to hear what he was saying.

I snagged a bottle of water from the fridge and then plopped down on the couch opposite my grumpy bodyguard. When he put his phone down, I asked, "Did you sleep?"

His face remained blank as he leaned back.

"You hungry?"

Silence.

Nodding, I sent Luca an "I miss you" text and turned to watch the sunrise.

TWENTY-ONE

"So many speedos." Miranda sighed dreamily. She pulled her sunglasses down her nose and smiled at me. "Thanks for inviting me."

"Of course." I took a sip of my margarita. "You're family."

"Why does that sound like a threat?"

"Because it is," Jazz, Imani, and Adriana said simultaneously, then burst into laughter.

I shot them a playful glare. "Shut up. You love me."

"We do." Imani smiled up at me from where she lay on her belly on a beach lounger. A colorful flower tattoo peeked out from under the low-cut back of her plum one-piece swimsuit when she reached for her cup.

Ashley reached for the pitcher of margaritas, stopping when she was leaning over Imani. "You have a tattoo?"

"Why do you sound so surprised?"

"I mean . . ."

We all shared a look, not sure what to say. The silence grew awkward, and we all shifted in our seats. The smile on Imani's face fell.

"Baby—"

"No!" Imani shoved up, adjusting the top of her strapless swimsuit so her small chest was completely covered. She stood, resting her hands on her wide hips. "You guys think I'm boring."

Maybe it was the tequila, or perhaps it was because none of us knew what to say, but not one of us told her she was wrong. Imani wasn't boring, but she wasn't exactly the life of the party, and that was okay. We all loved her for who she was.

She stomped her foot in the sand, and Jazz approached her slowly. "I'm not boring," she gritted out as she scowled at all of us.

Jazz took off her sunglasses and gazed down at Imani. "I know you're not boring." The heat of Jazz's stare rivaled the sun beating down on the beach. She ran her fingertips down Imani's arm, then laced their fingers together.

Imani tucked her lips and shook her head, her black spirals falling free from the scrunchy she'd stolen from my beach bag. Yanking her hand free, she stomped off, a confused Jazz following in her wake.

"What just happened?" Miranda asked.

Ashley adjusted in her seat to have a better view of the beach. "No idea."

Imani approached a guy near the water, Jazz looming behind them, occasionally glancing over her shoulder at us. Money exchanged hands, and Imani made a beeline back to our group.

"Incoming," Sarah mumbled as she sipped her lemonade.

"There!" Imani thrust a baggie of smelly weed in Ashley's face. "Now, who's boring?"

Ashley's eyes went wide.

"Now, let's smoke this shit!"

I gasped. I literally gasped. Imani didn't curse. She never got riled. "O-okay." Taking the small bag, I frowned. "Do you have papers or something?"

"I'll go get some." Jazz squeezed Imani's shoulder and walked to the small shop near the hotel.

I set the bag down, poured more margarita into Imani's glass, and handed it to her. "You okay?"

She pursed her lips and tilted her head. "I overheard Jazz and her mom talking about me. Apparently, I'm just the kind of woman she should marry because I'm so boring."

I cocked an eyebrow. "Jazz called you boring?"

Imani downed half her drink. "I think the exact word was safe. And you know what Jazz said?" We all shook our heads. "Nothing!"

"Uh, Imani?"

She sunk down onto her lounger with a sigh. "What?"

"Is it so bad to be safe?"

The cringe that twisted Imani's pretty face was all the answer I needed.

"I was the safe option, too." Adriana sat up, putting her floppy hat back on her head. "And believe me, it's a compliment."

"You think?" Imani's voice was soft like she wanted to believe her.

"Oh yeah. Any mother would want their child to be with someone that would keep their child's heart safe."

Imani's bottom lip trembled, and she set down her glass.

"Michael is safe," Sarah added. "I've never doubted his love, and he's never given me a reason to."

Miranda smirked. "Nothing about Oscar is safe."

Imani laughed, her shoulders finally relaxing.

"What's so funny?" Jazz handed me the papers and sat at the end of Imani's chair.

"I'm sorry." Imani threw herself at Jazz, nearly knocking them both into the sand.

"It's okay?" Jazz patted her back as she looked at me, bewildered. I shook my head.

Imani looked up at Jazz with a pained expression. "I don't want to smoke weed I bought from a stranger on the beach."

"I don't either."

Luca sighed into the phone. "I'm dreading tonight."

"You're being dramatic."

"I'm not."

"It'll be fun!" I plucked a piece of pineapple from the fruit salad. "A few strippers never hurt anybody." Luca groaned, and I barked out a laugh. "Why own strip clubs if you're not going to partake?"

"The only woman I want to see take her clothes off is you."

"That's all very sweet, but I know I'm looking forward to seeing a little skin tonight."

A door closed on his side, and my phone beeped, letting me know he was trying to video call me. Frowning, I accepted.

"What are you doing?"

On my phone's six-inch screen, Luca was unbuttoning his shirt. "If you don't know, I must not be doing this right."

Biting my lip, I skipped off to the privacy of my room. As my head hit the pillow, he shoved his shirt off. "I think you're doing a fine job."

Luca grinned and slowly unbuckled his belt. The fine leather slid through loop after loop, and I watched with rapt attention as he tossed it to the floor of his home office. "What do you want, Sasha?"

"Pants off." He unbuttoned his slacks and let them fall to his feet. "Damn."

Luca's hand trailed down his abs until he reached the band of his black boxer briefs. Toying with the elastic, he licked his lip. I pressed my thighs together, waiting to see what he would do next.

Luca didn't disappoint. He stroked himself over his boxers, his cock lengthening before my eyes.

"Boxers off," I demanded. He dragged them down until he was standing in all his naked glory. "Fuck me."

"I would if you were here." He squeezed the base of his cock with a groan. "Nothing feels better than you, baby."

Like a professional cam guy, Luca stroked himself. With every thrust, his abs and thighs flexed. His half-lidded eyes stayed trained on me as he fucked his fist.

My skin flushed all over as I squirmed under his stare.

"So fucking pretty and pink," he gritted out, which only intensified the heat in my cheeks. I swallowed, my mouth watering as I watched him please himself. Every little groan sent a thrill through me.

"My perfect fucking wife," he grunted, his hand speeding up.

"Luca . . ." I didn't know what to say. My husband was about to come from just looking at my face.

"And your voice. Fuck." Luca threw his head back and let out a deep, soul-satisfying groan. His throat bobbed as he swallowed. I marveled at how his body rippled and contracted. When our eyes met, he came moaning my name.

Suddenly, the phone went black, and Luca yelled, "Damn it, Ryan!"

Jarred from my sexual haze, I laughed, waiting for Luca to pick up his phone. When he did, he was delightfully rumpled, his forehead shiny from exertion. "Your cat is a menace."

"It's the risk you take when you prop your phone up for a little show and tell."

There was a light knock on the door and a quiet, "Sasha?"

"Uh, give me a minute." I grabbed the covers as if I was the naked one.

"Sasha?" Luca's voice echoed through the room. I faintly wondered if everyone had heard his little show.

"Uh, I think I got to go."

He chuckled. "All right. Have fun tonight."

"You too. Be nice tonight. No scowling at the dancers."

Luca smiled. "I promise. I love you."

"I love you too."

I tossed the phone and smoothed my hair—which was ridiculous. Not a hair was out of place, despite me feeling freshly fucked. *The power of modern technology.*

Standing, I adjusted my bikini and took a deep breath. When I opened the door, Adriana wasn't there. "Hello?"

"Over here," Adriana called from the pool.

I grabbed the platter of fruit and joined her poolside. Sitting on a towel, I put my feet in the cool water. "I thought you were taking a nap."

She grabbed a strawberry and shrugged. "Hard to sleep with all that noise."

"Ah."

"Yeah. Jazz and Imani were making up, and Miranda was in her room talking to Oscar, so . . ." She raised her eyebrows as she took a bite.

I bit back a smile. "I think Sarah's out cold after all that sun, and Ashley's doing a little shopping. So, it's just the two of us."

Adriana gazed out at the ocean as she took the last bite of her strawberry. "I need to talk to you about something."

"Okay?"

"I'm worried about Marco." She picked at her nail. "I didn't want to tell anyone about this until I knew more, but with Luca not trusting him, I need to tell at least you."

I covered her hand with mine. "What's going on?"

"My mom's sick."

"What?"

"She has breast cancer." My heart stuttered, but I didn't interrupt. "Our trip to Chicago was because Marco demanded she see a specialist there, and, of course, she wouldn't go unless we dragged her there. After my trip to the hospital, he's been making trips with Dante and me up there. That's where Marco's been—at my mom's house in Chicago."

My gut twisted. "Why wouldn't you just tell Luca?"

She shook her head, her eyes sparkling with unshed tears. "After the fire and everything else going on, I didn't want to put yet another burden on his shoulders. Then Chicago happened, and I was scared, and the lie just came out."

"Oh, honey."

"I know! And now Luca is watching Marco like he's an opp. I messed up."

I nodded, looping my arm through hers while staring out at the surf. "Are you okay?"

"Yes, or I will be. She's started treatment, so now we wait."

"If you need anything, I'm here."

"I know."

Adriana laid her head on my shoulder, and we watched the people running on the beach. I was scared but relieved to have proof that Marco wasn't a backstabbing asshole.

Glammed up and ready to enjoy our last night in Mexico, we strutted into the burlesque club, already tipsy. Gio and Tommy handled our covers and ushered us in, scanning the crowd.

"There's our table!" Ashley yelled over the house music. We bobbed and weaved around the small tables and laughing people. Ashley pulled out a chair in the middle of the table and bowed. "You sit here."

"Why, thank you."

She shared a smile with Sarah, and out of nowhere, a glittering crown materialized in front of me. "You've got to be kidding me." I picked it up and was shocked by its weight. "Am I supposed to wear this?"

"Well, yeah," Sarah said as she inspected the bottles of champagne chilling in the buckets on the table.

"Put on the damn crown, Sasha." Jazz took the bottle from Sarah and started pouring glasses of bubbly for everyone.

"Fine." I rolled my eyes but set the sparkling monstrosity on my head.

Imani grinned at me. "I knew it would look great on you."

I fingered the largest gemstone and begrudgingly accepted the crown, if only for sweet, cornball Imani. Fluttering my eyelashes, I said, "You have impeccable taste."

Imani preened, and Jazz gave me an approving nod over her shoulder. If Jazz had her way, Imani would walk through life in bubble wrap.

"For our pregnant friend, sparkling grape juice." Miranda handed Sarah a champagne flute.

As everyone settled into their seats, Ashley stood and raised her glass. "To Sasha's last hurrah!"

"To Sasha!"

We clinked glasses, and the lights dimmed. The dark theater reminded me of the Monocle back home—a touch too warm and the smell of alcohol thick in the air. Glasses clinked, and people whispered before the music swelled, and the MC, a beautiful drag queen called Gigi Give-em-more, emerged from the red velvet curtain and welcomed the audience in Spanish. Miranda laughed at something she said and gleefully pointed at me. Clearly, her growing up in a Spanish-speaking household was an advantage that she was about to wield against me.

Wide-eyed, I watched the larger-than-life queen leave the stage and stand in front of our table. She said something, and Miranda doubled over with laughter.

"Ah, no habla—"

"We're fucking with you, honey." The audience broke into laughter, and Gigi grinned. "What's your name, gorgeous?"

"Sasha."

"Princess Sasha. Love it."

Sarah held up a black sash with the word bride bedazzled across it. "Bride Sasha."

Gigi eyed me critically. "And what's the lucky person's name?"

"Luca."

"Oh, fuck me." Gigi sagged to the edge of the stage. "Sasha and Luca. I bet he's tall, dark, and handsome?"

"I mean . . ." I leaned forward, taking a sip of my champagne.

"Of course. Bitches like you make me sick. Congratulations," she grumbled, and the audience laughed at the dirty look she threw my way. With a scoff, Gigi moved on to work the rest of the room, and we kicked back and enjoyed the show.

We drank many, many bottles of champagne and watched many, many beautiful women shimmy and tease themselves out of their clothes before the house lights came up and it was time to go.

Gio and Tommy ushered us out into the warm summer night, and we started to make our way back to the hotel. Our group laughed and carried on, deciding a late-night dip was in order. Despite the fully stocked kitchen, the girls wanted some junk food and popped into the convenience store, leaving Tommy and me outside. He was making a call, so I took my phone out and found a series of texts from Luca and a picture from Frankie of a bored Luca getting a lap dance.

Mid-laugh, a pair of women bumped into me, knocking my phone from my hands and into the alley between the buildings.

"Fucking assholes," I mumbled as I stepped next to the dumpster, searching for my phone. "Can knock you over, but don't help you—"

A firm grip on the back of my neck pulled me up, forced me further into the alley, and shoved me against the rough wall. "All alone?" I opened my mouth to scream, but they turned my face until I couldn't move my jaw, let alone let out more than a whimper. "Stay quiet. Wouldn't want me to kill your little entourage."

Swallowing back my screams, I focused on my assailant's voice. It was familiar, and that sent a shiver down my spine.

"Good girl." He inhaled deeply and released a harsh breath against my neck. "God, you smell good."

"What do you want?" I whispered, not sure if he could hear me.

"I just wanted to say hello."

"Sasha?" Tommy's panicked voice called from feet away.

"See you in a few weeks, Sasha." He kissed the back of my

head and walked down the alley—his steps unhurried as if he hadn't just scared the ever-loving shit out of me.

I stayed plastered to the wall, my face throbbing.

"Sasha, what the hell are you doing?" Tommy gently peeled me from the stucco and guided me back toward the convenience store. When the glow of the yellow streetlights hit us, he frowned. "What happened?"

I shook my head and gestured to the alley. "Some women knocked my phone out of my hand, and it bounced down that way. I was looking for it when a guy shoved me against the wall."

"Did he rob you?" Tommy stood in the mouth of the dark alley.

"No, but he said he'd see me in a few weeks. Do you think he means at the wedding because—"

"I need to call Luca." Tommy took my hand and led me back to the store, where my friends came pouring out.

Gio scowled and shared a silent conversation with Tommy. Without a word, Tommy peeled off into the alley.

"What happened?" Ashley ran her thumb over the scrapes on my cheek. "Your lip!"

I let out a light chuckle. "Two girls knocked into me, and I fell. Leave it to me to have a drunk hit and run."

My little performance must have been convincing because they all laughed and started toward the hotel, chatting about the snacks they'd bought. Ten minutes after we'd made it back to the suite, Tommy showed up without my phone and with an irate Luca on his.

"Sasha?"

"Hey, Luca."

"You okay?" His voice was tight, hard.

I gave the girls an apologetic smile as I went into my room, shutting the door while they all hooted and hollered.

"I am. Tommy scared whoever it was away." Luca remained silent. "I'm fine. A couple of scrapes, but nothing too serious."

"I want you home."

"And I'll be home tomorrow."

"That's not soon enough." The way he was talking, I expected him to reschedule the flight. I could picture him pacing his office, a little tipsy and a whole lot pissed off. Even hundreds of miles away, I felt protected.

I smiled, and the cut on my lip started to bleed. "I know."

TWENTY-TWO

After my chat with Luca, our flight was magically bumped up, so our tired and hungover little party made it to the airport hours earlier than originally planned.

"There better be food," Jazz grumbled.

"The chef packed up our breakfast," Ashley mumbled as she disappeared onto the plane.

Imani shook her head, her tawny skin losing its glow at the mention of food. She took a deep breath, then followed Jazz up the steps.

While the flight to Mexico was rowdy, the flight back was a somber affair. Parting with half-assed hugs, we got into our respective cars and headed home. Tommy wisely kept the radio off and his lane changes to the minimum.

When he pulled into the driveway, I finished the last of the water in the bottle and sighed. "Can you grab my suitcase? I feel like I might die."

Tommy pursed his lips, clearly holding back a laugh as he got out of the car.

I took a deep breath and prepared myself to open the door, get my body out of the car, walk up flights of stairs, strip out of my clothes, and land face-first into bed.

Tommy opened my door.

One step down.

"Sasha?"

"Give me a second."

He rocked back and forth until he eventually rolled his eyes and held out his hand. "Give me your keys."

"You're not allowed in the house if Luca's not here."

"I know. I'm just going to open the door and set these inside."

I dug through my huge purse with a limp hand, slapping around until I landed on my keys. "Here."

Bracing myself for the worst, I shoved out of the car and took a moment to let the head spins settle. Tommy stood on the porch, grinning as I shuffled toward the door. "Shut up."

"I didn't say anything." He dangled my keys in front of me, and I snatched them away.

"Your thoughts are very loud." I shut the door in his laughing face and let out a sigh of relief. Ryan came running from the kitchen, meowing up a storm. "Hello to you, my darling." With a grace I didn't know my hungover self possessed, I bent over and scooped up the loudmouth cat, and he started to purr. "Now, let's go take an obscenely long nap. Mommy's feeling rough."

Ryan yawned and shook his precious little head. I trudged up the stairs, embarrassingly exhausted when I finally made it to my room. Setting my little furry angel on the bed, I pulled my clothes off and swan-dived into the middle of the bed.

Hours later, the room was much darker, and my phone buzzed nonstop from somewhere nearby. I groaned and rolled from the bed to the floor. "Why?" I whined as I crawled to my purse.

"Hello?" I laid my head on the expensive handbag, closing my eyes against the dwindling light.

"Sasha?" Sarah's panicked voice woke me right up.

Despite the headache and nausea, I shot up. "What's wrong?"

"I can't find Michael, and I'm cramping."

"Shit." I jumped up and pulled on my wrinkled travel clothes. "Do you need to go to the hospital?"

"Mom's on her way, but I need Michael." Her voice broke, and it was like an arrow to my heart.

"Let me see if I can track him down."

"Thank you, Sasha."

"I got you. I'll call once I find him."

A woman on a mission, I rushed downstairs, grabbed a sports drink, and ran out the front door. Tommy startled from his spot on the porch swing, and I chucked my keys at him. "Come on. We need to find Michael."

Tommy beat me to the car, opening the door for me before jogging around the hood. Once he was buckled and ready to roll, he looked at me expectantly. "Where to first?"

The headache made it hard to think, but I came up with a few places, and we were off.

———————————

Half an hour later, we hadn't found him, and I was worried. Michael wasn't involved in the criminal side of the Moretti family, but that didn't mean he couldn't get caught in the middle.

Tommy answered a call as we left Michael's office. "Hello?" I side-eyed him as he remained silent, the person on the other side of the phone barking out orders. "Marco? I—" More muffled talking and Tommy's eyes widened in what looked like fear. "I'm with Sasha right now looking for Michael. As soon as I drop her at home, I'll head to the casino." Tommy glanced at me, his jaw tight. "You got it, Boss." He dropped his phone in the cup holder, his body tense. "Luca talked to Michael, and he's heading to the hospital now."

"Good. Where's Luca?"

"I'm taking you home."

"No. You're taking me to Luca." I folded my arms, glaring into the side of his face.

"There's nothing going on that you need to see."

I huffed. "If you take me home, I'll just drive myself there. The difference is I might get there too late to keep Luca from making a huge mistake."

"He's going to kill me," Tommy muttered but changed directions.

As we pulled up to the construction site, I got a sick feeling in the pit of my stomach. Five cars, including Luca's, were parked behind the Moretti Construction sign. "What the hell?" I muttered as I got out of the vehicle.

"Sasha!" Tommy yelled after me.

Instead of waiting for him, I broke into a sprint. I wound through the jackhammered parking garage, stopping when I heard the first hint of masculine voices.

"Who?" Luca roared, his voice echoing off the walls. The sound of fists hitting flesh and groans made me flinch.

Tommy ran up behind me, not even a little out of breath. "Sasha, I think we should go."

"Hey!" a deep voice shouted from the shadows.

Tommy spun around and pushed me behind him. "It's Tommy and Sasha," he said loud and clear.

"What the fuck are you doing here?" Mickey snarled. There was something in his stare that set me on alert.

"I need to talk to Luca."

Marco strolled up, his face grim. "Follow me."

"I think we're just going to—"

"Sasha!" Luca bellowed, making me jump.

Marco jerked his chin toward where a floodlight was on.

"I guess we're going over there," I said with more confidence than I felt.

Chin up, shoulders back, I walked toward Luca's silhouette. His face was shadowed, but anger rolled off him in waves. The closer I got, the more my legs shook. In Luca's hand was a gun, complete with a silencer. Just feet away, the Marino twins knelt on a black tarp, beaten and bloody. Paulie stood behind them, holding a gun.

"Tough day at the office?" I joked.

He pulled me to his chest, gently tilting my chin up and running his thumb over the scrapes on my cheek. "Are you okay?"

I nodded, my eyes wandering to the two men glaring at me from the ground. Luca kissed my forehead, shocking me from staring at the soon-to-be-dead Marino twins. Marco joined us, maneuvering me behind him while Luca stalked toward Tommy.

Wordlessly, he raised the gun in the air and brought it down across Tommy's face in a punishing blow. To Tommy's credit, he remained standing and recovered long enough to look at Luca before another hit came down on the other side. Luca grabbed Tommy's jaw and said, "You shouldn't have brought Sasha here." He glanced back at me and shook his head. "Next time you're guarding her, she better come back intact. If even one nail is broken, I'll kill you. Understand?"

"Yes, sir."

Luca patted his shoulder, cuffing his ear. Tommy kept his hands behind his back, letting the blood from his nose and mouth pour down his chin. There was pride, a kind of nobility, in the way Tommy watched Luca. He'd been pistol-whipped and still looked at Luca like he was his hero.

Luca gestured for him to stand next to me. "Now. Where were we?" Luca rolled his neck, his eyes falling on his prey.

"Fuck you." The twin with a scar through his eyebrow spat.

Marco kicked him so hard that he fell into his brother, and when he wound up for another, Luca shook his head.

"Enough. Frankie?"

Frankie came out of the shadows, set a bag at Luca's feet, and came to stand next to me. Mickey joined him, leaving me surrounded by huge suited and booted men, but I could still make out the unfortunate assholes waiting for their execution.

Luca slid off his expensive jacket and handed it to Marco, who passed it to me. I crushed it against my chest, inhaling his cologne to try and soothe my rattled nerves. He set the gun down, rolling up his sleeves before unzipping the leather bag and rooting around. I gasped when he pulled out a knife as sharp as the ones he used in our kitchen, but no one spared me a look. All eyes stayed trained on Luca.

"Now. We're going to try this again. You tell me what I want, and I'll end this. You drag it out, and I'll break you down like a side of beef."

The twin with a scar spat at Luca while his brother shook.

Right there with ya, buddy.

"The shooting at the club the night Yanni was killed—" The trembling twin flinched, and Luca pivoted his body toward him. "You told them I was there, didn't you?"

When neither spoke, Luca palmed the crying twin's face and cleanly sliced off his right ear. Picking it up off the ground, he tossed it at his brother, hitting him in the center of his forehead. "Start talking, or the other ear goes."

The twin with a scar through his eyebrow glanced our way and grimaced.

Luca looked at Marco and jerked his head toward the twins. "You know anything about the night Yanni was shot?"

Marco licked his lips and shook his head. "Of course not. I'd never go behind your back."

"So, you didn't tell these fuckers to go to my cabin and collect Zoe?"

"Luca—"

"Shut the fuck up, Mickey, or you'll be down on your knees with these pieces of shit." Luca's eyes never left Marco as he put Mickey in his place. "Answer me."

Marco worked his jaw back and forth. "You know I did."

I bit my lip to keep from interrupting. Marco had fucked up there, but was it enough of a reason for Luca to kill him?

"So, what about the hit on Yanni Chronis or the attempted hit on Cy? Did you kill Pete?"

"You know I didn't do that shit." Marco took a step closer, only to be pulled back by Paulie.

"I don't know fucking anything. Why were you in Chicago if you weren't trying to kill Cy?"

Marco raised his chin, his lips pursed.

Luca nodded, a humorless laugh falling from his lips. "On the ground." At his command, Paulie shoved Marco down next to the twins. Luca pressed the muzzle of his gun between Marco's eyes.

"Luca—" Mickey and I called out at the same time.

Luca glanced over his shoulder at his cousin, his expression cold. "Your last warning, Mickey."

Mickey's jaw flexed, his hands fisting at his side, but he remained quiet despite his big brother kneeling with a gun to his forehead.

"Luca?" I tried again.

"Not now, Sasha." His tone was softer but by no means kind. "Tommy, take her home."

"No! Adriana's mom is sick!" I shouted, and all the men looked at me, confused. "Marco was taking her to get another opinion."

Luca frowned at me.

"He's loyal. You know he is," I choked out, hoping he believed me, hoping I could save Marco.

Luca let out a breath, raised his gun, and shot Paulie between the eyes. I jumped, letting out a scream that the empty garage amplified. Paulie fell to his knees and then onto the already sobbing twin. He tried to shoulder off the huge dead body, screaming for help.

"Did you just piss your pants?" Marco glared at the twins as he stood up and brushed off his knees. "Wasn't enough to cry like a little bitch"

"The fuck?" Mickey yelled, stepping closer to Luca and earning a backhand from him.

"Shut the fuck up. If you can't do that, I'll rethink your involvement." Luca gritted out.

Marco grabbed the back of his brother's neck, his face severe. "Your loyalty is to Luca. If I were working with these pieces of shit, I would deserve a bullet to the head." Mickey's shoulders tensed under the pressure of Marco's fingers.

"You're right."

Marco nodded and turned to me with a small smile. "You like me, Red?" It was not the time for Marco's weird humor.

"You're insane." I shook my head.

He leaned in, kissed my cheek, and whispered, "He already knew, but thank you. You're a real one."

"Get the fuck off my wife," Luca growled, and Marco let out a huff of a laugh against my neck.

Suddenly, it was comedy hour.

I caught Tommy's wide-eyed stare and Mickey's deep frown. He'd been left out of whatever Marco and Luca had planned, but it seemed like Luca calling me his wife broke his brain.

"You weren't supposed to shoot Paulie yet." Marco lorded over their captives.

"I couldn't look at that big fucker anymore. I guess we can't use you as a decoy now," Luca lamented.

"Since we're going off-script . . ." Taz stepped out of the shadows behind me, making me jump.

Squeezing Luca's jacket closer, I mumbled, "Any more of you lurking around?" Frankie nudged my shoulder, a rare sign of solidarity.

Luca sighed and gestured with the knife at the twins. "We know they tried to kill Tootsie. We also know they let us think Tootsie was dead. What I don't know is why. Marco didn't order—"

The now earless twin shrieked, "He knew!" He jerked his chin wildly in our direction. "He knew!" He cried out, folding in on himself until his forehead rested in a pool of blood draining from the hole in Paulie's head.

"Enough." Marco bit out, pulling a gun from his waistband

and shooting him in the leg, which, of course, only caused him to cry and scream more. "Give us a name."

Luca grabbed the hair on the back of the wounded twin's head, blood splattering his white shirt as he tugged upward, bringing them eye to eye. "Who knew? I want a name."

Sobbing, he shook his head, suddenly unable to follow through on ratting out his accomplice. Luca nodded and shoved the injured twin into his brother. As soon as Luca cleared the tarp, Taz filled the earless wonder with bullets. One bullet went cleanly through his arm and into his brother's. Unlike his twin, he just grunted, not a tear in sight.

I, on the other hand, struggled to remain standing. Frankie leaned into my side, propping me up without drawing attention to my weak knees.

"Now. Tony, tell us who you've been working with. I find it hard to believe you two dipshits are the brains of this operation." Marco circled the tarp, sending a swift kick from his expensive Italian leather shoe to the living twin's back. Tony fell forward, his face smashing into the ground with a sick thud.

Tony.

I'd never bothered to learn their names because the twins were fucking creeps.

Using the toe of his shoe, Marco rolled Tony's prone body over until he was on top of his dead brother and stared up at Luca with pure malice and a busted nose. Luca squatted down and wiped the bloody blade on Tony's shirt. "Why don't you tell us who you're working with, and I won't start carving off pieces of your face."

I could only see the back of Luca's head, but Marco stood over them with a grim smile. My stomach twisted. The residual hangover plus the scene before me was a dangerous combination. I shifted, trying to use Mickey's broad body to block the gruesome view.

"Fuck. You." Tony rolled his lips together as Luca pressed the tip of his knife into his cheek. Sweat from the heat and beating rolled down his forehead and into his eyes.

"You see that woman back there?" Luca asked, waving the knife toward me. "Your job was to keep her safe. Instead, you fucked with her brakes, let Cy's flunkies know she was at my club, left her alone in the middle of fucking nowhere, and had her followed."

Tony scowled. "Why would I have her followed?"

"Huh. Well, then the rest was all you." Luca sliced Tony's cheek wide open, and finally, Tony yelled and started crying. "That's all reason enough to fucking gut you like the scum you are, but you also betrayed the family." Luca flourished the knife and stabbed Tony right in the gut, twisting the handle.

"Luca?" Taz's gruff voice broke through the screams bouncing off the walls.

"Right." Luca nodded as he stood, leaving the knife in Tony as he stood next to Marco. "Your turn."

Taz approached, pointing a gun at Tony's head, and wasted no time pulling the trigger. Sighing, he slid his gun into his waistband and turned to his cousins. "So, what now?"

"We've got a traitor." Luca scratched his jaw, smearing Tony's blood across his skin. He didn't even notice because his attention was on the problem at hand.

"At least we have three less after tonight." Marco jerked his chin at Tommy and Frankie as he and Luca walked past us with Taz. "Get them in the hole and make sure the tarp covers everything."

Frankie squeezed my arm as he passed me. Mickey moved closer to his cousins, but not one of them spared him a glance.

"With the rehearsal dinner this week, we'll be able to feel out the out-of-towners." Luca turned to Taz. "We need to know when everyone gets to town."

"Done. I sent you the info you needed on the Chicago hit." Taz sighed. "I want my brother back. When this whole thing with

Cy is handled, I want Tootsie back in Chicago as my second. He never should've come here."

Luca's face remained neutral. "That's up to Tootsie. Before all this, he was set to be my consigliere. He'll have to answer for the past few months, but it's up to him where he wants to be after that. We clear?"

Taz's hands fisted. "Crystal. But if anything happens to my little brother, we'll have a problem."

Luca nodded and looked at Mickey. "What?"

"I'm sorry for interfering."

Another terse nod and Luca dismissed Mickey.

Mickey walked toward the cars, his attention on his phone.

"Keep an eye on him," Taz said, just loud enough for us to hear. His eyes narrowed at Mickey's back. "I don't think he likes you favoring Tootsie."

"Mickey's a good boy. He'll fall in line," Marco said, his voice sure.

Taz considered Marco's words and then ran a hand down his face. "You'll let me know if you hear from my brother?"

"Of course."

Taz hugged Luca, pounding his back, and did the same with Marco before walking off in the opposite direction that Mickey had gone.

Finally, Luca turned to me—face streaked red, his white shirt splattered with blood. "Welcome home." He reached a hand out, only to fist it and drop it to his side.

A sob-like laugh fell from my lips, and I threw myself into him. "What the fuck Luca?"

"Shh." He rubbed a hand down my back, his lips pressing against my hair every so often.

I leaned back and grabbed his chin. "Can we go home now?"

"Sure, baby. Once Frankie pours the concrete, we can go." As if on cue, Frankie pulled up in a cement mixer. Between him and Tommy, they got the ramp set up, and the hole filled in no time.

"Why don't you guys head out?" Frankie yelled over the noise of the truck.

Luca pulled out his phone and tapped away. "Can you handle this? Get the truck where it needs to go?"

"Sure thing. I'll double-check the area before the crew gets here."

"Perfect." Luca took my elbow and walked me to his car with Marco in our wake. He opened my door, helped me inside, and then walked around the hood as he shrugged on his suit coat. It covered most of the blood, but he'd be fucked if we got pulled over.

He got into the driver's seat and looked in the mirror while rubbing his jaw. "Another shirt," he muttered to himself.

I dove into my bag for my makeup removal wipes and handed them over. "Try these."

"Thank you." He cleaned what blood he could off his exposed skin, using every last one from the pack.

"What the fuck was that?" I looked between Luca and Marco.

Luca merged into traffic and sighed. "We made it look like Marco and I were on the outs so we could lure out whoever is trying to get rid of me. Unfortunately, only the Marino twins and Paulie were stupid enough to take the bait."

"Kicked your ass for no reason." Marco laughed, stretching out in the backseat of Luca's SUV.

"Tell that to your busted nose."

And because they were fucking lunatics, they started laughing. We dropped Marco off at his place—the rebuilt duplex next door to Adriana and Dante.

Back on the highway, Luca asked me if I was hungry. I shook my head, unable to vocalize just how ridiculous his question was.

Who would be hungry after watching three men die?

Luca. That's who.

As soon as we were home, he went into the kitchen and scrubbed his hands until they were no longer red from blood but from the hot water and nail brush. Once he was satisfied with his hands, he raided the fridge.

Numbly, I sat at the kitchen island and watched him slice green apples, gouda, and Havarti cheese as bacon sizzled in a skillet. "You're making a grilled cheese," I said matter-of-factly.

He dipped his head, his focus on assembling the sandwich.

"You killed three men, and you're going to eat a grilled cheese."

"We're going to eat a grilled cheese."

"I'm not—"

He set the knife down and pinned me with his dark stare. "You're hungover and have been through a tough couple of days. You're going to eat this fucking sandwich, even if I have to shove it down your throat." He didn't wait for me to agree as he fried up our sandwiches. The smell was amazing, even if I was still queasy.

The longer I sat in our beautiful kitchen, the more I relaxed. A part of me wanted to hold on to how wrong it was to go from an execution to domestic bliss, while the much larger part was willing to let Luca kiss it and make it all better.

When he put a plate in front of me, I started to refuse, but he merely lifted an eyebrow and took a bite of his own sandwich. It was time to pick my battles, and who wanted to battle against a delicious sandwich?

I took a big bite, and my eyes closed, savoring it. I hadn't eaten a bite all day. "Can you get me a glass of water?"

Luca nodded and got us both a tall tumbler of water. While I ate, I watched Luca. Even covered in blood splatter, he was exquisite. He braced himself with one hand, his bare forearm flexing as he gripped the edge of the counter. He slowly chewed every bite as if he could make the sandwich last forever.

But he couldn't.

As soon as there was nothing but crumbs, I asked, "Are you okay?"

Luca's eyes narrowed, and he scoffed. "Are you serious?"

"Yeah."

He picked up our plates and walked them to the sink. With his back to me, he said, "You watched me mutilate a man, then shoot another, and now you're asking me if I'm okay?" He turned the water off and wiped his hands on a kitchen towel before turning and leaning against the sink with his arms crossed. "I'm fine. Shit like that doesn't bother me—it hasn't in a long time. A better question would be if you're okay."

I crumpled a napkin in my hand, weighing my words carefully. "It would be a lie to say all of—" I waved my hand. "That wasn't shocking, but I feel weirdly okay. I mean, I get it."

"You get it?" Luca raised an eyebrow.

Nodding, I ripped my napkin apart.

Luca cursed under his breath as he joined me at the island. "Baby, you don't have to do that. I should be saying sorry. I got caught up in seeing you safe and wasn't thinking when I didn't send you home immediately. You should've never seen that."

"I've done worse," I mumbled, staring down at the butcher block.

"And you shouldn't have had to do that either." Luca pulled me from the stool, and white napkin confetti fluttered to the floor. Wrapping me in his arms, he said, for what had to be the millionth time, "I'm so sorry, Sasha." He buried his nose in my hair, inhaling deeply. "Things are going to get worse before they get better, but eventually, things will calm down. Yanni's death created a power vacuum in the Chronis family, and apparently, there's someone who wants to take me out. We'll find them, kill them, and life will go back to normal."

"I trust you," I said into his chest, realizing too late he was still in his gory shirt. Gently, I pulled back and gave him a timid smile.

"Good." He cupped my face, his thumb tracing the scratches on my cheek as a frown marred his face. "It's you above everyone and everything. I don't care who I have to kill. I'll keep you safe."

"Such a romantic."

TWENTY-THREE

After a short work week wrapping up all my open projects and finalizing the plans for our honeymoon, it was time for the rehearsal and rehearsal dinner. Hair swept up, makeup flawless, and dressed in the same gown I'd worn when we married, I walked into the cathedral on Luca's arm. Our parents and wedding party greeted us before our moms and the planner they'd hired ran us through the ceremony. The whole thing only took half an hour because Mom was in drill sergeant mode and didn't allow any side conversations or laughter.

Happiness and joy had no place at her rehearsal.

The entire wedding party moved to Moretti's for dinner. Besides our immediate families, groomsmen, and bridesmaids, our out-of-town family packed the dining room to the gills. Tommy and Gio stood at the front door, ensuring only those who should be there were there.

"Sasha!" My grandma rushed me at the door. Her perfume was overwhelming and comforting as she wrapped me in a hug that was sure to transfer her signature scent deep into my pores.

"Grandma. I'm so glad you could make it." I looked over her shoulder to where her second husband, Martin, stood smiling.

"And I see you brought a hot date." Martin scoffed as Grandma slapped my shoulder.

"Now, let me get a good look at your future hubby." She shoved me aside and grabbed Luca's arms. "He's certainly tall enough." She cackled as she craned her neck to look at his face. Grandma was shorter than Mom, but unlike us, she was a waif. Seeing the three of us in line was like watching one of those flipbooks about evolution. The final stage was me and all my glory. Grandma patted his arm and nodded. "He's a keeper. You'll have beautiful babies."

Luca laughed while I just stared. "Why don't you let us get married before you start crocheting baby blankets?"

She rolled her eyes, dismissing me, and walked Martin over to the bar.

"I see where your mom gets her . . ." Luca studied my grandma as she ordered an elaborate drink.

"Good boy. It's best not to name it. Is that your Nonna?" I tipped my head toward a table near the kitchen.

Luca's face lit up, and he dragged me over to the small but sturdy woman holding court over the Moretti aunts, uncles, and cousins. She looked every bit the matriarch Rosa described, with her salt and pepper hair tied into an elegant chignon and her ears, neck, wrist, and fingers dripping in diamonds.

"Luca," she said warmly. Marco helped her stand from her chair, clapped Luca on the shoulder, and headed to the kitchen. "Look at you." Luca bent over to allow Nonna to kiss his cheeks. "Such a handsome man." After looking her fill, she turned her attention to me with a tight-lipped smile. "And this must be Sasha." Her thick Italian accent caressed my name, making it sound romantic as hell.

"Yes, ma'am." I extended a hand.

Slapping it away, she stepped into me, gripping my biceps and air-kissing each cheek. She said something to Luca in Italian while looking me over. It must have been positive because Luca beamed at me while he responded.

I really need to learn more Italian.

"How rude of us," Nonna said, leading me to where she'd been sitting. "I take it you don't speak Italian?"

"No, ma'am. I—"

"Nonna. Call me Nonna." Luca pulled out her chair, and she sat.

I smiled at her, waiting for the dragon lady Rosa described to surface. "Okay, Nonna. I'm working through a program, but I clearly need to up my game."

She nodded and then asked Luca, "Are you going to sit?"

Luca glanced at the room full of people we'd yet to greet but seemed to decide that risking his Nonna's wrath wasn't worth the possibility of being rude to the rest of our friends and family. He pulled out my chair and then took the chair at the head of the long table. I hoped this was the seating chart our mothers had decided on.

"Luca, you should send Sasha to me for a few months. We could get her fluent in no time."

"I have no doubt you could, but I couldn't go that long without my wife." Luca covered my hand, a dopey smile on his face.

Nonna's face softened. "The honeymoon phase."

"The Sasha phase." Luca joked, picking my hand up and pressing his lips to my knuckles. Warmth spread through my chest, and my cheeks heated under his gaze.

Shouting in the kitchen interrupted our tender moment. "Sugar, if you're not getting out of my kitchen, I'm gonna need you to stir that." A voice with a soft southern drawl floated out of the open door.

As the door shut behind a waiter, Marco's booming voice cut through the noise of the party. "Answer my question!"

"I already did," the mystery woman said sweetly.

Luca stood from his chair and calmly walked to the kitchen door. The Morettis in the room watched with amusement while my family and friends shifted uncomfortably.

"Marco doesn't yell." Nonna's eyes cut to the kitchen, which had become quiet.

"He's got a temper on him, but no. Not usually a yeller. Unless it's Luca."

Nonna chuckled and took a sip of water. "Those two are more brothers than cousins."

"They're certainly a pair."

"What about you? Any siblings?"

"No, I'm an only child. Luckily, my cousin Sarah and I are close."

Nonna looked over my shoulder. "Michael's wife?"

"Yes. I actually met Luca at their wedding."

Luca and Marco emerged from the kitchen, Luca smirking while Marco had a stony expression.

"Everything okay?" I asked Luca.

His eyes slid to his cousin, and he pursed his lips. "Just a misunderstanding between Marco and the new chef."

"A new chef?" At this rate, Moretti's would go through every chef in St. Louis.

"Yes, a new chef." Marco cut in as his hands curled around the back of Nonna's chair. "Apparently, Mickey hired her this week. No one thought to tell me. And that b—" Nonna raised an eyebrow. "That woman ordered me out of the kitchen and then wouldn't tell me who she was."

I sagely nodded, biting back a laugh. "That would be confusing. What with her chef's coat and the whole cooking thing."

"That's why I asked. Her chef's jacket is this bright pink monstrosity. I figured she must be a new line cook, so I tried to help her out by letting her know the general uniform is white or black."

I let out a loud laugh, and Marco scowled at me. "That's too perfect. You tried to explain the dress code to the head chef."

"I am her boss."

"Sounds like Mickey's her boss."

At the sound of his brother's name, Marco straightened and stalked off into the crowd.

A thick, short woman in a hot pink chef's coat glided out of the kitchen and came our way.

"You must be the bride-to-be!" The color of her cheeks rivaled the color of her coat. "I'm Loretta Davenport King." She stuck out her hand, and I stood to shake it. Standing in my heels, Loretta came up to my chest, the neat, blond ponytail on top of her head giving her an extra inch. She pulled a small plate stacked with delicious morsels from behind her back. "I wanted to make sure you got a taste of the appetizers. Most brides nearly starve to death, meetin' and greetin'."

"You're an angel." I took the plate and inspected the tiny bites. "Is that fried chicken?"

"Good eye." Loretta winked, and her long, false eyelashes brushed the top of her round cheeks. I marveled at how great her full face of makeup looked after spending hours over a hot stove. Something caught her eye, and her smile dimmed. "I better get back in the kitchen before Mr. Boss Man comes to chew me out." As quickly as she came, she was gone.

"What an interesting woman," Nonna commented, her frown telling me she wasn't sure if it was a good interesting.

"I like her," I said, popping a fussy app in my mouth. Once I swallowed, I amended, "I love her. These are amazing."

"I thought you'd like those." Mom snuck up behind us. "It's time for everyone to get seated. You two are right here." She motioned to where we'd been sitting.

Once everyone was seated, Luca stood and tapped his glass, and the room fell silent. "Sasha and I would like to thank you all for coming to celebrate with us this weekend. It means so much to us to have your support as we enter this next phase of our lives. Greg, Maggie, thank you for raising the most magnificent woman I've ever met. Mom, you and Maggie have done an amazing job putting everything together. And Sasha, thank you for taking a chance on me and continuously picking me. I love you so much.

SASHA AND THE STALKER

You're stuck with me now." The table broke into laughter and cheering.

As Luca sat, I stood and raised my glass. "To the Morettis and Mitchells and the new family we're forming tomorrow." I gazed down at Luca and said just to him, "I love you. No matter what, it's you and me."

Luca swallowed thickly, waving his hand in the air. A team of waiters flooded the room, carrying plate after plate.

During the second course, Luca's cousin Tizzy Adamo stood to give a toast. She didn't bother to pull down the hem of her tight red dress, leaving a lot of her tan thighs on display. Like her brothers, she was tall and broad, but while their faces were blunt, she had the refined beauty of old movie stars—wide eyes, cheekbones sharp as glass, a straight, perfectly sized nose, and lips so full and pouty it was no wonder she was the princess of the family.

She was also high off her ass if her glazed-over dark eyes were anything to go by. Flicking her heavy curtain of black hair over her shoulder, she smiled at Luca and me. "I want to raise a toast to my cousin Luca and his total smokeshow of a fiancée, Sasha. I mean, seriously, how does a tight ass like him get a hot piece of—"

"Tizzy." Nonna cut her off. Down the table, my friends were all in various stages of silently laughing. Jazz was the only one not hiding her amusement and had a huge grin stretched across her face.

"Sorry, Nonna." Tizzy looked genuinely remorseful. "To Luca and Sasha and all the little Moretti babies to come!"

Everyone clicked glasses, but there was way less enthusiasm in the gesture than in previous toasts. I smiled at Tizzy, trying to relay the "It's okay that you're high as a kite and making a bit of an ass of yourself—we've all been there" message.

Taz stood after his twin—his expression far more suitable for torture than a joyous occasion like a wedding. "I'd like to make a toast to Luca and Sasha. May they have the kind of loyalty and love that does justice to the Moretti legacy."

Loyalty. Right.

He raised his glass, and everyone politely smiled, clicking their glasses.

Inspired by the cousins, Sarah popped up, her baby bump just visible. "To Sasha and Luca, a love like I've never seen." Her eyes filled with tears as she looked at Luca, a sob leaving her lips before she could say more. Michael stood and lovingly guided her back into her seat.

Luca cleared his throat, his face soft but unsmiling. "If there are no more toasts, I'd like to have them bring out dessert." There was a relieved chorus of agreement, and the servers presented each person with a dessert plate that was like a sampler of Italian treats. "The fantastic new chef of Moretti's worked at a bakery here on The Hill, and when it came time to pick the desserts, I couldn't." Luca chuckled and shot his cousin a smug look. "Enjoy."

The room fell silent, and I snuck a peek at the kitchen door just in time to see it swing closed, a flash of pink darting out of view before it shut.

When it was finally time to end the night, the relief I felt was immense. The only issue was that Luca and I were spending the night apart per tradition, which was, of course, ridiculous because we were already married. But Luca, ever the mama's boy, wanted to keep our mothers happy.

"I'm going to walk my grandma out."

Luca kissed my forehead and let me go.

"The Morettis are sure an interesting bunch," Grandma whispered as we passed Gio at the door, Tommy trailing behind us at a distance. "I do believe that young woman was high. If I had to guess, coke?"

I barked out a laugh and tightened my hold on her arm. Martin glanced back at us as he handed the valet his ticket. "What do you know about drugs, Grandma?"

She sniffed, adjusting her shawl. "Believe it or not, I do have a life and had one before I had your mother. I was a flower child."

"I bet you followed The Grateful Dead."

"I'll have you know, I was a deadhead for a summer."

"Why is it I hear another wild story every time I see you? Where was all this when I was a teenager getting into trouble for a little pot?"

"Wasn't my place to step in. I can't help that your mom's a square." The valet pulled up in their car, so Grandma gave me a hug and a kiss on the cheek. "Don't be boring like her."

I shook my head as Martin helped her into the car. "Don't be mean."

"You know I'm right," she sang as Martin closed the door with an apologetic smile.

I watched as they drove away before heading back inside.

"You ready to go?" Ashley asked, the other bridesmaids and women of the families standing in a cluster.

I sighed dramatically. "I guess. Let me say goodbye to Luca."

"You act like you aren't going to see him tomorrow." Ashley scoffed, pushing me toward the men congregated at the bar.

"I need to get Nicki home. I'll see you in the morning." Aldo patted Luca's arm, turning and almost plowing right into me. He gently touched my elbow and mumbled, "Sorry about that." I was sure that was the most I'd ever heard him say. Frozen, I watched him approach Nicki, her face lighting up only to fall when he jerked his head to the door without a word and walked away. She quickly gathered her things, a frown pulling her dark brows together until she noticed me. Before I could blink, she smoothed her features into the bland bitch facade she wanted everyone to see.

"You heading out?"

I stepped into Luca's body and hugged his waist. "Unfortunately."

He leaned down, his lips grazing my ear as he whispered, "I'll see you in a couple of hours."

A shiver ran down my spine as his fingers traced down my back. "Better not get caught."

"Never." He placed a not-so-chaste kiss on my lips, making me forget where we were until Frankie wolf-whistled.

Still wrapped around Luca, I glared over my shoulder. "Asshole." He only shrugged and downed the rest of his drink.

"Sasha!" my bridesmaids called from the door.

"I guess I have to go."

I stepped away from Luca and dragged my sorry ass to my cackling friends. "Shut up."

The gang chatted and joked all the way to my house and, surprisingly, didn't give me shit when I went up to bed early.

As the night wore on, the house grew quiet with everyone splitting up into the guestrooms and the living room, so I was left alone with my thoughts. Despite already being legally married, the idea of our wedding caused me a lot of anxiety. Not the saying I do to Luca—I would do that every day for the rest of our lives. It was doing all this in front of everyone I know and hundreds I didn't. After some tossing and turning, I fell into an uneasy sleep.

The bed dipped around two in the morning, and Luca gathered me into his arms, his scent and heat enveloping me. "Hey." I rubbed my eyes and propped my chin on his chest.

"How's my wife doing tonight?" He grinned down at me, kissing the tip of my nose.

"Better now." I shut my eyes and happily hummed as he kissed my cheeks and lips.

"Miss me?"

"Always."

Luca's rough hands caressed my back, moving lower until he had two overflowing handfuls of ass. Squeezing roughly, he rolled us, pinning me to the mattress.

"What are you doing?" I chuckled as he slid his hands from under me.

"What do you think?" He flexed his hips into me, and I moaned. "You need to be quiet. Your mom is next door."

Every filthy teenage fantasy roared to life. I'd done very little hooking up in my parents' house despite my rebellious nature. There was something deliciously naughty about the danger of being caught by my mom.

Best not to examine that one.

"Okay," I whispered, and Luca rewarded me with a kiss. He teased my bottom lip with light touches, his tongue grazing the seam of my lips until I sighed in frustration, and they parted. His tongue slipped into my mouth, his kiss becoming more urgent and fevered. I lost myself in it. Arousal coiled in my belly, and I wrapped my legs around him, trying to pull him closer.

"Shh, baby," Luca warned, shoving up my nightie and kissing down my body. I swallowed a moan when he bit my hip, pulling off my panties and spreading my thighs to accommodate his broad shoulders. "If you can't stay quiet, I won't eat your pussy." He slowly dragged his tongue up to my clit. "You're not going to keep me from devouring my wife, are you?"

I violently shook my head.

"Good girl."

Luca's hands gripped the inside of my thighs, and he practically dove into my pussy. His nose bumped my clit as he teased my slit. When I couldn't take anymore, he finally speared me with his long tongue. I gnawed the inside of my cheek to stay quiet, but when two thick fingers replaced his tongue, I moaned loud and long.

"Open," Luca grunted.

Blinking up at him in the dark room, I tried to make out what was in his hand.

"I said, open." The command left no room for argument. My mouth fell open, and Luca shoved a ball of satin past my lips.

My panties.

The faintest taste of me hit my tongue, and I groaned, the panties doing their job and muffling the sound.

"Fuck me. Look at you." His fingers thrust back into me as his mouth peppered my breasts with kisses, occasionally nipping until he captured the tip of my nipple between his teeth and pulled. I arched off the bed, coming around his fingers. "That's it," Luca murmured hotly against my ear. He slid his fingers from me and pushed his boxers down, lining his cock up and thrusting roughly until our hips met. I wrapped my legs around him, holding my thighs to keep the angle just right. He took the panties from my mouth, replacing them with his fingers. "Suck them clean."

Not one to argue with a good idea, I sucked his fingers to the last knuckle while he went absolutely feral. He pounded into me, fucking me into the mattress until I couldn't take a full breath. Slapping my thigh harshly, I moaned around his fingers, and he thrust them deeper until I gagged. "Quiet," he bit out.

Tears ran down my cheeks as another orgasm crested. Reading my body like the expert he was, Luca's thumb worked my clit as he ground down after every thrust.

"Come on, your husband's cock, Sasha."

Like a switch flipped, I came so hard I saw stars, my limbs going limp while Luca's body tensed, and he came with a grunt.

Panting and sweaty, we fell into a heap on the bed. "There's no way that was anything but good luck for tomorrow," I joked as I stretched my leg to make sure I didn't pull anything being wrapped around Luca like a pretzel.

"Absolutely." Luca kissed my forehead.

We lay in each other's arms for an hour before he got up and slipped from the house undetected. By the time I fell asleep, it was time to get up and start the long and arduous task of getting ready for my wedding.

TWENTY-FOUR

Hours. It takes hours to get ready for a wedding. As a woman who loves to primp, you'd think I would be in heaven.

Not even close.

I was exhausted, cranky, and getting side-eyed by my bridesmaids for a mystery mark on my collarbone that took the makeup artist half an hour to cover.

Abruptly standing, I said, "I'll be right back."

"The wedding's about to start." Ashley frowned.

"I just need a minute alone."

Jazz scoffed. "Are you about to pull a runner?"

"No, I just want to be alone for a second." I went out the side door. There was a small bench under a tree, but I figured sitting in the shade wasn't worth getting bitched out for a couple of wrinkles.

"Aren't you supposed to be inside?"

I spun on my heel and came face to face with Beth. "What are you doing here?"

"I was invited, along with every politician in the Midwest."

I sighed, shutting my eyes and tilting my face toward the sun.

"You never called me back."

She had to be fucking kidding. On what planet would I be

accepting her phone calls while she was trying to ruin the casino plans and talk shit about my husband? "What was there to say?"

"You're marrying a Moretti."

I pinned Beth with a glare. "That's none of your business. That stopped being your business three years ago."

"That was your choice, not mine!" Her voice was clipped as her chest heaved with the effort of her stilted words.

"You're right, so why are you still coming around?"

"I love you," she grumbled.

"No. You love what you want me to be. You hated the real me."

"I did not—"

"You did," I said calmly. The sting had gone out of my memories of my relationship with Beth. Being with Luca muted all that pain and insecurity. "You hate my choice of partner."

She rolled her eyes. "You can say husband. I know you're married." When I frowned, she pointed at herself. "Mayor. I have connections."

"About those connections. Are you really going to contest the casino?"

"If it's the right thing to do, yes."

"Unbelievable."

"What's unbelievable is that you're married to a man being investigated for murder."

"You seem to know an awful lot about what's going on in my life. Have you been watching us?" Beth blinked rapidly at me, her mouth twisting before turning toward the church to make a quick escape, but I grabbed her arm. "You have! You're watching us?" I hissed, my eyes scanning the area for eavesdroppers.

She ripped her arm from my hold, her heel catching a hole in the grass. "I paid a guy, but he went MIA."

Her words hit like a whip. "It was you." I shook my head. "You paid a PI to follow me?" Leaning in, I looked her right in the eye. "You could've gotten yourself killed. As it is, he paid for your curiosity."

She flinched, but it didn't slow her down. Her cheeks as red as my hair, her eyes shining with anger, she bit back, "And that's the family you want to tie yourself to?"

"You know what, Beth? Go. Fuck. Yourself." With that parting shot, I gathered up my skirt and stormed back into the church. Pausing outside the bridal suite, I took a calming breath as I listened to the most important women in my life laugh and carry on.

I must've put on a convincing smile because no one commented when I rejoined the group. As they continued to chat, I checked my face and found no proof of the Beth run-in. Despite feeling relief knowing she was behind the PI, having to actually talk to her on my wedding day was a real bitch.

Mom sat on the stiff couch in the bridal suite, watching the rest of us touch up our hair and makeup from the trip over. "I still can't believe my baby's getting married."

"Honestly, I can't believe I'm getting married. The whole 'the right person will make you do crazy things' is real. Hell—"

"Sasha," Mom hissed.

A portrait of Mother Mary holding a baby Jesus hung above my mom in the reflection of the mirror I was using. "Sorry. Heck," I apologized to the virgin mother, and Mom nodded. "Having kids isn't even freaking me out because I know he'll be my partner. Isn't that crazy?"

Mom's eyes shined with tears. She sniffed and gave me a small smile. "You don't know how happy that makes me."

"I have an idea," I teased.

Tricia, the wedding planner, popped her head in the doorway and said, "Time to line up."

The room broke into a flurry of excitement as my friends hurried out, leaving me alone with my mom.

"You really look beautiful, Sasha." Mom handed me the exquisite bouquet made of white roses and calla lilies.

Behind my eyes started to burn. As much as I had grown in

love and acceptance for myself, a part of me would always be ecstatic to receive her praise. "Thanks, Mom."

She took one more long look, giving me a watery smile as she held out her hand. "Let's get you married." I held on to her tightly as she led me through the hallways to the front of the cathedral. "This is it!" She squeezed my hand, shaking my arm out. An escort ushered her inside, and the enormous doors shut. The muffled sound of a string quartet playing something I didn't recognize kicked my nerves into overdrive.

I was getting married.

Dad looped his arm around mine, patting my hand. "You ready?"

"I think so?"

He chuckled. "It'll all be over soon. Try to enjoy the day as much as you can. Or at least pretend to because I saw some of what your mom has planned, and wow."

"Way to make me feel better."

The doors swung open, and Adriana started the procession. "Here we go," my dad murmured in the way dads can't help but narrate what's happening.

As each person left our little pack, I grew more anxious. My stomach flipped until I wasn't sure if I would throw up or faint.

Dante took the hand of my second cousin's kid, Libby, and started their adorable walk down the aisle. When the doors shut behind them, we took our position. Dad was the only thing keeping me upright. "Are you okay? Do you need to sit down?"

I shook my head so hard that the veil brushed against my cheek. "I just need to see Luca."

Dad smiled, every crease in his face deepening. "Then let's get you to the altar."

The music changed to an elegant string version of "Can't help falling in love," and the doors flung open. I paused long enough for Tricia to give me an impatient head nod. That first step was the hardest I'd ever taken. It wasn't until I looked to the front of the church and locked eyes with Luca that I was able to get my ass moving.

The intense love in his eyes made everyone else melt away, and Dad had to keep me from sprinting up the aisle. I could withstand the circus our mothers planned if he kept looking at me that way.

We reached the front of the cathedral, and as Luca took my hand, the doors flew open, and a swarm of police spilled inside, shouting for everyone to sit down. Luca used his body to block me from sight just as I recognized Detective Bennington at the front of the pack.

"Luca Moretti?" Bennington's voice echoed off the tall ceilings, carrying over the settling guests.

Luca squeezed my hand as he nodded at an approaching Bennington.

"We have a warrant for your arrest in the murder of Zoe Chronis and Torquato Adamo." Men dressed in swat gear surrounded Bennington in a strange juxtaposition to the formal wear of everyone surrounding them.

"I'm kind of in the middle of something," Luca said, his tone neutral.

"Sorry to interrupt, but the warrant was signed just half an hour ago." Bennington didn't sound sorry. No, he sounded like an asshole who delighted in ruining people's wedding days.

Nicki stood up, but her father pulled her down. "Can I see the warrant? I'm Mr. Moretti's legal counsel."

Bennington passed the warrant toward Gabe. The whole time, Nicki sat with a scowl on her face. After a tense moment, Gabe nodded and folded up the piece of paper.

Luca let out a deep sigh and turned to me. "I'm sorry, Sasha. Guess I was wrong. I love you." He pressed his lips to mine, and something cracked in my chest. When we'd made it to the week of the wedding, I really thought things would be fine. Clearly, we'd been delusional. Before I could wrap him in my arms, he was descending the sanctuary steps. I tried to follow, but Marco held me back. "Don't."

The group of heavily armed cops swallowed Luca up as Bennington recited his Miranda rights. The light glinted off the silver handcuffs as they clicked around Luca's wrists. I wouldn't have put it past the bastard to have shined them for the occasion. Blood whooshed in my ears as I fought to take a full breath as they walked him out of the church. Within minutes, the cathedral was free of cops. Over five hundred people sat in stunned silence.

"Luca!" I jerked away from Marco, throwing down my bouquet to gather up my skirt, and sprinted down the aisle on shaky legs. I made it to the front steps of the church as the cops pushed Luca into the back of a police car. Bright flashes went off in my face, and journalists shouted questions, but my eyes didn't stray from his silhouette in the back of the patrol car.

The squad cars pulled away, blue and red lights still flashing but with no sirens, and I was left in my wedding dress being hounded by the press.

"Come on, Sasha." Marco gathered me in his arms, directing me back inside. Tommy, Gio, and a few of the younger guys posted up by each door, their faces grim.

"Oh, honey! What's going on?" Mom searched me for injuries as if I was the one who had been arrested.

"I—"

"Maggie, let's get Sasha back to the bridal suite. I'll explain there." Rosa's patient voice cut through some of the confusion, and I allowed her to lead the entire wedding party away from the gathering crowd. As we passed the big doors, a familiar face caught my attention.

"Who's that?"

Rosa absent-mindedly glanced the way I pointed. "That's Luca's cousin Lorenzo from Chicago. My sister Gina's son."

No. No, he was the guy from Mexico, the one I saw at brunch in January. And now I wondered if he was the asshole from my bachelorette weekend.

There was no way he didn't know who I was, but how did I not recognize him? The weekend Rosa gave me a crash course in the family, she'd mentioned a sister, Gina, and that she'd passed on a few years ago. There was a cousin, Lorenzo, but I didn't remember seeing a picture of him.

"I'm surprised Lorenzo is even here. Gina and I were estranged before her death, and the boys have never been close." Rosa squeezed my hand before catching up with Marco and whispering something in his ear.

I looked over my shoulder and found Lorenzo staring at me. The smirk that attracted me that night in Mexico now made my stomach churn. He held my bouquet to his nose and took a deep breath. With one more intense look, he disappeared into the confused crowd. A chill went down my spine, and my stomach dropped to my ass. The surrounding chaos had nothing on what was going on in my head.

I'd fucked my husband's cousin, and now he was here to do what?

As soon as we hit the doorway, I rushed to the bathroom and threw up the continental breakfast I'd enjoyed that morning.

"Oh, sweetheart." My mom sat beside me on the cold tile, rubbing my back. "It'll be okay. I'm sure this is all some kind of misunderstanding."

Yeah, because Zoe and Tootsie were alive, but they wouldn't be surfacing until Cy was dead. I heaved again. Without them, Luca might be locked up for a while. They apparently had enough for an arrest. Would it be enough to hold him?

With my face resting on the toilet seat, I heard snippets of conversation.

"They found Luca's gun—"

"The blood matched—"

"Two eyewitnesses—"

"The fire report wasn't—"

Rosa joined us in the bathroom, shutting the door behind her. "I bought you a bottle of water and some crackers. It's what helped me when I was pregnant with Luca."

Shocked, I pulled my head from the toilet bowl.

"Pregnant?" my mom squealed, her hands covering her mouth as her eyes sparkled.

Before I could deny, deny, deny, Rosa added, "Luca told me they've been trying."

I shook my head, but the moms were too busy smiling with hearts in their eyes to notice my frown or plea that it wasn't true.

I should've told him I was still taking the pill.

"Well, that's a spot of sunshine in the storm." Mom brushed the hair off my face. "Everything will be okay, honey."

"From your lips to God's ears," I mumbled, resting my head against the wall.

EPILOGUE

"I'm sorry, ma'am. Visits are limited to Mr. Moretti's legal counsel."

I'd been told the same thing every day since Luca's bail was denied.

"It's been two weeks. Any idea when he'll be allowed visits from family? I'm his wife." It was the first time I'd tried throwing around my weight as the boss's wife, but if the look on the guy's face was anything to go by, it didn't mean shit.

He clicked around, and the grimace on his face told me I wasn't going to like what he had to tell me. "I don't know if I should tell you this." He looked up through the plexiglass partition.

"Please," I begged.

"Mr. Moretti's been allowed visitors since the day after he arrived. He set his visitor list to just his legal counsel."

"Ah."

"I'm sorry, Mrs. More—"

I raised my hand. "It's not your fault. Thank you for letting me know."

Stepping out into the July heat, I wiped under my eyes before putting on my sunglasses. My heels clicked against the hot asphalt as I walked across the parking lot to my huge SUV—a wedding gift Luca had insisted on. The trip inside had been so short that the leather was still cool when I slid inside.

Tossing my keys and purse on the passenger seat, I sat there, staring at the jail until the heat inside the vehicle became unbearable. With no plan, I turned on the car. The air conditioning blew my hair from my face as I reached for my phone. I needed answers. As I waited for Marco to pick up, the news cycle started with yet another story about Luca.

Muting the stereo, I muttered, "Fucking talk radio."

Thank you for reading Sasha and the Stalker, Book 2 in The Moretti Family Series. If you want to see the conclusion of Sasha and Luca's trilogy, read book 3—Sasha and the Heir.

Want to get sneak peeks, free short stories, and stay up to date on new releases? Join Stephanie's mailing list!

Acknowledgments

I want to thank all the readers that gave Sasha and the Butcher a chance and continued on to Sasha and the Stalker. You will never know how much it means to me.

Thank you to all the ARC readers for continuing on with the series, or jumping on in the thick of it. You are all beyond amazing.

A huge thanks goes to my best friend Bonnie for designing my covers, especially when I changed both the concept and title last minute. You're an angel.

And as always, I want to thank Jordan for supporting me in every way conceivable. From picking up the slack when I was MIA writing, to being the best alpha/beta/critique partner—this book wouldn't have happened without them being in my corner.

On to the next!

ABOUT THE AUTHOR

After becoming something of a romance fiend, Stephanie Kazowz decided to try her hand at writing some good old-fashioned love stories. Never one to narrow her focus, she plans to write the banging multiverse, weaving as many tropes and subgenres together as her smut-loving heart can handle—and it can handle a lot.

Stephanie lives in St. Louis, Missouri, with her husband, three bonkers babies, two codependent dogs, and two cats who are perpetually staring at her like she betrayed them by bringing the motley group home.

Made in the USA
Columbia, SC
22 November 2024